Journey of the Exiled

Jordan T. Bryant

Cover and Appendix Artwork by Jessica Adams
© 2021 Jordan T Bryant

Acknowledgements

 Thank you to my Parents, Wife, and the rest of my family for all the support they gave over the years for this goal. Thank you to Greg for being my springboard and helping me make this story better than I had ever imagined; Thank you to Jessica and Sophia for being willing to help with the artwork. Thank you to Jordan, Ashley and many others for being willing to give me honest feedback throughout the writing process. Finally, thank you to all my readers, I can't wait to see people enjoying this story. Hopefully you enjoy reading it as much as I loved writing it.

Table of Contents

Chapter 1 1
Exiled 1
Celenia 1

Chapter 2 21
Kaja's Escort 21
Kaja 21
Varen 26

Chapter 3 35
Caves 35
Kaja 35

Chapter 4 67
The Necromantic Disease 67
???? 67
Varen 92

Chapter 5 105
The Market 105
Varen 105

Chapter 6 149
Escape 149
Varen 149
William 155
Hjalmar 157
Kaja 160

Chapter 7 175
The Dancing Dragon 175
Varen 175
Hjalmar 178

Chapter 8 203

The Hunt 203
- Celenia 203
- Kaja 210
- Varen 222

Chapter 9 231

Elves 231
- Amara 231
- Varen 245

Chapter 10 253

Investigation 253
- Amara 253

Chapter 11 273

Picking Sides 273
- Hjalmar 273
- Amara 290

Chapter 12 295

The invitation 295
- Varen 295

Chapter 13 317

The Attempt 317
- Kaja 317
- Celenia 321
- Kaja 330

Chapter 14 335

The Council 335
- Celenia 335
- Amara 341
- Varen 348

Chapter 15 .... *351*
The Council's Decision **351**
Amara 351
Hjalmar 356
Amara 359

Chapter 16 .... *377*
The Chase **377**
Hjalmar 377
Amara 387

Chapter 17 .... *391*
Healers and Protectors **391**
Hjalmar 391
Amara 401

Chapter 18 .... *407*
The Duel **407**
Hjalmar 407

Chapter 19 .... *431*
Parting Ways **431**
Amara 431
Varen 437
Amara 441

Chapter 20 .... *457*
The Princess and the Paladin **457**
Celenia 457

Chapter 21 .... *479*
Egil **479**
Hjalmar 479
Varen 483

Chapter 22 .... *495*

Return to Vellara	**495**
Varen	495
Epilogue	***513***
Kaja	513
Pronunciation Guide	***i***
People	i
Groups	iii
Place	iii

Chapter 1

Exiled

Celenia

"Celenia and Varen Valbrandr, you are hereby exiled from the village of Vellara and the land thereof, by charge of the Gods." The cleric's voice boomed from the podium.

"The charges are as followed: the learning and practice of lessons deemed unholy and sinful, and the use of dark practices against humanity."

"We trained, yes, but we never used necromancy to harm anyone! This trial is completely out of line." My brother exclaimed.

"You dare question the authority of the high cleric?" He chided, his voice echoing off the stone walls of the church house, "Your charges have been set. Eternal exile is your punishment, and if not respected you will be put to death. Judgement is passed, you have until dawn. Use the seventeen hours to make your preparations and leave town."

I nudged my brother, "Don't question him anymore; If he declares we are dead to Vellara, we need to leave," I muttered, brushing a lock of my brown hair out of my face.

"But we didn't use them against humanity," he hissed back.

"No, but he believes that raising the dead is a crime against the people. We need to leave."

I let my brother out of the large building near the center of town that served as both church and town hall. If the Cleric who served as the head of the village and official lawmaker believed that we'd somehow used Necromancy for evil, then so be it. He also believed that he was a channel for the will of the Gods to be carried out, and he was as cracked as a log on a fire. Years ago, he believed that the gods sent him a prophecy in the form of a vision, of a young girl killing the village. She vanished shortly after.

"What are you thinking about?" Varen asked me as he righted himself.

"The little girl the Holy Crackpot had sentenced to death," Varen snickered at my nickname for the cleric, "And how he 'knew' that she'd destroy the village. I still feel so bad for that child's family."

"Cel, that happened years ago, and you were what, eight? Official town record says she was exiled, like we are."

"I know but, Varen, no one saw her leave. Not even the men on guard at the town entrance that night."

"Even so, we can't assume that she was put to death."

"What other explanation is there?"

"Maybe she found another way out of town, or maybe they are holding her somewhere. The point is, we don't know what happened to her."

"I guess. It still wouldn't surprise me. If you ask me, the Holy man is insane, but no one dares to stand up from him. I don't necessarily deny the existence of gods, but I can't imagine them working through someone like him.". I stopped and looked at my reflection in a well. My face was more pale than usual, probably due to the stress of the last few hours. My eyes were bloodshot, and there were dark rings under my eyes. My long hair was stringy and sweaty looking. I looked back at toward the town hall.

"Let's hurry and leave before he changes his mind and decides to have us killed."

"If needed, we could always fight back."

"What? And get killed?" I almost yelled, "No way in hell."

"Don't tell me you've cracked, too." I said, "There's no way we can take on the high cleric, let alone the town. Not with the limited ability we have now."

"Then we come back later. If you really believe that the cleric shouldn't be in charge then someone has to stop him, and no one else is going to do it."

"You really have cracked. Varen, where do you think we're

going to get any more practice? We've been exiled. Ellara can't continue teaching us, and where are we going to find another Master?"

"We were exiled from this town, and it's not as if she is the only master necromancer in the world."

"Even so, who's going to teach two exiles? Remember, he said 'and the land thereof'. Meaning we're going to have to leave the Kingdom." I replied as we approached home.

"And everyone we meet will know us as exiles right off the bat? Besides, it won't be hard to practice while on the road, there should plenty of dead animals," he hopped the small gate and walked up to the door, leading the way inside.

"Well, I'm not saying that they won't. I mean, it's kind of obvious where we're from. Vellara is one of few frontier towns, and we don't exactly look like we come from a city." I followed my brother inside, opening the chest by the door and rummaging through. Triumphantly I produced two water pouches made of animal leather.

"Maybe so, but it doesn't necessarily mean we were exiled, we could be on a trip to visit family or something." Varen suggested scanning the house for something. "Have you seen my Dragon bone staff? I hid it when the guards were approaching the house, but I don't remember where."

"You left it in the brush behind the house, remember?" I called from the yard, filling the water skins from the large barrel just outside the house, "You tossed it out the back door."

He stepped out the back door to look. "Ah there it is. Thanks!"

"Yeah, no problem," I responded. Focusing back on the water skins, I cursed as I noticed they had begun to leak. Well, these aren't going to be any use."

Varen poked his head out the door and spotted the leaking skins. "Well, that stinks like a corpse, looks like we're going to have to stop by the Valtr's shop." He went back inside, gathering other supplies. "You know, if we are leaving the realm, I doubt anyone will recognize what we are, news doesn't travel *that* fast."

"Remember what father always used to say? Word travel faster than feet*,"* I reminded him.

"Yeah, but now all he says is 'Nnnnnnnnn'," He joked.

"That's cruel."

"But funny," he grinned, putting clothes in a sack. "Did you grab the spell books?"

"I was going to," I passed him as I moved toward the cabinets, "but then I considered hitting you as hard as I could," I taunted. Searching underneath the cupboard, I found the small latch

Undoing the latch, I held my hands out for our spell books which fell out as the hidden door struck the wall with a loud smack.

"You know, sometimes I think I made that space just a little too tight a fit," I said, tossing Varen's book to him.

He looked up in time to narrowly avoid getting hit in the face by the flying bone-bound, leather covered, parchment book.

"Yeah, you have said so before, but I have told you if you made it much bigger, anyone could find it by bumping into it" He reached down, dusted off the book and slid it into the inside pocket of his robes.

Dawning my own robes, I slid my steel-bound, wood covered parchment book into a small pocket, "Yes, but I could have made it a tiny bit bigger, so the books would fit right."

"We really should have listened when Ellara told us to put the hideaway in the floor," he said picking up his own knapsack, "You have everything you need in the luggage bag?"

"Not yet. I'm looking for my scepter and dagger. Do you think they found it?" I asked.

"I doubt it, they didn't search the house that well. Besides, you hid it in the wall compartment with my bone knife, didn't you?" he asked.

"Oh yeah..." I said, kicking a small, well-hidden compartment low in the wall.

"All right, where is my cloak of shadows? Oh, and is my vial of poison still in the bone compartment of my knife?" He asked, looking around the closet.

"Uh, I haven't seen your cloak since you showed it off last. And what makes you think that the vial of poison wouldn't be still in your knife?" I replied, rolling my eyes and dawning my own riding cloak. "But where is my communication amulet?"

I searched around the house and found Varen's cloak in the cupboard next to the salt.

"I'm not asking, okay?"

"I hid it at the same time you hid your amulet in the salt," he replied nonchalantly.

"Why did I hide my amulet in the salt?" I asked, pouring the salt onto the ground and putting my amulet around my neck.

"Because we were finishing dishes when they were almost at the door, so we had to find a nearby place.

I cocked my eyebrow, "Did the trial really take so long that I forgot that...?" I mused.

"Stress does weird things to the mind," he replied, shrugging, "is that everything?"

"I think so."

"Alright, let's put our knives on our belts, grab some supplies, and get a head start," he said tucking his knife in the hilt in his belt and grabbing his pack bag.

"You seem to be taking this well," I eyed my brother, nevertheless I nodded and tied my dagger to my own belt beneath my robes. I headed out the door with my own pack and pockets empty as I dared leave them. The Valtr general store wasn't far from our home, but I couldn't help feeling more than a little uncomfortable and found myself frequently checking over my shoulder, concerned that the high cleric may have changed his mind about exiling us. Glancing over at my brother, it was clear he echoed my concern. I only relaxed slightly as we entered the store.

"Celenia! Varen! I've heard the bad news. Is it true you two were practicing necromancy?" The shopkeeper's daughter asked from behind the counter. Then realization dawned on her, "Oh, right, you're going to be needing supplies for the road, won't you?"

"Yeah, now that it's out, we won't be able to stay here," Varen said sadly.

"So, it's true then?" Her eyes grew wide.

"Yeah, it's true." Varen replied after brief hesitation.

It was no secret that Varen had a crush on this Auburn-haired girl. I couldn't blame him, she was a little taller than I was, probably 5 feet and somewhere between 9 and 10 inches. And her sky-blue eyes would catch anyone's attention. I was pretty sure even she had an idea that he liked her, but he remained oblivious to that fact. I almost felt bad for them but given the circumstances I was more worried about our lives than my brother's romantic feelings.

"So, what do you need?" She asked leaning on the counter.

"Well, what do you have?" my brother asked, looking at a basket of bone knives.

"Anything two brave adventurers would need," she said twirling a lock of her hair.

I saw Varen's face flush before he turned away, suddenly very interesting in the farming equipment on the wall. I shook my head and turned back to face Kaja.

"What kind of Canteens do you have?"

"Well, we have gourds, goblin and hobgoblin skin, and a couple bronze canteens, new just this week."

"How much do each of those hold and weigh?" I asked trying to imagine what a goblin skin canteen would look like.

"The heaviest is probably the bronze but it lasts a lot longer, the skins hold more, but aren't as strong, and the gourds hold the least."

"What's the difference between the goblin and hobgoblin skins?"

"The goblin skins are thicker, but the hobgoblin skins are larger and hold more," she stood up and pulled some from a box behind the counter, setting each in front of me.

I picked each one up, trying to figure out which one I wanted, finally I looked up at her "How much are two of the hobgoblin skins?
"

"Well, usually, twelve silver pieces, but for you guys," she almost unnoticeably glanced at my brother who had moved from the farming equipment and was now admiring some swords hanging on the wall, "I can give it to you for eight."

"This wouldn't have anything to do with..." I looked at Varen, "would it?"

"What? No," Kaja answered, a little too quickly, and blushed bright red.

"All right, we'll take them." I pulled out a small pouch I kept at my waist and counting out twelve silver pieces, "The rest is a tip."

"Okay let me write up the receipt," she replied, grabbing a second hobgoblin skins and setting on the counter.

She grabbed two pieces of parchment. One had a list of wares sold, and the other blank.

"What's the blank parchment for?" Varen asked.

Her only reply was to wrap her arm around the second as she wrote, preventing either of us from reading it. She folded it up and handed both pages to me.

She leaned close to me and whispered, "Don't open it until you are sure no one is watching" She grabbed Varen's shoulder just before he walked out the door, "please be careful."

"We promise," he nodded, "you don't have to worry about us."

We left the shop and began walking down the road, there were few people on the street, but each one was watching us carefully, fear in their eyes.

"We need to get out of here. Soon." I asked quietly, looking over my own shoulder to find nothing.

"Yeah, we're definitely not welcome here anymore." He replied, turning to walk backwards, which, oddly enough, wasn't out of the ordinary for him. Especially coming out of the Valtr's shop.

"But let's get somewhere we can open that parchment first." He whispered.

"Do you think our house is safe enough?" I inquired scratching my chin.

"I doubt anyone will come anywhere near it for a while. Do you still have the ward spells in case though?" he laced his fingers behind his head.

"I have the scrolls, but I've been waiting for…Deaths embrace!" I threw my head back.

"What?" Varen looked at me.

"The last order of supplies was supposed to have arrived at the Valtr shop today. I completely forgot to ask Kaja for it."

"Um, I think we better leave it for now," He said and pointed back toward the shop entrance.

"Why?" I turned and noticed Kaja's parents entering the shop.

"After the trial, we may not be welcome, not that we were very welcome before anyway," he said turning to face forward again.

I looked at my brother quizzically.

"Lately I've felt like her parents haven't liked us, or at least me. Anyway, they were in the crowd during our trial, and Leif seemed more upset than usual." He said gloomily.

"Why the sudden change? The Valtr's looked after us for a few years after mom and dad died. I never felt like they hated us."

"Well, even if they didn't before, I'm pretty sure we won't be welcome now.

"Well... let's just hurry and get it. I'm not going to let them stop me from getting it. Besides, it's already paid for" I mentioned, and looked pointedly at the shop.

"I'll follow your lead if you really want to, just hurry." Varen said.

I nodded, and we began to walk back toward the shop when we heard yelling and saw my scepter thrown out the doorway.

"You have got to stop leaving that places." I turned and saw my brother reaching into his robe for his spell book. I grabbed his wrist.

"You want to fight them?"

"I don't want to, but I get the feeling it might come to that."

"Well we need to avoid it we have barely been able to raise a single human, and then we had to sleep for days to get our energy back, we can't possibly fight them." I hissed.

"So, what do we do?" He said, frustrated.

"Unless you want to melee, there's nothing we *can* do."

"If I have to I will." he said, his jade eyes seemed to glow a little more than usual as he spoke.

"Calm down Varen." I sighed, "If you try to fight, you know we'll all just end up dead. If not from Kaja's parents, from the rest of the guard"

He didn't remove his gaze from the store front.

"Besides, you know how she can handle herself," I continued, putting my hand on his shoulder.

"I guess you're right, are you still planning on getting the supplies?" he asked looking at the doorway.

"I am," I nodded.

"Well then, let's hurry. The sooner we get them the sooner we can leave. He stabbed the end of his staff into the ground.

We ran down the dirt road in the direction of the store and I picked up my scepter from the ground a few feet from the doorway. We entered to find Kaja standing near the back of the store, a shelf knocked over and items scattered between her and her parents who turned as we entered, their faces paling slightly.

"Hey everyone," Varen said, stepping towards the counter nonchalantly, "we came back to pick up some supplies." He stopped speaking as if having just taken in the scene in the shop. "Oh, sorry we are not interrupting anything are we? Is there a problem here?" he asked cocking and eyebrow, as his hand almost imperceptibly reached into his robes.

"Yes, there's a problem here." Kaja's mother pointed at my brother, "You."

"Well, that was uncalled for. We just came to get some things to leave, I really don't suggest you insult us," he pulled out both his purse and his knife from his cloak and set both down on the counter directly next to him, "Or we might just do something we'll regret. After all," he glanced at Kaja, "We're dangerous exiles, remember?"

"But we'd like to avoid a scene just as much as you would," I finished, stepping into their view next to my brother, "Now, I'd like to pick up the supplies I ordered a couple weeks ago. They were supposed to be here today, yes?"

I felt myself use every bit of magic I could muster with that little sentence. I was attempting to charm the family man into focusing on us, giving Kaja a chance to slip out.

I could see an internal argument happening within him from the looks that flashed across his face until finally, her father went behind the counter and opened it.

"Fine. Buy it and don't come back." he spoke forcefully, placing the bag of items on the counter, the list of what's inside rolled up and bound to it.

"We don't intend to come back," Varen snapped at him, "Unless you haven't heard, we've been exiled."

Kaja's mother, glared at my brother as I paid; I took my sweet time, giving Kaja even greater chance to put distance between them, before we left. I made sure I grabbed my scepter this time, and Varen put away his purse and knife as we left.

"Well that went well, but if looks could kill, you would have died there on the shop floor," I laughed.

"Several times, it's not the first time I've gotten that look from them." My brother chuckled. "Now, let's go home, put up those wards, and read the message, unless you would rather leave now," he whispered to me.

"We should probably read the message first, in case there's something we need to do before we leave." I reasoned.

"To the house it is," he replied, leading the way.

We arrived and Varen hopped the fence once more. It was only a few feet tall, more to keep the cattle and wild animals out more than people. We made it up the path to the house. We stepped inside and immediately blocked all the windows and closed the doors.

"Will you set up the wards?" Varen asked, lighting a candle and setting it on the table.

"Doing that as we speak," I replied, taking a seat. I closed my eyes and reached out to the energy around me, drawing it in.

"Alright, do you need a scroll? I think I have one in my pack..." Varen said.

"Nope, I studied the spell this morning, so I'm good," I said, nodding in his direction. The next step was to set up some magic pillars as anchor points to keep the effects range constant.

"Okay, I'm going to light a few more candles so that we can read it," He said, opening some drawers and almost tripping over his bag once on his way back, "you done?"

"Almost," I said, "Just putting up the last anchor."

"Alright then," Varen said taking a seat across from me.

Once the last magic anchor point was in place, I reopened my eyes. His pale skin looked yellow in the light of the candles, and green eyes glowed slightly in the dark.

"So, what does it say?" he asked, hopefully.

"Give me a second." I pulled the folded parchment from my cloak pocket, slowly I read, "Meet me outside the village after dark. I will supply horses for us," I read, "Wait... us??"

"You don't think..." Varen asked with a worried expression, but I could see a hint in his eyes that he might have been more than a little hopeful.

"I do, actually," I said before he could complete his sentence.

Chapter 2

Kaja's Escort

Kaja

"I think that's everything," I said looking over my supplies one last time in the low lantern light. The horse dug at the ground eagerly.

"If you are going to leave the safety of town, don't you think you should at least take the sword and dagger your uncle gave you?" I froze at the voice behind me. Gathering my thoughts and reigning in my nerves, I turned to face my father as he entered the stable.

"I'm just going for supplies, dad, I shouldn't need it." I smiled innocently.

"Odd, we just brought in supplies last week, how could we already be running low?"

"I'm not sure, all I know is that when I took inventory today there were several things that we needed to resupply from Astor. Perhaps someone has been breaking into the store at night and making off with supplies."

"Ah," my father leaned against one of the stall gates, "Perhaps I should speak to the high cleric and get some men to keep an eye on it at night." He looked at the horse and sighed, "Of course the thief wouldn't need to break in if they had a key. That's a lot of supplies for a single day's trip for one person, Kaja."

"Do you think so?" I asked incredulously, "I just wanted to be prepared."

"Which, of course, is why you would leave your weapons behind."

I winced slightly, but reigned it back in quickly, "You're right, father, it was foolish of me to leave them behind."

"And even more foolish to lie to your father." He shook his head. "Do you really believe me so blind that I can't see what you are planning Kaja?" I opened my mouth to respond but he held up his hand, "No more lies; no more secrets. You were planning to slip out tonight and join the Valbrandrs in their exile."

"Yes." I couldn't look at my father anymore, so I stared at the ground.

My father sighed and smiled "You are so much like your uncle. Are you sure you aren't his child?" he teased.

"What do you mean?" I asked.

"Kaja, the Valtr family has been a merchant family for a very long time, and it was always expected that at least the oldest child would carry on the tradition."

"Isn't he older than you?" I asked.

My father nodded, "When we were born, we were each to inherit a share of the family shop once we were old enough to tend it. But my brother, your uncle, felt a call to adventure. He didn't want to spend his life as a merchant. He sold his share of the shop to me to get enough money to strike off on his own, wherever his journey may take him. And just like him, if this is where your heart is taking you, I know I can do nothing to stop you."

"You aren't upset?" I asked.

"If I'm being honest, your mother and I had always hoped that you would meet a young merchant and settle down and carry on the shop, but I've known of your feelings for Varen for a good while now. You don't hide it well, and he does even worse. Kaja, I want you to be happy, and while I'm sad that your happiness is taking you away from me and your mother, I would rather that than live out the rest of your life regretting that you didn't go with them. But if you're going to go, I simply ask that you be safe." He held out my blades once more.

I took them gently. "Thank you, dad." Then I stopped, "Doesn't mom want to say goodbye as well?"

An embarrassed look crossed my father's face, "Your mother doesn't know about this. If she did, we would both be dragged back and locked in the house for the next ten years." He chuckled lightly.

"What are you going to tell her?" I asked.

"Let me worry about that." He smiled momentarily before his face turned serious, "Kaja, I know that the Valbrandrs are exiled and it's not safe for them here right now, but I want you to promise me something."

"What?" I asked nervously.

"After some time, when things have calmed down and people have begun to forget them. Come back and see us. This goes against my instincts as a father, because a parent's greatest fear is to say goodbye to their child for the last time."

I nodded, feeling the pressure of tears welling up in my own eyes. "I will father."

"Good." He smiled and picked up a bag I had only just noticed at his feet. Moving to the other side of the horse he began moving things from this back to my pack bags."

"What is that?"

"I've packed you some things you may need. Basic medicinal supplies, a few cured meats, and some extra coin in case you need it. You should also take another horse with you. It will help spread the load, plus two horses should be able to carry the three of you. Knowing the Valbrandrs, they haven't entirely grasped the gravity of the situation. The need to leave, and the faster they can get out, the better. There will be no mercy if they are found." He knelt to check the saddle straps and nodded, satisfied. He stepped around and pulled me into a strong embrace. He held me there for a moment before releasing his grip. I kissed his cheek lightly and he turned to leave.

"Kaja," he stopped at the barn door, "please be safe."

"I will, dad." I smiled as I watched him leave the barn, and I felt tears well up in my eyes once more.

* * *

Varen

    I sighed lightly and looked back toward the gate. As far as the guards knew we had left more than an hour ago, but after getting out of sight we had ducked into the trees and quietly made our way back. My sister waited deeper in the trees for fear of being spotted, but the cover of the trees and the hanging clouds from recent rains provided enough darkness that my cloak made me near invisible.

    I cast my mind back, remembering years ago when our teacher, Ellara, had given it to me years ago, so we could slip out of town to get to the training field. I towered above other kids fairly early making slipping out of town more of a challenge than it already was. After all, it's hard not to notice someone who's eyes glow in the dark.

    "Hold. Who approaches the gate?" The guard's voice drew me from my reflection.

    "Relax, it's me. I'm going to gather some supplies from the next few towns," A female voice replied.

"Lady Valtr?" My ears perked up slightly at the sound of Kaja's family name, "Couldn't you wait until morning? The roads are dangerous after sundown."

"The supplies are needed quickly. Besides, I can handle myself."

I could see the guard she was addressing look at his partner.

"Do you intend to stop me?" She rested her hand on the haft of her sword.

"No Ma'am. Have a safe trip" he stepped aside, allowing her to pass.

"Is the whole town afraid of her blade?" I thought, holding back a half-chuckle. Kaja was probably one of the most skilled swordsmen in the town, at least for our age. Of course, her uncle was a grand adventurer and taught her any time he was in town, so she had a bit of an advantage. There were even a few times my sister and I attempted to spar with her. None of them ended well.

I spun as I felt a hand on my shoulder, "Varen, we've got to cut her off after the guards can't see us."

"Right" I nodded, staying close to my sister as we followed Kaja from the trees.

We had walked about sixty yards until the road turned and Kaja had moved out of the guards' sight. I looked back to my sister as I moved into the road and a felt a sudden blow to my chest. My hood slipped as I fell, dispelling the cloak's magic and leaving me visible on the ground.

"...Owww...." I groaned, trying to catch my breath as my sister cackled behind me.

"Oh, gods." Kaja whispered, "I am so sorry, I didn't know it was you," she knelt and grabbed my arm, pulling me back to my feet.

"Don't be, that was funny." Celenia snorted, "Do it again."

"I'd rather she didn't," I replied rubbing my jaw.

"Well, that's because you took the hit."

Kaja rolled her eyes "Are you two done joking around? If we are going to get away from the cleric, we should probably get going," Kaja interrupted.

Celenia looked at Kaja, holding up her fingers, "Whoa, whoa, whoa, what do you mean 'we'?"

"Well," Kaja stammered slightly, "I have to go get some things from the next few towns anyway, and I figured you two, being the big strong heroes, you are," she glanced my way, "I figured..."

Celenia cut her off, "Sorry, Hun, we're not heroes. We're criminals, exiled for blasphemous acts." She threw her arm to her forehead dramatically.

"Well, either way," she said to Celenia, "I figured you would be willing to...erm... escort me?"

Celenia turned to me and gave me a questioning look.

"Well, it could be a good cover; people are looking for a pair of exiles, not a group of three. Besides, we are heading the same direction. Where's the harm?"

"I guess you're right," Celenia conceded, nodding with her eyes closed and her arms crossed, "But you two'd better not go goo-goo over each other."

I felt my face heat up and I looked away quickly, hoping the cover of the night would hide my face.
"So how should we travel?" Kaja asked, "I have two horses with me. One is loaded down heavier with supplies, so only one rider there, but the other should be able to carry two."

"Why did you only bring two horses?" I asked, cocking my head to the side.

"Well, if I took one horse, my parents would think I followed you two on horseback. On the other hand, if I took three horses, they would know what I was planning. Two horses are enough for me and some supplies. It should throw them for a little bit anyway.," she said with an impish smile, """ She pat a small bag which made a slight jingling sound, "and it's not the first time I've gone with a couple horses to other towns to get supplies. By the time they realize I'm not coming back we should have at least a few days head start."

"I... suppose it makes sense," Celenia commented rather hesitantly, "but why did you say they would *know* what you were planning? What are you planning? You are planning to return, yes?"

"Well, erm-" Kaja struggled for words.

"Talk later. Incoming" I hissed hearing voices approaching down the path.

I pulled up the hood of my cloak. As I faded back into imperceptibility, Celenia stared intently at Kaja. Finally, my sister stepped back into the tree line, leaving Kaja apparently alone."

"Lady Valtr." The town guard approached, unknowingly running right past me, "Lady Valtr, are you all right? I thought I heard voices down here and I knew you had come through with your horses. I came to make sure you were okay."

"Voices? I didn't hear anything. Did you hear me? I stopped to recheck my supplies, and I was listing through them as I checked."

"No, it wasn't you, it was…" The guard hesitated.

"Yes?"

"Perhaps it's just the stress of the day," he shook his head, "But I thought it was the Valbrandrs. They left tonight as well. It's hard to believe that they were hiding such a dangerous secret. You should be careful while on the road, who knows what they are capable of. Are you sure you wouldn't like an escort to town? I'm sure we can find a few men; or I could do it personally if you would like."

"N-no, I think I'll be alright, thank you" she stammered.

I tried, unsuccessfully, to cover a snicker.

"What was that?" the guard jumped.

My sister, thinking quickly, did an impression of an owl to cover up for my slip. Personally, I think it was a poor impression, but it seemed to fool the guard.

"*This is what happens when you have a layman guard. Trained for combat, not intelligence*" I rolled my eyes as I moved quietly through the tree line to my sister.

"I best get going. The sooner I get to Astor, the sooner I can get back with supplies."

"Are you sure you don't need any help?"

"I'm fine." She asserted, probably a little more forcefully than she intended, "I assure you I can handle myself."

"Very well, miss Valtr." he sounded slightly dejected.

"Now, if there is nothing else, I should get going."

"Ah, there is one more thing.,"

"Yes?"

"I've heard that if you see the Valbrandrs, we are to report back their whereabouts."."

"Did the Cleric command this?" Kaja's eyes narrowed.

The guard nodded. "He didn't say why though. Probably to ensure they actually leave, but who knows. Anyway, if you see them let us know when you return. We've also been instructed not to make contact if we should see them. He says they are very dangerous."

"Thank you, I'll be careful.," She said, "Oh, and if you see my parents, tell them nothing of our meeting tonight, for, at least a week, I'm planning this trip to surprise them."

"A week? Astor is less than a day's journey. How far do you plan on going?"

"It depends. Some of the supplies we need can be a little harder to find. I may have to travel farther to get them. I hope to be back within a week but it's hard to say."

"All right then, safe travels." the guard waved as he walked back toward the town gate.
"Well, I don't think *he'll* be bothering us again anytime soon," My sister spoke up from behind me, causing me to jump slightly.

"I *hate* when sneak up on me." I nearly shouted.

"I didn't even do it on purpose this time, you were just too distracted by your *girlfriend*" she teased.

"We're not- I mean-" I floundered."

"You guys realize that just because you are invisible does not mean I can't hear you, right?" Kaja asked, shaking her head.

"Yeah, what's your point?" My sister said, grinning ear to ear.

"Let's get going," I shook my head, "before my sister has the chance to embarrass me again" I mumbled the last sentence, glad I had a cloak of shadows to hide my own flushed face.

Chapter 3

Caves

Kaja

I hoped the dim light of dusk was covering my flushed face. I couldn't see Varen, but he mumbled something under his breath that I couldn't quite make out. I'm was it had something to do with Celenia, since I managed to hear a lot of 's' sounds, but I thought better of asking.

"Shall we get going?" I suggested, the longer we sit here the longer it's going to take to get to Astor."

"Sounds great on all accounts," Varen replied from empty space nearby.

"On to Astor." Celenia cheered, preparing to go on foot, "Varen, you can take the horse Kaja supplied," she winked.

"Between the two horses, we should all be able to ride. If you'd rather ride alone Varen can ride with me."

"Listen Hun, as much as I like you, the last thing I want to do is spend the next few hours ignored while you two *lovebirds* flirt. Besides, someone should probably scout ahead so we can stay out of trouble."

I looked over at Varen and realized that I couldn't see him; For all I knew, he could have been making faces or shaking his fist at his smart-mouthed sister. I know I wanted to.

"You know we can't see you, right?" Celenia asked.

"For me that is rather preferable."

"Well, I would rather not look insane trying to converse with you on the road." I locked my eyes on a slight haze where his voice had come from.

"Well it's probably better than someone seeing you with me."

"Who are we going to run into out here? Vellara rarely gets visitors." I decided to change my tactic, "I want to see your face, will you take the hood off please?" I asked sweetly, taking a step towards him.

For a minute, he just stood there in the fading light it was getting even harder to make out his form.

"All right, you win," he finally sighed. He reached up and pulled the hood back snapping back into visibility. His green eyes were piercing in the low light. I watched as he eased himself effortlessly into the other saddle.

"Well, let's ride, shall we?"

He grinned and gave a nod, "Let's."

"Ugh, I'm going to be sick." Celenia groaned, "At least let me walk away before you start flirting." Celenia turned and started up the path.

"Is your sister always like that?" I hoped my face wasn't too flushed after Celenia's teasing comment.

"No." Varen replied and I was relieved momentarily. "I mean, she always teases me about my crushes, but it's usually worse. She's reigned it in tonight."."

"Your crushes? So, you *do* like me!" I nudged my horse closer.

"No. Well, yes but…" It was cute the way he stammered, though it made him look more than a little like a fish out of water.

"Varen, it's all right. I like you too. I have for a while now."

"…, you do?" I could see a grin slowly spread across his face.

"Yes, I do. I've just been waiting for you to get up the nerve to say something." I smiled back at him.

He gave me a strange look for a moment then started to laugh.

"What's so funny?" I asked sternly.

"I'm sorry. It just seems so unlike you."

"What does?"

"Waiting. You always seemed like the type of girl who would set off on her own to get something if she wanted it. You have a reputation of being one of the strongest people in the town."

I couldn't help but laugh as well, "Even I get nervous, Varen, and I had no idea how you would respond. No one likes rejection."

"I guess that's true." He nodded. Suddenly his face changed, and he looked down pulling an amulet from beneath his shirt. It seemed to be letting out a quiet hum as it pulsed yellow in his hand.

"What is that?" I leaned over to look. Varen didn't respond to my question, instead he quickly pulled his horse next to mine and put the reins into my hands. Before I could ask any more questions, he threw up the hood of his cloak and quickly blurred from sight.

"Varen what's going-" I stopped, suddenly hearing approaching hoof beats from somewhere down the path. The beats were heavy, much louder than the horses we rode. I waited in silence as they approached closer. Finally, the horse and rider came into view. The horse was much larger than most horses I had seen, and it wore plated armor. At its side rested weapons of various sizes and types. As intimidating as the horse appeared, the rider frightened me even more. He wore a suit of plate armor with only his head and hands were exposed, though I suspected the missing pieces were somewhere convenient should he need them. He was an older man, perhaps a decade or two older than my father. His hair was tinged with grey, and he wore a stern expression on his scarred face. He looked at me and nodded curtly as we passed. As we rounded the next bend Varen pulled his hood back and slipped back into visibility.

"Wow remind me not to get on his bad side."

"No kidding," I glanced over my shoulder, "I wonder why someone like him would be going to Vellara."

"I'm not sure," Varen took the reins back from me, "I saw some sort of emblem on his breastplate though, I wonder if he's a royal knight. Maybe it's Kingdom business."

"The King doesn't usually bother with Vellara; we're too far away."

"Must be something serious then."

"I guess…" I shook off my doubts and turned back to Varen, "How did you know he was coming? What was that you pulled out?"

"What, this?" Varen lifted his amulet.

"Yes. What is that? What was it doing back there?"

Varen smiled, "Celenia and I each made one with the help of our instructor. They are linked to each other; enchanted to be a sort of basic communication system. Let's use what just happened as an example. First Celenia, while scouting ahead, must have seen or heard the man we just saw as he was approaching up the path. Then all she had to do was reach up and touch her amulet while quietly saying a word like 'warning' or 'careful' the amulet then passes that to my amulet making it hum and glow yellow. Similar basic commands can be used. 'Danger' or 'Help' will make the other amulet hum and glow red. 'Safe' or 'clear' will cause mine to glow green. Because we set the commands to the common language, anyone can use them if they know how, making them far more versatile, we may need to make you one too."

"That's incredible," I replied, "that way one can give the other time to prepare for what's coming or call for help. Varen something like this would have revolutionized our town's alert system. Why didn't you take this to the Captain?"

"Well, we only made them a few months ago. On top of that they take a long time to make and cast the spell on for just the two of us, I can't imagine how long it would take to make enough for the whole town."

"Still the town would have pooled together to pay you for something like that."

"Or the Cleric would have demanded it and we wouldn't have seen a copper." Varen sneered.

I thought for a minute and had to admit he was right, but something else about the situation didn't make sense to me. "Varen, can I ask you something."

"Of course, What is it?"

"Well, you said that amulet's a protective measure, right?"

"Yes," Varen nodded.

"But as wizards studying necromancy, that can't be the only protective measure you used.

"If it was, we would have been caught long before now." He laughed. "Buy you're right; first off, we practiced at least once a week in a specific spot in the woods where we knew no one would accidentally walk in on us. Only we and our teacher knew the way there. On top of that we used wards that would warn us if someone followed us or tried to approach when we practiced. No one could magically spy on us either because we used anti-scrying fields. All things considered; it should not have been possible to discover us."

"Okay," I nodded, "So then, how were you discovered?"

Varen scratched the back of his head, "Well," He spoke slowly and carefully, "we have a theory, but there's no way to prove it. And if it did happen the way we think, it would have taken serious luck, or knowing both where and when we practiced."

"So, what happened?"

"It was a few night ago and, just like any other necromancy practice night, Celenia and I slipped out of town and made our way to our practice area. along the way, we activated the preset wards, the ones that would alert us if anyone was following us. It wasn't until we got to the grounds that we realized neither of us had brought the scroll that contained the anti-scrying spell."

"Scrying, that's the one that you can see things from a distance using a crystal ball or something right?"

"Yeah, although due to how expensive they are, only some mages use a crystal ball anything with a clear, still surface can be used. Most simply use a basin filled with water."

"I see, so you think someone scried on you."

"That's the theory, the problem is you either have to be looking for something or someone specifically, or you have to scry a specific area. Otherwise the spell can't find what you are looking for. That's why it's hard to imagine it happening, but it's also the only thing we can think of."

I see." I let silence fill the air as I wrapped my mind around what Varen had told me. Finally, I felt comfortable enough to continue. "So, as necromancers, what were your training grounds like?"

"It was a small clearing pretty deep in the woods. Clear enough for us to practice but the trees around were large enough to keep us out of sight from anyone wandering nearby, though that was unlikely. Off to one side we have all sorts of animal corpses all at different points of decay. A spell in place, to block the smell, as well as any further decay, in order to prevent that from giving us away and from animals trying to feed on the corpses."

I felt my stomach do a couple flips trying to imagine the rotting corpses piled up where they practiced. It must have shown on my face because Varen chuckled.

"I wasn't entirely comfortable with it either when we started, but you have to develop a stronger stomach. As Necromancers, our abilities are not always pretty... in fact, they rarely are."

"Yeah," I nodded, trying to calm my stomach, "So, where did the animals come from?" I wasn't sure that I wanted to know, but I didn't want him to stop telling me his story either.

"They could come from a few places," he shrugged. "We may find some on our path, sometimes we would go hunting beforehand. Sometimes Ellara would supply us some from what she had found."

"Who is Ellara?" I knew most of the people in the village, they all came through my families shop at some point or another, but I never heard of Ellara.

"Ellara is a Master Necromancer. She lives in the forest a good distance northwest of town. After our parents died, she came, claiming to be a friend of our parents who heard about the incident. She took care of us in our early childhood, and when we were old enough, and our abilities manifest themselves she began our training. She lived in our house and practically raised us. While she was there though, she went by the name Leeya."

"Leeya? I think I remember her. I was little, and my dad brought me to the shop. She came in and I couldn't help but watch her. There was something different about her, but I couldn't figure out what. I saw her fairly often until I was about ten, but after that I never saw her, when I asked my parents about it, they said she just disappeared."

Varen nodded, "My sister was 13 then, Leeya decided that we were old enough to take care of ourselves for our basic needs. In the cover of night, she snuck out of town and went back to live in the forest. After that my sister and I would sneak out to meet her for our lessons." A strange look crossed Varen's face for a moment, "I think we managed to get off topic a little bit."

"You're right! I'm sorry, you were talking about how you both forgot the scroll"

"Yes, the Anti-Scrying field spell. We could have prepared one there, but it could've taken hours; We could have turned back to get the scroll but if we got caught by the guards and they would have started asking questions. So, our only real options were either cancel our practice session and go home taking our time to make sure we aren't caught, or practice without the anti-scrying field. We had kept our practice location a well-guarded secret until that point, so the odds of someone wanting to scry on us was incredibly small. So, we decided to practice." Varen Chuckled, "I guess my sister and I should never gamble huh?"

"Is that why you two looked exhausted some mornings during the guard trainings?" I asked, Varen nodded in response. Then another question came to mind, "So that night was just you and your sister? I thought you said Leeya, or rather Ellara was training you. Why was she not there?"

"There is only so much you can learn from a teacher. If you really want to learn magic, you need to be able to study it yourself. Ellara was at all our training sessions as children, teaching us the basics of magic; but as we grew older, she would just give us spells to learn and we would show her our progress on the occasional session when she would show up."

"Okay, one last question. If Ellara has lived in that forest as long as you say she has, why has she not been discovered?"

Varen laughed, "Ellara is a master necromancer. She has been practicing magic in general for a very long time. She has Illusions, traps, curses, and who knows what else at her command. Several times we got lost trying to find it and she had to come get us."

I had to smile. *"Leave it to Varen to be able to laugh about getting lost."* I admired Varen, it was hard to believe that even now: Exiled from an area he has lived all his life, his parents and the woman who raised him gone, everything he ever knew taken away; he somehow managed to stay happy. It must have been hard to be necromancers even in town. The art was highly feared, so they must have had to watch their backs constantly, paranoid about being discovered.

"What are you two talking about?" Celenia's voice chimed as she came back up the path.

"Kaja asked how people found out we are Necromancers." Varen shrugged.

Celenia shot her brother a warning look. "Varen, you know we don't know how it happened."

"I know." Varen replied calmly, "I told her my best guess: The night we didn't have the anti-scrying scroll."

Celenia let out a sigh, "Well it's as good a guess as any, but even if that's the case we have no way of know who was scrying on us, let alone any ability to prove it."

"Celenia, you didn't come back here to lecture me," Varen changed the subject, "What is going on?"

Celenia looked at her brother for a moment then nodded her head towards the path "I found a cave up ahead and to the left, a little into the trees. I don't feel very comfortable out in the open in broad daylight. Especially when we are only hours away from the town. I say we stop and at least rest for a while before we continue."

"Well I think it would be better to get farther away from the town," I interjected, "but, you are right about being in the open in broad daylight, and the horses need water. Let's stop at this cave of yours and find a river."

"Right, just follow me."

We followed Celenia to the cave, well out of sight of the road with a convenient freshwater spring nearby. We quickly set to work to establish camp. Celenia brought a small bundle of twigs and some dry grass that Varen set up and lit with a spell. Meanwhile I took a blanket and tied it to a couple of stalactites, creating a rather effective curtain between the spring and the fire. We laid out bedrolls in the cave and tied the horses just downstream where they could drink.

"Well, I think with that our camp is good enough for now." Varen surveyed the area. "Is anyone hungry? I brought a little salted meat we could cook for dinner."

"I'm starving!" Celenia exclaimed, "Cook me something soon or we might be down to one horse!" Varen rolled his eyes, "Cel, how could you possibly be that hungry? You ate before we left!" "So? That was hours ago. It's time for food!" I couldn't help but chuckle at them, "Well, you two get it figured out, I think I'm going to relax in that spring for a while. Who knows the next time I'll be able to do that? "Do you need me to stand guard?" Celenia asked, a sly grin spreading across her face.

"I don't think that's necessary. I trust your brother." It was true. Maybe it was the loss of their parents played a role, but Varen and Celenia always seemed more mature than the others our age, despite their childish ribbing at one another. With a shake of my head I stood, grabbed a towel from my pack, and retreated behind the makeshift curtain, leaving Celenia to continue taunting her brother.

I approached the stream and peered into the clear water. Distorted reflections of moonlight and starlight danced across the surface. With a relaxed sight I stepped back toward the tree line. Hanging my clothes and towel carefully to keep them from getting dirty. No point bathing if your clothes are filthy. I approached the stream once more and dipped a toe in gritting my teeth against the chilly water. I didn't expect much else. This high up the source was probably mountaintop snow and Ice melting into the ground and coming back to surface here. I took a breath and forced myself deeper into the water making sure the curtain remained between me and the campsite. The stream wasn't deep, I had to kneel for the water to reach my shoulders. As my body adapted though the cold water felt rejuvenating. I tilted my head back dunking my hair into the water and ran my fingers through making sure that as much dirt was washed away with the stream as possible. Then I closed my eyes, allowing the current to carry the stresses of the day away with its trickling waters. I'm not sure how long I sat there before I opened my eyes and made my way back to the shore. I pulled my towel off the tree and began to whisk the moisture away with the rough fabric.

"Kaja?" Celenia whispered.

I jumped. A small shriek nearly escaped my lips before her hand pressed against my mouth.

"Shhh. It's only me, you're okay." Celenia said.

"Sorry, I just didn't expect anyone to come back here while I was *bathing.*" I emphasized the last work, but it seemed to be lost on her."

"Yes, well, if it weren't for the fact that I want to talk, I wouldn't have."

"Sounds important. Is something wrong?" I wrapped the towel around my waist and picked a relatively clean rock to sit on.
"Yes. I mean No. Well, I don't really know." She stammered.

"Cel, you can say whatever's on your mind. What do you need to talk to me about?"

"You... and my brother."

"Oh, okay," I could feel the blood begin to rush to my face.

"Look, I know you like him."

"Okay." I felt my face heat up a little more.

"And I know you want to be there for him."

"Uh-huh" I nodded.

"But I don't know that you understand what you are getting yourself into." That snapped me out of my embarrassment.

"What do you mean?" I asked confused.

"Okay, I am going to ask you what I asked earlier. This time, though, I want a straight answer," She fixed an intense stare on me, "why did you say they would know your plan was to meet us and go with us? You are planning to return, correct?"

"Well," I considered lying, but I knew it would catch up to me later. Besides, she deserved the truth, "No, actually, I have no intention of returning. At least, not without Varen."

Celenia leaned back slightly and sighed, "That's what I was afraid of."

"Look, I can take care of myself." I said, a little harsher than I meant for it to sound.

"I know you can. That's not what I'm worried about."

"Then what is?" I nearly shouted.

"It's just," She sighed again, "I know that you and your family have a good reputation in a great many towns."

"Yeah."

"But if word gets out that you are traveling with a couple of Necromancers, it will ruin you."

"I'm fine with that."

"Even if you are there's more. Necromancy is incredibly dangerous."

"Most magic is, isn't it?"

"Necromancy more than others." She shook her head, ". A single missed vowel could cause the spell to turn the very bodies you raised against you. A missed syllable could cause a spell to turn back and hurt you. A missed phrase and the spell will likely turn back and kill the casters."

"Okay," I said a little confused as to where she was going with this.

"The thing is," She sat down across from me on a stalagmite that had been broken off near the base, "My brother and I, we know the risks and have come to accept them."

"Right."

"There is a reason you usually hear about Necromancers traveling either alone or with other Necromancers. The spells tend to have an area effect, meaning, if misspelled the effects may not just stop at the casters, but those around them as well."

"I see." I replied, "Look, Celenia, you have to understand that it will take a lot more than that to frighten me off."

Celenia cut me off, "I am not trying to frighten you off. I tell you this so that you know the risks. And because I care for my brother. I know that he likes you, and if something were to happen to you because of him, well, he would never forgive himself."

"I see."

"I hope you do, for Varen's sake. And I expect you to make the right choice, whatever that may be."

"I will," I responded solemnly. Where did this girl come from? Not an hour ago she was silly, teasing, and being a pain in the hind quarters, yet here she was, talking to me straight, not hinting at anything and genuinely hoping for my welfare. I could see where Varen had gotten it from.

"Oh right, one more thing. Varen actually sent me back here to tell you the food is ready."

"Oh, all right, um" I looked at my towel wrapped body. "Tell him I will be out in a minute."

"Are you sure?" she replied wryly, "He will think you look

really good."

Well, wherever the old Celenia had been, she's back now.

"Just tell him"

"All right keep your pants on." She grinned as she left.

"This is delicious, what did you use to flavor this?" Celenia asked Varen as she wolfed down her meal.

"Thanks," he replied, "so, what took you two so long?"

"Are these carrots?"

"You're avoiding the question."

"What question?"

"What you two were doing behind our makeshift curtain?"

"What makes you think we were doing something? I swear these have to be carrots!"

I wasn't sure if Celenia was avoiding it to annoy her brother, or if she sincerely didn't want to discuss our conversation. I also wasn't sure if I wanted to get involved.

"Why are you avoiding the question?"

"Would it help if I told you we were talking about you? Are

those potatoes?"

"I'm not sure that did help," I finally decided to join in the conversation, "I mean, now he is looking at us suspiciously."

"He has every reason to be suspicious," Celenia giggled.

"What were you saying about me?" Varen asked

"That you're nosey," Celenia pointed at him with her fork.

"No, we weren't!" I amended quickly, trying to hide the fact that she was embarrassing me.

"Oh, c'mon, you know I don't mean it."

"Sometimes I wonder," Varen muttered.

"Aw, c'mon, you know you love me," Celenia replied, batting her eyelashes in false innocence.

Varen's response died in his throat as a deep growl echoed from within the cave.

"Varen, please tell me you have been practicing a ventriloquism spell behind my back."

Varen shook his head as a roar sounded.

Heavy footfalls could be heard approaching from within.

"Any idea what makes that kind of sound Kaja?" Varen asked.

"It's not any animal I've hunted. Actually, it sounds more monstrous if I'm being honest."

"Great, let me guess. None of us thought to check if the cave was already occupied." Celenia groaned.

Finally, an extremely large hand grabbed at the edge of the cave, behind it followed the large lanky creature. It scanned the area around it, its gaze landing on Celenia.

"Um, want some dinner?" she asked in a small voice holding out her bowl in the direction the towering creature.

It's eyes on the bowl, it began to emit a series of grunts and growls.

Celenia shouted in surprise as the top of her food caught fire.

"I'll take that as a no" I said.

"I think it's time to go." Varen slowly stood trying not to attract its attention.

"You think?" Celenia and I shouted simultaneously, startling the creature as it stepped back and let out another great roar.

The three of us took off toward the main road, not waiting to see if the creature would give chase, though it's lumbering footfalls behind us were answer enough.

"What is this thing? Varen asked, "I've never seen anything like it."

"It's hard to say. I didn't get the greatest look in the firelight, but it looked like it could have been trollkin." I replied.

"A what?" Celenia looked at me incredulously.

"A trollkin. As the name suggests they are most similar to trolls, but they have a leaner build and as we saw, a natural affinity with magic."

"Great," Celenia groaned, "Well, at least we seem to be faster. Its footsteps sound farther away."

"I don't think it'll stay that way for long." I shook my head, "That thing was a couple feet taller than Varen, and they are typically nocturnal. Most likely it's still groggy, but that won't last long."

"So, we have to fight it?" Celenia asked.

"My uncle has told me stories of it taking entire teams of people to take these things on, I doubt the three of us could do it."

"So, we can't outrun it, and we don't stand a chance fighting it. We've been exiled from town a full six hours and we're already doomed."

"Well," Varen piped in, "There may be one option."

Celenia and I both looked at him expectantly.

"We could give it something else to chase."

"And how do you propose we do that?" Celenia shook her head.

"Celenia we're out in the wild."

"And the animals are asleep."

"We could always wake some up."

"What we're going to find a den of wolves and poke them with sticks?"

Varen sighed, "You're not getting it. Kaja, you are probably the most skilled young fighter from the village. Do you think you could hold it off for a few minutes? Keep its attention on you?"

"I can try, but whatever you are doing do it fast. I don't know how long I can last one-on-one with that thing."

"Okay, we'll hurry. Celenia you grabbed your scepter, right?"

"Yeah, I've always got it, but- oh." She followed her brother into the trees.

Praying the thing was far enough away I dipped into the tree line, drawing a small blade from a sheath in my bracer. I closed my eyes and focused on my sense of hearing.

What am I doing? I can't take on a trollkin by myself. It's a predatory monster.

I shook the thoughts away; Varen has a plan, I just need to trust him.

Yeah, a plan for me to take the fall while he and his sister get away.

"Stop" I quietly growled at myself, "I've known them too long to think they'd do something like that. Especially Varen." I turned my focus to my quickly approaching opponent.

In order to stand a chance, I need to figure out how to approach him. He's a nocturnal predator, which means his night vision will be far better than mine, and his weapons will be teeth, claws, and of course magic. So, if I can stay out of range of his teeth and claws, all I have to do is keep him too busy to cast and I should be okay. I hope.

I heard the creature lumber down the road before coming to a stop. I could hear his breath as he began sniffing at the air.

Keen sense of smell, I won't be able to stay hidden long.

I sprang from my hiding spot, throwing my knife in the direction of the sounds. I scooped some stones during my tumble and landed crouched behind another tree. I heard the creature howl as it took a few staggered steps back. I poked my head out to see it cradling one side of its face in its large hand. As drew its hand away and blinked I saw the cut on its check just below the eye.

Blinding it would have been better, but not bad for aiming by ear.

I pulled a leather sling from a small pouch at my waist. Placing a stone in it I stepped out into the road and sent the stone flying in his direction, striking him in the side. He spun to face me and began to release a variety of grunts and growls.

"No, you don't." I grunted, releasing another stone into his jaw. The creature released a howl of pain as it reared up and slammed its large arms into the ground. I lunged into the tree line as he began to charge after me. I continued down the road running through the tree line as I heard the crunching of the trollkin charging behind me.

This isn't good. It's more awake now, more alert. It won't be long until it catches me.

A sudden roar behind me drew me from my thoughts. I looked back to see the creature stumbling wildly, swatting at something. Detaching itself from the creatures' leg I saw some sort of large rodent run down the path, followed closely by an owl. The creature chased after them, apparently forgetting all about me.

I closed my eyes and attempted to slow my pounding heart. My legs ached, and my lungs burned, but thankfully, I managed to hold it off without getting killed.

"Kaja?" I heard Varen call, "Kaja where are you?"

"Here," I pushed back to my feet, "I'm here." I stepped back out into the open road.

"Are you okay?" Varen ran up to me, his sister close behind.

"I'm fine. Just a little out of breath." I smiled weakly.

"So, what now? Do we go back to the cave?" Celenia asked.

"No way." I responded, "We may have distracted it, but that cave was likely it's home and it will return eventually."

"What about the supplies?" Cel asked.

"We likely bought enough time to get our supplies and find the horses, but we'll have to find somewhere else to rest."

"Cel and I found a clearing not far from here. That's where we found the corpses to... well, you saw."

I looked at him puzzled for a minute before it dawned on me.

"Wait, those animals were dead?"

"Yeah, we couldn't have given them command otherwise. It's only temporary though, you need a lot more skill and power to raise something permanently."

"How long will it last?"

Varen shrugged, "Half a day, maybe longer. Long enough to keep him out of our hair."

"All right then. Let's get our stuff and get settled in for the night." I shook my head, too tired to think about it any longer.

Chapter 4

The Necromantic Disease

????

"Morning patrols are the worst." Erlend yawned.

"Pay attention Erlend, we patrol the path to protect the city as well as the outlying towns. No matter how boring or how early the assignment, it is our duty to see it through to the best of our ability. We can't afford to be inattentive."

"Yeah, but we haven't even had any reports of trouble up this way. If there was, the captain would have sent more than two guards to patrol."

"Who do you think brings back the news of trouble Erlend? It's mostly the scouting guard."

"I thought it was the merchants and commoners that travel the road that report it." Erlend looked at me quizzically.

"Not if we're doing our job right. The idea is for us to find it and take care of it before it has the chance to affect the common people. If we wait, it's often too late."

"I guess that makes sense." He pouted slightly, "still I wish I could be doing something to prove myself more. I want to see some action. Take down some bandits or something."

I shook my head. I had to admit, I had many of the same ideas when I joined the Astorian guard. It was common really, the dreams of glory. It's never quite how you imagine it but try explaining that to a young guard.

"Sir Brunsvord, what kind of monsters are up this way?"

"You can just use my name Erlend. I'm a guard, not a knight. As for the monsters, goblins and their ilk are the most common troublemakers. Aside from that you have wandering beasts like wolves, maybe some bears."

"Anything that could do that?" Erlend pointed as some trees that leaned at odd angles. Upon closer inspection it appeared they had been pushed so hard that the trunk had separated from some of its roots.

"Nothing I've seen this way." I shook my head. "Yesterday's patrol made no mention of this, so it must be recent. Let's see if we can't follow the path to the culprit. Quiet now." I pulled my reigns slightly, redirecting my horse into the torn trees. Keeping our pace slow and careful we followed the damaged trail.

"I think it's leading toward the river," Erlend whispered, "It must be powerful to do something like this. Shouldn't we warn the town?"

I shook my head. "We need information. Warning them does

no good if we don't know what kind of creature it is and if it's actually a threat. It's one thing to damage trees, another if it's going after people."

"Won't we report it either way?"

"Yes, but the threat level will determine how fast, if at all, the guard will act on the report. Now keep quiet, I think I hear it up ahead." I dismounted my horse as quietly as I could and motioned for it to stay. Erlend followed suit. We crept our way through the undergrowth toward the source of the noise. We reached the trees nearest the riverside and I peered into the clearing. A large creature was hunched over drinking from the river. I scanned the clearing and saw it empty with the exception of what may have been a couple of animals at one time.

"What is it?" Erlend whispered.

"Nothing I've ever seen before," I shook my head, "Looks dangerous though. You need to report back to the town, be- "I heard him take off before I could warn him to caution. Unfortunately, I wasn't the only one. The creature spun on its heels as Erlend remounted his horse and took off. With a great roar it took off after him, completely ignoring me. They were both gone before I had time to recover from my shock.

"Great," I muttered "Erlend's gone with a monster on his heels. The guard better be ready." I shook my head and started back toward the road when something caught my eye. I stepped out of the trees to examine the carcasses I had noted previously.

"That's odd," I muttered to myself, "The bodies are torn apart, but there's almost no blood. If they were killed here the whole area should be spattered. They have also already begun to decay, but that creature couldn't have been here for more than a few hours." I shook my head, "no time to be looking too far into it, that thing will be chasing Erlend all the way to Astor." I ran back to where we had left our horses to find both of them gone. I let out a sigh, tossing my head back and looking toward the sky.

"Shh, someone's up there." I heard someone hiss from up the path.

I turned, hearing more voices muttering, though unable to make out anything further. I made my way up the path following the voices when they stopped. I scanned the path, searching for their possible origin when I felt the hair raise on my neck. I placed my hand on the hilt of my sword in reaction to the familiar instinct.

"I wouldn't." a voice warned behind me as I felt the point of a blade at the separation between my backplate and helmet.

I carefully removed my hand from the hilt and held it outward.

"Who are you?" The voice was feminine, but there was a sharpness to it that made it clear that the blade at my neck was not an empty threat.

"My name is Hjalmar Brunsvord, and I'm a guard for the city of Astor."

"What is a member of the Astorian guard doing out this way

alone?"

"My partner and I were on a routine patrol of the northern road when we saw some damaged trees down the path behind me. We followed them to a river where we saw a massive creature. I sent my partner to make a report but, in his haste, he drew the attention of the creature which chased him, scaring my horse in the process and leaving me with only one way back to town. On foot. There's little chance I'll make it back in time to help with my current situation, so hearing voices up here I decided to see if you happened to have faster means of transport."

"What did the creature look like?"

"It was tall, probably near 8 feet if it stood straight, as well as thin and lanky, with muscular limbs." The woman muttered something under her breath that I didn't catch. "You better come with me." I felt the blade withdraw. The woman stepped past me, leading the way up the path. She stood off to one side, never keeping very far. She motioned for me to continue following as she stepped into the trees. I tread carefully, keeping my senses sharp in the event I was being led into some sort of ambush. As we continued, I began to pick up voices. My hand moved to my sword, but I found a blade pointed at me in a flash.

"It's not in your best interest to make a move right now. We have no ill intention toward you as long as you show none toward us." I carefully removed my hand once more. She lowered her own blade but did not sheath it. She jerked her through the trees. I stepped past her, moving in the instructed direction.

I entered a small clearing, I saw two horses tied off to one side, various supplies were tied to the saddles.

"Don't stick that thing in my face!" I turned to see a brown-haired woman in some sort of robes glowering at a taller man near a boiling pot.

"What is going on?" The other woman stepped around me into the clearing.

"Oh, I'm just cooking breakfast," The young man gestured toward the fire with what looked like a large stick. The young lady in the cloak quite suddenly took a bite out of it.

"You know that was raw meat, right?" the young man looked at the woman quizzically.

"Yeah, so?"

"I can't believe we're related," The young man sighed.

"Is she okay?" I asked. The young man jumped, sending the stick of meat flying quite suddenly into the woman's face the juices splattering all over.

" ugh, really?" she wiped the meat and juices from her face.

"you brought him here?" The man looked at the woman closer to me, "Why?"

"Just hear him out, Var." she responded, "he said something that should concern us." She turned to me. "Well, introduce yourself and tell them what you told me."

"Well, my name," I said, "is Hjalmar Brunsvord. I'm an Astorian guard who was out on patrol with my partner when we came across a large creature. My partner, leaving to alert the town, drew the creature's attention and it chased after him. It scared my horse off in the process so now I have my partner and a creature heading towards Astor with no way to catch up. I heard voices up the path and decided to come see if you had a horse or other mode of transportation, so I can get to town and help fend this thing off."

The two by the cooking fire looked at each other, then at the woman who accompanied me.

"This creature was it fending off any animals?" the young man turned to me.

I shook my head, "No, but I did see some strange corpses in the clearing, they were torn to shreds without much blood. A bird and something else, I couldn't really tell."

The man looked at the woman who escorted me, "The trollkin?"

"I think so." She nodded.

"Death's embrace." The man threw back his head.

"Varen!" The woman next to him scolded.

"Hold on, you three knew about this thing?"

"Believe me, I wish we didn't." Varen responded, "but the three of us may have been the ones to anger it last night. Celenia, help me clean this up."

"But what about breakfast?" The woman beside him complained.

"There is a monster heading toward a town full of people and it's partially our fault Cel. We can get breakfast after we clean up our mess."

"Hold on just a second there. I can't let the three of you get involved here. This is a matter for the Astorian guard."

"This creature was on the road between Astor and Vellara, the town the three of us are from." The auburn-haired girl replied.

"What does that have to do with anything?"

The auburn-haired woman grinned, "Technically we're part of the guard for Vellara. The whole town is combat trained for a layman guardship."

"Are you sure you want to get involved with this? That creature looked nasty."

"If you want to use one of our horses then we come too." Varen looked me dead in the eye.

"Besides," the auburn hair girl continued, "We had to fend that thing off last night, if anyone knows how, it's us."

"All right," I shook my head, "I don't like it, but it doesn't sound like I can change your mind. I have one condition though."

"What's that?" the one named Celenia raised an eyebrow.

"If it gets too dangerous, the three of you will back off and let the guard handle it."

"Fine," The young man said, "But we'll judge when it becomes too dangerous. Now help us load this stuff up. The faster we pack the faster we can be on our way.

It didn't take long to get their things together. The three seemed to be traveling light. The young man, Varen, climbed up on one horse behind the auburn-haired woman I had first met. Leaving me sitting behind the one named Celenia.

"So, the three of you had a run in with the creature last night? You don't look any worse for wear."

"It wasn't intentional," Varen said, "We accidently made camp near it's den. It came out and got aggressive, so we ran."

"And it just let you get away?"

"No. It took off after us." Celenia said.

"So how did you get away?"

"Well, we had Kaja here hold it off while my sister and I… created a distraction." He spoke the last part of the sentence slowly, deliberately. There was something this group wasn't wanting to say.

"What kind of distraction? The three of you are the only ones who have dealt with this thing. I need to know what happened." Silence was my only reply, "What are the three of you hiding?"

Varen sighed, "You know the animal remains you found in the area where you found the trollkin?"

"What about them?"

"They were our distraction." He said.

"Varen!" his sister scolded.

"If we have to do it again, he'll know anyway, I'd rather he finds out like this."

"What do you mean? What would I find out?"

Celenia shook her head but said nothing more. Varen continued.

"My sister and I are mages, well, students anyway. Kaja held the creature off so my sister and I could cast a spell to get the trollkins attention away from us. We found the corpses of those creatures and we animated them. We instructed them to get the trollkins attention and lead it away from us."

"You animated the corpses? But that's- "

"Necromancy." Celenia finished my sentence, "My brother and I practice necromancy."

The three of them looked at me, gauging my reaction. No doubt this is what they were afraid of telling me. *This group had been defensive from the beginning, now it made sense. Necromancy is a taboo practice; it has been for most of my life.* I looked between the three of them. *Still, they had every opportunity to kill me and probably would have been safer if they had. I don't think they have any evil intentions; besides they are helping me get to town and take down a monster, none of which they had to do.*

"Your secret's safe with me." I shook my head, "Besides, if I'm being honest, I don't know much about magic in general, let alone necromancy. You two don't look the part though, I've always heard necromancy was magic cast by old wrinkly fellows who looked like they may die at any moment."

"Usually that's true," Varen nodded. "It's a side effect of the disease

"Disease?" Kaja looked at him.

At least this information is new to someone besides me.

"Yes, disease," Celenia jumped in, "You see, magic changes a person, especially if they practice a specific form. Most of the effects aren't so intense, or dangerous for that matter, but every necromancer gets this disease, it's sort of inherent to the system. It's what causes Necromancers to get old, wrinkly, and skinny as a bean pole early in life. Before the disease hits, a necromancer only has limited affinity for necromancy. Along with the disease comes a Necromancers full power. Most necromancers go through it around the age of twenty, but, because of our lineage, we go through it during infancy. Varen and I were lucky enough to survive."

"Your lineage?" I asked.

"The two of us are third generation necromancers, "Varen nodded, "Add to that our great great great great great grandfather was demi-lich who defeated a frost wyrm and making a staff from one of its wing bones," Varen pulled his staff from beside his horse. "This staff has been passed down through generations. That is, so long as the heir survives the disease."

"But if you already went through this disease, shouldn't you be old and wrinkly?" I asked.

"No, not necessarily. Since we are third generation necromancers, the disease affects us in a different way." Celenia said.

"Like what?"

"Well," Varen began, "The necromantic disease changes our bodies, brings us nearer to death in a way. It slows the bodily aging process, so the two of us will likely live much longer than your average person. Poisons and toxins have almost no effect, our bodies neutralize it. Also, because necromancy has been in our family so long our affinity is much greater than that of most necromancers."

"You said your "affinity" is greater, what does that mean?"

"Basically," Celenia explained, "it means that with enough training we can do things other necromancers can do, but with less effort."

"Is that all it does?"

"Well, we really don't know." Varen explained, "It's very possible it could have other effects we haven't run into yet. We're still fairly young, and with necromancy especially, it's rare to have this many generations that practice. Often somewhere an heir breaks off and studies some other magic with fewer risks or does something else entirely; if there is a surviving heir."

"This disease doesn't sound too bad. At least, not for the two of you" I said.

"Well, these are the aftereffects. How the disease changed us. The disease itself is horrible. It slowly brings you closer and closer to death. Starting with simple things like fever and chills and eventually progressing to organ failure." Varen said.

"I see. Any risk of catching it being around you?" I asked

"Not likely." Varen shook his head, "We were afflicted because of our bloodline. In your and Kaja's case it would take something like wild necromancy or contact with a powerful necromantic artifact. As long as my sister and I don't lose control of a spell or do something completely reckless, you should be fine."

"I see the gate up ahead." The one named Kaja called back.

I looked down the road. The large wooden gate had been smashed to pieces and the guards were absent from there post. We could hear the din of panic from withing.

"Well that doesn't look good," Celenia said.

"Way to state the obvious, Celenia," Kaja said.

"Well, it's our mess. Let's take care of it," Varen kicked his horse into action, charging into the town.

I held on tightly as Celenia as she followed suit. We road past a number of buildings from what I could see they were mostly intact with only minor damage to the outer walls. Passing this quarter, we entered Astor's open market area. The trollkin stood in the middle swinging his arms wildly as several guards attempted to hold it back. Behind them several more were ushering people toward the southern quarter.

Kaja grabbed hold of Varen's shoulders, hoisting herself from the saddle and rolling to her feet. She drew a small blade from her bracer and threw it, striking the creature in the shoulder. The trollkin spun to face the new attacker.

"Where did that come from?" Celenia shouted.

"I always have something on me, even when it doesn't look like it." Kaja winked.

"Remind me not to make her mad," I said to Celenia.

"You have no idea," She laughed.

Celenia brought our horse to a stop, pulling a small rod from a saddlebag. She caught my expression from over her shoulder.

"Basic magic is all I'm using," She assured me, "I don't intend to cause any more problems for me or my brother." A strange expression flashed across her face, replaced immediately by determination. Was it sadness? Regret?

"Watch your head!" Varen shouted, pulling me from my thoughts as a large beam from a stall flew just over our heads. The horse reared up, dumping the two of us from the saddle.

"You okay?" Celenia asked, pulling herself to her feet.

"Yeah, I'm fine," I stood, drawing my sword.

Kaja evaded another massive swipe. Then another. A small glowing orb struck the creature's shoulder. The smell of singed fur filled the air.

The creature howled with rage and searched for its attacker. It spotted Varen, another glowing orb growing in his hand as he chanted.

The creature dropped to its haunches; its eyes trained on Varen. There was no time to think. I drew my sword and charged.

As I reached the creature, he launched himself towards Varen. I swung, the tip of my blade barely caught its foot, but it was enough. It fell to the ground with a howl. Varen hurled the fiery orb, catching its cheek. The creature pulled itself to its feet.

Kaja drew a rapier from its sheath. She lunged in for a swing, but the creature spotted her. I swiped her away with a powerful arm, sending her into a nearby stand.

"Kaja!" Varen exclaimed.

The creature turned toward him once more. It lunged forward. I swung, attempting to distract it again, but my blade found only air.

Varen stood frozen. Celenia shouted a word unintelligibly. I watched as a wall of ice sprung from the ground in front of Varen. The Trollkin slammed into it, shattering the ice; but the delay was enough for Varen come to his senses and scramble out of the way.

Celenia fell to her knees, her exhaustion overtaking her. I moved quickly, placing myself between them and the creature. The creature turned and watched. I held my blade ready and tried to look for any opening.

At this rate we're gonna be dead. These kids are tiring out and we seem to have hardly scratched it.

"Celenia, Varen, get Kaja and fall back!"

"What? Why?" Celenia shouted.

"Because it's too dangerous! Now fall back!"

"Leaving you to die?" Varen growled, "I don't think so."

"I'm a guard. It's my job. Now get out."

As I spoke the words the creature howled and clutched its shoulder. I turned my head sharply trying to analyze the surroundings.

"Shield men approach!" a roar came from behind the creature. Several guardsmen circled around and forced themselves between us and the creature.

The creature eyed the new combatants. Then another yell from behind.

"Spearmen approach! If it tries to escape the circle, then strike!"

"Hjalmar!" I turned to the barrel-chested man approaching me.

"Captain!" I saluted.

"Stop saluting and get out of the way. You're blocking formation. You and your friends."

"Right! Celenia, Varen. The guard have this handled now, let's get Kaja and get out of their way."

The siblings nodded their head in response, Varen extinguishing a fireball before running to the collapsed stall.

"Kaja, are you all right?" Varen started shing aside the fallen cover.

"Yeah, I think so." Kaja gasped, "just give me a minute to catch my breath. That hurt."

"Well, if you're okay we need to clear out, so the guard has space to take care of this."

"Right," Celenia agreed, "We should probably find the owner of this stall later and apologize too."

"Hopefully it doesn't cost too much to fix." Varen knelt to look at the various beams and cloth.

"Ah, I wouldn't worry too much about it, lad." A large figure stepped from behind the building beside the stall, "The stalls are mostly supplied by the town, and the wares are hardy. If they are damaged, well" he shrugged, "Personally I'm just happy to see that the young lady is all right."

"I take it you are the merchant." I looked the man top to bottom. He didn't seem armed. "I thought the guard evacuated this area already. What are you doing here?"

The man looked back at me, "I saw some of the fight as I was leaving. Saw her get thrown into my stall. I wanted to make sure she was all right."

"Oh," Kaja looked embarrassed, "I can assure you I am fine."

"Yeah," Celenia interrupted, "The flight went great, she just needs to work on her landings."

The merchant let out a deep laugh, dispelling some of the tension. "Yer brave youths, I'll give you that. Where'd ye learn to fight like that?"

"We're from Vellara," Kaja pulled herself to her feet with some help from Varen. "We all learn how to fight in Vellara."

"I've heard of Vellara. You use a layman guard, right? Everyone is ready to defend should the need arise?"

"Yeah, exactly. Have you been before?" Celenia asked.

"Nah, never been myself, but an acquaintance of mine has before; but enough about that. Your friend here is right, we probably shouldn't be here while the guard are taking care of that creature. Do you three have somewhere you're staying?"

"No. We just got into town, so we haven't made any arrangements yet." Varen replied.

"Well, I may know a good place. The owner's a good friend of mine so if she has the space, I'm sure she'll put ye up. Follow me."

The man led the way down the alley taking us the long way to keep away from the commotion in the marketplace. After a few twists and turns he led us to 'The Drowsy Merchant' a local inn and tavern that was known for decent accommodations at a good price. It wasn't the nicest inn in town, not by a long shot, but it was a common spot for some of the less wealthy merchants that made their way hear during market season. The inside was crowded, probably a result of the market evacuation. The guard would have tried to funnel the crowds to any indoor space large enough.

"Ingrid!" The man shouted, "Ingrid"

"What do you need Will?" a woman shouted from the bar, "Can't you see I have my hands full here?"

"Let the barmaids handle it for a minute I want to introduce you to some folks."

"This had better be important, Will." The small dark-haired woman pushed her way through the crowd.

"It's me Ingrid, would I be bothering ya if it wasn't?"

"If your last visit was any indicator, then yes." She laughed.

"I'm hurt. I'll have you know tha' those drinks were for business purposes."

"Sure, they were." Ingrid smiled, "Now what is it you wanted?"

"I wanted tae introduce these fine youth to ye. This is Varen, Celenia, and Kaja. They helped keep the monster in the market occupied while the guard got everyone out."

"Is that so?" She looked the trio over, "Well thank you for your help. A lot of people are safe because of you."

"Ingrid." Will pulled her attention back, "They just got intae town and haven't a place to stay. Ye wouldn't happen to have any rooms te spare would ye?"

"I believe I had some people leave early this season thanks to that monster. Let me check my books." Ingrid vanished into the crowd.

"Do we have the money to pay for a stay?" Varen asked his sister.

"We can probably stay for a night or so, but we can't stay long; not just for money reasons."

"Dinae worry about the cost lads and lasses, I'll cover ye. If Ingrid decides to charge ye at all. 'Twas a great service ye did for the town." Will smiled.

"You really don't have to—" Varen attempted to protest but Will held up his hand.

"Nonsense lad. It's my pleasure an' I won't take no fer an answer."

"That's awfully generous of you, sir. May I ask why you are so eager?" I asked.

Will shrugged, "Ahm just grateful is all. Thanks to ye a good number of people are safe. Ah know it's yer job as a guard, but these three helped of their own will. Not out o' duty. That's not to say tha' yer efforts aren't appreciated too, friend. An if there's some way I can repay ye as well, let me know."

I opened my mouth to inquire further when a shout from the entrance caught my attention.

"Hjalmar!" Erlend shouted. "The creatures been taken care of and we're working on cleaning up the market area, so the Captain asked me to come find you."

"All right," I nodded and turned back to the young trio. "My friends, duty calls. Enjoy your time in Astor and come find me if you need any help."

*   *   *   *   *

Varen

We waved goodbye to Hjalmar as he ran to help with the reconstruction. *"We got lucky this time"* I thought. *"Hjalmar was willing to listen and work with us. As word gets out, I'm certain that others won't be so friendly. We need to be on our way as soon as possible before that happens.*

"Shall I take you to the rooms then?" Ingrid asked.

"Yes please." Celenia nodded.

"Follow me then." Ingrid led the way through the large crowd. She gestured to young blonde woman

"If you need food or drink during your stay here just pick a table and Eileen well attend to you." She turned back towards the counter and called, "Eileen."

"Yes, Ma'am?"

"This is Varen, Celenia, and Kaja. They are my special guests this evening. If they need anything, please get it for them."

"Yes Ma'am" Eileen nodded curtly before returned to her duties.

"Follow me." Ingrid made her way up to the second floor.

The stairs fed directly into a hallway with doors at regular points on either side. After a couple of turns we reached the end.

"These will be your rooms. Those two doors on the left are connected by a door so it may be more comfortable for the ladies to take those, however they are your rooms so you may arrange yourselves as you like. If you require anything else, please come find me." Ingrid smiled and walked past us, leaving us alone in the hallway.

"Well, what do you want to do for the room arrangements?" I asked

"Ingrid's suggestion sounds fine to me.... What do you think Celenia?"

"That should work fine. We have more important things to discuss." Celenia opened the door to our right as we followed close behind. I closed the door behind me.

"What do we need to discuss Celenia?" Kaja asked.

Rather than answering Kaja's question Celenia placed a finger to her lips. We watched as Celenia sat down near the middle of the floor then motioned where she wanted us to sit. We obeyed, creating a small circle on the floor.

"Varen would you like to."

"Yeah." I looked around the room carefully, trying to memorize it the best I could. The bed sat in the back corner of the room with a small nightstand sitting near it. A small window, which looked into an alley next to the inn, sat just past the foot of the bed. In the back corner opposite the bed sat a small chest, the key to which rested on the nightstand. Near the front of the room, opposite the bed and next to the door, sat a small dresser. I turned back to the center and closed my eyes, then I opened my mage's eye. I set anchor points in each corner of the room and finished the final words of the spell I had prepared that morning. The spell completed I could see it take shape in my mind, like a large bubble shimmering into my mental image. I opened my eyes.

"It's done," I told my sister, "Kaja, do you have a knife on you?"

"Of course, I always have at least one," She pulled a dagger from her waist with a sly grin, "Why do you ask?"

I pointed to the bed, then gestured to the window. The confused look on Kaja's face vanished as she nodded quickly. We each grabbed a corner of the blanket and drawing it over the window, we fastened it to the wall using our knives. Finished, we sat back down in our circle. Celenia opened her eyes and pulled a piece of chalk from her bag. She stood and drew a chalk circle around us as large as she could fit. Once she was done, she locked the door to the room before joining us again on the floor.

"What's the chalk for?" Kaja whispered to me.

I chuckled, "You can talk now. Celenia just marked the area that her spell covers."

"What spell?"

"It's called a circle of silence, a spell designed for privacy. This spell is basically a bubble that stops all sound travelling outside of it. In other words, no one outside this circle can hear what is being said inside."

"So, you are telling me that if all of us sat here and yelled as loud as physically possible..."

"No one could hear you scream." Celenia chuckled darkly.

"Someone has listened to too many scary bard's tales." I rolled my eyes.

Celenia just sat grinning at me for a moment then shook her head, "All jokes aside, we have to talk."

"What about? Is something wrong?" Kaja sounded concerned.

"No, I don't know that anything is wrong. At least, not yet. I just want to make sure we are all in agreement."

"What do you mean?" Kaja asked.

"Well, we have made some good friends here in town: Hjalmar, William, Ingrid..."

"Right," I agreed.

"But unfortunately, we have to think of our situation: We are exiles, at least, Varen and I are. We are supposed to be leaving this land. We can't spend too much time here; or anywhere for that matter. It doesn't seem that word of our exile has reached here yet, we can be sure it won't be long." Celenia stopped in thought for a moment. "Come to think of it, we need to find out for sure what the people know here. If they have heard about our exile, we need to get out immediately. "

"That's true." I nodded, "I was thinking about how lucky we

were that it was Hjalmar that found us. I doubt any of the other guards here would have been so understanding.", "This being said, as long as we are in town we should stock up. Who knows when we may go through another town with this much commerce?"

"That's true," Celenia nodded in agreement, "Especially since we will have an easier time staying hidden if we avoid cities."

"Exactly," I went on. "So, we'll need supplies, and I guess something to carry it all too."

"We have my two horses. If we can find a wagon, we will have plenty of space for travel supplies and anything else we may need. It's bound to be expensive though."

Celenia nodded for a moment, taking the information in. "Alright, here's the plan: As of right now the town recognizes us as the three strangers who helped get rid of the Trollkin. Only Hjalmar knows that we are the ones that caused the problem in the first place, and he doesn't seem the type to go telling anyone if he doesn't have to. With that in mind, we shouldn't draw any attention if we act like we belong. So, you two will go out and gather the supplies we need, see if you can get a wagon as well. View it as a date," Celenia gave a sly grin my direction, "In the meantime I am going to help get our stuff set up in our rooms. Once I'm done, I'll make a trip around town to the different taverns. If news of our exile has traveled here, I should hear about it there. Keep an eye on your amulet, I'll let you know if I get into any trouble. I want you two to keep your ears to the ground too, aside from the taverns the market is the most likely place to hear rumors. As darkness falls, we will meet back at the tavern downstairs and discuss what we found."

"Sounds good to me," I nodded, "What do you think Kaja?"

"Well, that depends," Kaja grinned, "does it sound good because it's a good plan, or does it sound good because your sister called it a date?"

"Great, now they are teaming up against me."

"Maybe a little of both." I shot back.

"Ugh, disgusting" Celenia teased, "Okay, if we are all agreed, let's get to it."

"Right," Kaja and I nodded. I stood up and then helped Kaja to her feet. "Do you need help?" I gestured to the chalk circle on the floor.

"No, I have this handled. You two have your coin purses?"

I pat the bag tied at my waist and heard Kaja's jingle as she did the same.

"Good. Take mine too." Celenia tossed the pouch after removing a few coins, "Between the three of us hopefully we will have enough for the wagon. If you see anything interesting the marketplace after that get it for me if we have enough."

"Right." I nodded as Kaja and I made our way for the door, "We'll see you tonight."

"One more thing," We stopped to listen. "Be careful you two." I could the concern in her voice, "If you get into trouble..."

"I know." Varen tapped his chest where his amulet was hidden.

"We'll be careful Cel, don't worry about us." Kaja closed the door behind us. She turned and gave me a smile as we began down the hallway. We had nearly made it to the stairs when we heard footsteps running up.

"Hey!" Celenia called out.

"What is it Celenia? Is something wrong?" I asked, a little concerned.

"No, no problem." She shook her head, "I just thought you two may want your blades back. They were still stuck in the wall."

"Oh," I couldn't help but chuckle, "Thanks Celenia." We took our knives and sheathed them.

"No problem little brother, enjoy your date; And good luck you two." Cclenia waved and walked back towards the rooms.

"Missing anything else?" Kaja asked.

I shook my head. "I think we should be ready to go now." I replied.

"Good." Kaja led the way down the stairs.

The tavern was nearly empty now. Only a couple tables were in use by people having a late lunch or an early dinner.

"So, what is our plan then?" Kaja sat down at a table.

"Well," I took a seat across from her, "The first thing we need to do is get the wagon. That is going to be the most expensive item."

"Right," Kaja agreed, "How much do we have between the three of us?"

"I'm not sure, but we need to figure that out." I pulled my coin purse, as well as Celenia's and set them on the table. Kaja did the same and we started counting out our coin.

"All right, what do you have?" I asked Kaja as I finished counting Celenia's.

"I have 180 gold, 20 silver, and 30 copper. What about you and your sister?"

"I have 120 gold, 13 silver, and 16 copper. Celenia has 73 gold, 22 silver, and 18 copper."

"So, between the three of us," Kaja sat quietly trying to figure it out, "We have 373 gold, 55 silver, and 64 copper. That sound right?"

"That's what I'm getting, yeah."

"It's going to be tight," she said, "Wagons aren't cheap."

"Yeah, but we have to try."

"Oh hello!" The girl that we saw cleaning the counter earlier came out of a door that I assumed led to the kitchen. "Let's see... It's Varen and ...Celenia right?"

"No, I'm Kaja. Celenia is still upstairs."

"Sorry about that. When Ingrid introduced you, I didn't get the chance to get a good look at you. I'm Eileen. Is there something I can get for you right now? Ingrid said it was on us, so anything you want. Ale? Skyr?"

"No, I think we are okay right now. Right Varen?"

I nodded.

"Okay, just give me a shout if I can do anything for you." Eileen grabbed a rag from behind the counter and began walking to another table.

"Actually, come to think of it, you may be able to help us." I said.

"All right, what is it?" she turned to face us.

"Well, we are supposed to be just stopping through here and we were planning on getting some supplies. The problem is, we have nothing to carry everything we need, and I am not familiar with this area. Do you know where we could go to get a wagon?"

Eileen shifted her weight and bit her lip in thought. "Well I know that there are stables and other horse related supplies a couple streets east of here. That may be good place to try. If they don't have them, I'm sure they can direct you to somewhere that does have them."

"Okay, we will try there! thank you for your help." I nodded. We grabbed the coin purses from the table.

"Not a problem, come back if you need anything else."

"We will. Thank you very much." I made sure the chairs were placed back nicely before we made our way outside.

Chapter 5

The Market

Varen

The streets outside had undergone a seemingly drastic change. the previously semi-empty streets were now bustling with people. Merchants, carts filled with wares, rode down towards the southern gate or up towards the open market. Locals were greeting each other, dressed in clothes of colors and fabrics which I had never seen. Guards were moving supplies from blacksmiths and carpenters in the direction of the open market. *"Probably to help with repairs," I thought.*

"Varen," Kaja laughed shaking her head gently. "Stop gawking. We are trying not to stick out." She continued to lead the way down the street, weaving our way through crowds of people. I found I could pick out people who had been to the open market as they showed off vibrant clothes and expensive jewelry. I got so distracted that I nearly lost sight of Kaja as she turned down another unfamiliar street. Lucky for me, while Kaja walked the busy streets with confidence, her leather and fur clothing made her stick out more than an Orc's underbite. We made one last turn and I saw the large wooden building that, while well kept, still looked out of place in the more well-built city. The large barn doors looked big enough to fit a carriage designed for a king if it was necessary. As the smell of livestock and feed entered my nose, I was reminded of the times we would help out the farms in Vellara using basic daylight and rainfall spells. We entered a smaller attached storefront displaying saddles and riding boots, bits and bridles and in one corner large bags of feed were stacked on top of one another.

"Welcome to Astor Stables, friends, what can I do for you?" The man behind the counter smiled.

"We need a cart and a strong horse to pull it." I explained.

"Ah, I see. Well, we have plenty of horses here. It shouldn't be too difficult to supply one for you. Would you like to come take a look at them?" He opened the connecting door to the barn. As we followed, I saw why the barn was so large. There were stalls lining either side of the barn, with plenty of room to work on any wagon or carriage that was likely to come through. Kaja got right down to business.

"Varen, come look at this one!" I walked to the stall where Kaja stood examining the horse. It was a large strong horse and still looked fairly young.

"You've an eye for horses, young lady." The young man laughed. " if you are looking for our strongest horse you have definitely found him. Though you may want to look at a different horse."

"Why?" I cocked an eyebrow, "You said he was the strongest right?"

"That I did. I'm sorry friend I didn't mean to offend. I meant that we have had some trouble with his training."

"What kind of issues?" Kaja asked

"Well normally he is a very well-behaved horse, but he startles easily, and something about storms." He shook his head.

"What about storms?" I asked getting slightly more upset by the minute.

"He just gets incredibly during storms. We not sure why, but we struggle to keep control of him when a storm blows through. We usually just have to keep him locked up in the stall until it passes. "

"Well if we can avoid it, we won't be traveling through any storms. So, I think we should be okay. He is your strongest horse?" I asked

"Without a doubt." The shopkeeper nodded.

"How much is he?" Kaja asked.

"Well because of his breed and the strength he possesses we are asking 325 gold. It would be more if it weren't for the issues I already mentioned."

I looked down at Kaja, who looked at me and nodded.

"All right, and how much for a wagon?"

The man sighed, "Unfortunately, that is where we have a problem."

"Why? What's the problem?" Kaja looked at the shopkeeper. Her voice, tinged with worry, took me by surprise.

"W- Well," The shopkeeper stammered, "After the attack in the open market we have had a wave of orders from the merchants for new wagons, and unfortunately we don't have any left that aren't already ordered."

"Please you have to have a wagon!" Kaja shouted before quieting down to a whisper, "please..."

The shopkeeper just stared at Kaja trying, I assumed, to understand this sudden emotion. He regained his thoughts after a moment.

"Well, if the blacksmith and the carpenter aren't too busy, we may be able to get one put together for you sometime between four days and a week."

"We can't wait that long! It may be too late by then!" Kaja turned and wrapped her arms around me, pushing her head into my shoulder.

"It's okay," I patted her on the back, "We can find another way." I wasn't sure what else I could say. This sudden change had me as confused as the shopkeeper. I rested my head against hers, "Are you okay?" I whispered. Her only response was shaking her head as she continued to cry.

"I don't understand, why are the two of you in such a hurry?"

"Great," I thought, *"Now we have to explain."* I opened my mouth to respond but Kaja spoke first.

"It's my grandfather, He recently moved down to Njord's port and we have just received word that he has fallen gravely ill and I wanted to see him one last time. My boyfriend is joining me for safety. He's a wizard, but he said he doesn't have any spells to get there fast. Please we really need your help so we can get down there before it's too late."

The man looked to me. "You're a wizard? What about teleportation spells? Something like that could get you there faster than any horse."

I shook my head, deciding to go along with Kaja's story. "No, I am a novice caster at best. Aside from that, I would have to have been there before in order to get us there through a teleport spell. I have never been that far down the mountains."

"I can tell," the shopkeeper nodded, it doesn't look like you get out of the forest towns much, let alone down to the ports." He looked over at the horse, then his eyes moved back to Kaja who still appeared to be trying to hold back tears. I moved up and put my arm around her shoulders. She turned and rested her head on my shoulder once again.

"All right, I will see if there is something we can do, but my hands may be tied when it comes to this. Just wait here." He turned and left through the door at the back of the barn.

"That was manipulative." I said once the shopkeeper was out of earshot.

"Yeah, I know. Kaja stepped back and pushed a stray lock of hair out of her face. "But we needed a wagon, and it's not like we could tell him the truth."

"Remind me never to let you pull that trick on me."

"I would never do that to you" she looked at me innocently.

"mhmm.... I don't know if I believe you. You seem pretty good at making things up on the spot. Like you have done this before." I gave a half smile.

"The trick is, you put a little truth in it."

"Oh? What do you mean?"

"Well, you are a wizard, we do desperately need a horse and wagon, and we do need to head to the port, or at least a port."

"What makes you say that?"

"As exiles that would be your best bet to get away somewhere you won't be chased. That Paladin was probably called by the Holy Cleric, which means before long, we're going to have people after us. Once word really starts to spread, how long do you think it will be before you start getting other people out to kill you?"

I stared at her, unable to argue. She obviously thought this through. Her lie was to try to keep us below notice in the city. That fight earlier would already bring us more attention than we really wanted, but we couldn't just leave it to destroy the town. I didn't like lying to this shopkeeper but Kaja was right, we needed to stay hidden.

I conceded, "I really don't like seeing you lie, but I guess staying hidden is more important right now."

The door to the barn opened and Kaja once again wrapped her arms around me. The shopkeeper approached us once again.

"I've had a look around and here's what I found. We have a small wagon that if the two of you sit close you can both fit in the front. It should be able to hold enough supplies to last you through a couple towns, if you need more carrying capacity, we carry supply saddlebags."

"How much do those cost?" I asked.

"Anywhere from 30 to 50 gold depending on the size of the bag."

I nodded, "I assume that the wagon comes with all the equipment needed for the horse as well?"

"It does. Each wagon is individually crafted so the equipment fits the wagon as well as the horse. Is there anything else I can do for you?"

"Well, it will still be quite a journey down the mountains. We may need feed for our horses." Kaja spoke.

"Can we afford that?" I asked her. We were already pushing the limits with the wagon and horse I wasn't sure how much more we could afford to purchase.

"Listen you two." The shopkeeper stepped in close, lowering his voice. "It sounds like you are in a pinch so here is what I can do for you. This horse has been a lot of trouble for us. If you purchase him, I will discount the price for you, and you can use the money to purchase the Saddlebags and the feed for your horse."

"You would do that?" I asked incredulously.

The shopkeeper nodded and Kaja threw his arms around him in a hug before quickly backing off. "Sorry about that. It's just, you have no idea how much that means to us."

"You're... Welcome," His face was starting to flush slightly. "Darren!" He yelled out the back door and a younger man came up to the three of us.

"Yes, sir?"

"Darren, I need you to take this horse and have Errol hitch him to the small cart out back, the one we discussed just a little bit ago. Then I need you to put a couple bags of feed in the cart and bring it here into the barn."

"Yes sir. I'll have it ready." Darren opened the gate and led the horse out to the yard.

"Let's get you two squared away then." The shopkeeper led the way back the smaller building where he pulled out parchment and pen and began listing the items and counting the cost. We waited patiently until he put his pen down.

"So how much do we owe you?" I asked.

"Well like I told you, I am discounting the price of the horse. I can do about 120 gold for him, another 100 gold for the cart. and 60 for the feed. So, your total comes to 280 gold. Is there anything else you need for your journey?"

"I don't believe so," I looked at Kaja who only shook her head. We pulled our coin purses out and counted out the money. "Thank you for your help."

"Hey, don't worry about it." He waved off the thanks, "Darren should have your cart set up by now. Let's make sure everything looks okay for you."

We re-entered the barn and took a good look at the wagon. It was a little on the smaller side, but he was definitely doing us a huge favor. He likely could have charged another 30 gold if not more. I felt a tinge of guilt for the lie that Kaja told. This man was helping us because he thought it was a family emergency. I wanted to correct it, but we needed the help, and to come clean would mean telling him of our status as exiles making it easier for anyone hunting us down to find us. We couldn't afford that.

"This is the most I was able to do for you. Will it suffice? The shopkeeper asked me.

"It's excellent," I nodded, "Thank you so much for your help. We really do appreciate it. I wish there was something we can do for you."

The shopkeeper shook his head, "Don't mention it, but if you really want to do something to repay me, spread the word about my shop in your travels. I always appreciate the business."

"We will. Thank you again."

"Is it ready to go?" Kaja asked.

The shopkeeper took a final look at the wagon before standing up and nodding, "Yeah, everything looks secure. It's ready to go."

"Great! Thank you again," Kaja climbed up onto the seat. The shopkeeper started for the barn doors as I climbed up in order to ensure they were open by the tame Kaja flicked the reins to set us off.

"So, that took a good chunk of our funds." I said once we had traveled a little way down the road, "I think we have 93 gold left plus our silver and copper. We still need to get food and water supplies; I'm worried we won't have enough."

"Let me handle that." Kaja responded as she took us around a turn.

"You aren't going to tell another phony story about your dying grandfather, are you?"

Kaja shook her head and sighed, "No, I hated doing that."

"Then why did you?"

"Well, I couldn't exactly tell him that we were a bunch of exiles, but we needed the wagon. It was a risk though. If he found out I was lying in order to get a wagon he probably would have called the guard. I needed him to think we were in an emergency where we needed the wagon without telling him our real situation. I didn't see any way around it."

"I guess so..." I still didn't like lying to the merchant especially as nice as he was, but she was right there was no way he would have helped us if he knew we were exiles. "Yeah, I guess you are right about that. I have one more question though, the boyfriend comment. was that just part of your story?"

Kaja chuckled, "You worry too much Varen." She brought us to a stop in front of the general store and handed the reins to me. She got down from the cart and walked into the store.

"I worry too much. What is that supposed to mean?" I wondered aloud.

As I waited, I couldn't help but feel guilty. Kaja was lying to people in order to protect us. The exile was ordered on me and Celenia, not Kaja. I started to feel like we were dragging her down with us. It was hard for my sister and I to leave Vellara. It was all we knew from the time we were children playing in the town, all through our period of guard training and even our magic lessons were just in the forest outside of town. Even so, I wasn't leaving anyone; Our parents died a long time ago and my sister was exiled with me. In order for Kaja to really join us like I wanted, she would have to completely abandon not only the town she grew up in and the people that she knew but her parents as well. On top of all that, who knew how we would support ourselves. Once word spread far enough of our exile it would be impossible to be given any sort of work. It was clear that Celenia and I were already being hunted but if Kaja is gone for too long a search will be out for her as well, and once it's discovered that she's with us we could all be in trouble.

The shaking of the wagon brought me out of my thoughts. I looked behind me to see a barrel-chested man placing crates in our wagon.

"Excuse me, I think you have the wrong cart." I called to him.

He shook his head, "You're with that Kaja girl, right? I was told to help load this stuff up."

I sat there shocked. "Yeah We're here together. You mean to tell me she got all that?" I gestured to the stack of crates next to him as he continued to load them on.

"Well, not quite," he responded, "There is still more coming."

"Thank you so much for your help." Kaja called back through the doorway as she left.

"It was our pleasure Miss Valtr." A voice called back. She turned and climbed back on top of the wagon.

"You used your real name?" I whispered in shock.

"I walked in and he recognized me, at that point there was no use to trying to lie."

"How much does he know?" I asked

"Nothing really. I told him that I was in a spot of trouble and needed help. I called in a favor he owed my family. That's how we got all these supplies."

"What's in all that?"

She shrugged, "Nothing fancy. Vegetables, breads, fruits, any sort of basic food he could spare, and a couple barrels of drinking water."

"I see. Is that why we came to this shop? Because you knew the owner?"

"No, I didn't know this was his shop, it was just the nearest general store I knew of around here. I haven't been in this area for years; and when I did come, I usually just stayed with the cart."

"I see." I handed the reins to her. "So, he recognized you, you told him you were in trouble and needed supplies, and he just gave you all this stuff?"

"Not quite. He didn't just give it to me, be he gave me the largest discount he possibly could. I think he actually lost money on this deal." She glanced back at the storefront.

"That was kind of him. Let's make sure we don't let it go to waste." I pulled out my knife and began unscrewing the compartment in the handle. Pulling out the vial of poison I handed it to her. "Hold on to this. I don't want to get it near the food. Oh, and don't open it or let the liquid touch you. I have been told that the poison needs to get into the blood either through a cut or by ingestion but I don't carry an antidote so I would rather not test that."

"Why don't you have an antidote?" Kaja asked and I detected a hint of panic in her voice.

It was my turn to shrug. "The poison doesn't affect me or my sister and no one else has ever handled the vial until now. Any other situation where this would have poisoned someone it would have been on purpose."

"*That* makes me feel comfortable," the sarcasm dripped from her voice, "What are you doing back there anyway?"

"I'm going to enchant these containers, assuming I can get the right symbols carved into the wood with all of the jostling"

"What kind of enchantment?"

"Just a preservation spell. It will keep the food safe from rot and decay, or rather, slow down the process of it. This way the food should stay good longer. We used these for the town crops all the time after harvest, some of the farmers even had us carve the symbols into their storehouses to make the spell permanent."

"That's why the town's food would keep so long? I always wondered why we were able to have fruit so much later in the year than other places. Why doesn't everyone use that?"

"Well, though most don't realize it, it's specifically a necromancy spell. Originally it was designed to preserve corpses. We were able to modify it for the use of preserving food. We never told anyone that the spell was necromantic for obvious reasons. Honestly, the town was pretty clueless to a lot of magic so we doubted anyone there would have known the spell to be of necromantic origin. Places like this though, the mages, if there are any, will likely be more knowledgeable so we need to get the cart back to the inn as soon as we can. The longer it is out in the open the more likely it is to be seen." I sheathed my knife as I finished the last symbol. "Let me know of any sudden movement that you are going to take before you take them, I'm going to start casting the spell and it's going to take a lot of concentration.

"Okay."

I closed my eyes and channeled the magic within me. Activating my mage sight. I opened my eyes and began to recite the spell. Normally it would be a simple spell, but I had to attempt multiple castings at once in order to affect only the contents within the individual containers.

"Turning left." Kaja said.

I braced myself for the turn and continued to chant. Now I had to set my anchor points at the proper symbols carved in each container. I focused on them and as I chanted, they began to glow and give off a field of energy.

"Road looks a little rough ahead."

I braced and held the spell in place until the road evened out. As I continued to chant, I manipulated the fields in my mind refining and anchoring to the other symbols I had carved into the containers until all the symbols glowed to my mind's eye. With a final word the spell anchored and stabilized. I slowly pinched off the flow of magic and cut off my mage sight as Kaja pulled the cart to a stop next to the inn stables.

Kaja jumped down and handed the reins to a stable boy, giving him some instruction. I jumped over the side of the wagon and onto my feet.

"Well," Kaja looked at me, "That's all we needed to do with the wagon and necessary supplies, and we still have a little while until sundown. Should we see the open market?"

"Sounds like fun." I grinned. She turned and with a great wave of her arm and started towards the open market with me close behind. "So, what is the open market anyway? What's so special about it?"

Kaja laughed, "Well the usual town marketplace is full of locals who import and sell from other places, the stores are constantly the same with a few new items coming in occasionally."

"Like your family's store back home."

"Right," Kaja nodded, "Now trade cities like this usually have an open market, where instead of having local citizens selling wares in permanent shops you have stands that people from outside cities will come and pay to use and sell their wares here. Places like this the kind of items you can get may be completely different from one day to the next because the merchants are constantly coming and going."

"I see, so we won't really know what to expect there?"

"Normally no, but I suspect that for the most part we will see fruits and vegetables-"

"Because the time of harvest just passed," I was starting to understand the idea.

"Right," she stopped and turned around to face me, "Okay, we're here. Are you ready for your first open market experience?" She grinned and bounced slightly.

"I think so." I chuckled.

She grabbed my hand and led me around the corner and into the crowds of the open market. The crowds were noisier than the guards back home during a goblin attack; though much less frantic and far more colorful. The people wandering the marketplace looked as colorful as the tarps over the stands. The clothing they wore here was odd to me. Celenia wore cloth rather than the normal skins and furs of Vellara, but her clothing had a functionality to it; at least it could keep her warm in the cold mountains. The clothing these people looked to be for show more than anything else.

"I've never seen so many people in one place. Is it always like this?" I asked.

"Only when there's not a battle with an angry trollkin." Kaja teased, "Stop gawking, the merchants are going to think you have never been to a city before."

"I haven't. I never had a reason to leave."

"I know, but some of the merchants will... adjust their prices if they think you don't know what it's worth."

"That's dishonest!"

"Yes, it is. Most merchants are too worried about the bad reputation to attempt it, but some of them have the silver tongue to get away with it."

"So how do you know what merchants are trying to overcharge and which are being honest."

"Unless you know what the fair prices are for the items you are purchasing, you don't. But if they can't tell whether or not you are versed in trade, they won't even try to cheat you."

"Okay, anything else I should know?"

Kaja tilted her head, "Well, it's really easy to lose each other in crowds, so let's stay close." With a grin she took my hand and led me into the crowds. "So, what do you want to see first? There's clothes, pouches, jewelry,"

"Why don't we start with something functional." I suggested.

Kaja looked off into the distance, "How about the weapons then? If we plan to avoid towns, we will need to fend off the creatures that live outside city walls."

"You don't have to try so hard to convince me to look at a weapon stand." I chuckled. She smiled in response.

"Okay let's see, if the weapons merchant is in the same place, he was this time last year he should be this way."

Kaja took my hand once more and led me through the crowds toting their recent purchases. We came to a stop at a corner stand with various small weapons displayed atop crates. The wares and merchant protected from the sun by the canvas cover.

"Welcome to my stand. Can I help you find something today?" A rather small man approached us.

"No, we are just browsing the market today." Kaja responded.

The merchant smiled, "Very well, let me know if I can help you with anything."

Kaja and I began browsing the weapons. He had a surprisingly large selection for the small stall he was occupying. I saw simple daggers and bows to the more exotic weapons that I would never have imagined existed. On top of one barrel I saw what looked like a coiled rope with a blade woven into one end.

"What is this?"

"Ah, that is a weapon far more common in the east, it's known as a whip dagger. Those properly trained with it can inflict fatal wounds from a distance no sword could reach."

"I'm not surprised, it looks pretty vicious."

"Look at these Varen." I made my way to where she stood. She was admiring a pair of small blades displayed on a wooden crate. The blades were pointed rather than edged and the handles were shaped like a small ladder rung with the upper half angling in to join the base of the blade. "I've never seen daggers like these before."

"Ah, the Katar," The stall owner surprised us from behind, "In basic terms it is known as the punching dagger." He picked one up by the handle, curling his hand into a fist the blade stuck out just below the knuckles. He took a couple jabs in the air. I missed the rest of what the merchant was saying because I was looking at Kaja who was watching the merchant very closely. I could guess she was trying to do. As the merchant finished, she picked up the other blade.

"It's used like this?" she took a couple jabs, mimicking the merchant.

"That's very good technique. Have you used these before?"

"No, not these. I have had a fair amount of experience in a

number of other small blades."

"That's quite a gift young lady. With proper training and enough practice, I can envision you labeled among the greatest of blade masters."

"Well, I'm not so sure about that." I could hear the embarrassment in Kaja's voice.

"How much do these cost?" I asked him.

"Well a standard Katar runs about 3 gold pieces, a pair I could sell for 5. If you want a sheath for them it's another gold piece for each."

Kaja nodded, "Sounds about right, unfortunately I have to save my money." She set the blade gently back onto the crate, "They are definitely something to look at in the future though. It would be pretty easy to hide and done right could also easily take someone by surprise. Should we move on Varen?"

"I wanted to ask him about a couple of these staffs but it's starting to get late, why don't you head down to the rings and amulets for Celenia."

"All right," she nodded, "You know where it is?"

"Yeah, I saw it on our way here."

"Then it's in the same place as before." Kaja turned and disappeared into the crowds.

"What is it you wanted to ask?" The merchant stepped up to the barrel where the staffs stood.

"What material are they?"

"Most of them are wood, but I have a couple that are iron."

"Why would anyone want a staff made of iron?" I looked into the crowds behind me.

There was a pause before the merchant's response, "Are you a mage?"

"Yeah, why?"

"No reason, it explains why you would question the use of a metal staff. You see, unlike the staves you mages carry to help focus and magnify your spells, these are designed for close combat staffs."

I turned back to get another look at the staffs, "Huh, so they are. I should have taken a closer look.

"Was there anything else you wanted to know about them?"

"No, but I would like to purchase one of those daggers."

"The Katar?"

"Yes, those. You said 4 gold for a dagger and sheath?"

"That's right sir."

I pulled my purse out and counted out the gold pieces, as the merchant took a Katar out of the crate below the displayed Katar.

"Now what kind of sheath would you like?" the merchant inquired.

"What do you mean what kind?"

"Well I have standard belt sheaths, but I also have leg strap and a couple of boot sheaths."

I stood in thought, "Well if I remember right, she already carries something in her boots. Which weapon it is I couldn't tell you."

"If I may," the merchant interjected, "It sounded as if the lady would want to keep it hidden and if the boot sheath doesn't work, the leg strap would be the best way to do that."

I nodded, "Let's get that then."

The merchant nodded and handed me the weapon carefully slid into the sheath and placed into a box.

"Thank you." I left the stall pushed my way into the crowds scanning the stalls until I saw Kaja admiring an amulet.

"Kaja!" She turned and smiled.

"There you are. You weren't very long."

"Yeah, the staffs were mostly martial style staffs. Not my style"

"but he still managed to sell you something." She gestured to the small box in my hand, "How much was it?"

"4 gold pieces."

"Can we afford that? After the cart and supplies we are already running low on money. We should be saving it for when we need supplies again, or if we need medical attention."

"It'll be all right. If we need money, we will find a way to get it. Even if it means doing odd jobs wherever we end up."

"I guess but…where will we end up Varen. What's going to happen?" Kaja asked softly.

"I wish I knew." I sighed, "I suppose you get your supplies and head back. Your parents will never know you accompanied us. As for me and Celenia, we keep traveling until we get out of the Kingdom. We can't live our lives in hiding after all. We will find some little town work until we have the money to buy a hut or a piece of land. It will take a while, but we will get on our feet."

"Varen, I haven't been completely honest. I don't plan on going back."

"Yeah, I know."

"You know?" her eyes widened

"It wasn't hard to figure out. You helped pay for a horse and wagon, which are expensive. You also have not yet bought any supplies for the shop back home. Once I realized that, I knew you didn't intend to go home; that you intend to keep traveling with us."

"You aren't upset?"

"To be honest, when we read your note, I hoped this would be the case. It will be fun traveling with you, and it will be nice to have another person on the road with us, but it still doesn't change the fact that my sister is right."

"What do you mean?"

"It would be far safer for you to go back to Valera, find someone with a good job who can take care of you, and settle down with them. They would be able to give you a better life. You don't deserve to be an exile with us.

"I'm confused. Do you want me to come along or not?"

"I do. Of course, I do it's just," I paused gathering my thoughts, "I'm glad you are her Kaja, but the future for us is full of questions. Where will we go? How will we get there? What will we do when we get there? and the biggest one right now is: Will we even survive long enough to get there? I can't answer any of these questions Kaja. Right now, I just have to trust in the gods and do the best I can."

Kaja grabbed my hand, "We'll see what the Gods have in store for us together."

I nodded in agreement and we just stood there until I finally decided to break the silence. "Did you find anything at the stall?"

"Well," Kaja led me to the displays, "There are a lot of rings that appear useful, but all of them are pretty costly."

"Excuse me young man, but will you pass me that ring next to you?" a woman gestured to the ring in question.

"Yes ma'am, of course." I took the small ring from the display and handed it to her.

"Thank you." She examined the ring for a moment before looking back at me. "Say, have I seen you somewhere before?"

I tried to keep the panic from appearing on my face. I couldn't keep my mind from racing: *Was this woman from Vellara? Was she at the trial? What will we do if she calls the guards? I don't recognize her.*

Kaja chimed in for the rescue, "No ma'am I don't believe we have met you before." She pushed gently on my shoulder encouraging me to turn around and start walking away.

"I swear I've seen you before." The woman furrowed her brow

in concentration.

"Come to think of it. Both of you look familiar." The ring merchant approached. I saw Kaja's hand gently migrate to the hilt of her sword.

"No, I don't think so." I insisted still trying to navigate away from the stall.

"I know! You were with Hjalmar fighting the trollkin right?" The woman beamed with a triumphant grin.

I released a breath I didn't even know I was holding. "Yeah, you got us None of you were hurt, were you?"

"That's funny, we were more concerned with the strangers who were running toward the monster rather than away from it." The merchant smiled.

"Especially about you," The woman looked at Kaja, "You owe this young man your life. If he hadn't distracted the creature, you probably wouldn't be here right now." She looked at Kaja for a minute and then looked back over at me. "You two would make a really cute couple."

"Um, thanks." I wasn't sure what to say. Kaja's face was flushed but I felt certain that mine was as red as the rubies set into many of the rings around us.

"You are embarrassing them." The merchant chuckled. "Come here you two." He led the way to a crate near the back of his stall.

"Ah, here it is." he pulled out a small wooden box. flipping the latch, he opened it to reveal two rings. Each ring was an ornate silver band with two stones set in each ring. One stone was black with white tones in vague flower shapes, the other was a simple dark blue stone.

"Those are pretty rings. What are they?" Kaja asked.

"They are a pair of very special rings." He took one and slid it onto his finger. "Young lady if you would like to put the other on. Now, these rings always come in pairs." He spoke a word that even the most novice mage would have identified as an activation word.

I shifted my focus to my mage sight. The ring glowed on his finger, active with magic, but aside from that I could see no change. I kept searching him but nothing else was showing up in my mage sight.

"What are you doing Varen?" Kaja asked

"I'm trying to see-" The words caught; dumbfounded by the light I saw around Kaja. I stepped up and looked closer. What I thought was Kaja glowing with magic was actually a field hovering just above her form.

"Trying to see what?"

"The spell" I replied.

"What? Is it affecting me? What is it doing? What does it look like?" I wasn't sure if Kaja's panicked state was from knowing the spell was in place on her or the fact that she didn't know what it did.

"It's not doing anything harmful. By appearance it looks like a defensive spell. Imagine a glowing bubble covering you." I reached out and tested the field. The bubble gave a slight resistance before letting my hand pass through. "For the expensive appearance of the ring it surprises me that it offers so little protection. What else does it do?"

"Nothing gets past you huh?" The merchant smiled, "Yes sir. The field, on top of adding that slight protection you observed, also lessens injuries received while the ring is active. It has a drawback though. The spell is designed to share the injury."

"I see, so whatever injury would have been inflicted that was reduced is given to the wearer of the ring that activated the shield, interesting. How much are they?"

"Well between the materials, spell, and the margin for profit I can't sell them for any less than 50,000 gold pieces."

I almost choked "50,000 gold pieces. I'm sorry but we can't afford that."

"Based off what you are wearing I had gathered that much already." The look Kaja gave him warned him to choose his next words carefully. I don't know if he missed it or ignored it, either way he moved on. "I have not been able to sell it because of the high price. Nor have I found anyone who would put it to good use. You risked your lives for the town and protected the city. As thanks I want to give these to you, but only with the promise you put them to good use."

"Yeah, we will, thank you." I could hear the shock in my voice I just hoped no one else did. The merchant gave a satisfied nod and placed the other ring in my hand.

"Are you sure about this?" Kaja asked.

"Of course. As I said I don't think I'm ever likely to find a buyer for them, and with me they will only gather dust."

He practiced the activation word with us until we both had it down. Once we had, Kaja looked toward the sky.

"Varen, it's close to sundown we need to meet back up with your sister. Are you ready?"

"Yeah."

"Thank you so much for your gift. We really appreciate it."

"You're welcome young lady. Don't forget that activation word now."

"I won't."

Kaja shook his hand and led the way back to the tavern.

"That was too close earlier. When they said they recognized us I thought word of our exile had traveled faster than we expected." I told her.

"I still wouldn't be so sure it hasn't. We may just be lucky for now. but a lot of people travel through this city. Just because we haven't run into anyone that knows doesn't mean there aren't any here."

"I guess that's true." I conceded.

"We are in a crazy situation," Kaja sighed, "We can't afford to drop our guard."

"Things will get better as we get away from Vellara." I tried to reassure her as I opened the inn door, but I couldn't help feeling it was false reassurance.

"Good evening Varen, Kaja." Eileen greeted us, "Celenia is at the table in the corner next to the stairs. I will have the specials at your table as soon as they are ready."

"Did Celenia pay already?" I asked realizing I had her money pouch.

"It's on the house tonight. Ingrid's orders."

"I see. Thank you, Eileen."

Kaja and I made our way to the table where Celenia sat using minor magic to move a mug back and forth between the ends of the table.

"Entertained?" Kaja laughed.

"Very much so, actually." Celenia gave a grin. "So how was

your *date*? You two didn't just run off and get married, did you?"

I struggled to keep a straight face as I held out my hand. "No, not yet. We got the rings, but we haven't agreed on a date yet."

I wish I could have had someone make a sculpt of Celenia's face. The shock was mixed with frustration and she was at a complete loss for words.

"Relax Cel, I'm kidding." I laughed.

"Explain." Celenia looked at Kaja.

Eileen came to our table and set plates of steaming food in front of us. "Is there anything else I can get for you?"

"No thank you, this should be all." Kaja replied.

"Very well, call for me if you need anything else." Eileen left to tend the other tables.

"All right," Kaja and I sat down. "What have you found sis?"

"Nuh-uh, you talk, I'll eat. Explain the rings."

"Please Celenia, I think your stomach can wait just a little bit."

Her eyes moved between me and her food for a few seconds. "No, I don't think it will." She put a small piece of meat in her mouth only to let it drop back onto the plate. "Ow! Still hot."

"Really?" Kaja rolled her eyes, "I thought the steam meant it was cold."

My sister crossed her arms and twisted her face into a childish pout. "All right, now that we have all had a laugh at my expense let's talk. How were things on your end today?"

"Well, after we left you Eileen gave us directions to the stables and cartwright. We got a great deal on a new horse and a wagon thanks to Kaja."

"How did you do that?" Kaja gave a scrutinizing look.

Kaja looked around and made sure no one was in earshot. "I fed him a story about my deathly ill grandfather in Njord's Port and that my boyfriend and I needed a fast way to get there."

"Is that right?" Cel glanced at me before looking back at Kaja, "How much did he blush?"

"Cel, that's not the point." I shook my head, hoping I wasn't blushing again. The look on Celenia's face told me otherwise. "After that we stopped at a shop to get supplies, we got a deal on those too. I guess he knows Kaja's family."

"He recognized you? Did he recognize Varen?"

"No, Varen stayed in the wagon. I told the merchant I was being sent for certain supplies far down the mountain and I needed the food and water necessary to get there."

"He believed you?"

"I think so. I have been sent for supplies before just never that far."

Celenia nodded, her mouth too full of food to say anything.

"After that we dropped of the cart at the stables here and went to the open market. I bought Kaja a new dagger. Then we went to look at rings."

"What did you find?"

"Any that were worth the price were out of our range. We had quite the scare when the merchant as well as one of the townsfolk recognized us."

"Why didn't you-" Celenia stopped when I raised my hand but not before a few of the patrons turned their attention toward us. I shrugged like nothing was wrong and wait for them to get back to their own conversations.

Kaja continued as I gave the go ahead. "They recognized us as two of the people who came in to stop the Trollkin rampage. As thanks the Merchant gave us the rings. They lessen injury and divert it to the other person."

"Interesting. I have never heard of a spell like that."

"That's what I thought" I nodded. "So, what did you find out?"

"From what I have heard there have been rumors of the existence of a couple of exiles from Vellara. No one knows who they are or what they look like. It seems we are safe for now."

"That's great." Kaja smiled.

"It is; Although I can't imagine it taking long for the information to get here."

"Oh," Kaja slumped in her chair slightly.

"Aside from that there has also been rumor of a storm heading this way from the port. I don't know how bad it's supposed to be, but I don't relish the idea of travelling in a storm."

"No, it doesn't sound pleasant." I agreed.

"That being said, we have drawn too much attention here. They see us as heroes now, but if someone comes looking for us, we will be too easy to find."

"Should we change inns?" I asked.

Cel shook her head. "It wouldn't take long for our new rooms to be discovered. Storm or not, I think it is too risky to stay here."

"I see your perspective Cel, but we have a wagon and supplies to consider as well. If that gets stuck in the mud because of a storm we become vulnerable."

"I still think we need to leave now. What do you think Kaja?"

"We are the talk of the town. The longer we stay in the public eye the more danger we are in, and the more danger the town is in by us being here. I don't want to get stuck in the storm, but people like to talk. You two are mages. Is there any way to make a bigger event than the trollkin? It would get people talking about something else..."

"Yeah, mages with specialty in Necromancy." Celenia pointed out, "It's too dangerous and I am not putting an entire town in danger just to become hidden."

"What about the illusion spells in our books Cel? I know we aren't well versed in Illusion, but we could probably figure it out. We don't have to put anyone in danger. We just have to make it look like the town is in danger."

"We wouldn't be preparing our normal spells tomorrow, and most of our offensive spells are out of the question." Cel observed.

"But if it works, we may be able to wait out the storm." I nodded.

"I can't say I'm entirely comfortable with this plan, but it looks like it may be the best one we have."

"So, what will you cast?" Kaja asked.

"We will figure out the details tomorrow when we prepare our spells, for now we should get some rest if we are done eating."

Kaja and I nodded, our plates empty. I said a quick goodnight and went to my room. I checked that all my things were still where I had hidden them. Satisfied, I lay in bed brainstorming ideas for the casting tomorrow until I finally drifted off to sleep.

Chapter 6

Escape

Varen

I awoke to someone shaking me and a voice in my ear, "Varen, young sorcerer, you must wake up."

Hearing the urgency in her voice the cloud of sleep quickly left my mind, "What is it?" I asked sitting up in my bed.

"You must leave. There are posters up around the town offering rewards for the three of you."

"There are what?" I nearly shouted. All traces of sleep were gone now.

"Quiet," Ingrid hissed, "I have already awoken your sister and girlfriend, and took the liberty of packing most of your things. Get dressed and come out in the hall, I will let you out the back door." She said, moving to the door.

"She's not my-" the door closed behind her, "girlfriend."

I quickly got out of my bed, gathering my spell book from the drawer of the nightstand. I quietly removed my bone staff from where I had hidden it along the bed frame. I got dressed quickly, no longer caring about making noise. Quickly double checking the room, I grabbed my cloak off the bedpost, grabbed everything that had been missed and exit the room.

"Come, we must hurry before dawn comes," Ingrid kept her voice low, "otherwise your cloak will do you little good young necromancer," She winked.

"Wait, hold up," I took a step back, "you know about that?"

"You and your sister? of course," she whispered, smiling sheepishly, "Only necromancers would carry around a dragon bone staff or a bone scepter, let alone the blade on your belt."

"Yet you intend to help us get away?" I said warily.

"Why wouldn't I?' She asked, a confused expression crossing her face, "You saved us, now I can truly repay you. Now come, hurry."

I was led down the hall into a small dining area. I was ushered gently through a pair of double doors before I could get a very good look at the room. I was cautiously guided around obstacles for what felt like an hour before we stopped. In reality it had probably only been about ten minutes.

"You are directly in front of the back door," Ingrid spoke quietly, "Your friends should be waiting for you outside."

"Thank you, for everything."

"My pleasure," she smiled, "Now hurry, you must get as far as you can before I open my doors. I can only delay probably another twenty minutes. Go now."

Still unsure, I slowly opened the door and winced at the pain caused by the moonlight.

"Varen, hurry!" Kaja called quietly.

"Right," I said, "I'm coming"

"Careful," a quiet, deep voice said, "That first step is a doozy."

This surprised me. I lost my balance and fell only to have a strong hand grab me by my upper arm and help me back onto the step.

"Careful there," the voice said, "Don't want you getting hurt."

"Thanks," I replied, stepping cautiously down the steps.

"So," the man stepped into the light where I recognized William, "Ah put some extra supplies in yer stuff, so ye should be prepared for the trip ahead. If ye need anything in the next town mention my name, most ov 'em will do their best to help ye."

"Thank you again William, there is no way we could have done this without your help." I heard Kaja say.

"And I doubt you will get much farther without mine," I recognized Hjalmar's voice, "The rest of the guards have likely locked down the gates by now, there is no way for you guys to get through the gates, but I can take the horses and get through if you guys can find another way around."

"Are you sure Hjalmar? Won't that put your standing with the guard at risk?" Kaja asked

"We don't have time to debate it right now. Ingrid can only keep those guys off your trail for so long."

"Well, I don't suppose there is any way to find out if we don't try" Celenia said.

"That's for sure," I replied, "So is all our stuff on the horses, or are there things we are missing?"

"Everything's here," Kaja said, "All that's left for us to do is get it out."

"The stuff is easy," William said, "Ah'll help, Ah was planning on leaving tomorrow anyway. Ah'll smuggle yer stuff out the south gate, the guards 'll think it's all mine. The problem is getting you three out. Hjalmar can exit the east gate and meet us around on the south side."

"I can sneak out easily enough with my cloak, but I'm not leaving without Kaja or my sister making it out as well."

"Ah would ne'er suggest it." William shook his head. "But leaving through the gates is out of the question; We will have tae work something out, but first, let's get away from the Inn."

We led our horses through darkened streets. The small homes were quiet, most people probably trying to get into the Inn, hoping to get the reward.

We weren't very far before Celenia whispered, "So, any ideas as to how Varen, Kaja and I are supposed to get out of the city?"

"I have an idea, but it's risky," Hjalmar said "There is a place where the river enters the city on the southeast side, there are grates to keep people from entering that way, but the grate on the east wall has loose bars that can be fairly easily pulled out allowing you through."

"How is that risky?" Kaja asked, concern obvious in her voice.

"Well, as you probably noticed yesterday, there are guard towers at every corner of the city and one on each side of the city entrance gates. Here's the problem: by exiting through there you wind up almost right underneath a guard tower and you are fighting the current, so unless you are incredibly quiet the guards will hear the disturbance of the water and spot you."

"What about a cloak of shadows?" Varen asked.

"What do you mean?" Hjalmar cocked his head at him, confused.

"Well with a cloak of shadows, they will hear the water, look down and see nothing, unless they have something that allows them to see through the illusion."

"That might work, but you are the only one with a cloak,

aren't you?"

"That's true, but my cloak should float. After I have made sure that the guards didn't see me, I place my cloak in the river, I make my way along the wall until I'm far enough to make it to the trees without being spotted, and the next person comes through, wearing my cloak and does the same thing."

There was a long silence. My plan was risky, I knew that, but it was also the only possibility I could see. If the guards spotted me running along the wall, an alarm would be raised throughout the city. If that happened, neither Kaja, nor Celenia would get their chance to escape.

"It's smart," Will spoke up. "risky, but we Dinah have time fer somethin' foolproof."

"I agree it's our best bet," Hjalmar conceded, "but that doesn't necessarily mean I like it."

*   *   *

William

"Ah ne'er thought ah'd be 'elping a pair o' young fugitives escape." I chuckled to myself, "'f someone 'ad told me ah'd be doing this one day, ah probably never would've believed 'em."

I could see the south gate ahead of me. I took a moment to relax as I approached, doing my best to look normal.

"Halt," A guard shouted, "Who approaches?"

"'S only me, lad." I called.

The guard's stiff posture relaxed slightly.

"All right, come on through, Will."

"Thank ye lad," I approached the gate quickly.

"Wow, that's a lot of equipment Will," The other guard chuckled, "Are you sure you didn't spend all your money this trip?"

"Sometimes ah wonder 'f ah even makin' money when ah come," I laughed.

"I think everybody does. Isn't it a bit late to be traveling though?"

"ah wanted to get out fahst 's possible after tha' trollkin attack, on top o tha' ah can avoid the crowds."

The guard nodded, "All right, well, be safe, it's dangerous in the forest lately, I have heard a paladin is looking for a couple criminals in the area."

"Thanks, ah will!" I waved to him as I passed through.

*   *   *

Hjalmar

"Halt! Who approaches?" A familiar voice called as I approached the gate.

"Erlend! They put you on gate duty?" I smiled.

"Hjalmar, thank the Pantheon it's you.," He sighed with relief, "Yeah, almost everyone is out tonight after that paladin stopped by the guardhouse." He paused, "I know it's cowardly, but I really hope the two Necromancers don't come through this gate. I know t's my duty to stop them, but I don't want to try fighting someone with death magic."

"It's not cowardly to wish to avoid a fight you don't think you can win, Erlend." I smiled at him, "Look at the trollkin this morning. I sent you back to warn the city." I smiled.

"But you still ended up fighting him." Erlend pointed out.

"Not by choice though, lad. I went toe to toe with that beast because if I didn't far more would have lost their lives. It's not a matter of standing up to every monster. It's about being willing to put yourself in the line to protect others."

"Thanks, I needed that." Erlend smiled "So why are you over here Hjalmar? I didn't think you were called on patrol."

"I wasn't originally, but they sent for me to bring some horses and help search outside of town just in case they had already made it out."

"Well, if they have gotten out, it will be hard to get very far with an abductee." He replied.

"Abductee?" I asked surprised.

"Yeah, rumor has it the girl that was with them. Braya or something."

"Kaja?" I interjected.

"Yeah! Official report says she was abducted."

"Is that why her posters say that they want her alive?"

"Yeah, her parents just want her back, but if she is an abductee, I wonder how long they will keep her alive."

"Yeah," I replied, wondering if I was doing the right thing. *'What if the reports are true?'* I shook the thought from my mind; Too far in for second guesses now.

"Well, you should probably get those horses out before they wonder where you've gone."

"Yeah, I should. See you Erlend."

He saw me off with a wave and I walked quickly through the and followed the path into the tree line. Once I knew I was out of sight I turned off the trail and slowly made my way to the south gate. I moved cautiously, stopping several times to make sure I wouldn't be spotted by the guard towers. As I reached the path from the south gate, I heard clopping hooves and creaking wheels in the darkness.

"It sounds like you need to put some grease on those wheels," I stepped out of the trees carefully and came up directly next to Will.

"Aye, ah wince e'ry time the' creak," He chuckled nervously. "Are we far 'nough away from the towers? Or will they see tha signal?'

"Only one way to find out."

*   *   *

Kaja

"Varen I really hope this works." Celenia whispered nervously looking up at the guard tower.

"Yeah, me too," Varen chuckled.

"It has to work," I chimed, "If it doesn't, we will all be dead."

"Not an appealing thought" Celenia agreed.

"Hide!" I hissed, and we ducked into a tiny alley between two houses as a guard approached with a lantern. They stopped and examined the area cautiously. I held my breath, mentally willing them to move on. Apparently satisfied, he continued down the street. I exhaled softly

"There!" Varen hissed pointing out around the other corner into the air, "That must be the stream that Hjalmar told us about."

I looked where he pointed and saw the stream in question. As he had described, it entered from a small barred archway.

"All right, Varen. You're up. Are you ready?" Celenia looked to her brother.

"No choice really." He smiled softly. With a deep breath Varen flipped his hood up and he faded until I could only see a slight shimmer which vanished a moment later. Only the splashing water told me that he had reached the river.

"Okay, once he sends the cloak back, you're next," Celenia spoke quietly into my ear.

"What?"

"I said-"

"I know what you said, but you should be the one to go next."

Celenia shook her head gently, "Varen and I can communicate with our amulets, but if you separate from us, we have no way to signal you. Its better you stick with one of us or the other. You go next and Varen can signal me when you have made it." As if in response, her amulet pulsed green a couple times. "It looks like he's clear. Watch for his cloak coming down the stream."

I wanted to argue with her, but she made a good point. I didn't really want to be left in the dark. I nodded wordlessly and carefully made my way to the stream. The moments felt like hours before I saw the cloak float down through the gap where the bars had been removed. I waded into the water to grab hold of it. I drew the cold fabric around my shoulders and pulled up the hood. I looked at my hands to check if it was working, but I could still see myself.

'what's going on? Did the stream somehow nullify the magic? What if I get spotted standing here in the river?" my mind raced.

"Kaja!" Celenia hissed, "The cloak doesn't affect the perception of the wearer. Now get going before anyone spots where you're standing."

"Okay," I calmed my mind, grit my teeth against the cold water rushing past me, and began to make my way against the current. It was difficult with the cold water up to my waist but soon enough I reached the wall. I ducked down and squoze myself through the small gap and out the other side. Once there, I scrambled up the bank. The night air did little to warm me as I did so. There was still some distance before I reached the tree line, but it would be easier to stay hidden without the water swirling around me. I crept quickly, instinctively keeping low to keep out of sight despite knowing the cloaks magic alone should keep me hidden.

Varen stood waiting as I reached the forest. I pulled the hood down and shook out my wet hair.

"Here, let me help you." He chuckled. I turned and he lifted the wet cloak from my shoulders. He wrung it out a bit as I rubbed my arms in a vain attempt to warm up.

"Was it cold?" I didn't have to look to hear the grin in his face.

"You are well aware of the answer to that." I glared teasingly. He chuckled as he set his cloak in the river once more. I stepped over to him and rested head against his chest. He gently place his arm around my shoulders in response.

After a few minutes I felt his arm drop away.

"Is something wrong?" I asked. He shook his head no and pointed to the sky south of us where a bright light streaked through the sky, looking not unlike a shooting star going the wrong direction.

"The signal." Varen muttered, "Will and Hjalmar got out of the city okay."

"We need to meet up soon." I replied. I turned my head to search down the field, looking closely I could see the grass flattening under Celenia's invisible feet. I followed Varen as he met his sister at the edge of the tree line.

"Alright, let's get moving before we are caught by someone at ground level." Celenia said, handing Varen back his soaking wet cloak. He took it and wrung it out a bit before tying it around his shoulders. With a nod he led the way through the trees, carefully avoiding places where the cover overhead could reveal us. He almost tripped a couple of times over roots from the trees, and Celenia and I would grab him before he injured himself.

"Why doesn't he watch where he is going instead of the branches above us?" I asked Celenia.

"He's being careful of not being spotted for our sake, especially your sake. That's how he has always been. His entire life he has put others before himself. I respect it, but I worry it's going to get him killed one of these days." She shook her head, then chuckled. "I remember once, when you were sick, and your family wasn't doing so well for food, he went without food for a week so that you guys could eat. I told him it was stupid, but he wouldn't listen to me."

"I don't remember him ever doing that."

"That's because he didn't want you to know it was him. He would leave handmade baskets full of food on the porch of your store at about midnight, then when your parents would open up shop, they would find it and bring it in."

"Wait! I do remember that, they tried to figure out who it was for weeks so that they could thank them."

"They never figured it out because he never left a trace of who it was. At that time, his cloak was too long for him and the end would drag in the dirt erasing his footprints; And because it was at midnight everyone was asleep but the guards on duty."

"I can't believe he would do that."

"I tried to talk him out of it several times, but when it comes to you the boy doesn't listen." She rolled her eyes.

"Hey," Varen hissed from up ahead, "I hear horses ahead, it's probably not a big deal, but probably best to be careful anyway."

Celenia and I nodded silently.

Varen slowly led us through the underbrush, taking

care to lead us through the clearest path as to prevent alerting someone to our presence. As we approached the edge Varen peered out around the trees for a moment. Then turned around and motioned to us and walked out onto the path.

We followed to see our horses, and a cart of supplies with Hjalmar and William standing nearby.

"Do ye think they saw't?" Will asked nervously.

"I should hope so," Hjalmar replied, "It shot high enough to be seen from the center of the city, but I brought a spare just in case, if they don't show up in the next few minutes, we'll-"

"Hey guys," Varen said, startling both of them.

"Varen!" Hjalmar gasped, "Don't do that."

"Sorry," an obvious lie, but I wasn't going to say anything. Mostly because I couldn't trust myself not to laugh. Celenia wasn't holding back though.

"No, you're not." She laughed.

He shrugged in response and grinned, "No, you're right, I'm not."

"You are not a very nice man," Hjalmar chuckled.

"Me?" Varen spoke in a slightly higher voice, widening his eyes with feigned innocence.

"A'right," Will chuckled, "Well, 'ere are yer horses and all yer equipment. Ye may want to stop at the tavern jes'down the path, they get a lot o' local rumors floatin' 'round, maybe ye can find som'un who can help get ye out 'o these parts an' onto another continent. But be careful, we 'ave no idea how far the news of ye has spread, so try not tae draw too much attention tae yerselves."

"Right," Celenia nodded.

"What are you going to do William?" I asked.

"Oh, Ah'm gonna 'ead down the road a little bit, but ah'm splittin' off a the next fahrk, if ye want tae travel down the mountain, yeh'll want tae stick t'the left path." He turned "Wha's yer plan Hjalmar?"

"Well, after this blatant subversion of the guard, I don't think It'll be safe to go back. My best bet is probably to go into exile with these kids, besides they look like they could use the help."

"Who are you calling children?" Celenia pouted.

"Tha's probably yer best choice 'n the circumstances," Will ignored Celenia and looked back toward the city, "Ah would get goin' though, 'oo knows how long it'll be 'fore they decide tae search out 'ere too."

With a nod, Varen and I climbed up on the wagon front. As Celenia and Hjalmar got into the saddled of their horses, I flicked the reigns gently, urging the horse into a good even pace. Will followed silently until we reached the fork in the road.

"Well lad's 'n lasses, this is where we part ways. But fahrst. Here," He put a bulging pouch of leather in my hand. "Use it wisely." He gave a final wink before grabbing the reins of his horse and leading him down the path.

"What is it?" Celenia asked.

I shook my head, unsure and unable to take my eyes off the pouch.

"Well, open it," nudged me.

I gently tugged at one of the small leather straps, the knot easily coming loose. I reached a couple of fingers into the pouch and felt the touch of cool metal.

"They are coins of some kind. But I can't tell what kind without any light."

"Well William said there was a tavern ahead, right?" Hjalmar jerked his head down the path.

"Yeah, but I don't know if it is the smartest idea to go there right now." Celenia replied.

"Why not?"

"Well for starters we have people after us who want to kill us." Celenia sounded surprised he even had to ask.

"Yeah, but they are searching Astor right now. That could take days if they are doing a thorough job. As long as you didn't leave any clues behind the danger should be minimal." Hjalmar responded, "Besides, *some of us* had to skip dinner to help you guys get out of town."

"I still don't think it's a good Idea." Celenia retorted.

"It would be faster than preparing a meal, sis." Varen pointed out, "plus we can try to prep some spells while we wait. Two blasts with one cast."

"I know, but it's public. We would be putting people in danger just by being there." Celenia retorted.

"Well, if we're being honest about it, the man who was looking for you made it sound like your very existence was dangerous."

"Not helping," I hissed.

"Ah, sorry, I didn't mean it like that. I only meant that the guy following you seemed pretty determined to catch you; and he didn't seem the type to give up easily either."

"Which means the longer we stay here the closer he gets. We need to decide what we're doing now."
Celenia folded her arms in silent debate. Finally, she looked at the group and sighed, "All right, we will go to the tavern, but we are only staying long enough to eat. As soon as we're done, we

need to get back on the road."

"That sounds fine." Hjalmar responded urging his horse down the path. With a flick of the reins our wagon fell in behind.

We rode in silence for a time. All of us surely worried about the man searching for us. It was Varen who finally broke the silence."

"Hjalmar,"

"What is it Varen?" Hjalmar slowed his horse until he was riding alongside the wagon.

"I wanted to thank you for helping us out of town, but how did you know we needed it." Varen's hands were unusually active while he spoke.

"You don't have to bother with a spell, boy. I've nothing to gain in lying to you now. If I was going to betray you, I would have done back when I still had men to back me up. By helping you I've made myself an exile, just the same as you."

Varen rested his hands in his lap. "Sorry."

"Don't be," Hjalmar replied, "Caution is good. It'll keep ya alive. Anyway, it was mostly luck that I knew you needed help."

"Luck?" Celenia questioned.

"Yeah, luck. See, I had just gotten out of a meeting with Captain Sterrid and was sitting down to have dinner, when a large man donned in full-plate armor knocked at the guardhouse door. He said his name was Olmar and that he had been hired to hunt down two necromancers and a girl they had kidnapped!"

"Kidnapped!" I shrieked, "They didn't kidnap me! Who told him I was kidnapped?"

"I don't know, but he said he was certain that they came into town and he was asking the guard to help track them. Obviously, they agreed, and I slipped out in the commotion. When I got to the Inn, Will was already there waiting. He said he had found a wanted notice and that he was there to help you get out. In fact, the man was willing to stand in my way if I was there to take you in. I have to say, if nothing else, the man was devoted to your safety." Hjalmar scratched at his chin.

"What happened next?" I asked.

"Not much," Hjalmar shrugged, "I convinced Will that I was also there to help and shortly after Ingrid brought out Celenia and Kaja, then went back in for Varen. The rest after that, you know."

"Anything else we should know?" Celenia called from back behind.

"Yeah. Although I couldn't see well enough to be sure. From the insignia on his armor, I think he may have been a paladin."
    Silence once again enveloped us as we tried to take in this information.

"It must be the same man we passed the night we left." Celenia spoke quietly, "but we were already exiled. Why would they bring in a paladin?"

"Fear does strange things to people," Hjalmar shook his head, "Maybe they thought they couldn't trust you to stay away. Worried you would come back for revenge. Either way, if he is a paladin, we need to do everything we can to avoid getting caught."

We all nodded in agreement as the tavern came into view down the road.

"All right, we need to move on quickly so let's get some food and get back on the road" Celenia said.

"While we're stopped, we should probably check all of our stuff." Varen suggested, "I would hate to be missing something important, or anything that could lead that paladin to us. You guys go in and order. I'll just do a quick check of everything."

"For safety, we should probably stay in pairs." I suggested, hoping I wasn't being too obvious, "I can stay out here with Varen. Hjalmar, why don't you go in with Celenia and order."

"All right, I get it," Celenia teased. Then she was all business, "Just hurry, we need to get back on the road fast."

Chapter 7

The Dancing Dragon

Varen

As Celenia and Hjalmar walked away I began to check the wagon. The first thing I made sure to find were my staff and Celenia's scepter. Thankfully, I was able to find both tucked away in the wagon; Safe from a quick look over, but if any of the guards stopped to actually look through the wagons contents they would have easily been found.

"Varen," Kaja worked at the opposite side of the wagon checking bags of food and other general supplies. "Do you ever miss your parents?"

"Where did this come from?" I asked incredulously.

"Well, I've been away from home and I'm already homesick. Don't misunderstand, I don't regret leaving with you, but I can't help but worry about them." She sighed, "Then I think how you must feel. Your parents died when you were how old?"

"I was about five years old. Celenia was seven or eight, I don't remember exactly when it happened."

"Do you ever use your Necromancy to, y'know talk to them. Get to see them again?"

"We have before, a couple times, with the help of our master." I finished going through the last bag on my side and moved on to one of the horses, "It's a very complicated ritual; and you need to have something strongly connected to the individual you are trying to contact."

"and that pulls them to you?"

"Not pulls exactly. The ritual lets them know someone is requesting their presence, the object acts as a beacon to guide them. They still have to be willing to speak with the caster."

"I see. Did they ever tell you what happened?"

"No, they never wanted to talk about how they died. They were more interested in learning about our lives and what we were doing. The village told us it was during one of the goblin raids though."

"I'm sorry. It must have been rough."

"It would have been a lot harder without Celenia and Ellara. The townsfolk helped a lot at the time too. After a while it was as if I had never known anything else." I stopped as my hand touched a wooden box, looking at one of the saddlebags.

"Kaja, this is one of your bags, right?"

Kaja walked over and inspected the bag, finding the Valtr seal on the flap. A shield with a weight scale on it.

"Yeah, it's one of mine. Why?"

"Well I didn't want to invade your privacy, but I was wondering about this. Is it something personal?"

Kaja gently took the chest from my hand. It was black with silver trim and a heavy lock. The key was tied to the top with some rope.

"I don't know what's in that…"

"You didn't pack it?" I asked, confused.

"No. I've seen it before though. In my father's room. He never let the key away from his person, except when he slept. Then he hid it somewhere; I was never able to find it. He came and talked to me before I left town and put some things in one of the bags. He must have given it to me then."

She untied the key from the box and let the string fall to the ground. Carefully, almost fearfully, she put the key in the lock and turned it. The lid popped open just a crack. She gently lifted it, neither of us sure what to expect. Inside was a large book with leather covers and black binding. I gave a light gasp as I saw the name written on the cover: *Kaden Valbrandr.*

Hjalmar

"There they are." Celenia stood and began waving her brother and Kaja over to our table near the back.

Like most taverns, this was still pretty full for how early it was. It also had its fair share of drunk, noisy patrons and bards telling the same stories that every child knows by heart by the time they are ten. I had come to find out that the Dancing Dragon was as much a theme for the tavern as it was the name. Each table had its own sculpture carved out of a deep red wood. Each one had the same couple locked in some sore to elegant dance.

"Did you already order?" Varen asked as he sat down, cradling something in his arms.

"Yeah, we just ordered basic meals for all of us. Will gave us about 50 gold so we could have gotten better, but we thought it wiser to save it for an emergency. What do you have there?"

"You'll never believe this Cel. Before she left, Kaja's father gave her some supplies for the journey, and with it a black box. We unlocked the box and found this." Varen slid the object across the table. Celenia blinked at it a few times as if she couldn't believe what she was seeing.

"Is that?"

Varen nodded, "I think it's Dad's spell book."

"But why did your dad have it?" Celenia looked to Kaja.

"I don't have a clue." Kaja replied, "I told Varen that I've seen the box at home before but never seen inside it. I can't imagine why he had it or how he got it; but I can only think he gave it to me so that it could get back to you. I would've had no use for it."

"I guess so." Cel nodded, "Let's take a look later. We'll have time on the road that we don't have right now." She set the book at the far end of the table. Varen picked up the statuette and looked at it closely, turning it in his hands.

"What are you doing, Varen?" Kaja giggled quietly.

"I just- I'm trying to figure out what kind of dance they are doing."

"If you haven't figured it out yet brother, you probably won't." Celenia chuckled.

"Oh, I'll figure it out." Varen muttered stubbornly. I chuckled despite myself for kids who found themselves in so serious a situation, the seemed to know how to make the best of it.

"So what path are we taking?" I asked, "there are a couple roads from here that lead to the nearest port. One has plenty of places to stop to resupply. The other is more direct with only one or two town between here and there, but it's less used and less patrolled, making it far more dangerous."

Celenia shook her head, "The biggest threat to us at the moment is that Paladin; and the more we are around people the easier it will be for him to track us." I heard Varen mutter something, but I ignored it and focused on Celenia, "We only stopped in Astor because we needed supplies. From here on we need to avoid towns as much as we can. Besides, between the four of us we should be able to handle most things we're likely to run into." Celenia stopped nodded her head to look behind me, where someone was approaching our table.

"Here are your- oh," The tavern maid, mugs in hand, stood there transfixed on the table. following her gaze, we saw the figures from the statuette doing an elegant dance. One unlike any I had seen before.

"Varen." Celenia hissed.

"What?". He blinked a few times as he came out of his transfixed state. The figures danced back to their pedestal and returned to their original pose, becoming motionless once more. "Sorry." He said sheepishly, I wanted to see their dance."

"What's up with those anyway. I see them at every table, but it doesn't make sense to me."

"It's part of the theme. This is the Dancing Dragon." She set the mugs of water down as if her explanation actually answered the question.

"I get the dancing part," Kaja responded, but where's the dragon.

"Have you never heard the legend of the Dancing Dragon?" she asked as if it was the strangest thing she had ever heard. Our blank looks were apparently all the response she needed.

"Aelton! Aelton, I know you are here somewhere!"

"I'm over here Astra. Excuse me friends." A colorfully dressed young man left another table and approached us. "What is it?"

"This table has never heard the legend of the Dancing Dragon; and I know it's one of your favorite stories that you have locked in that bardic beartrap of a mind. Would you mind telling it so I can get back to work?"

"You owe me Astra." Aelton chuckled.

"Yeah, put it on my tab." Astra gave a teasing wave of her hand as she walked off.

Aelton muttered something I didn't catch as he grabbed an empty chair and brought it to the table. He gently set his lute off to the side.

"So, you want to hear the Legend of the Dancing Dragon? Well, it happened a long time ago in a distant land."

"How distant?" Celenia squinted at him suspiciously.

"Friend, this tale is so old I doubt anyone knows where it happened anymore. That's if it's anything more than legend, and I have seen nothing to suggest that it was real."

Celenia rolled her eyes and motioned for him to continue.

"In this unknown land there was a kingdom. A Kingdom of unknown name." He glanced at Celenia with a teasing grin. "The Kingdom was powerful and wealthy. The King was a man who dealt sternly, but fairly with his subjects. His Queen both his support, and his adviser. Together they were great rulers and managed great things in their kingdom. They had but one child, a daughter, adored by the Kingdom and sought after by suitors from throughout the land."

"This isn't going to be one of those stories where the helpless princess is kidnapped by the ferocious dragon, so the knight in shining armor slays the dragon to save the princess and they live happily ever after garbage is it?" Kaja asked cocking her eyebrow. We looked at her in shock. "Don't give me that look! I hate those stories!" laughter spread around the table.

As we settled back down Aelton continued, "For many years this Kingdom flourished, but then the farmers began complaining that someone was stealing their livestock. The King sent his guards to watch over the herds and deal with the thieves. The next morning his guards had returned with a report. It was no man stealing the cattle, but a Dragon."

"That's a dangerous situation," Varen muttered.

"Is that so? What do you know of dragons, friend?"

"Only what I have learned from bard's tales and books." He shrugged, "Massive creatures with an arsenal of claws and teeth. But those are only minor inconveniences compared to their magical abilities. *If* one can manage to kill a dragon, their various parts have many uses from their flameproof hides to their very bones which can be used to focus channel and, when used properly, even enhance the magic of the wielder."

"You're well read on the subject, friend. Very impressive."

"He couldn't read enough about them as a kid." Celenia teased.

"Well friend, here's something you may not know. Among their numerous magic powers, is the ability to shapeshift into human form."

"That *is* news." Varen nodded.

"No one in this kingdom had this knowledge either; and while the king and his men deliberated on how to get rid of it, the dragon entered the town in humanoid form. The very same night, the princess, bored of her pampered life in the castle, slipped out of the castle and went to a nearby tavern. There she met a man. Unaware that this man was the dragon who plagued the kingdom, they talked, laughed, and dances. They agreed to meet again the following week and dance again. They followed this pattern for months and, over time, fell in love."

"Is that the end?" Kaja asked, as engrossed in the story as a child listening to a father's bedtime story.

"No. One night, after dancing in the tavern, the man led the princess outside the kingdom and to his lair, where he revealed himself. He promised the princess that if she stayed with him, they could live together, and dance every night. When the King discovered what happened, he sent his fastest and strongest Knights to find the lair of the dragon. They never did. In fact, they say that princess agreed as long as the dragon stayed in human form and allow them to have a normal life. The dragon promised and they left for another kingdom to start new lives there. Eventually, they had children together. First, was a pair of twins. It wasn't until their birth that the princess realized something was… different. Though human in shape, the children has serpent like eyes and scales. Their nails were sharp and strong like claws. Out of fear they took the children and left hiding away. The children grew and over time had children of their own. They say even now these dragon-human descendants are hidden away, creating a society of their own. That my friends, is the Legend of the Dancing Dragon."

"Wow, that's a fascinating tale. But what does it have to do with the Tavern?" I asked.

"Nothing, really." He smiled and shrugged, "I guess the owner just loved the story enough to make it the theme of his tavern. I can't tell you how many times Astra has asked me to tell patrons that story."

Celenia opened her mouth to speak when her face suddenly blanched. She pointed subtly to the entrance.

We all turned to look where she gestured.

"Death's embrace!" Varen muttered quietly.

There, in the doorway, stood Olmar. The same man who requested the guards help finding Varen and Celenia.

"Is there a problem? Who is that guy?" Aelton asked.

I shook my head, unsure of exactly what to tell him. Not the truth, certainly.

Kaja jumped in "Okay here is the situation, I ran away from home because I'm in love with this man." she gestured to Varen. "The man in the doorway was hired to track me down and bring me back. This man here," she gestured to me, "is helping us get away."

"What about her?" Aelton gestured to Celenia.

"I'm his sister. I unfortunately got dragged into this romantic mess." She sighed, feigning annoyance.

"I'm going to try to throw him off the trail. They can't have figured out I've helped you escape yet, so I may be able to do it. I stood and straightened into a soldier's posture, making my way toward him.

"Sir Olmar." I saluted. My heart was pounding with fear, but I did my best to stay composed.

He turned to face me, "Ah, one of the Astorian guardsmen, right? What are you doing so far outside the city?"

"Sir," I stood at attention, hoping that by showing him the proper respect he would be more likely to believe me, "As a precaution in the event that the individuals in question may have already found a way out of the city, I was sent to investigate the nearby area. My belief is that if they are on the run, they would be attempting to make it as far away as possible meaning they were likely heading to the port city. In order to learn if my hunch was correct, I stopped to interview the people here in the tavern just in case any of them may have seen anything."

Olmar nodded, "And what have you to report?"

"Unfortunately, nothing sir. No individuals matching the description have been spotted in the area. If they did head this way, they didn't stop here. That being said, I can't imagine they would have been able to leave with much. Most likely they would have head to the nearest town for supplies. Of course, that's only if they have managed to escape the city."

Olmar scanned the crowd again, then nodded "I too thought that this was the direction they would move. They probably didn't stop here for fear of being seen, especially if they are aware that I'm looking for them. Very well, continue your search. I will return to Astor and try to pick up their trail again. They will not get away from me." I watched as he left the tavern, mounted his horse, and rode back toward Astor.

I finally relaxed, "Hopefully, that will keep him busy for a while, but we obviously can't let our guard down." I was just glad he didn't spot them. I turned around and walked back toward our table, when I realized that Kaja and the siblings were gone. Aelton still sat at the table but I no longer knew any of the people at the table. One of them motioned me over.

"Is he gone?" one of the individuals asked, which caused the table to erupt in laughter, "Our voices too? I'm impressed."

I ignored the question, "Where did my friends go?"

Aelton laughed and stopped playing his lute. As the notes faded, so too did the strange figures at the table; replaced once more by the familiar faces of Varen, Celenia, and Kaja.

"How did you do that?" I asked Aelton.

"A few bards, such as myself, know how to weave music to make you see what we want you to see."

"Which is a very bardic way of saying that some bards can use music to cast spells." Varen rolled his eyes and laughed.

Astra approached the table and began placing before each of us plates with a little bread and a bowl of chicken stew that was more stew than chicken. She also refilled our clay mugs with water.

"Sorry about the wait on this everyone, we have been pretty backed up tonight. Is there anything else I can get you?"

"No this should be fine thank you." Kaja nodded.

"All right, holler if you need anything. Aelton I think the table over there is calling for you." Astra smiled at him as she moved on to the next table.

"So it is. Excuse me friends. It was good meeting all of you."

"Likewise, Aelton." Varen replied taking a bite out of his bread.

"So, what do we do now?" I asked, taking a bite of the bread.

"What do you mean?" Varen asked.

"I bought us time, but I don't think Olmar will be thrown off the trail for long. He's skilled, determined, and doesn't seem to be the type who will just give up. I don't think he will stop until either you two are dead, or he is."

"I don't want to kill anybody." Varen said sternly, taking a bite of stew.

"I know Var," I had never heard Celenia, or anyone, call him by any sort of nickname, "None of us do; but the only way we get a choice is to get so far away he can't follow us, and I don't think that will be easy. We are exiles, renegades in the eyes of society. It's not about right or wrong anymore. If it comes to it, we need to do what we have to in order to survive."

Varen nodded slowly, not taking his eyes off his stew.

"So, with all that in mind, what *is* our next move?" Kaja asked.

"We need to take advantage of the time we do have to get ahead of him." Celenia asserted.

"We have a whole city that knows of your exile now. On top of that, it's a trade city, meaning it won't be long for news to spread by way of the merchants leaving the city. It won't be wise to visit any towns for a while. On top of that it may not be the safest to travel in daylight."

"You're right Kaja. That means we have to use as much of this night as we can to get ahead then we will hopefully find a good spot to duck into the forest and rest." Celenia nodded. "Lacking a spot to stop we can probably travel a few extra hours with some minor illusion spells. Changing hair color and facial features should do as long as we don't get too close to other people."

"Sounds good to me." I agreed, finishing the last dregs of my stew.

"Well, I guess if we are ready let's pay and get out of here."

Kaja replied and counted out the coin at a speed I had only ever seen experienced merchants accomplish.

"That should cover the meal plus a little extra." Kaja stood up and led the way out to the stables.

The stable boy must have seen our approach because he was already hitching the horse to the wagon.

"Almost ready, I just need to adjust the harness, the other horses are already saddled up in the stalls." He called.

Celenia made her way straight back and mounted her horse. I found mine and climbed into my saddle.

"There, your horses are ready for travel."

"Thank you for your help," Kaja placed a few copper in his hand then climbed into the wagon. Varen Climbed up the other side.

"As of now we just need to get out of here," Celenia said, "Let's continue down the road until it forks, then we will take the one with the fewest settlements if we can."

Kaja nodded and gave the reins a flick. As the wagon lurched into motion Varen turned around and waved his hand and muttered something.

"What did you do now?" Kaja snapped. Varen looked surprised at the outburst.

"Everything's okay Kaja," Celenia soothed "It was a simple mind affecting spell. He won't have any clear memory on the past little while."

"What does that mean? He's just forgotten everything then?" Kaja exclaimed

"No, it's a specific span of time." Celenia responded, "It depends on how long the caster extended the spell."

"I did it for about ten minutes. That way, it shouldn't affect his work. Unfortunately, if he's questioned that means he will still remember us coming here, but he shouldn't be able to say where we went."

"It still doesn't seem right, to alter his mind without telling him." Kaja pouted slightly.

"I'm not happy that I needed to do it either, but our first priority has to be keeping ourselves safe right now. I don't want to make it easy for Olmar to follow us."

"Speaking of spells," I interjected, "back there in the tavern, Aelton cast a spell to disguise you right?"

"An illusion spell, yes." Varen nodded.

"I thought only wizards like you and Celenia could cast spells."

"You haven't had much experience with spellcasters, have you

Hjalmar?" Celenia asked.

"I don't even really know how magic works," I confessed, "I have a cousin back in Astor who is training under a local wizard, but we don't really get along."

Celenia and Varen looked at each other for a moment, their expressions thoughtful."

"It's… kind of a difficult thing to explain." Varen started, "Especially to someone who is unfamiliar with the basic concepts."

"He means that explaining spellcasting is easier to someone who has the ability to cast spells." Celenia explained.

"I will do my best to explain it clearly to you." Varen said, "Imagine, if you can, that there is this energy that surrounds everything. It's not stagnant, however, it moves and interacts with the world as if it were alive. In fact, many wizards are convinced that it is alive."

"And that's what magic is?" I wasn't doing very well at wrapping my head around the concept.

"Not quite." Varen shook his head, "That's just there. Magic as most people know it, would be the way we interact with the energy. See, magic users, no matter what kind, are able to feel this energy, able to interact with it and manipulate it."

"And that's spellcasting, right?"

"Now you're getting it!" Varen smiled.

"So that's all it takes?" I asked, "You just have to feel the energy and tell it what to do?"

"Well, that's the watered-down version," Celenia laughed, "It sounds so simple when you say it like that."

"What is that supposed to mean?"

"My sister means that it is far from simple. We have been studying this from a very young age, probably a good ten to twelve years now. Even with that much time we are only learning apprentice level spells and we have a natural inclination toward magic. Learning the arcane language alone takes years and if it's spoken wrong the results could be disastrous."

"I see." I sat in thought, "Varen, if you need to command the energy through that ancient language how did Aelton do it just by playing his lute?"

"Well, when you use magic it changes you. As you practice it, your ability to feel and interact with it grows. It's why master fire mages always feel warm to the touch and ice mages feel cold; most necromancers age unnaturally quickly, and healers are more resilient against disease. If a family practices magic, these attributes and heightened sensitivity are more likely to be passed on. Over time people were born with so heightened an attunement to the energy, they can interact with it naturally, in new way. This created whole new branches of magic, there may even be some we don't know of yet. Bards like Aelton have learned to use music rather than words, and while I've never seen it myself, I have heard of casters so magically attuned that they just have to focus on what they want."

"So, do you have to have a natural inclination to magic in order to be a caster?"

"Not necessarily, no. Anyone can learn magic but, just like anything, those who have a natural inclination towards it are going to have an easier time understanding it. I have heard that they have academies in the major cities where they teach magic. Are you interested in learning?"

"I think I'll stick to daggers thanks," Kaja laughed.

"You're not interested at all Kaja?" I asked.

She shook her head, "You haven't seen these guys when a spell goes wrong. One night, Varen miscast a spell to light a candle, he was walking around without eyebrows for a week and he had to cut his hair. one of the few times I have seen it that short. "
"How does a fire spell that small explode that badly?" I asked

"You misspeak the command that establish the boundaries of the spell. Took it from an inch to a foot." Varen chuckled, "But that's nothing compared to Cel's fire spell mishap. Show him, sis."

Celenia pulled up her sleeves and turned her palms up showing her arms. They were spattered with darkened scars.

"I was trying to learn how to cast a fireball," she explained, "I got distracted and misspoke. Rather than launching forward as it was supposed to, it exploded in front of me. I had just enough time to raise my arms to cover my face.

"Are accidents frequent?"

"Yeah," Varen shrugged, "Just like with anything you learn you are bound to mess up a few times. As long as you take the proper precautions though, you should be relatively safe."

"Okay, and anyone can learn the language? So, if you wanted to you could teach it to me for example?"

"Anyone can learn it in theory," Varen nodded, "but I don't think we would be able to teach you."

"But you're wizards, right?"

"Well, yes. But the ability to perform magic, and the ability to teach it are two different skills. You would be better off with an actual teacher." Celenia reasoned.

"Why are you interested in it anyway Hjalmar?" Kaja asked, "You are an experienced guardsman, trained with a sword. What would you need magic for?"

"Don't you think it would be useful? Using illusions to psych out your enemy or blasting them with fire out of nowhere."

"Personally, I think it would draw too much attention. If you were faced against a group like ours, what would you do?"

I thought for a moment. "I'd have to find a way to get past you and stop Varen and Celenia casting. It would be too much of a risk to go toe to toe with you while also having spells hurled my way."

"Exactly. Take out any ranged threats first, if possible."

"Thanks, Kaja. That's comforting really." Varen responded.

"It's just basic strategy." Kaja shrugged, "If someone could get past me, your defenses would be easier to breach. Once you're down it makes me a much easier opponent."

"That doesn't seem fair." Celenia pouted.

I laughed, "I learned a long time ago that fair fights only happen in duels; and sometimes not even then."

"The goblins never fought fair." Kaja pointed out.

"Your combat experiences have been very different than mine I would be interested to match blades with you."

"Hjalmar, how much combat have you actually seen?" Celenia asked. "As a town guard wouldn't you just be dealing with a lot of drunks and stuff?"

"We dealt with a good number of disorderly individuals," Hjalmar nodded, "but don't underestimate the Astorian guard. Our duties also involved the roads around the city, so we also raided encroaching monster camps and dealt with bandits along the road as well. Occasionally we were called on to defend a visiting dignitary. The life of a guardsman was never boring, I can tell you that."

"Now you've got my competitive streak chomping at the bit." Kaja grinned.

"At least wait until we stop for camp." Celenia rolled her eyes, "This isn't the time to be bashing each other like trolls. We need to put some distance between us and Olmar."

"All right," Kaja shifted in her seat, "but as soon as we stop for camp, we're gonna have this match Hjalmar."

"Are you sure about this Kaja?" Celenia cocked her eyebrow.

"Of course! I'm going to take him down." Kaja laughed.

"You're going to try." I retorted. She reminded me of a new guardsman just out of training. Overconfident in their own abilities and eager to prove something. "What makes you think you can win?"

"You come from a cushy town protected by great stone walls. I come from a frontier town where we have to be constantly on guard. The creatures we deal with don't know what a fair fight is, they fight by instinct. You can't expect them to fight with the same honor that mankind tends to have. It's less like fighting and more like hunting. You outsmart these creatures in order to beat them."

A smile tugged at the edge of my lips. I could tell where this was going.

"Hjalmar, I can teach you a thing or two, if you are willing to train with me." Kaja offered,

"All right, Kaja. Once we stop for camp, I'll spar with you."

We didn't stop for a few hours, and in the meantime I had the Valbrandrs continue to explain the basics of magic. Once we found a suitable place to pull off where we would be adequately out of sight from the road, Kaja was eager to go. She leapt off the wagon and quickly searched the area until she found a couple branches. She removed the smaller offshoots and handed one to me.

"I don't want to hurt you, so it's probably best if we don't use our real blades. Let's use these instead."

"Whatever you think best." I replied, "Are you two okay with starting set up without me?"

Varen waved me off, "Kaja won't be satisfied until the two of you have your match. So, the sooner you get it over with, the sooner you guys can come help."

"All right," I shrugged and the two of us moved farther into the grove, away from the cart and horses. "So, what kind of match do you want? What are the rules."

"Well, like I said," Kaja grinned, "I don't want to hurt ya. So, let's say anything goes, but first one knocked off their feet or to give up loses."

"All right." I agreed, adjusting myself into stance. She did the same.

"Ready?" She asked. I nodded. "Go!" She shouted.

She quickly came at me with a number of light, rapid blows. She obviously preferred speed to strength. Made sense, her build would allow her to be nimbler than the average opponent. I parried each blow then countered. She moved her branch to block but I broke through with sheer strength and she fell to the ground.

"Hjalmar: 1, Kaja: 0" I smiled and held out my hand to help her to her feet.

Chapter 8

The Hunt

Celenia

"It's getting close to dawn. We should probably find a spot where we can get the wagon into the forest." Hjalmar suggested.

"There's a spot up ahead on the left that we may be able to squeeze into. What do you think Varen?" I asked.

Varen scrutinized it as we approached, "It will be a tight fit, but we should make it through."

"Hopefully we find a good spot to train." Kaja's commented.

"You are definitely improving." Hjalmar chuckled in response.

"Improving?" Kaja teased, "I'm gonna take you down this time!"

"Kaja, it's been a week and a half, and you have only beaten him once. And that was because he misstepped and tripped." I laughed.

Honestly, though Hjalmar was right. Kaja had always been one of the best back in Vellara, but their first match proved that didn't mean much in the wider world. When she and Hjalmar started, their matches would last a few seconds before she would be defeated. Now they could go several minutes of back and forth. Hjalmar still inevitably would win almost every time, but the matches seemed far more even now. I had to admit her progress was pretty astounding.

"Hey, I positioned myself so he *would* trip over that root. That was intentional and the win was legitimate!" She argued.

"Yeah, well let's just see if you can manage a second win." Hjalmar grinned.

"Ladies, you're both pretty." Celenia rolled her eyes as we pulled as far as we could off the road and out of sight. Once the wagon came to a stop Kaja hopped down and pulled her branch from the wagon. They started bringing them along, so they didn't have to find a new one every time they stopped, though Hjalmar had broken a couple of Kaja's.

I dismounted from my horse and helped Varen start pulling out camp supplies. Varen was looking in one of the barrels when he called my name.

"Celenia, come look at this." I walked over and peeked in the barrel. We had nearly reached the bottom of it.

"How long will the rest of that last us?" I asked.

Varen shrugged, "Probably a couple of days if we use it sparingly. We're running low on feed for the horses too. If the two of us stopped eating it could probably last us a couple extra days."

"We could… but I don't think those two would allow it." I jerked my head in the direction of our sparring compatriots.

"Well, we're still at least a week from the port. No matter what we do, we are going to need to stop in a town to resupply."

"Is that going to be safe to do? Who knows how far word has

travelled?"

"Well, we haven't seen Olmar for a week now." Varen argued.

"That doesn't mean he's stopped looking," Hjalmar interjected as he ducked around a tree to evade a strike from Kaja.

"Which is why you have to keep focused." Kaja chased after him.

"I don't like the idea of having to go into town." I looked at my brother, who shrugged in response.

"Neither do I; but if we don't, we're not gonna make it to the port. We've been cautious. We haven't seen another soul in days and by travelling at night, we've made sure they haven't seen us. To most people, we've probably just vanished." He suggested.

"Yeah, especially since we have been travelling at night." Kaja called. "Actually, if Olmar has doubled back, there's a fair chance he passed us on the road."

"That sounds like a good thing now," Hjalmar grunted, attempting a swipe at Kaja who nimbly dodged, "But that could be a much bigger problem if he finds out we haven't made it and decides to wait for us a port."

"That's true," I admitted, "But if he is, we can catch him by surprise as long as he has no way to get news of our location. I say we stay hidden."

"If we go into town, we can find out for sure if he's passed us. I don't think he'd pass up the chance to ask about us at a town. If he's been there, someone is sure to have seen him. I say we stop and ask around. We can go in disguise if we have to." Varen argued.

"You guys," Hjalmar interjected, "This whole argument is useless unless one of you actually knows how far it is *to* the next town. As much as I like the idea of knowing where Olmar is, our first priority has to be keeping up our strength. Let's use what we have and if we need to, we can stop in the next town, or we can start to try to forage along the way. There's surely some wild fruit that's safe to eat. On top of that, I'd imagine we all know how to hunt." He parried a blow from Kaja and struck with a counter. She stumbled back slightly, but still stood.

"That may be our best option. I'd like stopping in town to be our last resort. I think the longer we stay hidden the better off we are." I said, "If Olmar did pass us, and I'm not sure he has, news of us has already spread to the towns ahead."

"Even if he didn't pass us with the news someone surely has by now." Kaja avoided another blow.

"Right, and you never know who may be able to connect us to the reports of our exile." Varen sighed but agreed.

"All the more reason to stay away from towns as long as we can." I replied, "Once we reach the port we can get out of the Kingdom, after that we can finally find a place to can settle down again and start over."

I pulled more things from the wagons to continue to set up camp. Varen stopped to watch the sparring match for a moment.

"Hjalmar! Are you holding back or something? You're matches never last this long."

"Hey! Whose side are you on?" Kaja exclaimed.

"I'll say this for your girlfriend, Varen. She is excellent at using this terrain in her favor. She's giving me a far more difficult time than usual."

"That's to be expected, Hjalmar." I called, "We're from Vellara. This kind of terrain is normal fighting grounds for her."

"Vellara has a layman guard, right? You all learned how to defend yourselves?" Hjalmar side stepped a tree to land another blow, this one against Kaja's shoulder.

"That's right." Varen nodded not bothering to look up from the food he was starting to prepare, "Why?"

"Well," Hjalmar stepped in for another strike, pushing his advantage with blow after blow, "That means you three have sparred before, right? You and Celenia know some close quarters combat too?"

"Sure," I shrugged, "But it's not our preferred. You are definitely sparring with the cream of our crop right now. We've tried to go two on one with her and she took us both out."

With a final blow Kaja was on the ground. Another win for Hjalmar.

"Well, my uncle helped teach me. Now though, I'm realizing he wasn't teaching me as much as I thought." she stood and brushed herself off.

"It's not your skill that's the most lacking, Kaja." Hjalmar replied.

"Oh, and what would it be then?" She grabbed a cloth and wiped her brow.

"It's your humility. You were the best in your town. But you've grown too accustomed to it, you overestimate yourself and underestimate your opponent. The moment you can overcome that, you become twice the threat you currently are."

Kaja looked stunned, then thoughtful. "Maybe you're right. I definitely was too cocky when I first challenged you. In a real fight that probably would have gotten me killed."

"I won't argue with your logic." Hjalmar said, "I know it's not a comforting thought, but your ability to recognize that will only help you in the future."

"Well, I'm glad you two are enjoying your matches, and learning from them. Now perhaps you guys will be able to help set up camp. Varen's cutting veggies now, but we're gonna need a fire started."

"I can gather some wood and help with the fire." Kaja volunteered.

"I'll unload more from the wagons then." Hjalmar responded. "Is there anything you need me to get out for you Varen?"

"Well, I've almost got these all chopped so if you can get me a pot of water from the barrel, I'd appreciate it."

"Of course," Hjalmar dug through to find the pot. "So, what's the plan for rest time?"

"Well, I'm sure you and Kaja are at least a little worn out by your match. Why don't I take the first shift?" I offered.

"Sounds fine to me. I only need a brief rest so I can take the next."

"I can take third." Kaja returned with an armful of branches.
"I guess that leaves me for the last shift." Varen dumped the food into the pot Hjalmar brought over. "Works for me."

"Well then, let's finished setting up camp while Varen's cooking. Then we can eat and the three of you can get some rest."

Kaja

"Kaja, wake up. It's your watch now." Hjalmar's voice brought me from sleep.

"Okay," I replied, sitting up groggily, "I'm coming." I stood, letting the light blanket fall from around my shoulders and onto the bedroll. And walking out to where Hjalmar sat.

"Quiet watch?" I rubbed the last bit of sleep from my eyes.

"Yeah," He nodded, "Celenia's was too, by the sound of it. I doubt we've anything to worry about immediately."

"That so?" I mused, looking to the woods around us. Then a thought occurred to me. "Hjalmar, you said you know how to hunt right?"

"I do. Probably not as efficient at it as you, but it was part of our training in the guard. Never knew when you would need survival skills."

"Good enough. Come hunt with me."

"What?"

"Come hunt with me. We're gonna need food within days and these woods should be teeming with wildlife. Even if we can just catch a couple things it will help."

"What about watch?"

"You said yourself that it was quiet. And with two of us we can catch more at once. If we catch enough now, we may not have to worry about food for the rest of the trip; and that means that we can make it to the port without getting ourselves noticed."

I watched as he debated internally for a few minutes. In the end, he must have come to the same conclusion I had that the benefit outweighed the risk.

"All right just let me get out of my armor. If I'm making noise with every step, I'm going to scare away everything we hope to catch."

Hjalmar set to unbuckling his armor while I went to the wagon and pulled out my hunting supplies.

"So, do you know what you're hoping to catch?" Hjalmar asked, placing his armor in the wagon.

I shook my head, "I'm not familiar enough with the woods this far down the mountains to know what's here but look how lush it is. There's sure to be something to hunt."

"True, but let's be back before too long. I don't want those two waking up and worrying about us."

I looked back at where Varen slept. His tousled, greasy hair messily framing his face. I nodded in agreement, no need to cause undue concern.

I quickly restrung my bow and shouldered it. Letting it rest just above my quiver.

"So, what's the best way to do this?" Hjalmar asked.

"I saw a river back that way when I was gathering wood for the fire." I pointed into the trees a little east of us. "That's likely where the local animals in this forest drink. So, we're most likely to be able to pick up a trail somewhere over there."

"Lead the way." Hjalmar gestured with a sweep of his arm.

We made our way toward the river, doing our best to keep our steps quiet as we moved along. I knelt a couple of time by bushes where it was clear animals had recently been and laid some snares before moving on. Time enough to come back and check those later. We kept low as we approached the river, keeping an eye out for any movement.

"Okay, it looks empty."

"So, what now?" Hjalmar asked, "Should we move upstream or down?"

"Not enough here to be able to tell" I shook my head, "But nothing is going to approach while we're here. Probably best to pick one and just go with it. We're about as likely to find something either way."

"Probably best to move downstream then. We're just after harvest season for the farmers which means most animals are either getting ready to settle in or moving downward to keep with the food supply."

"Good call." I clapped him on the shoulder as I passed, leading the way once more. It wasn't long before I spotted something. I leaned in to get a closer look.

"What have you found?" Hjalmar whispered.

"Droppings," I replied quietly, "and some tracks." I knelt and pointed at the indents in the ground, "This looks like a deer. The hooves are separated, and the size looks a little small, so it's likely a female or a younger male. They head further downstream."

I led the way carefully, being sure to stay downwind and out of sight as much as possible. as the tracks became more difficult to follow, I looked for trampled brush and broken branches. Hjalmar stayed close behind, doing his best to match my movements.

"These tracks look pretty fresh." I pointed, "We're catching up."

He said nothing but nodded in response. My steps became increasingly cautious as we closed the distance. Finally, I spotted it drinking from the river. Quietly I drew my bow and knocked an arrow. I closed my eyes and felt to see if there was any wind. Just a light breeze, not enough to throw it off too bad. I drew back and adjusted my shot, ready to release the arrow when the creature bolted.

"What happened?" Hjalmar asked, "Did it notice you?"

I shook my head, "I don't think so. We're downwind and I was being extremely quiet."

"Well what spooked it?" Hjalmar scanned our surroundings.

"Shhh," I hissed.

"What is it?"

"Listen." I replied.

We sat there in almost complete silence; and that's what had me so on edge. The river rushing was about the only noise. Up above I saw a branch shake slightly.

"Hjalmar, roll!" I heard the arrow whistle overhead as I rolled away from the bush and onto my feet, hand on the hilt of my sword. An arrow embedded itself in the ground only inches from where I had been.

"That was impressive. Truly a skilled hunter, but I advise you to put down your weapons." I heard a pair of feet land gently on the ground. I looked up to see a slender woman approach. I glanced at Hjalmar who already had his blade drawn, ready for a fight.

"Who are you?" He asked, sword ready.

"The only question right now is whether you choose to follow my commands willingly or if we will have to force you." A few more women emerged from the trees.

"Why should we? Who are you to command us?"

"You hunt on Elven lands, now you will be brought to answer for your crime. *You* will relinquish your weapons to Nalia over there and come silently or else I will signal my archers to fire."

"I don't think we have a choice, Hjalmar. I know you're good and I'm improving but I don't think we can take this many at once."

Hjalmar hesitated, studying each woman. "I think I'd have to agree with you there." Hjalmar sighed and sheathed his sword, removing it from his side.

We carefully approached Nalia and handed her our weapons. I considered attempting to hold on to my more hidden weapons, but I thought better of it. Who knew how they would react if they found out later? "This may take a minute." I began unsheathing the weapons from my gauntlets, boots, and belt. Nalia's face became more concerned with each weapon I removed.

"All that just for hunting?" She raised an eyebrow.

"Nalia! Don't talk to the prisoners."

Nalia snapped at attention and more archers emerged from the to surround us.

"Follow." The first, whose name we still hadn't gotten, commanded.

We were urged forward in a steady pace. Over the course of our march some of the archers would disappear into the woods while others would emerge. In total I thought I counted seven in their in their ranks but with the constant shifting it could have been more. Under orders from their leader, they didn't speak to us. Occasionally she would give command in what I could only assume was Elven, and the others would respond in kind. We walked for a while and as best I tried, all the turns were throwing off my sense of direction. Instead I attempted to make my footfalls heavier without them noticing. Finally, we stopped. The leader spoke something and the one carrying our gear saluted and disappeared into the tree line.

"We are going to search you both once more, if you are hiding anything else now would be the time to confess, otherwise the consequences will be severe."

We shook our heads as they searched us. Despite the uncomfortable feeling of being disarmed, I was glad that had given them all of my weapons earlier. I had no interest in finding out what those consequences would be. As they took the last of our equipment, Nalia returned carrying two sets of leather cuffs and a small slender creature.
She brought the creature close and it moved its head around as it smelled the air next to me. It rested back in her arms as it finished with me, then she took it to do the same thing to Hjalmar. Satisfied she nodded and strapped the leather cuffs around our wrists. She turned to the leader and said something I couldn't understand, but it apparently satisfied her.

"Follow." She commanded us as she led the way through the brush. We passed through a small opening into a large city build into the forest.

Some of the buildings looked to be carved into the trunks of great trees while others were built up in the high branches. A few here and there even seem to be built from where multiple trees entwined themselves. The sight was such a shock I had unconsciously slowed my pace to get a better look.

"Keep up." The leader snapped at us. I snapped out of my awe and followed her to what appeared to be a typed of Palace created from the combined trunks of four or five colossal trees. Two guards stood at attention as we approached. After a quick exchange I didn't understand the commander led us through the gate.

Once through, she turned and faced us. "You will stay with me and say nothing. The slightest attempt to escape will be met with deadly force."

"Better do what she says," One of the guards chuckled, "If there is one person in this city I wouldn't want to get on the wrong side of, it's Korryn."

"Come!" She snapped from up ahead.

She led us into the large building to a small room with an older elf working at a desk. He looked up and said something to Korryn. A question, by his body language.

They conversed for a few minutes before the man gave a sigh and motioned her forward with a shake of his head. He said something more, but she chose to ignore it.

She led the way through a pair of large doors. The room appeared to be a large Audience Chamber similar to ones I had heard of in human castles, but this one appeared to be made entirely of living wood. Decorations hung throughout the hall and a woman busied herself about. She would say something and with a wave of her hand the wood would bend, stretch and move to whatever shape she desired.

"Magic." I thought as I watched her work.

After waiting a few moments, our captor said something. The woman turned to face her then looked at us for a few moments.

"Korryn, my za'rola. We cannot bring humans here to be accused of something in a tongue they don't understand."

She spoke something else, clearly protesting, but a look from the woman clearly subdued her as he spoke her next sentence.

"Mother, you know how I detest using their disgusting tongue. We are elves and proudly so. Why should we stoop to speaking their tongue simply because they are not refined enough to understand ours?"

"You are being overly dramatic dear. Speaking their language will not corrupt you."

"Fine." She spat, "We arrested these two *humans* for hunting on elven lands. Upon asking them to relinquish their weapons this one pulled out more weapons than would be necessary to hunt. And the other's shirt bears an insignia likely from some sort of human army. Likely their true mission was to seek us out so the rest of their force could attack."

"That's not true!" I defended.

"Silence *human*!" Korryn snapped at me.

"Korryn, that's more than enough." Another elf entered the room.

"You have no right to criticize me."

"Your sister is right Korryn. They deserve a chance to defend themselves."

"Fine. Perhaps after they speak Amara will see that I was right to bring them in and that her sentiment toward them as a species is foolish and will only bring trouble to our people. I had one of the members of my unit take a list of the items we have confiscated. See for yourself."

The woman gracefully took the list and read through it. She turned to us with an unknown word and a wave of her hand. "Perhaps you were right to take such measures. Speak humans. Why would you carry so much weaponry if your intentions weren't malicious?"

I panicked, unsure what to do. *'I can't tell them about Celenia and Varen, especially if they think we come from an army. Mentioning anyone else would only make us look more suspicious."*

"She is the daughter of a merchant family sent to sell wares and retrieve supplies on her family's behalf." Hjalmar interjected, "I am a mercenary who was hired to defend her from any dangers she might encounter on the roads. By her request we secured a number of weapons she asked me to help train her in for safety's sake. After stopping to rest we decided to search for something to eat, either safe wild fruit or animal. This woman found us as we were on the trail of a deer."

The woman eyed us for a moment, as if trying to decide whether or not to believe us. "And what of the insignia you bear on your shirt?"
"I was once part of a city guard before I struck off on my own. The shirt is a memento of that time in my life."

The woman looked at us for a moment more then sighed. "You are likely unaware of the enchantments in place here, but they allow me to know when a lie is told. The story you just told was far more lie than truth. I don't know for what reason you lied, but if there is any truth to the accusations Korryn brings against you we must know for the sake of my people." She turned away from us, "Korryn, take them below to the cells."

"Yes Mother." Korryn bowed, "Follow me." She grinned as she led the way out of the chamber. We were led down a series of corridors and the light grew dimmer as we moved. I couldn't tell if it was a purposeful lack of light sources or if it was simply growing later.

A voice echoed from the darkness of the corridor ahead, greeting Korryn. There was a brief exchange between the two in elven before we were allowed to pass through the door. As we did, two more guards fell into step behind us, preventing any attempt to get away; not that we were going to try. We suddenly came to a stop and the guards opened a cell on either side of us.

"Get in." Korryn commanded. We obeyed and the cells were closed and locked behind us.

She turned to the guards. "No one gets to visit them. Not even my sister."

Varen

I bolted upright. Celenia repeatedly shouting my name had shattered my sleep.

"What's going on Cel? Your shouts could wake the dead easier than our magic could." I squinted in light. "What time is it?"

"It's late afternoon, around when I was supposed to be on watch, but your girlfriend didn't wake me for it. Hjalmar's gone too."

"What, in the dead's true name, are you talking about?"

"I mean, my groggy brother, that Kaja and Hjalmar have vanished, and I have no idea where!"

I leapt to my feet, my tired mind finally waking up and grasping what Celenia was saying. I looked around, taking in the campsite. Hjalmar's bedroll was still there, and it looked untouched. Whatever happened Hjalmar wasn't able to get to bed.

"Did we get attacked or something? Hjalmar didn't even make it to bed."

Celenia cocked an eyebrow at me, "You are a heavy sleeper, Varen. But I don't think even you could miss the sounds of combat. Besides," she gestured with her arm, "The campsite is still in one piece, nothings out of place. They were either lured out or left willingly."

"What could lure them away without waking us?"

"Nothing probably. I just found Hjalmar's armor in the wagon." Celenia held up one of his bracers.

I stepped over Hjalmar's bedroll and joined my sister at the wagon. "Kaja's bow is gone too. Which means most likely they went hunting."

"Why do you say that?" Celenia looked at me quizzically.

"Well if they were lured away, Hjalmar would have been wearing his armor, but it would have been too noisy to hunt in. Not to mention we talked about possibly needing to hunt to keep up our food supply. They probably thought this was a good time to do it."

"So, should we just wait for them to come back?"

"I don't think so. They have been gone Kaja's whole watch, and part of yours. I don't think they would have gone for that long intentionally;

something must have happened. We better go find them."

"I found some tracks at the edge of camp. That's probably where they entered the woods. What do you think happened?"

"No idea," I shook my head, "best case, they managed to get a lot and are having trouble bringing it back, or maybe they got turned around and are just having a hard time finding their way back."

"You don't really believe that, do you? Kaja's sense of direction borders on the uncanny."

"No, but I'm not sure what else to think at this point. I just know it won't do any more good to stay here." I wove my way through the trees doing my best to look for signs of where they may have gone. Celenia hesitated for a moment before following behind.

The forest grew denser the further in we got, branches snagged on my robes and my cloak every few feet, and the plants beneath our feet were quick to spring back up after being trodden down. The longer we moved the more anxious I got. What if they came back while we were out searching? What if Olmar managed to find them? What would he do to them if he did? I didn't have an answer.

"Varen, look!" Celenia pointed ahead. I looked to see something brown poking out from behind a bush. I edged my way around, unsure of what to expect. It didn't move as I approached and, once it was fully in view, I knew why.

"It's a hare, caught in a trap. It's set up like the ones we use in Vellara, so there's a good chance it's Kaja's."

"Good," my sister replied, "Then we're on the right track. Where from here?"

"If she set traps, she was planning to come back. That means she probably would have used an easy to follow landmark."

"There's a river up ahead somewhere, I can hear it."

We pushed our way forward as we neared the bank; I saw footprints in the wet ground.

"Are they theirs?"

"I don't imagine many other people wandering these woods. Besides, I think it's too close to Kaja's snare to be coincidence. It looks like they moved downstream. Let's go."

We followed the tracks as far as we could before they turned back onto drier ground. I only hoped they kept to the same direction. Celenia was being far less cautious as she trampled through the brush behind me.

"I hate these bushes," She complained, "They grab at my cloak every few feet and don't get me started on many times I've nearly tripped on the undergrowth. Have you found anything else yet? Are we even still on their trail?"

"Yeah, I think I just found something."

"Really? What?" She asked, freeing her cloak from another branch before coming to look herself. An arrow was embedded in the ground ahead.

"One of Kaja's?" Celenia asked, hopefully.

"I don't think so. I've never seen an arrow like this."

Celenia's eyes wandered from the arrow to the surrounding area. "Varen look at the ground around here, there are a lot of footprints."

She was right, several pairs all facing towards the area where the arrow was embedded.

"It looks like someone found them." Celenia said quietly.
"Yeah, and they were outnumbered pretty badly. I don't see any signs of a major struggle though; and no blood anywhere."

"So, they just gave up?" Celenia looked at me quizzically, "That doesn't sound like them."

"I don't think they were given much choice."

"Yeah," Celenia agreed as she knelt, analyzing the prints herself. After a moment she began chuckling to herself.

"What is it Celenia? Find something?"

"No," she shook her head trying to stifle her laughter, "it's just that, compared to all these slender footprints, Hjalmar's looks like a hill troll stomping around by comparison."

"That's not funny Celenia!' I lied through my own chuckle I failed to restrain. After a few moments I was able to recompose myself.

"It looks like they crossed the river," Celenia continued, "Who knows where they're taking them."

"Let's go after them." I said making my way toward the river."

"Varen wait. We can't keep going- "

"We don't have a choice but to try. If they were ambushed into a surrender, we need to find out who and why."

"I know, Varen. But we can't go unprepared. We haven't even had time to prepare any more spells and I don't know about you but the ones I still have left won't be much use if we get in a fight. I know you are worried, but we can't just charge in."

I just stared at my sister. She would have us return to camp to get our gear, then take a couple of hours to study? On the one hand, we would be prepared going in, but on the other we would be losing precious time. What if they were on the move? What if they were hurt? What kind of trouble were they in? What if we never saw them again?

"Varen, you're flaring, calm down" Celenia warned, "If you lose it you will cause even more trouble for us."

"I am not flaring," I lied. I closed my eyes and focused inward. I felt the churning energy at my core with the occasional lash of magical energy striking outward. "Okay, maybe I'm flaring a little bit." I took several deep breaths to calm my emotions, before opening my eyes.

"Feeling better?" My sister questioned.

"I'm still worried."

"I am too Varen, but we don't know what's out there, we need to be careful."

I sighed, "You're right, but let's hurry, I don't want to lose them."

"We've already lost them." Celenia pointed out.

"You know what I mean." I gestured back to the camp and Celenia began leading the way back.

"We'll find them, you know." Celenia asserted,

"I know. I'm worried about what happens when we do."

Chapter 9

Elves

Amara

Nestled in the upper branches of the great tree that made up the North wing of the palace, I watched as the sun set in the distance. As the last of the salmon color had gone from the sky, I heaved a sigh and made my way back down through the branches before landing on the balcony outside my room. I moved inside and knelt on the padded rug facing the balcony doorway. I took a deep breath and released it as I let my mind wander its way into a meditative half-slumber. My mind continued to wander, reflecting on the various boring events of the day until the moment Korryn brought the two humans to the palace. As much as she tried to hide it, the woman's piercing blue-grey eyes betrayed her fear. In my mind their gaze landed on me startling me back to full consciousness.

"I'm not going to get much sleep tonight until I know what happens to them, am I?" I sighed to no one in particular. I stood, ran my hands through my hair in an attempt to make myself semi-presentable, and stepped out into the hallway.

Normally the quiet evening hallways seemed peaceful in their stillness; but tonight, there seemed to be a foreboding to it. I shook it off, attempting to reassure myself that it was just my nerves.

I approached the doors to the Audience chamber and took a deep breath and refocused. I knocked at the door thrice.

"Enter." I heard mother's voice from within.

I opened the door gently. "Good evening mother."

"Amara?" she looked at me over the sheet in her hand, "You have usually gone to rest by now, is something wrong?"

"uh, well yes mother" I stammered.

"There's no need for hesitation Amara," She set the page atop a nearby stack. "You are free to speak your mind to me."

"Yes Mother, I know."

"Then why do you hesitate? what's bothering you?"

"It's the humans that Korryn brought in earlier. Korryn seems convinced that they are malicious but a part of me wonders if that's only because of what happened to father. Sorry" I apologized as a flash of pain crossed my mothers face for a brief moment.

"It's all right, Amara. It was a long time ago."

"Doesn't make it any less painful though."

"The loss of a loved one isn't something you get over, Amara. It's something that you always carry with you. The days get easier as time goes on but that doesn't mean that the pain goes away. You simple become stronger, and more equipped to handle the pain." Mother took me in her arms for a moment as she spoke. "But you didn't come here to discuss your father. You came to discuss the humans. Though you haven't yet explained why."

"It's just… Korryn is convinced they are a threat, but the people she brought in looked scared and bewildered. Not menacing."

"Perhaps they were afraid they got caught and their mission failed."

"I suppose, but I'm not convinced."

"They did lie to me Amara." Mother reminded.

"Yes, but we both know that spell only lets you know that there *was* a lie, not what was specifically lied about. It could have been something completely innocent."

"You're right Amara, it could have been." Mother sighed and looked at me quietly for a moment. Her expression difficult to read.

"Amara," She started, "As Queen my priority has to be to protect my people. If we release them and they do pose a threat, then I am directly responsible for putting our people, the people who trust me and rely on me, in danger. I would sooner put two humans through unnecessary pain to ensure our peoples safety than put thousands of our people in danger through an act of trust." Despite the bite to the words, my mother didn't raise her voice. There was no spite or malice there, only concern for the safety or our people.

"I suppose so, but it doesn't seem right."

"My daughter," She put her arm around my shoulders and brought me close once more, "Much as I wish it were so, what is right, and what has to be done are not always the same. As a leader, I have to put my people first."

"I understand, Mother. It still doesn't feel right, but I understand."

A knock came at the door.

"It seems I'm to be kept busy tonight," Mother smiled slightly, "Enter!"

One of the stewards opened the door and stepped in with a deep bow. "I hope am not interrupting anything important, your majesty."

"No Galan, my daughter and I were just talking. What is it?"

"One of the guards just brought word that there is a human approaching the city gate."

"The city guard?" Mother inquired.

"Yes, ma'am."

"How did they get so close to the walls? What happened to the scouts?"

"Korryn took a few members of her team back out on patrol about an hour ago. We haven't heard anything from them since then, but we likely wouldn't for another couple hours at the soonest."

"This human managed to get past my sister's patrol?" I couldn't keep the surprise from my voice.

"It would appear so, Miss Amara. What will you have me do Ma'am?"

"If this individual seeks entrance search and remove all weaponry from their person and find out their intent."

"Yes ma'am."

"I'm going to the gates with you."

"Miss Amara, I don't think-" He hesitated.

"Galan, that wasn't a request." I warned

"Y-Yes Miss Amara. As you wish." He sighed. He turned and led the way through the doors of the throne room.

My mind raced with questions as we traversed the city. How did this human get past my sister's patrol? They should have easily been able to catch anyone wandering through the forest. On top of that the city walls were designed to blend in with the forest. How did they find it? The only plausible explanation was that someone told them of our location, but who? I couldn't imagine any of our people even having casual conversation with a human, let alone be willing to tell them the location of our city.

"Miss Amara!" One of the guards saluted at my approach.

"I'm here to see the woman approaching the gate."

"She is waiting on the other side of the gate. We told her she had to wait for approval before we let her in."

"I see. I need you to come with me."

"Yes Miss Amara."

We approached the gate and I got my first look at the girl that approached the wall. She was shorter than I was and was wearing a riding cloak over a basic tunic she carried a strange looking instrument at her side.

"Miss, please stand back." I said as I stepped out of the gate.

"It's about time." She responded, "What takes you people so long. This place certainly isn't visitor friendly is it?"

I ignored her remarks, "Miss if you want to be approved for entrance to our city you will have to follow all of my instructions."

"Really?" She sneered, "No wonder you aren't used to visitors. Fine what do you need?"

"First I need you to tell me why you are here."

"My brother and I are here to speak with whoever is in charge here."

"Brother?" I scanned the forest around us.

"Varen, we are at the gates, you can come out now." A tall boy stepped out from behind some of the trees. His green eyes pierced the darkness of the night and he carried a large walking stick.

"How did my sister miss someone like that? How did the guards miss him for that matter?" I wondered. Something about his appearance seemed familiar, but try as I might, I couldn't place it.

"So, we can enter the city?" The tall boy pulled my mind from its cogitation.

"She said we have to do some things first." The girl sneered.

"Oh, well I guess we better listen. The sooner we can do this the sooner we can leave."

"I guess you're right. Fine. What is it you need us to do?"

"First, I need you to state your reason for coming here."

The two looked exchanged looks.

"What is your reason for coming here?" I asserted.

The boy looked at me and stood straight up. "That is a matter that can only be discussed with the leader of the city."

"You seek an audience?" I was shocked by the sudden change in the boy, one moment he didn't sound like he cared about anything, but now he sounds like he is here for the most important reason in the world. *"This could be interesting"* I thought.

"Yes. Is there anything else?" The girl shot back.

"Only one other thing. I need you to relinquish all weaponry to the guard here before you enter the city. Then we will have to make sure that that is all the weaponry on you."

"You are going to search us?" The girl questioned.

"I don't think arguing will do any good Cel. Let's just get it over with." He pulled out a white handled dagger and looked closely at it before handing it to the guard. The girl just sighed as she pulled another dagger and placed it in the hand of the guard.

"Take those to the chest and send two more to search these two." I commanded.

Two more guards came out and thoroughly searched the siblings making sure to check the sacks they carried as well.

"They don't seem to have anything else dangerous on them." The guard reported.

"Are you satisfied now?" The girl sneered.

"Yes, I suppose that should do. Please follow me."

I looked back at the humans occasionally as we walked. The boy seemed to be in deep concentration about something and the girl, Cel as he had called her, had a look of curiosity about everything around her. *"The boy seems focused, determined. Whatever they were here for was serious."* Despite myself, I wanted answers. Hopefully they would come when they met with mother.

"Welcome to the palace of the Vene'ta'ri."

"The Venetree?" The girl struggled with the pronunciation.

"Vene'ta'ri it is the name of our people." I opened the door and led them down the corridors to the audience chamber.

"Is mother ready?" I asked the steward.

"Yes, the Queen awaits the human- er, Humans inside."

I watched as what little color was on the girl's face drained as my identity dawned on her. I smiled as I opened the door.

"Mother, I've returned with our visitors. Would you like to meet them?"

"Yes dear, bring them in."

I led the humans into the chamber and the guards closed the doors behind us. I gave a deep bow and the humans made a clumsy attempt to do the same.

"So, the report I received moments ago stated that you desired an audience with me." Mother began. She leaned forward in her throne and peered at them closely. No doubt attempting to spot any physical sign of dishonesty.

"That's right, your highness," the young man stepped forward attempting another clumsy bow. These humans obviously weren't used to being around royalty of any kind, let alone elven. Though I doubted anyone but myself would be able to come to that conclusion.

He continued, "We believe that a couple of friends of ours may have been brought here."

"Is that so? And how have you come to that conclusion?" There was warning in her voice, but the boy gave no sign of having noticed.

"Well, we found their tracks in the woods where it looked like they were confronted by other people. From there we followed the tracks here."

"I see. And who are these friends of yours? For that matter who are you and what are any of you doing in our woods?"

"My name is Varen Valbrandr and this is my sister Celenia. The two we're looking for are my… girlfriend Kaja and a man named Hjalmar. As for your forest, I'm certain that no harm was meant to you or your people. See, for reasons difficult to explain my sister and I have to travel away from home. We are heading to a port so we can leave and those two decided to join us. I believe they entered the woods because our food supplies are running low and where we come from, we hunt for much of our food."

"But they hunted on elven lands."

"We didn't even know you and your people were in these woods.

Let alone know what lands belong to your people. I assure you that no wrong done was done intentionally."

The room fell silent as mother sat eyeing the humans before her.

"Why doesn't she say anything?" I thought, unwilling to break the silence myself, *"Mother is usually very decisive. So, what has her deliberating so long?"*

What broke the silence was a knock at the door.

"Enter." Mother responded at last.

The door opened and my sister entered the room with a bow. "Mother, I've returned from another patrol." She stopped, suddenly taking notice of myself and the humans. "I was unaware of the capture of more humans. Did one of my scout groups catch them?"

"Not at all sister." I felt the grin tug at the corner of my lips but did my best to keep a straight face, "In fact your scouts must be sleeping on the duty because these two approached the gate and requested an audience."

"Impossible." She hissed, her demeanor souring considerably. "No human has ever found the city, let alone made it to the gate. How did you do it?" She growled, turning towards them. They didn't respond; only looked at her with a mix of confusion and fear.

"Korryn!" mother reprimanded, "Your sister speaks true. They have sought an audience with me and as such are to be treated as guests until I command otherwise, or they commit a heinous crime against our people."

"They *are* a heinous crime against our people." She muttered. "Fine, then what do they seek?"

"Well, it appears that they are acquainted with the humans you brought in earlier. They claim they were traveling, and their companions were hunting due to a shortage of food."

"Weak lies," Korryn laughed, "We saw the weaponry they carried. It was far more than a common hunter would have."

"Korryn, the spell has not reacted to anything these two have said." I retorted

"That's impossible!" She spun to face the humans. "What did you do to the magic here?"

The two humans stood stunned, giving no response.

"Korryn! That is no way to speak to guests." Mother chided

"Humans aren't guests, mother, they're parasites that should be disposed."

"Mother accepted their request for audience, giving them permission to enter. Do you now outrank her to rescind that?"

"Korryn, Amara, Enough!" Mother silenced us. "It is obvious we are not going to come to a conclusion on this tonight."

"Perhaps you are right, mother" Korryn nodded solemnly, "Truthfully this is probably a matter for the council to decide."

"What do you mean by that?" I narrowed my eyes at her.

"Simply that with the appearance of these two and the location of an elven city potentially exposed, this becomes an inter-racial issue. This decision could affect all of the other elves as well."

"I thought you were accusing them of hunting on elven grounds. How exactly does that affect the other elves?"

"No, their charge was trespassing on elven lands. They were the ones that said they were hunting. With the appearance of these humans, however, it seems possible they were actually spying for a larger group possibly with the intent to invade us."

"But the spell- "

"Is magic, and as such can be countered with magic. We know humans have the capability, after all, they taught you magic when you ran away."

"Yes, but magic is more rare among them. I found one of maybe two mages in the whole town."

"So? If even one of them was a mage and was able to recognize the spell they could have interfered for both of them."

"But- "

"We can't discount the possibility, Amara." Mother shook her head, "and if this does potentially pose a threat to the other elves, I don't think I have a choice but to call the council together. It will take a few days for them to convene on short notice though."

"Then what are we to do with these two in the meantime?" I asked.

"We'll have them put up in an inn for now. They won't be allowed to leave the city until a decision has been reached. Though, I doubt they will try without your friends. Still better to be safe. Korryn, get a message to the guards to make sure they don't leave. Amara, have Garran take them to the Inn and make arrangements for their stay. I need to contact the council."

"Yes, Mother" My sister and I responded with a bow.

Varen

The princess who had brought us before the queen led us back outside the large chamber. As the large doors closed behind us my sister leaned in and whispered, "Did you understand anything after that other girl came in?"

"Not a word." I responded.

The princess spoke to one of the guards who stood at the door. With a quick nod they walked away, only to return several minutes later with an older man following behind. The princess spoke briefly with the man who glanced at us several times throughout the conversation. With a bow to the princess he turned to us."

"Greetings humans, my name is Garran. I've been tasked with arranging your lodging for the time being. The two of you will please follow me." the Chamberlain said.

"Oh good, I can understand you now!" I smiled tightly, the annoyance from the past few minutes only thinly veiled."

"What do you mean arranging our lodging?" Celenia asked.

"Her Majesty has asked that we put you in rooms in the city until the situation can be sorted out. Now please, come along." He turned and began walking swiftly back the way we had come.

"Wait, what needs to be sorted? We explained the situation. They should be released."

"I'm afraid it's not so simple. The information you have provided will certainly be considered, but whether or not your friends will be released will be up to the council to decide."

"Council?" My sister looked at the chamberlain quizzically.

"Though queen in title, Tei'ara only has the power to make decisions in regard to our people when it has possible repercussions on the other elves, the Council of Elders must be called for a decision to be reached. They are a collection of leaders over the various elven communities. They gather on these affairs in order to maintain order and cohesion among them"

"And how long will it take for this council to reach a decision?" My sister asked.

"The messengers will likely be sent tomorrow in the morning. I would expect the councilors to arrive no more than three days after, with a decision made by the end of that day."

As we arrived, the Chamberlain knocked at the door of the inn. A few moments later the door opened a crack.

"Yes?" A bleary- eyed elf rubbed the sleep from his eyes."

"Apologies for the interruption, I was sent to make arrangements for they stay of these guests."

The elf's eyes narrowed at us. "I don't house outsiders."

"This order comes from the queen herself." Garran responded.

The elf continued to glare at us for a moment longer. "Fine." He opened the door allowing us entry. He rummaged behind a counter for a key.

"There. Down the hall, last room on the left. And do try to keep it clean. I don't need to spend a fortune on cleaning up after barbarians."

"We'll try not to break anything too important." I retorted. The Innkeeper shot me a look of annoyance.

"Thank you, sir. Rest assured you will be properly compensated for the inconvenience. However," Garran's voice took on a stern tone, "If we hear that these guests have been mistreated by you, your staff, or your other patrons. Consequences will certainly follow."

"Y-yes sir."

"Have a good night you two." Garran gave a curt nod to us.

"Thanks." I muttered, taking the key from the counter.

"Mhmm," the innkeeper's response was equally unenthusiastic.

"One last thing, you two. I'll stop by sometime tomorrow to update you on anything and make sure everything is going well. Try not to get into any trouble, just because you were allowed into the city doesn't mean you will be welcomed with open arms by the people here."

"Yeah, I can see that." I shot an icy look toward the inkeep.

"We won't stir up any trouble, sir. Thank you for your help." I responded as respectfully as I could muster. Garran gave a nod and left, his elegant robes flowing slightly behind him.

The innkeeper closed the door clearly unhappy with the

arrangement. In a half groggy-half grumpy shamble he pulled out a book and quill.

"Like I said, your room is down that hall, the last one on the left, let me know if you need anything." He dipped a quill in his inkwell and hastily scribbled something in a small ledger.

I nodded and quickly made my way to the room, Celenia struggling to keep up.

"Varen, calm down." She warned from behind.

"Ease up?" I snapped, "We are stuck here playing a waiting game while our friends are being held in a dungeon with who-knows-what happening to them. Meanwhile it's only a matter of time before-"

With a word and a motion from my sister the rest of that sentence was silenced.

"Varen, first off get a grip, your eyes are flaring. Second, we are at an inn, an elven inn at that. You know as well as I do that we can't discuss our situation in the open like that."

As sternly as she spoke, the look on her face reflected the emotional storm coming down inside me. With a slow heavy breath, I closed my eyes and my mind to calm the emotional storm that seemed to be welling within. Seconds ticked by and finally I opened my eyes.

"You okay?" She asked quietly.

"I'm...... better. I'm not sure okay is the word."

"It'll have to do." she took the key from me and insert it into the lock. The door opened with a small click.

We entered and I closed the door behind me. After a quick scan of the room I activated my magesight and began to cast anchor points in each corner, the bubble of magic shimmering into existence thereafter.

"Okay, the room should be safe. We can talk without anyone hearing us." I said, turning to my sister.

"Good. What about you? Are you sure you're okay?"

I sighed "Honestly, I'd love nothing more than to charge in and pull Kaja and Hjalmar out of there, but I know there's almost no chance of that succeeding. If we want to get them out, we'll need a plan."

"Are you suggesting we just break them out?" Celenia asked.

"Well, I don't see that we have much choice. Do you trust this elven council to just release them? We were given permission to enter the city and we aren't exactly being welcomed with open arms. Kaja and Hjalmar were brought here as criminals."

"Falsely." My sister corrected.

"Yeah well so was the belief that we would one day use our necromancy to lay waste to the village. That didn't stop the Holy crackpot from exiling us."

Celenia rubbed her temples, "But the Holy crackpot has done that kind of thing before. Remember the little girl who was never seen again because he said her arrival was a deadly omen of the future?"

"Cel, our own village supported his decision, for what reason I still don't know, but if our own village could do that to us, what will complete strangers be willing to do to Kaja and Hjalmar? No, we have to get them out before the council can come to a decision."

Celenia threw up her hands, "All right, all right. You have a point Varen, but let's think this through for a minute. We don't even know where they're being held, and we don't know this town at all. The way things stand it would be impossible to get them out without getting caught ourselves. The only way we got as close as we did was our magic and, honestly, probably a significant amount of dumb luck."

"So, what do you propose we do Cel?" I shook my head, "We don't have a lot of time here so if we are going to plan, we have to do it quickly."

"I know. From the sound of it, we only have three days to make a plan and execute it successfully. I say tomorrow we go out into town and get information. Map out the city and figure out guard patrols. The more information we have the easier this will be to plan, but we can't draw attention to ourselves."

"How do you suggest we get guard patrols? I don't suspect that they'll just let you follow them around."

Celenia smiled. "I think I have an idea, but let's get some rest. I'll fill you in tomorrow."

Chapter 10

Investigation

Amara

A sharp rapping at my door pulled me from my meditative state.

"Strange," I muttered, "I thought I requested a later wake up time today."

"Amara!" The rapping came again. "Amara, are you awake."

With a roll of my eyes I stood and made my way to the door. "What are you doing Korryn?" I asked as I swung it open.

"Mother has a job she wishes for you to do," Korryn looked at me, "though why she wishes to give it to you is beyond me. If you ask me, I'm more suited to the job."

"What's the job Za'rola?"

"Mother has requested my help in preparing the chambers for the council. But she wants someone to keep an eye on our human visitors. Mother's not entirely sure if she can trust them, and frankly I'm quite certain I can't."

"I understand. Inform mother I accept the task and will depart." My sister gave a nod of acknowledgment and left. Once she was gone, I set about gathering what I needed

"*Korryn has a point, though. Korryn is the better scout, that's why she leads her own scouting unit. So why does mother want me on this job? Why doesn't she have me helping prepare for the council?*" I opened the oak chest at one corner and pulled out my old scouting gear. Leather armor and a uniform designed to blend into the woods. The dark green cloak had a few small holes. I chuckled and muttered "I guess it really has been a while since I've been out. Better fix these." Focusing on the holes, I muttered a word as the cloth seemed to reach like tendrils across them until the fabric had mended itself. Next, I grabbed my bow and after stringing it, made my way to my balcony.

I looked around, trying to find the fastest way down. A series of branches starting just below my balcony seemed to be my best bet. I climbed onto the wooden balustrade and dropped to the first branch. I landed a little harder than I intended, causing the branch to rock for a moment. Once it stopped, I dropped quickly from branch to branch until I reached the ground below. I quickly made my way out the gate and began scanning the street.

"All right the first step in every hunt is to find your prey." I recalled the words of one of the palace scouting trainers "So I need to figure out where those two were taken for lodging."

I turned to one of the guards by the gate. "Excuse me."

"Ah! Princess Amara." He took a deep bow, "What can I do for your highness today?"

"First off, I'm not my sister there's really no need for the formality. Second, I have a task to keep an eye on some visitors in our city. A couple of humans. Perhaps you know where they were put up for the night?"

"Humans you say? I heard rumors about that around the guardhouse, I didn't think they were true though."

"They are, but please keep it to yourself. Though I'm sure it won't be long before people know, we don't need an uproar among the citizenry. The humans are currently under royal protection. I just need to know where they are."

"Of course, princess. Again, I have only heard rumor but according to that, they were put up at the Grand Mirkoya. I can't say whether or not they are still there."

"It's a start. Thank you."

"Yes, princess." He smiled as we parted ways.

"The Grand Mirkoya? Is that where they were lodged? Garran doesn't do anything halfway, does he? Then again, it was mother's order; doing anything less would be a black mark on his otherwise perfect record of service to the royal family."

I wove my way through the morning crowds, hoping no one would recognize me before I found the humans. Being the closest inn to the palace, I found myself standing in front of the Grand Mirkoya's elegant doorway within minutes.

"Probably another reason they were put up here for the night." I thought. I stepped inside and scanned the room, finding nothing out of the ordinary. Only a bunch of elven folks stopping in for the Mirkoya's breakfast.

"Princess Amara!" one of the servers spotted me. "Are you here for the breakfast special today?"

"No, sadly," I smiled, "I'm actually on errand at the moment."

"Oh? Is there something I can do to help?"

"Now that you mention it, maybe. I've been tasked to keep an eye on some guests we have here in the city. I've heard rumor that this is where they were staying."

Her eyes widened. "The humans?" She whispered.

I nodded in reply.

"Are they dangerous? What are they doing here?" She asked.

"It's nothing to worry about." I assured, "They should be gone in a few days. I just need to know where they are. Can you tell me?"

She bit her lip in thought, "Well they came down for breakfast not long ago, then headed toward the west side of town. They didn't say where they were going, though."

I nodded, "Thank you."

"Of course! Let me know if there is anything else, I can do."

"I will." I nodded as I stepped back outside.

"They headed west? And it doesn't sound like they asked for directions either." I thought as I wove through the streets. *"Is Korryn right? Do they know more about us and the city than they are letting on?"* I shook the thought from my head. Korryn hated humans ever since father's death, so it was no surprise she didn't trust them. If I wanted the truth I would need to observe, not make baseless assumptions. Perhaps that was why mother chose me for this.

I was so lost in thought that I almost didn't spot the humans standing near the entrance pf a small tavern near the city gate. The one named Celenia was speaking animatedly to her brother, who listened with great intent. I didn't dare get any closer than I already was for fear of being spotted. I reached in my pocket rubbed a smooth stone, debating on whether or not to use it. I decided against it. In the crowded streets there was too much of a chance I wouldn't be able to get it close enough.

I chose instead to duck into the nearest shop and watch discreetly from the window. The one named Varen gestured in the general direction of the palace and then in the direction of the gates. Celenia's face scrunched and she said something in rebuttal then made a few other motions. He nodded and handed her his cloak before walking into the tavern. Celenia pulled the cloak around her shoulders and fastened it. Next, she began to approach and speak with people on the street. Most of them simply pretended she wasn't there and kept walking. Others purposely skirted around the area she was standing.

"The other elves calling me soft for humans may not be so far off" I though as I found myself sympathetic to her situation. A part of me wanted to go and try to help her but I shook it off. It wouldn't do to reveal myself just yet. Several minutes later a few of the guard approached her. She turned and began to speak to them. One of them responded and began gesturing down the street as he spoke.

Celenia nodded and spoke once more. The guard gave a slight wave in response as she merged into the crowd in that direction. The guard began to walk away when he stopped looking where she had previously stood. He picked up a small object and turned to call out to her. He searched the crowds, confused. I too, realized she had quickly disappeared in the crowd. With a shrug he placed the object in a small pouch at his belt before rejoining his compatriots and making their way back to their posts.

"Heads of the founders!" I cursed. Searching the street, "How did I let a human girl get away from me?" I took a deep breath to calm my nerves.

"All right, the girl's gone. What are my options?" I thought, *"She asked the guard directions. I could try to follow her based off the pointing I saw."* I shook my head, the odds of finding her that way were far too slim. *"What if I find the guard and ask?"* No, that wasn't likely to work either. By the time I found the guard and found out where she was going, she could have moved on to somewhere else. I mentally kicked myself, Korryn never would have allowed that to happen.

I needed a new tactic. The girl was a lost case for now; but her brother went into the tavern and I hadn't yet seen him leave. That was my best shot at picking up the trail again before I lose it completely. I tugged my hood farther and walked in quickly, trying to get as far as I could before being recognized. Thankfully, the tavern's late morning crew was dying down and I was too early for the lunch crowd. I stepped up toward the counter and began to scan the crowd. I pursed my lips, no sign of the human boy. The bartender approached for my order, a mixed expression of surprise and curiosity on his face.

"How can I help you, princess?" I put a finger to my lips ordering him to keep it down. He nodded and leaned closer, keeping his next words down, "It seems you're not here for an early lunch."

"No," I agreed, "I'm looking for someone. I know he came in here, but I don't know where he is now."

"I see. Can you describe him?" The barkeep cocked an eyebrow.

'In a single word: human."

"A human boy? Wouldn't that just be the next fitting scandal for princess Amara. Does your mother know about this?"

I was used to this opinion of me, but I didn't have time to sit here and contest his gossip. It was time to take a page from my sister's book. I grabbed him by the shirt and pulled him down until his eyes were level with mine.

"My mother is the one who gave me the mission to keep an eye on him." I growled, "Now you can use that pathetic muscle you call a tongue to continue gossiping so I can haul you to the palace for impeding my investigation, or you can use it to give me the information I need. The choice is yours."

Korryn would have been harsher, but I could tell I got my point across by the blanching of his face. "The boy you're looking for was in here about an hour ago. He asked if there was somewhere, he could get a map of the city, and asked some general questions about your highness and the rest of the royal family. After that he ate a small meal and left toward the marketplace, probably to find the cartographer. I have no idea where he is now."

"Thank you." I smiled, "You have been very helpful." I stood, pat his cheek, and walked out the door.

"So, the rumors about me still float around, huh?" I muttered to myself. Though used to it, the bartender's words still bothered me. I shook it off; I couldn't afford to become distracted at this point. I took off down the street, hoping my knowledge of the city and where everything is would give me the edge I needed to catch up to the boy.

I slowed my pace as I approached the shop, not wanting to bring too much attention to myself. I peered through the window first. No sign of the boy. I pulled open the door and stepped inside.

"Princess Amara!" The young shopkeeper bowed with respect, her chestnut hair falling over her shoulder. "What brings you in to my humble shop today? In need of a map for an upcoming journey."

I motioned for her to stand. Normally I would have complained about the bowing but, after the barkeep, it was a welcome change. "No actually I'm searching for someone I was asked to keep an eye on. A human boy who managed to slip away from my watch. A barkeep told me I may find him here."

"Ah. Yes, I did have a human visitor in my shop. Pray tell, what in the Queen's name is a human doing in our town?"

"There are two of them actually; and for now, they are under mother's protection. I was tasked to keep an eye on them though and make sure they aren't up to anything."

"but they slipped out from under your watch?"

"Unfortunately." I sighed, "But you said the boy was here?"

"I did. He came in and browsed for a few minutes then asked if I had any maps of the town. I was hesitant but, seeing as he was already in the city, I didn't see what harm it could do. I pulled out a few different ones and he picked one out that he liked: A moderately detailed overhead map of the town. He did ask some strange questions though.

"What did he ask you?"

"He asked about the architecture of the palace. Said he met with the queen the other day and loved the architecture. He wanted to know if I had any imagery of it or where he could get some. I told him I didn't have any and I wasn't sure if any local art merchants would either but that he could try. After that he left."

"I see. The trails cold now then. Even if I could try every art merchant in town, I doubt he'll be there long." I put my head in my hands, defeated.

"Do you know where they are staying?"

"Yeah, I do." I pulled my head up slightly, "I guess I could wait there and see when they come back, but it won't tell me where they've been, or what they've been doing."

"Well you may not have to wait to long for him there."

"What do you mean?" I looked at her quizzically.

"He bought a map of the town, Your Highness. Most likely he's going to want to sit down somewhere and look at it."

"That's true." I smiled, "and I actually think the one they're staying at is nearby. Thank you for your help!" I said as I rushed toward the door.

"My pleasure. Oh, and Princess!" She called.

"Yes?" I looked back at her.

"I don't mean to speak out of turn but be careful around that boy. It may have been a trick of the light or my imagination, but his eyes seemed to glow with some sort of intense power. His demeanor was calm; but something tells me there may be more to him than what can be seen on the surface..."

"I'll be cautious. Thank you." I pulled my hood back up before stepping back into the street. As I made my way to the Grand Mirkoya my mind was analyzing the previous conversations. If the boy was looking for maps and pictures of the palace, they may be trying to break their friends out; but how were they going to do it? On top of that how were they planning to get past the guards and make their escape?

I scanned the room as I stepped inside. It didn't take long to spot the young man sitting at one of the farthest tables from the door. Though he seemed to be watching the entrance intently he didn't even seem to take note of me. I made my way to a table on the opposite side of the room, keeping my distance in the hopes that even if he did notice me, he wouldn't be able to see me clearly enough to recognize me.

I watched him for a time as he just sat gazing at the entrance. As time went on, I began to wonder if they caught wind of me watching them and this was simply a distraction. Then he stood and waved his arm. I looked toward the entrance and saw his sister making her way towards the table.

As she sat across from her brother, I could see her mouth move to speak but I couldn't hear anything over the din of the restaurant.

"All right then. Time to use a trick I learned from my human magic teacher." I drew a small stone from my pouch carved with an arcane rune. I spoke a word and the rune glowed for a moment before fading. I waited until the space was between my table and theirs was clear, then tossed it in their direction. The stone skittered across the floor, nearly getting kicked off course by a passing barmaid before coming to a stop beneath their table. The siblings didn't seem to notice.

I closed my eyes and focused on the arcane mark on the stone. Slowly the sounds of the tavern faded, and I could hear the voices of the siblings.

"- you get the map?" I heard the girl ask.

"I got the one for the city. They didn't have anything for the palace."

"Did you really expect him to have some?"

"No. I knew it was a long shot, but it would have been helpful. At least we would know we're going instead of trying to navigate blindly. Did you figure out the guard patrols?"

"I think so, assuming they don't change them daily or something. I'll mark it on the map once we get to our room. I also figured out where they're keeping our gear, I'm pretty sure I even saw Kaja's stuff in there. The bad news is that they are in the guard house so if we are going to get them, we're going to have to time it so that there are as few guards there as possible and probably use your cloak to slip past them. Has your ring reacted at all?"

"No, but that could go either way. Either they found hers and took it, which would mean I have no idea what's happening to her; or they have been too preoccupied to do anything to her today."

"Hopefully the latter. They do have to prepare for this council to arrive. Who knows how long that takes?"

"Yeah, but we have to prepare too. The council will be here in a couple more days, and we need to have them out at least before they pass any sort of judgement. Personally, I'd like to have them out before the council even arrives." Varen said.

"Yeah, I know. At least with what we have we can plan how to get out of the city once we get them from the palace, but I don't know how we're going to plan for the palace. I tried a scrying spell but the whole place must be covered with anti-scry. We need to figure out a way to get in unnoticed; and I'm not sure the cloak is going to cut it this time."

"I was worried that would be the case. We already knew someone at that palace had to be capable of magic from the truth detection zone in that throne room. I had hoped that would be the extent of it.

Unfortunately, that doesn't appear to be the case."

"So, we need a way into the palace without attracting suspicion. How would we do that?"

"I don't know, Cel. They are the only reason we have to be in the palace right now and they won't let us in just because we ask. We would have to secure some sort of official invitation. That, or sneak in undetected and that place is guarded tighter than a bandit's purse."

"Man, the more we look at this the more it seems like it would be easier just to let this council run its course."

Varen disagreed, "Even if we could trust them, which I don't feel we can, we just don't have the time to wait. Every day we're here is another day the news about us travels, if it gets too far ahead of us, we will never make it to the port let alone beyond it. Plus, there's Olmar."

"It sounds like they're on the run. What did they do? And who's Olmar?" I thought

"You're right Varen, but what do we do? I know you just want to rush in and save everyone, but we have no idea what we're going up against. We have to find some way to study and map it out, and we were lucky to even get in the city with little issue. It's not like we can just fashion ourselves some guard uniforms and slip in, especially not knowing what kind of wards they may have magical or otherwise."

"I know that Cel, and I want to take the time to give us our best shot, but it doesn't change the fact that we can't sit and wait. Kaja and Hjalmar can't afford it, and neither can –"

"I'm not saying we do nothing, Varen. I want to help them too, all I'm saying is that we have to be careful, if we even had some way to contact them that would be something but I don't think the royal family, let alone the Royal guard, will do us any favors like that."

The young man had very rapidly taken a fall from his seat, holding his face as if something had struck him.

"Varen, are you okay?"

"I'm fine Cel, but we have to hurry."

"You're ring reacted." Her tone wasn't a question.

"Yeah. The good news, she still has hers. The bad news is, I think the interrogator finally got some free time."

"I'm honestly surprised they didn't take it. Then again you got your ah, 'walking stick' an my 'instrument' through so they must not analyze that closely. They probably didn't realize it was more than a simple piece of jewelry."

"If Korryn was here the two of you would be dead on the spot. We'll have to talk to the guards about their due diligence when searching suspicious people."

"That's it!" Varen replied, "What about transmutation? We're in the middle of the forest and it's not like that palace is completely sealed from the outside it can't be that strange for forest animals to get in on occasion."

"Varen, we're not transmutes, the closest spell we know is a glamour to make us look like another person. Besides, even if something like that is normal, I'm sure they don't allow them to just freely wander the palace halls. Beyond that I'd rather not cause panic by using our magic, and we saw how that worked out last time. Let's not forget that the trollkin in Astor was our fault."

"Unintentionally!" The boy interjected

"But our fault nonetheless, Varen. We were foolish and reckless, and we were lucky it didn't get anyone killed. This time it's Kaja and Hjalmar at risk. Do you really want to go in with a half-baked plan?"

The boy looked like he wanted to reply, but eventually hung his head in defeat.

"Varen," The girl reached across the table and placed her hand on his arm, "We'll get them out, but let's go up to our room and figure out a solid plan. Okay?"

"Yeah, let's go." The boy nodded gently. They stood and retreated up the stairs.

"Well, that was interesting, but it really didn't tell me much besides that they are planning to try to break out their friends. That and they are on the run from something. I still need more information and I don't think I'm going to get much more than that. I guess it's time to head home.

I went and picked up the runestone from beneath their table. No reason to leave any evidence I was there. As I stood, I noticed a faint line in chalk around their table. A silence field.

"That's why they were so open in their conversation. If not for my rune, I could have been sitting right next to them and heard nothing."

I retrieved the stone and hurried out of the tavern. I made my way back to the palace taking the tree limb path back into my chambers. I needed to gather my thoughts before I did anything more. I knelt on my meditation pad and attempted to gather my thoughts.

"We can't trust them…. We can't sit here…." The boy's voice echoed through my mind. I shook my head to clear it.

"I want to help them too… we don't know what we're up against… let's figure out a solid plan." The sister's voice this time.

"Stop it." I demanded under my breath. "Stop it."

"Do you really want to go in with a half-baked plan?"

Unable to focus, I stood up quickly and paced the floor of my chambers. Their conversation wouldn't leave my mind.

"Who are these two?" I muttered, "They obviously aren't innocent passersby, that much is clear. They are criminals, guilty of some crime in their own civilization. I should have arrested them, Korryn would have. So why didn't I?" I threw myself onto some cushions and groaned.

"Why are you having so much trouble with this Amara? The humans trespassed on human lands. Humans are warlike and constantly at war with one another, that's why they have such short lifespans. You've been told this all your life, so why hesitate?" Deep down I knew the answer, but I didn't want to admit it. Before I was willing to face it, I had to know a little more about these people, and there was only one place left I could do that.

Chapter 11

Picking Sides

Hjalmar

I lay on the bench of my cell trying to find something, anything, to keep my mind busy. For the past while I had been mentally reviewing the various combat forms I had been taught in the guard. I actually thought I may have come up with some new techniques, though my ability to test them was nonexistent at the moment. The low torchlight had been constant since we had been brought here, making it impossible to distinguish the passage of time.

I sat up and peered through the bars. Preliminary experimentation already told me that everything about the cell was likely magically reinforced. The cell floor appeared to be dirt, but it was as hard as any stone. The bars felt strong as iron but by all appearances were nothing more than tree roots. The cells were opened with magic, which meant that neither Kaja nor I had any hope of being able to open them ourselves. We could take a chance when the guards come to check on us, but the odds of success were low. After all, they wield magic and I don't even have a sword.

I looked across the hall where I could barely make out Kaja's silhouette. She sat on the bench of her cell, one leg hugged to her chest, the other dangling below her. She had been brought back from being interrogated by the princess only a short time ago.

Kaja…" she didn't even react to my voice. I sighed, "Kaja, are you okay?" The elven interrogation techniques weren't anything I hadn't been prepared for so far. In honesty they weren't so different from human tactics in my experience, though with their outlook on humans telling them that would probably only serve to aggravate them.

"Yeah, Hjalmar. I'm okay."

"Good," I sighed a breath of relief.

"Hjalmar, have you ever been captured and interrogated before?"

"Not for real, but guard puts you through training to help you learn how to withstand interrogation and torture."

"Do they train you for mental attacks? "

"What do you mean? Did they do something different to you?"

Kaja sighed, "Not at first. The Princess brought me in and started asking questions. Every time I gave an answer she didn't like, she'd strike. After that wasn't getting anywhere, she turned to magic. At least, I think it was magic. I started seeing things at one point I thought I saw Varen come to rescue me, then saw him killed by the guard. I think she wanted to crush my hope. "

"Well don't let them succeed." I encouraged.

"I'm trying, Hjalmar. But that made me question everything. How do I even know this conversation is real?"

I was going to respond, but I realized I could hear voices up the hall. Kaja must have heard them too because she moved closer in an attempt to hear.

"… no one is allowed to see the prisoners." I heard a man's voice

"I wouldn't care if she said the Elven Council wasn't allowed to see them; You will let me in, or I will have you reassigned to gate watch for the next five years." A woman's voice threatened.

"Great, here she comes again." Kaya hung her head.

"No," I responded, "Her voice is different, a softer tone. Unless she's purposely disguising it, but I don't think so."

As footsteps approached down the corridor, we both tried to steel ourselves to whatever was about to come. Despite her exhaustion, Kaja forced herself to stand a taller. Finally, the woman came into view. She eyed us both for a few moments before turning to me.

"What's your name?" She demanded.

I drew myself to my full height, about a head taller than her. "Give me one reason I should tell you anything."

Her eyes narrowed at me. "Let me give you two. A pair of humans named Varen and Celenia."

"How do you know them?" Kaja snapped.

She turned to face her. "They arrived in our city last night, only hours after the two of you were imprisoned."

"They weren't arrested?" I asked, the surprise tinging my voice.

"Not yet. Though after spending today watching them I have more than enough evidence to arrest them."

"Arrest them for what? An elven law they have no means of

knowing about?"

"No." the woman spun on her heels to once again face Kaja. "I overheard a conversation in which they discussed a plan to break out a certain pair of prisoners. Now, if you don't want me to go and arrest them immediately you will tell me what I want to know."

Kaja and I were silent, a sign she took to mean that we agreed. She placed her hand on the wall to one side of Kaja's cell and a series of symbols began to glow brightly. She turned and did the same to mine.

"What is this?" Kaja asked.

"The glyphs are empowered with a latent antifalsity charm that anyone who knows how can invoke."

Our blank stares bored into her.

"It's a spell that will let me know if you lie." She sighed.

"Why didn't you just say that in the first place?" Kaja asked.

"All right," She ignored the comment. "First, I'm going to test the glyphs so Miss, if you will please answer this question with a lie: Where are you from?"

"Astor" Kaja responded flatly.

I watched as the glyphs surrounding her cell turned a dark red color it remained that way for several moments before returning to a cool white.

"Excellent, thank you. Now if you will tell me the truth."

"…Vellara." The glyphs remained their cool white.

"And what's your name?"

"Kaja. Valtr."

"So Kaja. You said you are from Vellara. That's a good distance farther into the mountains, what are you doing down here?"

"Traveling."

"I've gathered that much. For what reason?" she asked.

Kaja stood silently, glaring at the woman.

"The less information you give me the less I can help you." She urged.

"I'm not even convinced you want to help us. Your princess refuses to listen to reason and not a single one of you people has treated us with anything but hostility. All of this over completely fabricated charges, I might add. So, what reason do I have to tell you anything when it may only be a ploy to get information?"

We stood in silence. It was impossible to tell how long. Finally, the woman sighed. "I'm sorry."

"…What?" I asked, more out of shock than anything else.

"I said I'm sorry. My sister, the princess who's been interrogating you, holds a grudge because our father was killed by humans when trying to unite our races. As for our people, and the Elves in general, well, we live for a long time. Which has its benefits, but it also makes us cynical of races with shorter life spans."

"Why would your lifespan affect your view of other races?"

"Well, take you humans for example. Your lives are too short to be able to see the long-term impact of your actions. To elves that means you lack wisdom. In a way they see you as only slightly above wild animals. As humans expand, they destroy nature around them: clear trees, displace animals and change ecosystems; but he ones that do all of the destruction aren't around long enough to see that damage they cause. So, ages ago, in response, the Vene'ta'ri - my people- staked their claim on large portions of forestland and have vowed to stop any attempt to destroy that land. As generations passed and those borders weren't being encroached as often, our people retreated into the woods to avoid contact with the 'lesser races'. Though patrols still watch those borders in case they need to be protected once more."

"So, what, you see us as some sort of barbarians?" Kaja asked.

"My people do, yes."

"Isn't that a little arrogant?" I questioned, "according to legends, your people have committed their own atrocities, even against your own."

"It is arrogant. And I never said I agreed with it, simply that it was the general opinion of the elves."

"So, you claim to be different then. Why should we believe that?" Kaja asked, the suspicion absolutely dripping from her voice.

"Because unlike most of my people, I've spent time among humans. Though most everyone else prefers to pretend it never happened; Humans are kind of the sworn enemy after all."

"How do we know you aren't lying?" I asked, "You would probably say anything to get us to say something that would condemn us."

"Believe it or not I feel conflicted. On one hand I am a Vene'ta'ri princess, a potential future leader of our people; my loyalty should be completely to them. On the other, it's not just to condemn people based on their race. There's also the matter of a human who helped me once upon a time, and if it's right, I need to repay the favor."

"So, you do believe that we're innocent?" I probed.

"Well, that's what I came to find out. Because the one thing I won't do is bring harm to my people. So, before I can do anything, I have to be sure of you."

"That still doesn't prove it. Prove you want to help, or we're done talking." Kaja shot.

"I… can't. Nothing I could do would adequately prove to you that I am an ally. Even if I went into one of the cells you could accuse me of tampering with the spell."

"You can tamper with the spell?" I asked.

"Not really. They are pretty rigid spells, but there's no way to prove that to you."

I looked at Kaja who had regained her usual sharpness. She quickly turned this questioning back on the princess with good result. She was now in her customary role of the hunter. The look in her eye said that she had found her prey and she was going to chase it to the end. The princess was right, no proof that she could provide would be enough. As impressed as I would normally be, if Varen and Celenia truly were here planning a breakout, this could be our one chance to help them. I couldn't let that go to waste.

"Fine, you can't prove it to us. At least give us a reason to trust you. You already talked about your people, but you said you were different. Like you don't count yourself among your people because you spent time among humans. Why should that make us trust you?"

The princess glared at me and I was certain that not only had I ended any chance of her helping us, but she was going to see to my death personally. Finally, her expression softened. She opened her palm towards the floor and muttered something. Plant life grew from the ground beneath her palm and pushed its way up until it sprouted into a single leaf, green and bright. Then the growth began to grow outward creating and hardening a wooden outer layer until it was thick enough she could sit down.

"Honestly, that's about the best proof I could give you that I want to help."

"What, that you can do magic? How is that any proof? A lot of people can do magic. My boyfriend can do magic!" Kaja shocked herself into silence with the last statement. Whether it was because she referred to him as her boyfriend or that she didn't mean to tell her I wasn't sure. Either way the princess brushed it off and continued.

"That's true, but a few decades ago I couldn't. As a Vene'ta'ri princess, my sister and I were to be taught all the different arts and skills of our people. One of those skills is magic. Every member of the royal family is to know magic, but no one was able to teach me. No, it's more like I just couldn't learn. When the royal instructor failed every mage in town tried to teach me. When I couldn't learn from them, high mages were brought from other elven towns until, finally, one denounced me as unteachable. I was a disappointment. From then on, I was a princess by name only. Though they would never outwardly show it, even the townsfolk were ashamed of me.

For a time, I tried not to let it bother me, but I couldn't keep it up for long. So, rather than continue to be looked down on by my own kinsmen, I decided to try my luck among humans. Despite being enemies, surely they couldn't treat me any worse than the elves already were. At least, that's what I thought; I left the woods and went to the closest human city I could find. I went up the mountain and that town happened to be one called Astor.

The people there despised me. Cursed at me and spat at me. The kind ones just pretended like I wasn't there. I had nothing and spent a month out in the streets until a man appeared from another town. He looked tired and stressed, but he stopped in front of me and smiled. The first time in human lands I received any look that wasn't filled with spite. He knelt down and gave me a few coins and some food he had let over from a nearby tavern. I'll admit I was suspicious, and I refused to speak to him. It wasn't even until after he left that I tried the food. It didn't seem to bother him. Over the weeks he would stop by, give me a few coins and a bit of food. Occasionally he would bring a full meal.

One week I fell very Ill. He asked me what was wrong, but I was still too proud to talk to him. So, he walked away. I thought that was the last I would see of him. I laid down in the small alleyway and prepared for the Illness to overtake me. Sleep took me first and I welcomed it, hoping I would at least avoid pain at the end.

The next thing I knew I awoke in a small room with modest furnishings There was a woman with Auburn hair, in a seat next to the bed. She faced away from me, working on something at a small table. I tried to sit up but, she immediately turned and placed a hand on my chest. She told me to take it easy and that I needed rest. She said her magic had done what it can to heal any damage and ease the symptoms, but it would still take some time for the illness to go away. I asked her where I was and she told me that I was in a room at the Inn that she was temporarily working out of, and that a man named Kaden had brought me there. She introduced herself as Altea, a local mage who mainly focused on healing arts. As she spoke the man entered the room and asked how I was doing. I told him I was fine, and he nodded.

Altea asked to speak with him and they moved to another room. I drifted off again. Over about the course of a week Altea looked after me, and the man named Kaden visited. Slowly, we began to speak more, and he inquired after my presence in a human city. I told him of my shame, and he offered to teach me. I warned him that many before him had tried but he seemed unconcerned.

Once I felt well enough, we began lessons. It was difficult, human magic is very different than what the elves taught. But over time his lessons made sense and I began to be able to put them into practice. He taught me other things too, things about human life and culture. As he and the healer Altea grew closer, I also learned a small amount about human romance and courtship. Once my skills had developed to a satisfactory level, the time came for me to return to my people.

So, I returned here to the elven city, eager to show off my newly learned skill and be welcomed back. Unfortunately, it didn't go as well as I had hoped. The high mages refused to believe I could have learned from a human over them. Even after demonstrating my abilities many tried to take credit themselves, which I adamantly denied them. Then they claimed that my magic was somehow tainted by human practices. After a long argument with the council over whether or not to allow me to use human taught practices, I convinced them that Magic was magic whether taught by a human or an elf. In the end, I was allowed to practice what I was taught, but forbidden from telling the story of how I learned it. But thought the rest of my people have forgotten it, I never have. Kaden changed my life, and I don't suspect I will ever be able to pay him back. But by helping you, I feel like I repay him in a way. I just have to know this won't cause harm to my people before I can I decide if I should get involved."

Kaja and I sat stunned. I searched for a response, but none came to mind. The princess sat patiently, silently. None of us moved or spoke for several minutes.

It was Kaja that broke the silence. "I'm sorry. We can't tell you anything. It's not our story to tell."

The princess was quiet as she looked sadly at us. Finally, she stood and with a motion of her hand the plant that had sprouted withered and dissolved within moments.

"Then there is nothing more I can do. I'm sorry, I did try." With a word and the glyphs above our cells faded until they looked like nothing more than faint marks in the stone. Satisfied that they were deactivated she turned and began to walk back down the hall.

"Wait," I called out. I heard her footsteps cease although I could no longer see her. "Will you give us a few minutes to discuss?" Kaja appeared like she was about to protest but the look I gave her warned against it.

My question hung in the air for a moment before her response echoed back. "I'll give you five minutes from the time I leave. When I return whatever answer your give me will be final. I won't have another opportunity to get down here, so this is your only chance."

"I understand. Thank you."

She gave no response, but I heard her footsteps fade from hearing.

"What are you doing?" I hissed at Kaja.

"What?" She glared at me; the warning clear in her tone.

"No, Kaja. Don't even try getting me to back down. She wants to help us."

"You're blind Hjalmar. They have been trying to get information from us for I don't even know how long now because there is no way to tell time here! Her sister has tried by force and mind games and haven't gotten anywhere with either so now they are trying this. They figured a new face and a sob story would get us to tell them what they wanted to hear. It wasn't sincere."

"Kaja, I've been a guard for years. It's not the first time I've had to figure out if someone is lying to me. I'm not blind, but I think you've become jaded. If she just wanted us to say what she wanted, why activate the spell that alerts her if we lie? Look, we got ourselves into this and now Varen and Celenia are out there trying to get us out. She offers to help us and you're too stubborn to accept it."

"Hjalmar, right now we are the only ones in trouble and I'd rather keep it that way. What do you think they will do when they find out that Varen and Celenia are exiles? Right now, they are concerned that we might be working for someone else, so they are being careful. If they find out no one is coming for us, it won't end well."

"But we aren't the only ones in trouble here; she said that she had the evidence she needed to arrest them. She came to us first. And when that council comes things are only likely to get worse. I say we take the risk of trouble coming a little early. If she's can help us at least we're doing something to help Varen and Celenia. Can you really tell me that you are okay sitting here doing nothing while those two are struggling trying to find some way to help you?"

Kaja didn't have an answer for that, but I could tell she still wasn't comfortable with the idea.

I sighed and shook my head. "Look, she's going to come back any minute and we have to give her an answer. I'm going to take the chance."

Kaja's glare was piercing, but I continued. "I know you think it's the wrong call, but I can't sit here and do nothing anymore. If I'm wrong, we're dead, but if I'm right then we all have a better chance of getting out of here. If there's one thing I've learned, it's that Celenia won't leave without her brother and Varen won't leave without you."

Across the hall I could almost make out the internal debate going through her mind. "Fine," she conceded, "but Hjalmar, we tell her we were heading to the port city to move or something. We do not tell them about Varen and Cel's situation under any circumstances. Are we agreed?"

I opened my mouth to argue but heard the door opening down the hallway. I shook my head "All right."

Amara soon came back into view with an unreadable expression.

"So? What did you decide?"

"You really want to help us?" I asked.

"I know it's difficult to believe, but I truly do. If I can." She nodded.

"Then I'll tell you what I can, though it may not be as much as you'd like. When I met Varen and Celenia, the two trying to get us out, they were moving away from their hometown towards the port to the west. When they arrived in Astor, we were under attack from a trollkin, and they helped us get rid of it. As a member of the guard, I felt I owed them for helping us, so I decided to travel with them to help protect them. When we were low on food Kaja suggested hunting for more and I agreed. That's when your people found us."

"And what about her? I noticed she was absent from your story aside from hunting being her suggestion."

"Only because I thought your concern was our relation to Varen and Celenia and what their intentions are." I shrugged, "Kaja was there with Varen and Celenia when I met them. Beyond that you'll have to ask her."

"Well, what do you have to add?" She turned to Kaja.

Kaja peered at her for a moment. Seeming to analyze her as she would an opponent in combat before finally sighing, "Fine. I'll tell you what I feel is my place to say. But if you're wrong about this Hjalmar I will take a dagger to you myself and it won't be painless."

"There will be no need for that. You have my word." Amara calmly replied.

Kaja scoffed "I have no reason to believe your word. The only reason I'm going along with this is because you appear to be our only chance of helping them from in here." She leaned back against the wall, "I grew up with Celenia and Varen in a town called Vellara. While we were there, they got in trouble with the cleric who leads our town, so they had to leave."

"And you aren't going to tell me why, are you?"

"No. I'm taking enough of a gamble as it is telling you this much."

"All right at least explain to me why it is you are traveling with them. Certainly, you had family where you're from?"

Despite the dim lighting I could see Kaja's face contort in embarrassment.

Amara let out clear chiming laugh

"I see," she managed to get out between bouts of laughter. "Well, I think you have given me what I needed to know. You don't seem to have any ill intentions, so please be patient and I will do everything in my power to assist your friends."

She turned back towards the entrance and her footsteps faded. We heard the door open and close again and faintly heard her speak as she left.

"I was never here, and if you speak a word to the contrary, I will make your next decades of life hell. You will wish it was my sister punishing you."

"Yes, your highness!" we heard in harmony.

Amara

I stood nervously at the doors to the audience chamber. After talking to the two in the prisons, the next few hours had been spent pacing my chambers planning the best way to assist them. I had finally come up with my plan, but the first step was to get my mother to agree to the idea. I gathered my courage and knocked on the door.

"Enter." Mother's voice came through the door. I pushed the door open to see my mother focusing her magic to add and change the furnishings to transform the audience chamber into a council room.

"Your pardons mother. I don't mean to intrude." I bowed.

"It's of little consequence Amara, I'm certain you had good reason for it, else you would have come to me tomorrow. What is it you need?"

"It's regarding the situation with the council, mother. If I may speak on it."

"Stop hesitating dear and tell me what you came to say." She chided.

"Yes, apologies mother. It's simply that I know the Council members will begin to arrive tomorrow night to meet the day following over the situation here; yet, what have we to tell them. I have heard nothing of the results of Korryn's attempts to coerce information out of the prisoners but judging by her mood yesterday it hasn't gone well. I'm concerned about how the council will view us calling them out on such a long journey with accusations and no proof."

"I see," mother paused and leveled her gaze at me, "and what were you hoping to do about this?"

"Well, the hunts master always said that if you can't drive the hunt where you want it, lure it there..." my statement hung in the air

"And how do you intend to lure the information that your sister has failed to force out? Be forward dear, you're hesitating."

"Yes mother. I would like to invite the two at the inn to a dinner with us. You, myself, and Korryn. I believe if we can change how they view us we may be able to get more information from them without trying to force it out."

"You would invite them into the Palace?" there was warning in mothers voice but if my plan was to succeed, I had to press forward.

"It would be safer to bring them here where there are guards and wards. We can also use their friends as leverage should it become necessary. And when it comes to the food it would be far safer for our own cooks to prepare the food than allow them any access to the cooks."

"That's going to rather great lengths Amara, and we do have the council arriving tomorrow night and we must be available to greet them, and I have to finish the Chamber before the Council meets."

"I will take care of all of the arrangements mother. If you would just be there, I will make sure everything is handled and we will be done in plenty of time to greet the council."

Mother hesitated for a moment, a long internal debate taking place in her mind. Finally, she bowed her head, "All right Amara, if you will organize everything, I will ensure that both Korryn and I are present."

"Thank you, Mother!" I bowed and bolted for the door.

"Amara," Mothers stern tone stopped me in my tracks, "If anything goes wrong, it's your responsibility. Ensure that there are no incidents. The council would not be pleased if anything were to happen and even less so if you were the cause."

"Yes Mother, I understand." I bowed and quickly retreated out the door.

Chapter 12

The invitation

Varen

"Cel, can you open the door please? I have breakfast." I called through the door, balancing a tray in each hand. I heard rustling inside as Celenia came over and unlocked and opened the door. I stepped through and she closed it immediately behind me.

I set the trays on the floor and sat down resting my back against the bed. Celenia sat across from me and leaned against the wall studying her tome closely as we ate.

"You know, people call our magic evil… but you know what's really evil? Whatever these elves do to these vegetables." I said as I took another bite of food.

Celenia scoffed, "I dunno, I actually think they taste really good."

"That's the problem." I retorted, "Vegetables are healthy, they're not *supposed* to taste good. I'm telling you, it's witchcraft!"

"You're just upset because you no longer have an excuse not to eat them." Cel shot back, chuckling.

"Well technically I still have an excuse not to eat anything, but I enjoy food too much."

"Except Vegetables." Celenia mocked.

"Except vegetables" I agreed.

Celenia shook her head, a grin spread across her face. I could tell she was going to retort but we heard a knock at the door to the room. We both stopped and stared at it. Who could it be? Only a few people knew we were here, and even fewer knew what room. A few moments passed and the knock came again.

I called out, "Who is it?"

"My name is Nikal, I am a courier and I bring an Urgent message from the Palace for the two humans staying at this inn. I was directed by the Innkeeper to this room."

"Give us just a moment please." I looked at my sister who was just as wide eyed as I.

"A message from the palace?" I mouthed to her.

"What could they want?" she mouthed back.

"Is something wrong with Kaja and Hjalmar?"

"How should I know?" She shook her head toward the door, "Answer it."

I looked at the door and nodded. Standing up I walked over and as calmly as I could, opened the door. Nikal bowed grandly and from his satchel pulled out two letters each bearing a seal that I guessed belonged to the royal family.

"These are your invitations."

"Invitations? To what?" I took them carefully.

I was not told sir. Only that I was to deliver them to the two humans staying at this inn and that they were of utmost importance coming from princess Amara herself."

"I see. Well thank you for bringing them to us… I think."

"It's an honor to do the task sir. But if there will be nothing else, I'll be off. I have many other deliveries to do."

"Of course. Thank you again." I waved him off and re-entered the room, closing the door behind me.

"Invitations?" Celenia cocked her head in curiosity.

"That's what he said. What would we be invited to?" I handed one of the sealed envelopes to her.

"I guess there's only one way to find out." She shrugged and broke the seal on her letter.

"Greetings," she read, "You have been invited to join the royal family for a dinner organized by Princess Amara. Come to the palace this evening and show these invitations to the guards at the gate. You will be accompanied to the dining area. Signed, Amara Ventai." She looked up at me. "There's a wax seal next to her name that matches the one that sealed the invitation."

"Huh." I smiled, "This is great news."

"What do you mean this is great news? Do you suddenly trust the elves?"

"Not at all." I shook my head, "But, this is our opportunity to get into the palace. If we can even learn where Kaja and Hjalmar it can help us plan to get them out. If nothing else, it will answer some of the questions we have."

"I don't know Varen; It's a little too convenient. It could be a trap."

"It could be," I agreed, "but you and I both have been keeping an eye on the palace gates. There is no other way we're getting in safely. It's too heavily guarded and we don't know- "

"Varen shut up." Celenia cut me off.

"What?"

"I said shut up. look at the letter with your magesight."

"What?" I opened my mage sight and stared at the letter. "You're right. There's a trace amount of magic leaking from the seal by the signature." I slowly peeled off the seal, releasing the magic. in my mage sight I could see tendrils of magic make their way across the page, erasing and transforming the words until a new message appeared.

"What does it say?" Celenia asked, peeling the seal from her own invitation.

"Varen and Celenia," I read "I have designed this dinner as a means to help you, though my mother and sister are unaware of it. Your friends in the cells have spoken to me somewhat regarding your situation. Though they refused to give any significant details, I have been informed enough to trust that you pose no threat to us and that my sister is making a mistake. My mother and sister will be hoping to get some information out of the two of you. My mother I can guarantee to be kind and diplomatic, I can make no such promises for my sister. Though hope is that she will be reserved in her attempts, her prejudice against humans can make her unpredictable. Regardless I will escort you to the dining room and we will pass the prison door along the way. I can't take you in, and I can't point it out to you, but it will have two guards posted at the door. Signed, Amara Ventai."

I put the letter down and looked at my sister.

"What do you think?" I asked.

"I still don't trust it... but it's our best chance of getting in without arousing suspicion." She sighed. "Honestly, I don't think there's a choice to make here; but if we go, we go in ready. Prepare any spells you might need. if things go badly, I don't want to be caught off guard."

"Right, we better renew the illusions on our weapons as well." I nodded.

*　　*　　*

That evening we arrived in square in front of the castle. Two guards stood before the gates.

"Hold. State your name and purpose." One guard called as we approached.

"Our names are Celenia and Varen." My sister responded, "And we were invited to dinner" She held the invitation out. The hidden message we had read faded hours ago, restoring the original invitation.

The guard took the envelope and read quickly. He turned to the other and nodded. The second guard stepped through the gates and closed them again behind him.

"Wait here just a minute please." He handed the invitation back.

A short time later the second guard returned followed by princess Amara.

"You've arrived, excellent. Now before you enter, we just must search you. My apologies but in order for my family to agree to this I had to assure them I would take the utmost precautions. Li'nar, if you please."

"This again?" Celenia complained, "You guys took everything off us when arrived at the city."

"True." The princess responded, "But you have also been in the city for a couple of days now, it's not impossible for you to have bought or crafted more weapons."

"Nothing to report, Princess." Li'nar bowed.

"Good. Now, Ciara."

The guard named Ciara approached us with the small creature and brought it close to us. It bobbed its head around intently as it appeared to be smelling us. Moments later it chirped gently and curled up in the guard's hand.

"Clean, your highness." Ciara reported.

"Excellent. Now if you will please follow me." She turned and opened the gate, leading the way into the palace.

We were led down ornate hallways and I took in every detail I could so we could later construct our escape plan.

"So, it's Amara, right?" Celenia asked.

"Yes, and you are called Celenia, correct?" Amara responded.

"Yes, that's right. If I may ask, what was with the dinner invitation all of a sudden? You and your family haven't exactly been our biggest fans since we arrived. Not to offend of course." She quickly amended seeing the look on Amara's face. "It's just that it seemed sudden, we really weren't expecting this."

"You're right." The princess sighed, "We haven't been very welcoming, and that's part of the reason for this tonight. Consider it an apology, at least in part."

"And the other part?"

"Well, as you are aware, the council arrives here tomorrow. My mother would like to hear the events from your point of view in order to better discuss the matter with the council."

"Uh-huh... and what side is she on?"

"What do you mean?" Amara raised an eyebrow.

"Well, to be perfectly honest, it's a little ridiculous that things have gotten this far over a simple mistake. We came to get our friends and leave and now it becomes a matter for every elven kingdom for some reason. It's stupid."

Amara stopped and turned quickly, "Miss Celenia, with all due respect, just because you have a story doesn't mean we can take it to be truth. Mistake or not, the accusations of my sister are quite serious and could create a war between humans and elves. And though most elves prefer to avoid contact with humans, it will not stop them from amassing their armies if they believe a war is coming to them."

"I apologize for my sister. We didn't realize the situation was so serious. I assure you she meant no offence by the statement." I shot Celenia a warning look.

The princess took a deep breath and when she spoke again her tone was calm. "I understand your frustration, but please be respectful in the presence of my mother and sister. Respect goes a long way when working with my mother."

"Of course, your highness." I bowed slightly.

"All right," Amara nodded, "let's not keep my mother waiting."

"You're supposed to be looking for the dungeon and a way out." I heard my sister's voice enter my mind. Well, that's two spells that seem to work within the walls of the palace.

"How am I supposed to focus on that when my sister, who's supposed to keep them distracted, is bent on getting us kicked out instead!"

"Ow! Don't yell in my mind."

"Just don't offend them again, we're here to help Kaja and Hjalmar; not make things worse for them."

"All right! Just keep looking."

Amara continued to lead us down the winding corridor and down one hall I saw the door. Guarded, as she had said. It looked to be made of wood, but my magesight immediately told me it was magically altered. The two guards appeared to be highly alert, but it was impossible to say whether that was usual or if they were keeping up appearances. I focused on it for every moment I could, absorbing every detail.

"Found it. Now we just need to get through this dinner"

"Right, that shouldn't be too hard."

"As long as we're careful not, to say anything that might offend them."

"Will you drop that? It was one misunderstanding."

"Yeah, with the princess that's supposedly on our side. Imagine if it was the princess that hates us, or the queen who has the power to order our deaths."

"All right, I've got it. I'll watch myself. Who's the older sibling here?"

"I find I've been asking that a lot myself lately."

"So, Varen was it?" Amara interrupted our mental conversation, "You haven't said much. Are you as angry at us as Celenia seems to be?"

"Well, I can't say I'm exactly happy with how things have occurred. You have two of our friends locked away somewhere, and we have only your word that they are still alive. I understand that there are accusations against them, but you continue to hold them without proof of any of it. I am certain that your people have a process for these things, but the way we have been treated doesn't exactly fill me with hope that things will turn out okay for us."

"That would be a yes." Amara sighed.

"Look, it's been clear that your people mostly either fear or detest us because we are human. I just hope that cultural outlook doesn't blind you to the truth of things, and that your council is more interested in the truth than in vilifying some humans; but I suppose that's why we are having this dinner."

"Yes, and the dining room is right down here." Amara gestured as we continued down the hall.

As we rounded the corner, we spotted the other princess conversing with another elf dressed in light leather armor and wearing a dark colored riding cloak. The elf placed something into the satchel she carried and bowed. As she left the princess turned to us.

"Ah, there you are Amara! And these must be our guests, Selina and Warren?" she tried.

"Celenia and Varen, but close." My sister responded, "And your name was?"

"Ah, of course. I am Korryn Ventai. I am Amara's elder sister."

"Korryn, I would have thought you'd have been waiting in the dining room already." Amara commented.

"I intended to, but due to the council's arrival tomorrow and being preoccupied with this myself, I had to make some changes to the patrol teams. She just left to take my orders to the guardhouse.

"I see. Well if you have no other business to attend to, shall we go inside?"

"Please," Korryn nodded and motioned to the door next to her, allowing Amara to lead us inside.

The room was simple but elegant. It wasn't large enough to be a banquet hall. I would guess that this was where the royal family commonly took meals when they didn't have guests. While nothing in the palace was particularly lavish, this room felt plain in comparison to the rest of the castle. It has an opening to a balcony near the head of the table the queen sat. There was also a small pedestal in the corner opposite the balcony. There was an object atop the pedestal, covered by a cloth. An elven woman, a servant I guessed, stood beside the pedestal."

"Good evening." The queen greeted us.

"Good evening your highness," I bowed awkwardly. Out of the corner of my eye I saw my sister follow suit.

The queen let out a chiming laugh, "Please, this dinner was suggested by my Daughter, Amara that we could discuss the situation at hand in a... less formal setting. Certainly, in light of this we may dispense with honorifics for tonight. You may call me Tei'ara. Take a seat, and please make yourself comfortable. Elia, please take their cloaks." The woman who stood by the cage approached and held out her arms. We placed our cloaks in them and she gave a gentle nod.

"Would you like me to store your walking stick as well sir?" she asked.

"Ah, if it's all the same, I'd like to keep it nearby. It's rather sentimental to me." She bowed and left the room, taking our cloaks with her.

"Amara, do you have the amulets? I'd much prefer to allow conversation to flow easily."

"Yes, Mother." Amara picked up a small pouch from the corner of the table, from it she pulled out several amulets. Looking closely at them she nodded. She put one on herself then handed one to each of us, beginning with Celenia and myself, then handing one to Korryn and took the last to her mother.

"I'm sorry, what are these?" Celenia asked, turning the amulet over in her hands.

"Nothing to be concerned about." Amara responded, "They will serve to translate so we can both speak in our native tongues and can be understood by all who are wearing these amulets."

Celenia looked at me, I could tell she still wasn't sure. I looked at her and shrugged, putting the amulet around my neck. Once nothing appeared to happen, my sister followed suit.

"Now we can all speak without struggle and everyone can understand." The queen stated.

Celenia and I had learned a fair amount about ways to communicate magically in our studies, but we had never had a chance to use it. When the queen spoke, my ears were undoubtedly hearing elven, but my mind understood it perfectly.

"That's strange." My sister said, echoing my own impression. "Cool, but strange."

"It does take a little bit of adapting, but that shouldn't take long." The queen smiled gently. "Now please, have a seat." She gestured to the spots nearest us.

Obediently, we pulled our seats out and sat down. The chairs were of a dark wood and had some subtle but intricate carvings along the arms that I had not previously noticed. They were also very comfortable, my guess was that was done magically, but I didn't dare activate my magesight here in case they had some way to detect it. My staff and cloak had made their way in without issue, but I didn't want to push my luck.

"Well, I believe that the cooks should have our food sent out shortly, but in the meantime let's begin with proper introductions. I am Tei'ara Ventai I am the leader of the elves in these woods. These are my daughters: Korryn, my eldest. She leads a specialized scouting and tracking unit of the guard. Amara, my youngest, keeps an eye on the internal matters of the city."

"It's an honor meet all of you, and a greater honor to dine with all of you." I responded, "My name is Varen Valbrandr and this is my sister Celenia Valbrandr."

"Well Varen and Celenia, it's good to meet you, though I do wish it were under less strained circumstances. I don't expect any of us to truly put aside the situation at hand, but if I can make a request please enjoy tonight as much as you can. Amara put great effort into planning it and convincing us to hold it tonight."

"We'll try your highness. Right, Varen?" Celenia nudged me.

"Yeah…" I responded, trying to pull my mind away from the fact that Kaja was in cells not far from us.

The queen gazed at us for a moment, then nodded. "I suppose I can't ask any more than that. Have the two of you found your stay agreeable at least?"

I shrugged, "As agreeable as I suppose I could expect, all things considered."

"What does that mean? Are the accommodations sub-par for you?" The older princess's tone was level and calm but there was no mistaking the intention behind the words.

"Korryn." Tei'ara warned.

"What I meant was that your people are rather secluded here, we've been treated with fear, distaste, and hesitancy. Your people act as if they have never seen a human before."

Tei'ara nodded, "Humans are rare, most of our people have no need to go outside of the woods here. And our patrols are usually vigilant enough to ward off any outsiders before they actually enter elven lands."

"So, why were our friends arrested instead of being 'warded off' as you put it?" Celenia questioned.

"There had been recent reports from one of the nearby Vene'ta'ri towns they had been having some problems near their borders," Amara responded, "in response my sister pulled some of our people from the patrols to provide support to their town. That apparently left enough of a hole in our guard that your friends managed to get well into elven lands before they were discovered."

"So, it was because you had fewer scouts out that the situation has progressed here?" I muttered to myself "That hardly seems like their fault."

"Let's not forget who intruded where here." Korryn interjected forcefully. "If you humans would stop attempting to expand and be content with what you have, we wouldn't have to guard our borders so closely."

"Korryn, that's enough." Tei'ara spoke sternly, "the events that occurred are unfortunate, but they have nevertheless occurred and no amount of debate on whose fault it is can retract them" she sighed and readjusted her dress, "For the sake of all involved please allow me to lead the discussion regarding the matter at hand."

"I apologize, mother." Korryn hesitantly offered.

"Yes, your highness, of course. I apologize as well; I didn't intend for my observation to cause things to escalate."

"Looks like I'm not the only one who needs to watch what I say around them." Celenia's voice smugly chided in my mind.

"They hit a nerve; it won't happen again." I retorted.

"So, you're highness. If I may change the subject for a moment, these amulets are supposed to translate anything we hear in another language to our own, right?" I asked.

"They are specifically designed to translate between elven and Merchari, but yes."

"But there was one word you said before that didn't get translated. Vene'ta'ri, that's the name of your people, right?"

The Queen chuckled "That's right. The word 'elf' in your language actually is more of a general term for our races. Vene'ta'ri is our specific race of elf."

"How many races are there?" Celenia cocked her head slightly.

"There are five different races of elf, each with their own unique culture and lifestyle. We are known as the Vene'ta'ri. The other four are the Vessi, the Vc'tri, the Shakari, and the Ugathri."

"And are all these races represented in this council? Or just the Vene'ta'ri?" I asked.

"There are eleven individuals that make up the council, myself included. The number of representatives from each group differs, but each is represented to ensure we all have a say in matters that will affect the elves as a whole."

"That's fascinating if I'm being honest. So, you are in charge here, but if something has the potential to affect the other races then you don't have the power to act. The council has to be called. Do I have that right?"

"Yes, that would be correct." Tei'ara nodded.

"So, by all technicality it's becomes a council matter simply because they're human?" My sister questioned.

"Yes. Though were accusations that could bring war not made, I would have had a little more authority to handle it myself."

"I see..." I mused to myself.

"Well, I guess that's understandable." Celenia said, "It's not that you wouldn't act it's that you couldn't."

"That's an apt way of putting it." The queen agreed. As she spoke the doors opened servants filed in carrying platters of food. Large trays were set near the center of the table while smaller platters were placed before each of us. Elegantly crafted cups were set before us each filled with a clear liquid. The covers were removed from the trays simultaneously, revealing the meal in one grand motion. It was a meat dish that could have been deer, but I wasn't certain. It was topped with some kind of mushrooms, with vegetables on the side.

The dish was so artistically presented it seemed tragic to destroy it, but the aromas emanating from the dish were making my mouth water. Platters were arranged carefully around the table arrayed with various pastries and fruits. Once the table was set all the servants stepped back. All looking to the servant who stood next to the pedestal. The servant nodded and the other servants left with a bow.

"Well, that was fancy." Celenia commented picking up her silverware.

The Queen let out a chiming laugh, "My apologies if that seemed overdone, I told them to treat this dinner as practice for when they serve the council tomorrow."

"Well they definitely impressed me." My sister grinned.

"Well let's hope the council is equally impressed." The Queen smiled, "So Varen, where are the two of you from?"

"We're from a small village to the northeast, closer to the timberline."

"I'm not sure I'm aware of one there. The only one to the north of here was the settlement I believe is known as Astor."

"Astor is the furthest major city up the mountain, but our home town is a few hours journey further up the mountain path."

"I see." The Queen nodded.

"What is it like there?" Amara asked, "How do you live?"

"Well, we're a small town made up of mostly farmers and tradesmen. We rely on one another for survival. For example, small hunting parties are occasionally sent out to gather meat and furs for the village."

"So you have hunters. Does that make up your fighting force as well?"

"Korryn!" Amara cried.

"It's all right," Varen held his hand to calm her, "if it helps clear our friends, I'll tell you. That far up the mountain we don't benefit from the organized guard of major cities. Most of the town learns the basics of combat from a young age in order to protect against wild animals and goblin raids. We rotate guard duties and patrols through the members of the village, but we don't have the skilled men or the large force that would be necessary to do much more than fight off goblins, wolves, and other natural dangers. We definitely don't have the kind of force necessary to attack another town. Let alone one that, up until a couple days ago, I didn't know existed."

Korryn sat back in her chair, obviously dissatisfied with my answer.

"My apologies for the forward nature of my eldest daughter." The Queen spoke gently, "However, as the conversation has approached the subject, I would like to know what it is you and your friends were doing in our lands, especially where it's so far from home."

"Well you're highness, I will tell you what I can but to give a full and detailed account would not only take quite a bit of time, but would breach into subjects that my sister and I would rather not discuss for more personal reasons." I took another bite of my food.

"That's certainly your right. However, if you and your friends are truly innocent, surely leaving things out is not in your best interest."

"Respectfully your highness, no one in this world is innocent. Certainly, everyone here has made mistakes, including us. The things we are guilty of, however, do not include the crime of which our friends are currently being accused. I will tell you how we came to be here, with all the details I feel comfortable including, and you can decide whether you feel the story sufficient."

"Very well, I suppose that can only be seen as fair." The queen smiled subtly and nodded. "Go on."

Chapter 13

The Attempt

Kaja

I cracked my eyes open as I heard the guards approaching the cells. I wasn't sure how long it had been since I slept but I was certain it was too long. I could barely keep my eyes open but any time I started to doze off something would jolt me awake. My head was pounding, and my body ached. Looking out I saw the guards dragging Hjalmar back into his cell. He let out a grunt as they dropped him on the floor. As the guards were locking the cell another elf approached them. The as the guards turned the new arrival came into view.

"Do you come with news?" One of the guards asked

The elf nodded. "Dinner has been served. Korryn's plan is in motion. The targets won't survive the night."

"What are they talking about?" I tried to think clearly through the pain, *"Targets? Are they trying to kill someone?"*

"Who are the ones making sure?" The second guard asked.

"Na'var and Tavaran will be on watch to ensure the mission is a success"

"Good. I hope the chefs cooked well tonight. After all, they should enjoy their last meal." The third laughed.

"Last meal? Dinner? So, it's evening and it sounds like they are

planning to kill someone at dinner."

"Indeed, I would love to see the look on their faces as they realize what's happening. You're lucky that you get to be out there with the action." The first guard sighed. "Keep us updated, won't you? I hate being stuck down here. I don't see why Koryn saw the need to post extra guard down here tonight."

"Well, feel free to ask her. Let me know how that goes." The third answered.

"I'm annoyed, not stupid. The last person who complained about their post got gate duty for a year."

"She doesn't take people questioning her well, that's certain." The second agreed.

"Keep this to yourselves, but as much as she makes an excellent captain, I dread the day Lady Tei'ara dies and the crown is passed." The first guard said.

"Well there are two heirs, it may be Amara that takes the throne." The second responded.

"Not a chance." The third retorted, "The choice of successor is a council decision, and Korryn would be the choice of the Vetri."

"There are more council members than the Vetri, there is a chance." The second argued. "Plus, even the council's vote can be overturned on the matter of succession if enough of our people disagree with it."

"The Vetri haven't lost a council decision in centuries, I don't see that changing anytime soon. And the Vessi recently lost a seat to put some youth on the council, giving the Vetri even more power." The first let out an exasperated sigh. "and I don't think enough of our people will overlook Amara's scandal to appoint her."

"Well, hopefully we still have a lot of time before that decision has to be made. Now, if you will excuse me, I have to check the status of everyone else."

"And we had better make our rounds. Keep us informed." The first guard nodded.

"Certainly." The third elf responded before leaving.

The two guards went back in the direction they brought Hjalmar and I waited for their footsteps to fade.

"Hjalmar did you hear that?" I whispered.

"Not, really." He groaned pushing himself to a sitting position. "What happened?"

"I'm not really sure, but it sounds like one of the Princesses is behind a murder plot."

"Which princess, and against who?"

"The mean one. I'm really not sure who though, they weren't clear on that. But whoever it is, is eating dinner with them tonight."

"Why are you so interested in the elves political intrigue? I mean, granted, there's not much else to talk about but it's not as if there's anything we could do about it."

"But what if it's Varen and Kaja? They could be in trouble."

Hjalmar stared at me for a moment before letting out a combination of laughter and groaning from the pain it caused.

"What's so funny?" I challenged.

"It's funny that you think it's Celenia and Varen. Kaja, why would they be having dinner with the Elven royalty? I would guess that talking to them would have been the first thing they tried. Knowing Varen's impatience, I doubt they are going to wait until this council makes a decision."

"Yeah," I sighed, "You're probably right. But I still can't shake this clenching in my gut."

"Oh, did you get hit there too?" He chuckled as I glared at him. "Don't worry Kaja, I'm sure they are just fine."

*   *   *

Celenia

I sat back in my chair slightly, as Varen told the story. The food had been delicious. The meat was savory, the fruit sweet, and I found myself agreeing with Varen's sentiment on the vegetables this morning; they had to be magically altered.

Throughout Varen's tale the queen barely moved aside from taking the occasional bite of her food. Amara seemed very interested in various aspects of our life back home, but that interest faded as we approached the part of the city where we entered the Elven city. Korryn, however, was the greatest mystery to me. Throughout the story she had the face of a master gambler, the kind you would see in the darkest corner of the tavern or maybe a back room, but occasionally a smile would creep across her face and it was impossible to tell what she was thinking.

As Varen finished, the Queen sat up in her seat. "Well, I must say that it is an enthralling tale you've told us."

"But you don't believe it to be true?" Varen looked somewhat deflated.

"In honesty, it's difficult for me to see it as anything but; However, it is not solely my decision that matters. The council has very strong opinions of humans that will be difficult to overcome. It took bravery to come after your friends and even greater bravery to come before me here in an Elven city. If nothing else, you have impressed me. I will do what I can to sway the council, but I can make no promise."

Korryn waved one of the servants over to refill our glasses and Amara looked at her with curiosity. As we continued whatever was beneath the cover began to stir. As it began it was only very brief, rapid sniffing sounds, then it turned into a small growling and chirping sound.

"If I may ask your highness, what is under there?" My brother asked curiously.

The Queen smiled and motioned for us to approach. "They are known to us as the Mirkoya. I don't believe your people have come across them to give them a name of your own." She motioned for the guard to remove the cover.

As she did so we saw an intricate cage with a furry large weasel like creature inside. Its skin hung loosely making it look like a little like it was melting. As we approached creature arched it's back aggressively and hissed.

"What's wrong with it?" I asked.

"Guards, search them please." The Queen calmly ordered.

"What?" I turned to face the queen.

"What's going on?" Varen inquired.

"Do not resist." Korryn barked preparing to draw her own blade.

"Korryn! Stop that!" Amara shouted. "Mother, we searched them at the gate. They had nothing."

"I understand." The Queen responded calmly, "However when the Mirkoya reacts we must take it seriously."

The guard approached the cage, and another entered the room. Opening the door, she held out her arm and the creature climbed atop it. The guard approached us.

"Please make no sudden moves and spread your arms apart."

My brother and I obeyed.

"What's going on?" Varen repeated.

"The Mirkoya is a creature well known to our people for its ability to sniff out poisons. The way it behaved as you approached is it's way of alerting us that it has detected some."

"Why didn't you leave your poison vial?" I hissed in my brother's mind.

"Celenia, my knife was taken by the guards at the gates before we entered the city. I don't have my poison vial."

The guard took the creature in both her hands and started bringing it near us. The creature was unreactive as she brought it near my brothers' torso and limbs, but as she reached up to bring it near his face it began to hiss. The guard's eyes widened as she repeated the action on me with the same results.

"Your highness," the guard turned to the Queen. "It appears the guests didn't bring poison," she hesitated, "they were poisoned."

"What?" the Queen stood up.

"Death's embrace." My brother and I thought in Unison.

"Get the healer." Amara shouted. "Find out what this is and get the cure."

"No!" I shouted as everyone stopped and stared at me. I stammered looking for something to say.

"What my sister means is that with all due respect without knowing who has made this attempt on our lives it is difficult to trust any of your servants. My sister and I are somewhat of herbalists, so we will be taking care of this ourselves."

I nodded in confirmation as I gathered our things.

"Na'var, Tavaran!" Korryn called. Two more guard entered the room, "Accompany these two back to their inn. Ensure nothing happens to them."

"No, we're fine." I protested.

"This is not a matter up for debate." Korryn responded, "You can either allow them to accompany you or I will have them follow you."

"Very well." I relented.

"I'll grab the plates for analysis."

"Take the cups as well. It is possible it may have been in your drinks." The queen said.

"Shei'ra, fetch their cloaks and meet them at the front gates." Amara ordered.

"Yes, your highness."

"Thank you for taking the time to hear us out, and we appreciated the evening." I gave a rushed bow in the queen's direction and ushered my brother out.

Varen led the way quickly down the corridors with the guards close behind. He had studied the path well, as he pressed forward never wavering in what turn to take. The palace was a maze to me, but he acted as if he had grown up here. Then again, my brother always did have an excellent memory. As we approached the gates two other servants were waiting with our cloaks. We walked past them taking our coats without stopping.

The Guards continued to follow close behind us, keeping a keen watch probably for the onset of any symptoms. As we turned down the main street of the square one of them spoke.

"How are you two feeling?" I believe it was the one called Tavaran that spoke.

"Fine for now." I responded shortly.

"You two really should have let our healers help." Na'var said.

"Even if you are herbalists our healers would know a lot more about local poisons."

"Would you remain in the place where someone had tried to assassinate you?" I shot back. "Let's not forget that it was someone within the palace that tried to poison us, and I have no reason to exclude you from the possible attempters."

"We have been entrusted with your safety." Tavaran responded.

"By a princess who, even with what limited time I have spent with her, I can tell she couldn't care less what happened to us." I shot back.

"Are you slandering Princess Korryn?" There's was warning in Na'var's voice.

"A bit touchy, aren't we?" My brother asked, "All my sister was saying is that it seems she doesn't have a high opinion of us. If we're wrong, please feel free to correct us but your reaction convinces me that she hit the mark rather directly."

The two guards looked away and remained silent. We walked the streets in a tense silence. I could feel the guard's eyes on us, analyzing any detail.

"Varen, this isn't good. We have no idea what they used or the effects it will have on us. If they are with us much longer, they may realize something's wrong. And if they are part of the attempt, they will know something's not right."

"Calm down. We're almost to the inn. Once we're there, we can send them on their way."

"I hope you're right." I thought back.

As we completed the trek to the inn. The two guards stepped in front of the door.

"What are you doing?" I hissed.

"You two were just targets of an assassination attempt from within the palace. Allow us to enter before you and ensure that no one is here to make a second attempt."

"I suppose this isn't something you are going to let us say no to." My brother observed.

The two guards shook their heads. Na'var reached for the door handled until we heard footsteps quickly approaching up the street.

"Serei, what's going on?" Tavaran called out to an elf running in the direction of the palace.

"Tavaran? Na'var? What are you doing here? Get back to the Palace, the Council is Arriving! I'm on my way to tell Queen Tei'ara." She once again took off running. The two guards looked at each other.

"Well, what are you two waiting for?" Varen smiled, "We'll be fine. It sounds like you have to get back." The two guards hesitated. "Unless of course you want your council to see you accompanying a couple of humans to an inn." My brother shrugged, "It's up to you."

"Let's go Na'var, we best make sure the rest of the guard is ready for the council." Tavaran led the way back to the palace, his associate on his heels.

"Let's get inside." I urged and my brother nodded, opening the door and entering the inn. We made our way down the hall to our room. Locking the door behind us, Varen moved to the window.

"Well, this council enjoys making an entrance. They brought a whole entourage."

"Unless all those people are the council." I responded.

"I guess it's possible..." Varen nodded.

"Varen, Celenia, Are the two of you okay, can you hear me?" I jumped at the voice that pierced my mind. My brother's expression made it clear he heard it too.

"We're fine." I hesitantly responded, *"Who is this?"*

"It's Amara. Listen, I apologize for what happened tonight, I had no idea that someone would attempt to harm you."

"How are you communicating with us?" I asked.

"The translation Amulets. The two I gave you I prepared beforehand with an additional spell, but I had to wait to activate it until I could slip away. Are the two of you okay? Were you able to neutralize the poison?"

"Ummm... Don't worry about that." My brother responded, *"If you have something to tell us, you better do it quick. A guard just ran by a few minutes ago saying that the council had arrived."*

Amara let out a string of Elven that the Amulet seemed to have trouble translating, saying something along the lines of "Arrows cutting ears." I was pretty sure she was cursing. Once she had calmed down, she spoke again in our minds.

"Listen, if the council has arrived then I don't have long. I have a

plan to get the two of you into the palace to help your friends, but the timing will have to be perfect."

* * *

Kaja

As time went on the guards began to speak more frequently and their conversations became more frantic. I couldn't understand much of what was being said since they had started speaking in Elven, but I was certain that they were not happy.

We heard a commotion upstairs and a few of the elves retreated further down the hall. The door of the of prison blew open, slamming against the wall as heavy footfalls approached down the stairs. We heard a hand slam on the desk near the entrance. As a voice began shouting in Elven, I knew who it was. The steps continued toward us and Korryn came into view.

"How could you have messed this up so badly?" Korryn shouted at one of the guards in front of our cell.

"Captain Korryn, with all respect, the poison was correct even the Mirkoya detected it."

"Yes, about that." She turned to another guard. "You were supposed to ensure that the Mirkoya used for this dinner would not be able to detect the poison in their food."

"It wouldn't have, but it was having no effect, so we kept adding more. By the end of the dinner there was enough poison in their food that it would have killed an Ugathri."

Korryn stood there for a few moments, stunned. "How could two humans survive enough poison to kill an Ugathri?"

The guards stood in dumb silence non. None of them daring to break it. Suddenly a hearty laugh echoed through the cells. Everyone began looking around until we realized it was coming from Hjalmar's cell across from me.

"Hjalmar. I don't think this is the time to be laughing." I hissed.

"Your friend has sense, boy. I'm in no mood for your joviality."

"I can't help it Kaja. I know who they attempted to kill."

"What?" The princess and I spoke nearly simultaneously.

"Kaja, I was wrong earlier. It was Celenia and Varen her for dinner. And these guys tried to poison them." He succumbed to another bout of laughter. I had to think for a moment before realization hit me and began to laugh as well.

"How could you possibly know that?"

"Well," Hjalmar said, "You aren't exactly welcoming to humans, so I don't suspect there are any other humans in this city."

Korryn's face hardened. "Fine, perhaps you do know. So, tell me this. Why won't they die?" She stared a Hjalmar.

"Why would I tell you?" He stood to his full height, looking down on the princess. Intimidating to anyone else, but Korryn seemed unfazed.

"If you don't then you'll be put through greater pain than you could possibly imagine."

"Oh, so you'll torture us?" I laughed again. "That's been going on for the past days. You're going to do it again whether we tell you or not. So, we choose not."

Korryn clenched her fists tightly, then an unnerving calm seemed to wash over her.

"It doesn't matter. Tavaran and Na'var will ensure their end if the poison can't."

The door opened again, another elf running down the steps.

"Tavaran. Are you here to announce the death of the humans?" Korryn smiled wickedly.

"Forgive me captain, but no. We didn't get the chance." The elf breathily responded.

"And why not?" Korryn snapped.

"The council has arrived. The runner was approaching down the street as we were preparing to attack. We had to rush back here. Otherwise we would have been discovered."

"Aww," I faked, "It sounds like you won't be able to torment us tonight after all."

Korryn stepped up to my cell her face maybe a foot away from mine. A wicked smile spread across her face as she whispered.

"Oh, I'll make sure we have time. And it will be the worst night of your short miserable life."

She stood upright and turned to two of the guards. "Prepare the chambers. I'm going to have a lot of venting to do after greeting the council."

"Yes Ma'am" They bowed.

Chapter 14

The Council

Celenia

I jolted awake in my bed. I looked around the room, searching for what could have so rudely brought me from sleep. It didn't take long for me to realize it must have been the noise coming from down below me. Getting up and quickly throwing my robes on I moved toward the window. Overnight the street below had become a bustling thoroughfare. Strange Rhythmic shouting seemed to come from beneath me.

I finished dressing and left our room finding Varen waiting outside in the hallway.

"You saw the street?" He asked.

I nodded. "Do you think this is because of the council?"

"I don't know. But I saw people that I know weren't here in the city the past few days."

"Yeah," I nodded. "We better figure out how far this goes. Let's grab something quick to eat and go investigate."

Varen nodded and followed me as we descended the stairs. Our first sight at the bottom was a large, stocky elf sitting at the counter with an equally large, half empty tankard in front of him. The tavern was packed with elves, most of whom looked very different from the ones we grew used to seeing over the past couple days.

The large elf spotted us and spoke to the bartender. "Ah........City....Humans...."

I looked down at my amulet. It still seemed to be in one piece.

"My apologies sir, but I am not fluent in the Ugathri tongue." The bartender spoke apologetically.

The large man nodded. "Ah ma apologies, Ahm not used to being this far down from home. Ah was sayin' that it's some change ye've made in yer cities lettin human folk in."

At the word "Humans" the tavern went silent, all eyes turning to us.

"Ah, well these two are an exception. The royal family requested that we put them up here. Wouldn't be doing it otherwise."

Slowly stares moved away from us back to various meals and conversations.

"I think things are about to get a lot trickier." I said to my brother.

"Yeah," he sighed. "Looks that way."

We ordered from the bartender and found an unoccupied table in the corner. As we waited, I looked around the tavern. It looked like elves came in all sorts of kinds. Some looked regal, dressed in whites and golds. Others, like the large one with the strange accent, wore furs that looked like they could crush Hjalmar with their bare hands. There seemed to be a few other kinds too, but it was impossible for me to discern where they came from.

The food came, and my brother and I ate quickly. We didn't want to spend any more time in the tavern than we had to. The large elf's comment may have been smoothed over but I couldn't help feeling the occasional glances our way. Varen had a very serious expression on his face as we ate, and I noticed the slight bags under his eyes.

"Did you get any sleep last night?" I whispered.

"Don't worry about it." He stood as he took his last bite and started for the door.

"Varen." I called after him. I quickly gathered my scepter, still disguised as an instrument, and followed him out nearly bumping into an elf on his way in.

"I'm sorry."

"No worries there, miss. You seem to be in quite the hurry." He laughed.

"Sir, we don't have time for this." the woman following him checked an amulet at her neck.

"Stop looking at sand dwellers and enjoy the coral La'vee." He waved off her comment. "There's always time for breakfast." He smiled at me one last time before entering the tavern. And I heard one last comment from the man as I left.

"La'vee, I think we're going to be late."

I spotted my brother weaving his way through the crowds in the direction of the palace. I pushed my way through to catch up to him and finally managed to grab his sleeve. He turned and looked at me. There was a penetrating intensity in his eyes, and I couldn't help but be concerned.

"Celenia. Let go."

"What are you doing? It's not time yet." I hissed under my breath so only he could hear me. I found myself wishing we had renewed the thought connect spell this morning. The amulets only seemed to connect us to Amara, not each other.

"I don't care Celenia. Kaja is in there and I have to get her out. I can't wait any longer."

"Varen, remember what Amara said? If you go in there now the guards will catch you almost immediately. You won't have a chance to rescue her, and honestly, they may not even decide to imprison you. They'll just kill you and what will Kaja do then?"

My brother's eyes flared brighter for an instant before he closed them and took a single deep breath. The next time he opened them they were back to their normal, subtle glow.

"You okay?"

"No, but I'm in control. I just want to get her out."

"I know Varen, but we can't get ourselves caught. That would defeat the purpose. I know you know that, what's going on?"

He shook his head and looked away. "I can't." He finally mustered.

"Can't what, Varen? I don't understand."

"I don't want to talk about it Celenia."

"Why not?" I urged

The answer came in another flash of his eyes and another slow, deep breath. Whatever it was, it had seriously upset my brother.

"Okay, then we won't talk about it. Just try to stay calm, okay? We'll get them out, but we have to be smart." My brother only nodded. "Okay, let's take a look at the stands. Maybe we can find something useful, plus we can keep an eye on the palace gates. Just be ready to move."

Varen nodded mutely. He didn't seem to trust speaking. I watched him for another moment before turning down the street towards the palace. As we walked the streets, I saw even more strange elves than I had noticed in the tavern. Some were tanned and dressed in little more than tunics or vests with some sort of form fitting pants, and I spotted a few that were head to toe with strange, loose fitting clothing. One of these elves was running a stall.

"Greetings, Miss." My amulet translated "What can I do for—" the elf stopped short, "You're a human."

"Is that a problem?" I cocked my eyebrow.

"Not for me." I couldn't tell because of the cloth covering their face, but I thought I heard the barest hint of a smile. "Though it is rather unexpected to find a human in a Vene'ta'ri city."

"That's fair." I confessed. "So, what are you selling."

"Clothing of Shakari make. Designed to keep off the hot sun and keep you cool even in the hottest environments."

"Shakari huh? That's what you are?" The elf nodded. "So, is the clothing you're offering the kind that you are wearing right now? That doesn't seem like it would keep you very cool. How does it work?"

"That is a Shakari secret, but it works effectively. All of our people wear these."

I looked the elf over head to toe one more time and felt a smile spread across my face.

"Hey Varen, come here. I think I have an idea."

* * *

Amara

I smoothed my dress hoping my nerves wouldn't show. The council met fairly frequently to discuss elven matters, but usually the meetings were held in the Vetri capital. The last time the meeting was held in Vene'ta'ri lands was my own trial upon my return from human lands. The memory was still all too clear in my mind.

My mother stood in front of me, off to my left. On the other side of her stood my sister, in slightly higher spirits than last night. Various servants bustled about making sure everything was ready.

"Calm yourself, my child." Mother spoke over her shoulder to me.

"I'm sorry, Mother. I'm nervous I can't help myself, the last time I was here I was the one under scrutiny. I think some of the council members would still have preferred throwing me out."

My sister threw me a sidelong glance, and it could have been the morning light, but her expression seemed to soften for a moment, but it disappeared as quickly as it came.

"Even if that were true," My sister spoke flatly, "The Council cannot go back on a decision they have made. You have nothing to fear Amara."

I opened my mouth to respond to my sister's unexpected attempt at comfort, when the chamberlain entered followed by a herald.

"Your Highness," the chamberlain bowed "The council has begun to arrive. Shall we begin?"

"Yes, Garran. Please begin to show them in. We mustn't keep them waiting."

With another bow, the chamberlain stepped outside leaving the herald behind. Moments later the servants opened the large doors wide. An elegantly dressed servant entered, speaking to the Herald.

"Entering, the representatives for the Vetri: Miavel, Daleen, Siele, and Thistelle."

The four Vetri councilors entered the room dressed in the finest of clothing in whites and golds, an entire entourage of servants followed them in.

"I thought each councilor was only supposed to bring one advisor." I whispered.

My sister nodded. "That's how it's supposed to be. But typical of the Vetri to decide the rules don't apply to them."

"Quiet girls, they are our guests." Mother chided.

The Councilors bowed almost imperceptibly, and Mother smiled and bowed in acknowledgement. They sat at the table directly at the head of the room.

Once they had settled in Garran continued, "Entering, the fellow representatives for the Vene'ta'ri: Ve'stil and g"

Ve'stil and Talise were relatives of ours. Ve'stil was my mother's cousin and he used to visit often when I was a child. Talise I knew of by name, but his line branched off several generations back and traveled to a distant forest to make their city.

The two entered with their advisors and bowed, my mother greeting them with a smile and a bow. They moved past us and took seats at the table next to my mother.

"Entering, the representatives of the Ugathri, the brothers... Tevar and... Ureya." The Herald seemed to struggle with the somewhat strange names.

Two unbelievably large elves entered the room with their two equally large advisors trailing behind slightly. Even bowing they were taller than my mother. And while there was a rule that no weapons were allowed in the Council chambers, I had no doubt that these men could do as much damage with their bare hands as they could with any weapon.

"How do they get so large? That's not natural to elves." I whispered.

"I'm not sure of the truth behind it," my sister admitted, "but legend has it that they descend from elven adventurers who made their home high in the mountains and they mixed their bloodline with those of dwarves and giants. They are said to be incredible warriors, and their weapons are said to be forged with powerful magic."

Mother bowed to them and the men moved to the table to the right of the Vetri.

"Entering the representative of the Shakari: Aderon"

The man entered, his advisor following close behind. They were both clothed head to toe in some sort of robes. Out of the corner of my eye I saw many of the councilors shift in discomfort.

"Why is everyone so nervous? The Shakari are just desert dwellers, aren't they?"

"Haven't you done any studies on the origins of the races?" Korryn hissed, "The Shakari descend from elves who were exiled to desert lands. Their ancestry is made up of Elven Criminals. It wasn't until father approached them that they become recognized as a group important enough to have a seat on the council and they were only allocated one."

"But that was ages ago. Descendants of criminals are not necessarily criminals." I protested quietly. "Now they are just desert dwelling elves, aren't they?"

My sister hesitated. "From what I understand of Shakari law, it's a lot looser than typical elven law, unless you are endangering someone's life, most anything is acceptable activity. I haven't studied it though, so I can't say for sure."

Mother greeted the Shakari as she had all the others and the robed elves moved to the table on the left of ours.

Mother turned toward the Herald expectantly. He stood for a moment in waiting, then looked at my mother and shook his head, bowing.

"Is there not another?" Mother calmly asked.

"No, your highness, it appears not." He frowned, looking again at his list.

"What?" The Vetri known as Daleen shouted, "Where is Master Avareen?"

"He makes a mockery of the Council." Thistelle growled, "He should be removed immediately."

"Calm yourselves councilors. Certainly, Master Avareen has just been held up. He is sure to be here shortly." Miavel responded.

"Thank you, Miavel." Mother smiled gently.

"Perhaps he was killed by the assassins we've been receiving threats from." Siele mused aloud, "On that note, your guard on the council chamber seemed a little light considering we've been receiving death threats your majesty. I don't mean to criticize of course, but would it be possible to increase our security?"

My mother opened her mouth to respond but I interrupted gently.

"Allow me, Mother. I'll find some extra guards."

Mother nodded as we heard chatter from the doorway. Finally, a servant entered with a sheet for the herald who cleared his throat.

"Entering, The representative of the Vessi, Eizel Avareen."

A fairly young elf, somewhere around Thistelle's age, entered the room. A red band of some sort held back his shining black hair. He straightened his tunic and smiled.

"Apologies my friends, I was held up." He smiled.

"You always seem to be held up, Eizel." Thistelle sneered. "Or you don't make it. I've begun to question how seriously you take your position. It was a mistake on the part of your people to give up a seat of power to us to put one such as *you* on the council. Pray tell, what held you up this time?"

"Breakfast." The man said simply, his smile never wavering.

"You kept the council waiting, for breakfast?" Thistelle glared. "How irresponsible."

"Well, my dear Thistelle, one simply mustn't work on an empty stomach. And not all of us have the benefit of bringing our personal chefs into the council with us. We lowborn elves are only allowed a single Advisor. And let's not forget that if my people hadn't given up a seat, you wouldn't be on the council."

Thistelle opened her mouth to respond, but Mother held up her hand. "Councilors, please stop this bickering. We benefit nothing from it and it only uses up more time. Amara, please honor Siele's request and go find some more guard for the chamber."

"Yes mother." I bowed quickly and left the council chamber. Once out of sight I reached for the amulet around my neck.

"Varen, Celenia. The last member of the council has just arrived but wait until I contact you again to move. I've just received an opportunity to make our plan easier."

I waited several long moments. I began to wonder if the amulet's spell had worn off when Celenia's voice pierced my mind with a single word.

"Understood"

*   *   *

Varen

We stood on the outskirts of the shopping commotion in the square waiting to hear once more from Amara within the Palace. I shifted the bag on my shoulder as it attempted to slide off. I couldn't deny that the marketplace was impressive and the various types of elves fascinating. Under normal circumstances I would have explored and learned as much as I could about these people and their wares; but under normal circumstances I also would have had a full night's sleep and would not be concerned about a plan to break Kaja and Hjalmar out of prison, or that plan requiring us to rely on an elf, one of the very people who imprisoned them in the first place. Certainly, Amara had proven helpful so far, but this would end in disaster if she tricked us.

"We have everything from the inn, right?" I asked my sister. "Once this is done, we won't have time to go back."

"Yeah, we've got everything," She nodded, patting the bag next to her. "And then some." She paused looking at me, "What about you? Are you okay?"

"I'm fine for now, but the sooner we get this over with, the better."

My sister looked like she wanted to respond, but instead nodded in agreement.

"Okay you two, there's been some guard reassignment, your path is now about as clear as it's going to get. Go now."

"Got it." I sent my thought through the amulet's spell.

My sister and I casually retreated further away from the market off to one side of the Palace. The palace was fairly well defended using the large tree branches one could get out through the upper levels of the palace, and presumably in if you knew where to begin. None of the trees could be climbed directly however as they all stood too far from the palace and there were no branches at a reachable height. I closed my eyes and willed open my mind's eye. There set into the base of one of the trees was a marking, invisible to the naked eye but perfectly clear to us. We knelt down next to the tree and my sister spoke the trigger word taught to us by Amara the evening before. The tree began to shiver and twist, branches moving down the trunk and new ones sprouting until the branches created a path into the upper canopy giving us a direct path into the palace to a room that Amara assured us would be unguarded.

"Hopefully no one is using any sensory magic out this far." My sister commented.

We moved cautiously, neither my sister or I very adept at climbing and the process took far too long for my tastes, but finally we reached the balcony.

"Do you see any guards?" My sister asked as my feet hit the ground.

"No," I shook my head, "It looks clear."

"Good. Let's get changed." My sister pulled the bag from my shoulder.

*　　*　　*

Chapter 15

The Council's Decision

Amara

I re-entered the Audience chamber and approached the center of the room. It appeared the cooks had already brought some small sampling dishes. The Ugathri Councilors were chewing on some sort of dried meat chunks while Eizel, who had several small swirled objects sitting on a platter in front of him with a strange looking meat inside. enthralled them with stories of sea Voyages. As they countered with stories of great beasts slain in the highest peak. The Vetri were the image of refined dignity, their own chefs having prepared their meal. The chamber fell silent as I reached the central point

"I have done as you requested mother and increased the guard on the council chamber." I bowed.

"Thank you, Amara. Now please, take a seat."

I bowed once more and moved to the Advisor seat on the right of my mother. A plate had been set out for me as well on a small table beside my seat.

My mother stood, drawing all attention towards her. "Thank you all for agreeing to meet on this occasion. Now, if all desired pleasantries have been exchanged, perhaps we may begin. Shall we begin with current events?"

"If I may," Miavel slowly stood, "You all know that I have been on the Council a great many years. Why every face in here differs from those that were here when I began, I am an old elf, and many have speculated on my retirement. I announce it today. This will be my last meeting as a member of the Council."

"Thank you, Master Miavel" Mother smiled "You are a dear member of the council and began around the same time as my father. You must see fit to stop by sometime."

"Certainly, your highness." A gentle smile crossed his face.

"Who will be spokesman for the Vetri in the meetings to come?" Aderon asked.

"I have already asked Daleen to fill that position, He will speak on our behalf in this meeting and those to come."

"Has it yet been decided who will be the new Councilor?"

"Not as yet, however only a small handful remain for consideration. It should not be long before one is selected."

Several nods around the room in response.

"Is there any other news from the Vetri?" Mother asked.

"No, your majesty." Daleen responded, "What events transpire in the lands of the Vene'ta'ri?"

"We have had some skirmishes near the borders to the deep forest, however a team from our own city has been dispatched to assist with the problem."

"I see." Daleen nodded, "What news from the Vessi lands?"

Eizel stood, smoothing his colorful vest. "The Vessi are currently on a path of economic prosperity, trade is spreading and strengthening. A few small groups are looking for new coasts to settle. No further news at the moment."

Daleen nodded and turned to the large elves sitting nearby. "What of the Ugathri tribes?"

One of the men stood. "The Ugathri busy themselves preparing for winter in the peaks and the creatures that come with it. We make every effort to keep paths clear up the mountain. The lowlands gather supplies to be sent to the peaks. No other news at the moment."

"What of the Shakari?"

The Shakari representative stood "Matters in the Shakari lands remain unchanged." He sat.

The council sat uncomfortably for a few moments, thinking the same thing I was, *"What does that mean?"*

"All right," Daleen broke the silence first. "Your highness certainly called the Council here for more than an update on current events, though there was very little detail in your message."

"Yes, I apologize for the vagueness of the message, but it is a matter that I would much rather be kept to the council as much as possible as it could cause a lot of problems if the wrong individuals discovered it."

"The matter sounds rather critical Tei'ara, I hope you didn't delay in sending for us."

"But master Miavel, what could possibly be of such import? I for one can't think of anything." Thistelle spoke.

"Patience child," Siele chided, "we are about to find out. My apologies for the interruption, your highness, please continue."

"It's quite all right Siele. The matter at hand, Counsellors, is one involving humans."

Shocked gasps came from the Vetri and quiet murmurings from the rest of the room.

"Please, Counsellors, allow me time to explain the situation. Two humans were discovered in our forest on one of Korryn's, routine patrols. She believes them to have been a scouting party sent by someone. When brought before me however, they claimed they were hunting for food and were unaware of our existence."

"Typical lies from humans." Thistelle grunted.

"How can you prove they were lying Thistelle? Have you some information you're not sharing?" Eizel leaned back in his chair. "With all due respect to you and your eldest daughter, your highness, it seems awfully like her word against theirs and we have no confirmation regarding either. I do hope there is more to this story."

"Of course, Master Avareen, I wouldn't have called this meeting if there wasn't." Mother soothed, "I had the two taken to the cells until I could get to the bottom of things and shortly after two more humans appeared at the gate of our city. They were looking for the two that were arrested. They came before me claiming that the two were friends of theirs and that they were traveling to the coast, and their friends had come hunting for food."

"Your highness," Thistelle cried, "You can't tell me that you believe their tales. We know humans to be liars, they—"

"Thistelle, enough!" Siele snapped.

Miavel reached out and placed his hand on Siele's shoulder. "It's all right Siele; Thistelle doesn't know about this place."

"What does that mean?" Thistelle inquired.

"Thistelle," Mother turned to her, "You and Master Avareen are the two newest members of the council, so you may be unaware of the spells that are active in this room when it serves as my audience chamber. One alerts me when an individual is lying, and while a few lies were spoken most of their story appeared to be true, or at least they believed it to be so."

"It's a very interesting situation," Daleen spoke, "but cases such as this are why the council was created. Do the counsellors have any questions for Queen Tei'ara?"

Hjalmar

It was an eerily silent down in the cells. Most of the guards who had been here last night were positioned elsewhere. I looked to Kaja's cell where she currently sat cross legged near the center. She frequently shifted sitting positions and I was guilty of the same; aftermath from the painful events of the night before.

Kaja was difficult to read, since being returned to our cells she had sunk into silence, but whether it was contemplative or depressive I wasn't sure. What I did know was that as we sat here our fate was being sealed somewhere up above us.

"What do you think it is?" Kaja finally spoke. Her voice was quiet, as if the question was directed at herself as much as me.

"What what is?" I cocked my eyebrow.

"Amara's plan. She said she has one, but she never told us what it was."

"I don't know, but she better put it into action soon. With the way these elves seem to dislike us, I doubt this council will take long to decide what to do with us."

Kaja sighed gently, "I wish Varen was here, he may have known a way to get us out of here."

"Yeah, well-" I was cut short when I heard a thud near the entrance followed by the door opening. I heard hushed voices as footsteps approached, and shortly after a pair of robed figures came into view.

"Kaja? Hjalmar?" One pulled the head cover and I recognized Varen, "Are you two here?"

Kaja stayed silent for a moment before jumping to her feet. "Varen? Varen is that really you?" Her voice quivered.

"Kaja, are you okay?" Varen stepped up to her cell.

"I'm all right now," She smiled gently. I watched as she reached through the bars and placed her hand gently on the back of his head. They leaned closer to each other until their lips met briefly. Then I heard a ringing of bars as Varen crumpled to the ground doubled over and grabbing his stomach.

"What happened?" The other asked.

"What happened is that I'm not an idiot." Kaja responded, "I'm just talking to my friend here about how I wish he was here and like magic he shows up? I'm not falling for another one of your Illusions, princess."

"Kaja it's really us." The other pulled away her covering, and I saw Celenia's face, "Amara helped us get into the palace so that we could get you out before they decide to sentence you."

Varen slowly got back to his feet. He gripped the bar for a moment before quickly pulling it away in case Kaja decided to strike again. I saw a small glint on his hand as he brushed off his robes.

"The ring..." Kaja stood, stunned. "Have you had that active this whole time?"

Varen looked dumbstruck, "Well, yeah. I wanted to be sure you were okay."

"High Cleric's beard, it is you. Varen, I didn't know, I thought it was a trick."

"It's okay," Varen replied, still breathing heavily, "Don't worry about it."

Celenia pulled out a ring of keys from within the sandy colored robes. She unlocked Kaja's cell who promptly sprung into Varen's arms, then she turned to mine. I stood, trying not to wince from the aches that ran through my body with every movement.

"All right, we have a plan to get you out, but you need to change first." Celenia spoke as Varen pulled more robes out of the bag he carried. "Varen, go get that guard at the entrance, we'll put him in one of these cells." Varen nodded in agreement and as he left, she turned back to us, "Be quick you two, we're not sure how much time we have, they could send someone for you at any time."

* * *

Amara

As the Council meeting progressed my anxiety grew. I had no idea of where Celenia and Varen were or if they had gotten their friends and made their escape already. All I knew was that they hadn't been caught otherwise they would have been brought before the council immediately. That, and that this meeting seemed like it would never end.

"All I'm saying," Eizel continued, "Is that what we have is two humans, only one of which appeared to be heavily armed, and with small weapons at that, who are here in this city being held on charges that I see no support for."

Thistelle shot back, "The humans are shortsighted, warlike, and dangerous. They destroy the land around them to make room for themselves and spread like a plague. That's why our people are so wary of them. The fact that you argue so vehemently in their defense says only one thing. That you, Eizel are a fool, and your people even more so. Why they chose to give up a seat on the council to put you in a position of influence I'll never understand, I am however grateful that with a single seat your decisions can't put our people at risk."

"Calm yourself La'vee" Eizel put up his hand as his advisor stepped forward, "Her insults amount to little more than displaying her own childishness."

"This bickering is getting us nowhere." Daleen rubbed his temples, "Does anyone have useful insights to bring to the table?"

"Well, I do have one, Master Daleen." Eizel stood, "But not many are going to like it."

"Whatever it is it must be better than sitting here with the discussion going in circles." Ureya, one of the Ugathri councilors, spoke.

"I must agree with my brother." Tevar nodded. "We have spent some time arguing and are no closer to a decision. Whatever your suggestion is Master Avareen, I support it as long as it aids in the argument going forward."

"I thank you friends," Eizel gave a sweeping bow, "I think if we cannot come to a decision with the facts as they are presented, then we must bring the prisoners here to defend themselves, in hopes that some new evidence may come to light to sway in one way or another."

"Traitor! You would bring humans into the council chamber?" Thistelle growled.

"Thistelle, Temperance is your greatest ally at this moment." Siele chided. "This suggestion, however, is rather unusual master Avareen. Humans have never been trusted to be brought near the council."

"Unusual perhaps, Siele," Eizel nodded, "but I see no other option to come to a conclusion. And as no one has spoken up in any capacity other than support or distaste for my suggestion, it seems no one else has any ideas either. What say you Daleen?"

"I can't say I entirely feel comfortable with the suggestion, as effective as it sounds," Daleen responded, "but as the host to this Council I will leave the decision to you Your Highness."

Mother was silent for a moment, in contemplation, the entirety of the council watching her as the tension grew from anticipation. "I think Master Avareen is right, bringing the humans in question in may be the best course of action for the progression of this meeting; And from my experience with these humans I don't believe there is any danger to the council from them." She waved one of the attendants over. "Get one of the guards and bring the two humans in the cells before the council." The attendant bowed quickly and retreated from the chamber.

After a few moments hushed chatter spread around the room. I sat in silence trying with everything I had to look unconcerned as my fears grew internally. I wanted to use the amulet and contact them, but in a room full of Elven leadership someone would be sure to notice.

"Where are they right now? Have they made it inside the palace? Are they going to be discovered? What should I do if they are brought before the council?" I looked at my sister who didn't seem any happier than I about our mother's decision. If one didn't know her, she would seem calm and collected. But in her eyes, I could see that she was concerned as well. Mother sat calmly, seeming unconcerned. Surveying the room, I found that most of the room continued to debate among themselves regarding the guilt of the humans that were soon to come before the council.

Suddenly the large door opened, and the attendant came rushing in falling to her knees before the council.

"Your highness. I'm sorry to bear concerning news but the prisoners are gone. There are also reports of four Shakari assassins leaving the palace through a balcony in one of the bedrooms."

A ripple of panic washed through the room everyone speaking over each other.

"It seems the concerns of the Vetri were not unfounded" My sister muttered.

"Yes, it does." I agreed, "It's hard to imagine assassins here in the palace. How do you think they got in?"

"I couldn't say. The better question is: if they are leaving, what did they want? And did they get it?"

"What of the guard at the door of the cells?" Korryn asked the attendant.

"He was discovered unconscious in a room nearby." The attendant replied shakily.

"If Shakari assassins were here" Daleen said, they must have arrived with your entourage." Daleen turned to Aderon. The noise in the room faded, all eyes turning to the Shakari Councilor.

"I don't appreciate your insinuation, Daleen." Aderon stood slowly. "And while I am fully aware of what the other races think of us, I would have thought more of the counselors than direct accusations." He looked around the room, and all eyes continued to stare. "Now if I hold everyone's attention, I have some observations as well. Surely if you fear the Shehazari then you are aware of their reputation."

"What reputation?" Eizel's advisor, La'vee, asked. Though it was rather unusual for an advisor to directly speak out in a council meeting, no one complained. Likely we were all thinking the same question.

"The Shehazari are said to appear as suddenly as a sandstorm in the night and vanish just as quickly. They would not have been found so easily unless they wanted to be, so who's dead? All you have is an unconscious guard, and any possible target I can think of is here in the council chamber. Daleen, I don't believe the individuals you have seen to be Shehazari. Who they are I cannot say, but Shehazari they most certainly are not."

"Then who could they be?" Siele wondered aloud, then turned to the attendant. "What causes you to think they were Shakari assassins? These

"Shehazari"?"

"They were wearing Shakari robes and were not spotted until they were leaving. This is what led us to believe they were Shehazari"

"So, they must have been Shakari at least..."

"Not necessarily, Siele." Eizel replied absently.

"Why do you say that?"

"When I was on my way here, I stopped around the marketplace outside the palace gates and I spotted a Shakari stand selling robes. It's possible those robes were purchased to disguise the intruders' identities."

"I'm not usually one to take guesses counselors," Ureya spoke, "But is it possible that two of those individuals could have been our missing prisoners?"

"But what of the identity of the other two, brother?" Tevar asked.

"Your highness," Miavel spoke oddly calmly, "you mentioned another pair of humans in the city, did you not?"

"I did." Mother nodded, "Was there anything distinguishing about these individuals?"

The attendant hesitated, "The guard reported that one of them carried some kind of staff, but he said there was something strange about it."

"Strange?" Eizel leaned in, "Please explain if you can."

"Well, he wasn't entirely sure himself. He said it was a normal staff but for a moment he said it changed and looked like it was pure white, like it was some sort of Ivory or something. He also said he could see the man's eyes. Bright green he said, as if they glowed."

"Your highness, do these details mean anything to you?" Eizel asked.

"That does sound like one of the two humans here in the city." Mother nodded.

"Then it seems our prisoners are on the run." Daleen observed.

"True," Eizel said, "However, they have yet to be determined to be guilty of anything."

"Master Avareen, they are on the run." Daleen reasoned, "What could that signify other than their guilt?"

"Simple." Eizel shrugged, "They are afraid. You would be too if you were in their position. They were brought, accused of something they may or may not have done, personally I've yet to see any evidence they have, and the people have been more than openly hostile to them, seeing as their humans and we're elves. Reverse the roles, Daleen. If you were being held by humans in a similar situation you would assume that no matter what you say they are going to find you guilty. In which case, should the opportunity come to escape you would take it without hesitation."

"So, you don't think we should go after them?" Ureya asked, stroking his scruffy beard.

"I see no reason to, my large friend. They haven't been proven guilty of anything, only accused. It's a waste of manpower to go after someone based solely on an accusation."

"They escaped from the prison!" Thistelle interjected, "in doing that they broke the law and should be brought back to face judgement."

"I'll agree that the escape was wrong." Eizel raises his hands to his shoulders, palms out, "but given the situation it is an understandable action. And it's questionable whether they should really have been arrested for trespassing into our lands in the first place. I have no reason to mistrust that it was accidental."

"Eizel Avareen, are you siding with humans?" Siele accused.

"It's not nearly that simple, Siele." Eizel shook his head. "The Vetri and the Vene'ta'ri remain the two elven groups the completely cut themselves off from all but other elves. The remaining groups of the Ugathri, Shakari, and Vessi have some contact, however limited, with other races. And we work hard to keep the beneficial relationships we have. We also worked hard to develop those, and it was not easy to do due to the reputation elves have of being prideful, to put it kindly. A reputation built over the course of a couple thousand years. As such I find it our job as a council to ensure our judgements are fair and unbiased, so unless we have some sort of real proof of their guilt, I move that we allow them to leave."

Echoes of conversation filled the room. Eizel returned to his leaned back position with his feet on the table in front of him. Thistelle looked infuriated, and I could tell Siele was also irritated despite her calm exterior. A few minutes passed and Daleen stood.

"Councilors, I thank all of you for your input, and in light of the current situation and all that has been said regarding it I move for a vote. Should we send a group to retrieve the humans currently fleeing the city? As with all motions each counselor will have a single vote, and we will proceed by group. Each vote, once cast, is final. Does anyone have any objections to this vote?"

The room was silent, everyone looking around at one another.

"Then we will proceed with the vote. Attendant," Daleen pointed to a servant standing to one side of the room, who came forward and bowed. "While the scribes will record the events as they unfold, I wish for you to count the vote and report at the end."

"Of course, sir." The servant bowed again and was lent a parchment and pen from the scribes.

"Then let us begin with the vote. We shall start with Aderon of the Shakari."

Aderon stood, smoothing his robes as he did so. "In Shakari law we must have evidence, a decisive witness, or a confession to proceed to judge ones who are accused. As such I find myself having no interest in this trial of conjecture. My vote is no." He sat once more.

"Very well," Daleen nodded, "let us move on to the Vene'ta'ri. Teiara, ve'stil, and talisa. Your votes."

Ve'stil stood. "In analysis of the possible risk, despite lack of proof, I find it in our best interest to see this to the end. I vote yes."

Talisa stood next, "I have yet to hear any certain evidence that the humans lied. As such I can't find reason enough to drag these individuals back here. I vote No."

Mother stood, "I have met the humans and spoke to them, however limited the time. I haven't felt strongly in their innocence or their guilt. So, in presence of such strong doubt and weak knowledge, I too must vote no."

Daleen smiled gently "Next the Ugathri, Tevar and Ureya. Your votes please."

Both men stood, smiling. "What do you think Ureya? How should we vote in this matter?"

"Well, the Ugathri view our people's worth by their accolades. Are they strong, smart, and bold? Excepting only if the problems they cause are greater than their worth to the people. In this instance the individuals under scrutiny have managed to get away, that shows that they are clever, or that they are connected to someone clever who is willing to risk themselves to get them out. That makes them of value, at least to the Highland Ugathri. Under lowland law I believe they would still be tracked back down and put on trial."

"But you forget brother," Tevar slapped Ureya on the back, "These are not Ugathri, nor are they elven. They are outsiders."

"True," Ureya nodded, "So they wouldn't have any direct benefit to this people."

"So, do we vote to bring them back?" Tevar cocked his head.

"Ah, but Remember Tevar, if we shunned outsiders as the Vetri, the Ugathri would not exist as we do. We have much to be grateful for that came from the races around us."

"True, our people have learned many things from the people who have aided us." Tevar scratched his beard, "So you're saying a connection to them may be of value?"

"It could be, but after what we've heard that connection is yet to be forged. One needs to be made before they can be of any use."

"I follow your reasoning brother, but I'm not sure if I understand what it means. How should we vote?"

"Well making that connection is up to them. In this circumstance, I say that they've been beaten this time." Ureya laughed.

"All things considered; I would have to agree." His brother joined him.

"Ureya, and Tevar, your votes, please." Daleen urged.

"Simple," Ureya waved his hand as if he was shooing away an insect, "We vote no. Both of us."
Tevar nodded, a smile still on his face.

Daleen nodded, "Now we, the Ve'tri will vote. Miavel, as the eldest councilor, we will begin with yours. Followed by Siele, Thistelle, and finally myself.

Miavel nodded, then stood scratching beneath his long, well-groomed beard. "Perhaps it's that I'm part of an older generation of elves, I served on the council with Tei'ara's father after all, but I feel that the lack of evidence should make us cautious, and ensure there is no danger before we allow them to leave. I vote yes, we should go after them."

Siele stood as Miavel sat. "I don't believe it to be simply your age Miavel, we act as judges on elven matters. A threat, even a potential one, should not be allowed to slip through our fingers. I vote yes, we bring them back."

Thistelle was on her feet before Siele managed to be seated again. "Not to scrutinize votes, but I don't understand the argument against going after them. Elves have always mistrusted humans for good reason. They lie, cheat, steal, and destroy everything around them. I don't believe that creatures who are capable of such things could be harmless. I have no doubt that they pose a threat despite what they said. I say yes, of course we should go after them."

Daleen stood. "Thank you, councilors, as for my own vote... I hold the opinion that the elven council is in place to benefit the elven people, regardless of how other races view us. A potential threat should be seen as a threat until proven otherwise. It is my belief that we should act in this manner and as such, I vote yes. We go after them. Attendant how stands the vote?"

The attendant cleared his throat, "The vote currently stands at five votes in the positive, and five in the negative. With one vote remaining."

The room fell silent, stunned. All eyes turned to the remaining councilor.

"Well, Master Avareen." Daleen spoke firmly, "It seems you have the final say, how will you vote? In the interest of the elven people or in the interest of humans?"

"Daleen, I don't care for your attempt to sway my vote. The high elves hold great power in the council and decisions over the past centuries have aligned with high elf beliefs, but we are a council, and that means we together must decide on what is the right course of action. That being said many excellent points have been made over the past few minutes. I would like to take a moment to discuss with my advisor before I cast my vote." With a word, a string of runes flashed around his table allowing him and his advisor to speak privately.

I looked around the room. Hushed conversations happening all around, most probably wondering which way this vote would go.

"He'll vote yes." Korryn muttered certainly, "Despite everything he's said so far, he won't dare oppose the high elves. No one does. That's why Daleen chose for the high elves to vote before Eizel; to force him to vote the way they want him to."

"You think he'll give in?" I asked.

Korryn shrugged, "The councilors before him did, I see no reason that would change now. The high elves still hold more power than any other group on the council. I've heard it's dangerous to cross them."

"Dangerous how?" I looked at my sister, her arms were crossed, and she focused directly ahead in thought.

"Well, they're just rumors, but there's some who think that tragedies that have befallen past councilors have been caused by the high elves. Sabotage, assassinations. No one can prove anything of course, and some councilors I doubt have any part of it. Still, the rumors are out there, as hard as it is to prove anything, the possibility can't be eliminated either."

"But how could they do that?" I asked, stunned.

"Once again, sister. They are just rumors. But I suspect the high elves to be more prideful than any other group of elves. If they had their way, I'm sure they would-"

"Korryn. That's enough." Mother chided. "There's no reason for speculation. In the end Eizel's vote is his own. He has a choice to make. To allow himself to be pressured or to vote however he feels is best. Perhaps the two are the same, perhaps not."

With a wave of his hand Eizel could once again be heard. He stood, smoothing his outfit with great flourish.

"Well, Master Avareen. Have you reached a decision?" Daleen asked impatiently.

"Daleen, I have heard a good many arguments and Votes as well as the ways individuals came to the decision and one thing is clear. Each councilor voted in a way that they felt was best for their people and that is what I too must do."

Daleen nodded in approval.

"Thistelle, earlier you made a condescending comment about my people, saying that they were fools for giving up a seat on the council in order to put me in this position, but they did so because they wanted someone whose actions reflect their desires; And, my dear Thistelle, even a small ripple can create a wave. My vote is no, do not go after the humans."

For a few moments, there was another stunned silence. The attendant fumbled with the parchment for a moment then cleared his throat once more.

"The vote fails with five votes for and six against."

"Traitor!" Thistelle cried out, pointing at Eizel. "Why would you turn on your own people?"

"Didn't you hear me Thistelle? I did this for my people." As Eizel spoke La'vee move to stand between the two. "And if you call me traitor, do you intend to accuse all who voted differently than yourself of the same? After all, my vote may have decided, but many others voted the same as I."

During the commotion, my sister stood and began to walk for the door.

"What are you doing?" I rushed over to question her.

"What does it appear to be? I'm going after them." She replied taking some equipment from an attendant.

"But the council just decided-"

"The council's decision can be fed to the Mirkoya, it's just as poisonous. I will not allow our people to be harmed by the consequence of letting these humans go. The Council is wrong. Mother is wrong; and I don't intend to be." She turned to one of the guards, "Gather my rangers. We hunt."

Chapter 16

The Chase

Hjalmar

We managed to get out of the palace and the city without too much trouble. On our way out Varen used his cloak to slip into the guardhouse and retrieve our weapons.

"Cel, you sure you remember the path?" Varen asked from the tail end of the group.

"Not the path necessarily," Celenia shook her head. "But I remember coming to the gates from this general direction. If I remember correctly there should be a small clearing up ahead. We'll stop there for a moment to rest and get our bearings. I just want to put some distance between us and the city."

Varen said nothing but nodded in response.

"So," I asked following behind Celenia, "How did you two come up with the escape plan?"

"Honestly," She ducked, missing a tree branch, "Most of it inside the palace was Amara's idea, the elven princess. We had been working on an escape plan, but she had better inside information on the affairs within the palace. The only part that was our idea was the cloaks."

I nodded, "And how did you knock out the guards at the entrance to the prison? Did you use a spell?"

Varen smiled slightly, "There was only one guard, and yeah. The spell's called 'sneak up and hit him in the head with my staff."

Kaja laughed a genuine joyful laugh; a sound that I hadn't heard in what seemed like forever. Our time in the prison wasn't even an hour behind us but it seemed like Varen being there made her forget, or maybe it just allowed her to move past it. I tried my best to hide the pain as we moved but I couldn't help the occasional wince if I mis stepped.

"So Varen, how did you know I still had my ring?" Kaja asked, "Even I was surprised they didn't take it."

"I didn't know. But I thought it was better to have it active in case you did. The first while I thought that the elves probably had taken it because it never reacted. Then last night..." he trailed off, probably not wanting to continue. He may not know exactly what happened but if he was sharing a portion of her pain during that time then he knew enough.

"Is that the clearing up ahead?" Kaja called.

Celenia looked ahead, "Yeah, that's the one." She slowed as she entered the clearing. "Hjalmar, can you keep an eye out? I'm going to start casting."

"Of course." I put my hand on the hilt of the sword Varen mistakenly took for me from the guardhouse. It was a little smaller than I was used to, but it would do. "What is it you're doing?"

Celenia opened her mouth but her brother interrupted, "We don't have time Cel, just cast." Celenia nodded and sat down, closing her eyes and focusing. I looked at Varen quizzically.

"Yes, Hjalmar. I'll explain." He chuckled "Do you know how everyone had a sort of internal directional ability? The one that lets you instinctively know what direction you're generally going? And how that same sense allows you to find your way back to a place that you've frequented?"

"Yeah, I know what you're talking about. For training sometimes they would take members of the guard out to the forest in blindfolds and they had to find their way back."

"Right, well one can use a combination of that sense, one's memory of that area, and magic to find their way somewhere. In this case Celenia is trying to figure out the way back to camp."

"So how does the magic help find the place you want to go?" I asked.

"Well, it's kind of like getting directions from a person. Magic is everywhere so it can find anything, but in order for it to work you have to be clear on what you're looking for. The better the image and general direction in your mind the better the chance of the magic finding where you want to go."

"I see, so that should be a pretty easy spell then."

Varen nodded, "It's one of the basic spells, yes, but it's also the magic basis for all transportation type spells. If we were good enough, we could find the camp and teleport us all there, but unfortunately we haven't reached that level of skill."

"Varen, come look at this." Kaja called from some bushes at a close edge of the clearing.

"What is it?" Varen responded walking towards her.

"It looks like an old helmet. I mean really old and rusted." She turned around to show him and as she did, I heard a whistling by my ear. I watched as she gave out a cry and stumbled back before falling to the ground, an arrow suddenly protruding from her shoulder.

"What happened?" Celenia snapped her eyes open. I didn't respond, instead choosing to draw my blade and looking to the woods as Varen knelt next to Kaja, calling her name.

"The natural consequence of running away." Korryn emerged from the woods, several of her soldiers forming a semicircle before us. "That one was a warning. Now you have a choice. You can return willingly; we have healing mages who can heal your friend; or you can attempt to run and die here."

"May the Reaper's icy kiss be bestowed on all of you." Varen spat the curse. He stood taking a couple of steps away from Kaja.

There was something off about him, something I couldn't quite place. The best I could tell is that there was a new intensity to him.

"Have I upset you?" Korryn smirked. "You are the one who decided to break them out, in a way, you are the one that brought these consequences on her. Of course, you humans are too short-sighted to realize any of that."

"Deaths embrace, you are so prideful. You elves think everyone to be below you, but you fail to see anything beyond your forest."

"My my, racial insults." Korryn smiled, "I have upset you. Who is she, a friend? Lover?" Varen didn't respond, "No matter. It seems you have no intention of returning. Now she's only one more pest to be eliminated."

Varen's eyes flared brightly, and I heard Celenia curse.

"Hjalmar run to Kaja. Now." Celenia commanded. The tone in her voice told me not to question it, so I ran. A couple more arrows shot past me, but both missed. I saw Kaja only a few feet ahead of me. Suddenly something struck me from behind. I twisted around as I fell and saw Celenia was tackling me to the ground. Laying on top of both me and Kaja, I heard her say two words.

"Keep down." She hissed, then spoke something in the magic language they use.

"What has her so scared?" I thought. I counted about eight elves in the clearing, with a couple probably in the trees behind them, keeping hidden.

"Why? We can handle them." I muttered to her, trying to push myself to my feet.

"Keep down" She growled. She pressed her arms into my chest, shoving me back down.

"Obviously I'm missing something." I looked around again and glanced at Varen. "Does he look a little, hazy?" I looked closer and the air did seem to shimmer around him, and his breathing was strained.

"Your friends have the right idea." Korryn and her elves took a few steps before Varen's hand shot out.

"Don't touch us." He struggled to say.

Korryn laughed, "You don't seem in any condition to fight us. Your friends are cowering behind you." She shook her head and raised a hand. "Aim for the bodies behind him. Leave him to me."

She dropped her hand and I heard the whistling of arrows. Suddenly everything was illuminated a bright green color. I looked an found Varen was at its center. Every few moments a new wave of green pulsed through the clearing. The grass around Varen withered and died. A couple elves had made their way towards him. The green waves took them to their knees, vomiting. I stretched my arm toward Varen and within moments my arm grew pale, then started to wrinkle. Celenia quickly pulled it back in to the pile of us. The elves closer to Korryn fell to the ground clutching their stomachs. Korryn was trying to keep her composure but her entire body quivered. With fear or sickness, I wasn't sure.

Something made a thud next to me. I looked over and saw a small figure, it took me a moment to discern it as a bird through the waves of green light. Slowly the creature stood back up, but its movements were shaky. As it stood, I saw the glazed, vacant expression in its eyes.

"The light killed it then reanimated it," I thought, *"The light is magical. No, wait. The light is magic, visible magic!"*

The next thing I knew dirt was hitting my face and I could hear tearing and grinding sounds. I shook it off an looking I saw people rise to their feet. Some appeared to rise from shallow holes in the ground, but along with them rose some of the elves nearest Varen, who began to turn toward their comrades.

Celenia shifted on top of me, taking hold of her scepter and stabbing it into the ground next to her.

"Stay down, stay still. Don't move and you'll be safe."

"What is going on Celenia?" I asked, though I think I already had it partially figured out.

"Remember what we said about Varen having a large reserve of magic? Well, you are seeing it uncontrolled, and unleashed." With that statement, she turned and started crawling away towards her brother.

When she reached him, she pulled herself to her feet and grabbed his shoulder. He turned to look at her, his eyes almost unperceivable through the bright green light emanating from them. I couldn't hear what was being said, but I saw Varen's shoulders slump and, slowly, his eyes faded back to their normal appearance. The light in the clearing faded until only the late day sunlight illuminated it.

"You can get up now." Celenia said, turning back to us, "It's safe."

I got up slowly, shaking. From the aches or the sudden adrenaline rushing through me I wasn't sure. I looked at the animated dead around the clearing. They stood, as if waiting for something.

"Is Kaja okay?" Varen started to work his way to us slowly, holding his head in one hand.

I turned to look at her. The arrow was still protruding from her shoulder. I knelt next to her and Celenia and Varen joined me soon after.

"I see quite a bit of blood." I said.

"Not as much as I'd expect from an arrow wound like this though." Celenia said. "It's possible they missed anything major, but it's also possible the arrow itself is keeping the wound sealed."

"So what do we do Cel?" Varen asked, his voice quivering slightly.

"You just released massive amounts of magic, Varen. Hjalmar and I can treat her a little bit, you go recover. You can't do any good right now." Varen opened his mouth to argue, but Celenia shook her head. "I promise Varen, we will do everything we can and then we'll all get her to a healer, but the way you are right now, you would just be in the way."

I could see the dejection in the fall of Varen's shoulders, but he nodded.

"Hjalmar. Do you know how to treat wounds?" Celenia asked.

"I know a little battlefield medicine but I'm no healer."

"I observed some field treatments from stray arrows on the training ground, but nothing this bad before."

"Okay so what do you want to do?" I asked.

"We need to do what we can to prevent it from getting worse here, but that's the best we can do. After that we need to get her to a healer." She leaned in to take a closer look at the wound.

"How do we start?" I asked.

"I can't tell how deep the wound is. There is less blood than I would have expected but like I said that may mean the arrow itself is keeping the wound sealed. Because that's a possibility, I don't dare remove it."

"It's going to be in the way when I try to wrap it though." I pointed out.

"Then we'll have to cut it at the shaft. But be careful when you wrap it. We don't want to push the arrow in any further." Celenia drew a knife and started sawing through the arrow.

I looked at the area around us and came to a realization.

"Varen. I need your help." He jumped to his feet in a blink and looked at me.

"I need you to find a long strip of cloth or something to wrap Kaja's wound. Maybe one of the elves has a field kit."

He shook his head. "It would be corrupted if they did." He removed his cloak and robes, so he wore only his Vellarian tunic. Then, removing his knife, he began cutting the bottom of his robe into strips along its width. Piling them in his lap he held his hand over them and muttered a few words. He closed his eyes for a moment and nodded, satisfied. He picked them up and handed them to me.

"They're cleansed already, so they should be safe to apply to the wound." He looked at me as I took them. "Hjalmar, please take care of her."

I nodded in response.

Amara

All the Councilors and their entourages milled about the Palace courtyard and overflowed into the town square. Mother went around to each group wishing them safe travels and thanking them for coming. Eizel and his group stood nearest me at the gate. I watched as Master Miavel approached him.

"Master Eizel," the men shook hands, "I'm glad to have been a member of the council long enough to see members as yourself come in."

"My people chose me to represent them, and I intend to do just that."

"Honorable," Miavel smiled, "but some will fault you for that honor. I believe you Vessi have a saying 'even the great shark must watch for whales' is that right?"

He sighed, "thank you for the warning friend. The High Elves have been in uncontested control for a long time and I'm aware of the danger, but it's time to change currents. The Elves cannot continue on this path."

"Perhaps you're right." Miavel nodded, "But you need allies if things are going to change. Remember not all who opposed you are necessarily your enemies, nor are those who sided with you necessarily your allies. Choose who you associate with wisely and you may very well come to change the entirety of elven society." Miavel leaned in and whispered something in Eizel's ear that I couldn't make out, but Eizel looked at him with contemplation.

"Look!" someone called out pointing toward the woods toward the entrance of the city. It was a good way out, but it appeared to be a pulsing green light.

"That's the direction Korryn would have gone." Mother gasped.

The Ugathri brothers looked at Mother before drawing their weapons.

"Men, with us!" With that cry every member of their entourage began hefting massive swords, axes, and other weapons.

"Guards, go with them. Bring my daughter home." Mother ordered.

I turned to the servant nearest me.

"Bring me my armor." I commanded.

Hearing my words, mother turned to me. "You intend to go out there?"

"Korryn can irritate me, but she is my sister." I responded, "I'll make sure she gets home mother."

"Don't allow me to lose you either." She responded. "I know what you are capable of, and you are going against a real enemy this time. Don't hold back."

Chapter 17

Healers and Protectors

Hjalmar

We rushed down the road, Varen carrying Kaja in his arms. Over the past couple hours Celenia and I had both offered to carry her, but he had only shaken his head in response. I wasn't entirely certain what was going through his mind, but I was certain guilt was at least part of it.

"I don't think the town should be much further." Celenia said. She had enough time on the spell to give us a general direction of the road, but she wasn't able to get us back to camp. With Kaja's condition we decided we couldn't concern ourselves with finding camp and just to head to the next town and find a healer.

"You're right. I think I can see the gate up ahead." I responded. As we pushed forward, I thought about everything that had occurred. Meeting these two and rushing to fight the trollkin back in Astor. Helping them escape the paladin hunting them, and the time in the Elven city.

"Varen, Celenia, stop."

"What is it Hjalmar?" Celenia turned.

"We can't stop. We have to get her to a healer." Varen continued forward.

"If you want to get her to a healer and not get stopped and arrested on the way you'll stop and listen to me."

Varen stopped, then spun on his heels.

"Was that a threat?" His eyes flared mildly.

"No Varen, it's not a threat; but I've thought of something that is."

Varen's expression wavered.

"What are you talking about Hjalmar?" Celenia asked.

"Olmar." I said gently. "We threw off his trail outside of Astor, but we spent several days with the elves, he's bound to double back and keep looking at some point. How do we know he hasn't already been there and put your faces on every street corner?"

"So what do you suggest?" Varen asked gruffly, "We don't know how critical Kaja's injury is, so we don't exactly have time for a scouting mission."

"Let me take her." I offered, "Olmar has only seen me once and had no suspicion of me working with you. Even if he became suspicious later, he probably doesn't remember what I look like, especially without my Astorian guard armor. I can get into the town without arousing suspicion. You two can wait out here and I can bring you word."

"No." Varen responded firmly

"Varen…"

"I'm not leaving her."

"Do you not trust me, Varen?"

"This isn't a matter of trust Hjalmar. I am not going to leave her."

"Well at least let me take her and you can follow with your cloak, but that leaves Celenia here by herself. Unless your cloak can hide two people."

"No," Varen hung his head "… It can't."

"Well, I might have a way to keep hidden. Varen will need to take my mage robes though."

"What are you talking about Cel?" Varen asked

"You don't remember? Well, you have the cloak, so I guess it's not so critical that you know it. Just trust me. Hand Kaja to Hjalmar, careful of the wound, then come take my robes." She started to tug them off by the sleeves.

We followed Celenia's directions, Varen gently placing Kaja in my arms, careful to avoid moving her injured shoulder too much. Then he reached to and took Celenia's robes.

Celenia placed her hands in front of her, pressing them against each other. She began chanting gently, and while I didn't know the arcane tongue it sounded like the same phrase repeated several times. As she did so the features of her face began to soften and shift. Her usually round face stretched longer sharpening her chin and jawline slightly. Her short dark hair grew in length past her shoulder blades and lightened in color until it was nearer to a blond. Her complexion darkened a couple of shades and her eyes enlarged slightly. Finished, she stopped chanting and dropped her hands. Had I not seen her transform before me I would not have believed it was Celenia standing there.

"You're right Cel." Varen chuckled, "I did forget about that spell. Probably because I never liked the feeling."

"What just happened?" I asked, stunned.

"It's a very simple spell to alter your features," Celenia explained, "You can only make very minor changes, but do enough of them and you can look like a totally different person. Our teacher taught it to us a long time ago and made us memorize it. We don't need a spell book for it because it's so well carved into our minds, come to think of it, it was probably in case something like this happened."

"If you both knew how to do that, why haven't you been using it this entire time?"

"It's not very feasible in the long term. The spell only lasts a few hours at the most and anyone in tune enough with magic can tell there is a disguise spell in place. It should last long enough to get us to the healer's cabin and get Kaja taken care of, but not much more than that."

"Ladies, we don't have time for chit chat, remember?" Varen chided, "We have to get Kaja to a healer."

"Right, Sorry." I turned and regarded the town. It was fairly simple and from what I could see was much smaller than Astor. The gateway was made of bound logs and it lacked any real walls. To see something like that we were certainly much closer to the base of the mountains where beasts and raiders are less frequent. As we passed through the gates, I could see the occasional passerby. I saw one child near a pile of rocks staring intently. Down the road from him stood a large single-story building. While only little taller than the others, it spread much farther out. An older man passed us heading in its direction.

"Excuse me," Celenia stopped him, "we're from out of town and our friend got hurt." She gestured to Kaja, unconscious in my arms, "Is there a healer in this town? We need to get her some medical attention."

The man glanced at Kaja, then turned and faced down the cross street next to us. "Take this road down to the next crossroad where you'll see a small store on the corner take a right there and follow the road until you see the Inn. I believe it's called the grim petal or somethin', either way it's the only one in town. Take a left and follow the road until you see a two-story building with flower boxes in the front. That's the healer's cabin. You should hurry though. Your friend doesn't look too good."

"Thank you."

The man nodded and looked off behind us before turning back toward the large building.

"Come on Hjalmar, we need to go. He's right, she's looking a little pale, and I mean more so than usual."

"Yeah, I'm right behind you."

We followed the man's instructions turning after spotting the small shop on the corner and approaching the inn.

"Grimrose, huh?" Celenia read the sign, "That's kind of a depressing name for an inn. Wonder if there's a story behind that."

"We don't exactly have time to find out at the moment." I turned down the street, accidently shifting Kaja, who let out a soft groan. In moments the hair on the back of my neck rose. "She's okay, Varen. I just bumped her a little." I muttered, hoping he could hear me. Not long later the feeling vanished.

"Hjalmar, up ahead, I think I see the flowerboxes."

I looked. "You're right Cel. That must be the healers' cabin." We stopped in front of the building, the strong scent of the flowers reaching our noses and I could feel my muscles relax slightly.

Celenia opened the door and held it as I carried Kaja inside.

The room was warm, but not hot. There was a small front area with a few seats and a cushioned bench next to the window. There was a counter in front of the entry and a door behind the counter that led to the rest of the building.

"Hello?" Celenia called out. "Is anyone here?"

"A bit quieter if you will please," A young woman's voice came from behind the door, "I'll be with you in a moment. Please have a seat."

Celenia sat down and I laid Kaja on the bench. I could hear the floorboards creak repetitively nearby.

"Varen," I hissed, "Stop pacing, the floorboards!"

They creaked a few more times then stopped. Unsure where he was, and not wanting to accidently sit on him, I leaned against the wall next to the bench. A couple minutes later a young woman came through the door behind the counter.

"Sorry for the delay," She spoke gently, brushing a stray blond lock away from her face, "What can we help you with?"

"Our friend was struck by an arrow," I gestured to Kaja's unconscious form, "We did what we could to treat it in the field but don't know what to do beyond that.

The woman glanced at Kaja on the bench and nodded.

"Gently pick her up and follow me." She commanded.

I bent down and threading my arm under her legs and the small of her back, gingerly lifted her once again. The blond woman opened the door to let us back and led the way down the hall. The hall was lit from windows at the end but also from candles of various colors placed every several feet. As we passed I noticed each seemed to have its own fragrance.

An older woman with dark red hair emerged from one of the rooms as we passed.

"Another patient?"

The blond haired woman nodded in response.

"What do we have Erinis?" she glanced back toward me.

"A battle wound from what they describe, I haven't been able to check the wound yet though, I don't know the severity."

"All right," she nodded, "call for me if you need me."

"Of course, Ibis."

The woman nodded and stepped into another room nearby as we continued down the hall. Our guide stopped and opened the door before her, motioning us to enter.

The room was not very large with a single bed centered at one of the walls and extending into the center of the room. A small set of cabinets sat opposed to it and a couple of seats were at either side of the bed.

"Rest the young lady on the bed, the injury is in her shoulder so place her with her feet to the wall."

I did as instructed and the healer, Erinis as she was called, pulled one of the chairs beside the bed. She removed Kaja's bracer and pressed two of her fingers against Kaja's wrist and closed her eyes. She opened them again and looked at Kaja with a strange expression. She made a few motions with one hand and spoke a word, I could feel a wave of magic emit from her and dark bruises began to appear on Kaja's skin I looked down at my hands and arms and saw the same thing appear on my own skin.

"What are you doing?" Celenia shouted, "You're supposed to be a healer, why are you hurting her?"

Erinis held up a single hand responded gently, "I have done nothing but show the truth. Someone else was attempting to hide injuries she already had, and ones inflicted on that one as well." She pointed at me. "Beyond that whoever is hiding in the corner over there, if you are friend to this group show yourself otherwise get out."

I followed her gaze and found that whatever her spell it had revealed a hazy outline where Varen stood. The figure reached up and pulled at his head and as the hood came down, Varen came into view.

"I apologize, I just didn't-"

Erinis held her hand up, "I'm not interested in your reasons as long as you mean no harm to my patient, but I cannot allow you to remain hidden. Do you know him?" She turned to me.

"Yes, he's with us." I responded.

She nodded, apparently satisfied, and turned back to Kaja. Slowly, she began unwrapping the makeshift bandages on her shoulder. The wound exposed, she leaned in close, muttering a few words as she did so. Time seemed to crawl as Erinis examined the room, looking touching, and gently moving Kaja's arm once or twice, who let out an unconscious groan in response. Finally, she stood and faced us once more.

"The wound is fairly serious. Though not critical, it could have been if you had waited any longer. The placement of this arrow is no accident, whoever did this was quite the marksman. Even if I can heal her, she will not be able to comfortably use the arm for quite a while. On top of that her body is weak from whatever caused all this bruising. I'm guessing that the bruises on you, sir, were a result of the same event. Speaking of which," she moved past Varen and bent down, opening the cabinet and rummaging around for a moment before pulling out a small jar, "This should help the bruising heal." She handed it to me. "As for your friend, I'm not sure how long a healing for this may take. It could be hours; a day or more if there's infection. Leave her here with us and go find the Inn, 'Grimrose' tell them you have a friend being taken care of here, they should be able to give you a room until she's ready. They may charge you a small fee, but I'm not sure how much. I'll send a messenger when we're finished."

"All right, thank you." I responded. I opened the door behind me, and Varen and Celenia followed me out the door.

***

Amara

I picked my way around the clearing, looking in awe and horror at the sight. It was the first time I got to really look at the area. As we had approached the walking corpses attacked, as if they were trying to keep us away from something. I attempted to fight but my arrows seemed to do nothing to them. The Ugathri, however, lived up to their reputation. It was a brutal combat to see, and many Ugathri were bandaging cuts and other wounds, but bone fragments and dead flesh scattered about were all that remained of the enemy. The clearing had a chill in the air, and an almost tangible feeling of death to it. The grass was grey, the trees at the edge of the clearing were an ashen color and dead leaves were quickly falling from them. Looking closely, even insect life hadn't survived.

"Miss Amara, your highness," Ureya approached, "Your sister is over here. She's unconscious, and looks rather sickly, but alive."

"Thank you Master Ureya. Please, take me to her."

He jerked his head in a motion to follow and made his way across the clearing. My sister was laid in a sitting position against a tree. Likely one of the Ugathri noticed her during the fight and moved her to prevent further harm. Her breathing was slow, but even. I attempted to gently shake her awake, but to no avail.

"Stupid. Why should I have expected that to work? If an Ugathri moving her in the middle of combat didn't wake her, why would that?" I muttered to myself. "Is this my fault? Was I wrong to trust them? To help them. Surely this happened because she chased after them, but to turn her rangers into undead… I just can't imagine them doing that…"

"You seem in thought, princess." Tevar joined his brother and myself, "I suppose I can see why. It is rather strange after all."

His statement pulled me from my thoughts, "What's strange?"

"Well," he gently rocked his head back and forth, in some internal debate, then continued. "Obviously at least one member of the group knew some strong necromancy, it's not easy raising a single corpse let alone the number that were here. And judging by the surrounding area the only reason there weren't more is because there were no more bodies to raise."

"I don't see what's strange about it, Brother." Ureya responded as he approached, "A necromancer raises bodies, that's what that magic does."

"Yes, that's not the strange part." Tevar nodded, "The strange part is when it happened."

A look of understanding crossed Ureya's face and he nodded, stroking his beard.

"What do you mean? Why is it strange? They used necromancy to escape from my sister, didn't they?"

"Yes, princess. They did; but necromancy and the undead are not magic to be trifled with. If we and our men hadn't been here the struggle would have been far greater and could very well have resulted in the death of most, if not all, who came." Tevar responded.

"A great reason we succeeded here is because of our Ugathri weaponry." Ureya agreed. "Our arms have been forged with magic. Some of our weapons can sever a corpse's connection with the magic or caster that animates it. We had problems with undead in the mountains before, we still don't know if it was wild magic, or the work of a necromancer; maybe a lich."

"Either way, we took care of it." Tevar grinned. "But if they had that kind of power, why wait until here to release it? Their friends were here for days before the council arrived, if they wanted to escape or break their friends out, depending on which human it was, they could have easily done it with something like this from the start. Why wait?"

"Maybe it wasn't the humans?" Ureya offered.

"Maybe…" Tevar didn't sound convinced. "But it seems terribly coincidental that Korryn, who was after the humans, ran into something like this."

My mind churned, trying to take in everything I was seeing and hearing. Finally, I stood and walked over to the edge of the clearing where we found the undead. Behind them was a large patch of ground that was still green. From that looking around nearby I found some crushed underbrush and broken branches leading away from the city and the clearing. I stood and adjusted the quiver on my back.

"Tevar, Ureya, will the two of you take my sister back to the Palace?"

The brothers looked at each other, "We can, but where are you going princess?"

"I'm going to find out what happened."

"Do you think it wise?" Ureya asked, "Whoever did this is dangerous. If they were willing to do this to your sister and her band, they could do it to you."

"I'll be careful; but I have to know."

Ureya drew a knife from his belt. "Your mother will probably kill us for letting you go, but it's not the first time an Ugathri looked death in the eye." He grinned, "But I won't let you go without having at least something to defend yourself."

I gently took the blade. It was heavier than the knives I was used to, but it gave some peace of mind. I looked up at the brothers.

"Thank you both." I smiled gently, "You'll take care of my sister?"

"She was never in safer hands." Ureya replied, "You be careful, I may not fear the pain that will come from allowing you to leave, but I do fear the strength and cunning of a Mother who loses a child. Return, and do so quickly."

I nodded once more in response before retreating into the underbrush.

Chapter 18

The Duel

Hjalmar

The tension in the room could be cut with even the dullest of blades. We all had the same question on our minds but none of us dared voice it. Even if we did no answer would come, not for a while. We all handled it differently; Celenia sat at the foot of the bed with her head in her spell book, studying intently. Varen attempted to relax a few times, sitting on the bed or the floor, but inevitably he went back to the same pacing he had been doing for a while now. I sat in nothing but my vest and shorts putting on the salve given to me by the healer. I winced as it touched my skin, it didn't really hurt, but it was cool to the touch, and got colder as it was on my skin.

"Varen, please sit down," Celenia groaned, "You've been pacing for hours. You're making me nervous."

"I'm making you nervous? How is that possible for me to make you nervous when our friend is in the healer's cabin, seriously injured? How are you not already at wits end questioning what happens now? We have no idea if she'll be okay. We also don't know how long we can stay here. Now not only do we have Olmar on our trail, we've managed to piss off a bunch of elves. Death's embrace, Celenia, I don't know how our situation could be much worse."

Varen's eyes hadn't had their same glow since the clearing, but I could see the flare to them as he spoke now. Something else was different about him though, a somberness that hadn't been there before.

"Varen," Celenia spoke more calmly this time, "There is nothing we can do but wait. She is in the hands of the healer's now and nothing we can do will affect what happens next. I know how you feel, but we can't lose our heads now."

"How could you possibly know how I feel Celenia? You've never felt for someone the way I do for Kaja. On top of that, you're not the one who…" Varen stopped, then shook his head. He turned and grabbed his cloak of the hook. "I'm going for a walk."

"Varen, we can't just--"Celenia's next sentence was cut off by the slam of the door. She sighed and rested her head in her hands, rubbing her temples.

"Are you okay?"

"Yeah, I'm alright. I'm worried though. I don't know if I've ever seen Varen as upset as he is right now."

"Do we need to worry about him losing control again?" I asked cautiously.

"I doubt it." Celenia shook her head, "He released a massive amount of energy in that clearing, I think it will take a while to be able to build his reserve back to where it was. I'm more worried that he won't let this go."

"What do you want to do?"

"I don't know what we can do. The only time I've seen him close to this upset about something was when our parents died."

"What did you do back then?"

"I couldn't do much back then. I was shocked and upset too. A lot of people in town tried to help comfort or console us. It was nice, and I came out of it with their help; but for Varen it was weeks before he would talk to anyone, even me. When he was ready, he came and talked to me, but it took him a long time. But he was a child then and can probably hardly remember that. I just don't know what to do now."

"Well we can't afford to wait weeks for him to come around. Whether Kaja pulls through or not," Celenia shot me a glare, but I continued, "Whether she pulls through or not it won't be long before Olmar tracks us down again. We need to be ready to move."

Celenia shrugged, "If you think it will do any good you can try to track him down and talk to him."

"You're not going to come with me?" I blinked, surprised.

"You saw how talking to him went just now. He won't listen to me… besides, someone has to stay here and wait for word about Kaja."

I opened my mouth to argue, to urge her to come help but she had a point. Someone needed to stay here in case a runner was sent from the Cabin, and based on Varen's reaction a moment ago Celenia going after him may only serve to make things worse.

"The longer you wait, the harder he's going to be to find. He took his cloak, remember?"

"All right." I conceded, "I'm going to go and see if I can find him. We can't afford to wait to track him down in case our paladin or elven friends show up again."

"Good luck, Hjalmar. I hope you can get through to him."

"I hope so too."

I closed the door gently behind me and let out a sigh. I made my way toward the dining area. A few patrons sat about with drinks or half eaten plates of food. Hardly anyone looked up as I entered. The staff busied themselves cleaning empty tables and other tasks in preparation for the dinner meal.

"Excuse me ma'am.," I approached one red haired woman cleaning a table nearby, she glanced up at me. "My friend left our room a bit ago and I need to find him. I was wondering if you know where he went. Tall young man with dark hair and bright green eyes."

"Oh, him. Yeah, he passed by several minutes ago."

"Do you know where he went?" I urged again.

"Hmmm… Hey Anabelle, did you see which way the young wizard went?"

The young woman at the counter looked up, "Which wizard? The cute one with the glowing eyes?"

The first woman looked at me and rolled her eyes, "Yes that one. He's the only wizard that's passed by within the last few hours."

Anabelle either didn't notice or ignored the tone of her coworker. "Well he went out front and headed toward the east side of town."

"What's over there?" I asked.

"Not much," Anabelle shrugged, "The Eastern gate, a guard training ground, a couple of shops. The only thing that I can imagine being of interest to a wizard is the Academy. But he seemed too old to be interested in that."

"What do you mean?"

"The academy is for children who want to learn magic. Usually when they are his age, they've joined some sort of trade to continue their magic training. That or their family is wealthy enough to send them to a higher mage school in the city."

"I see... you're sure that's where he went?"

She shrugged, "that's the direction I saw him leave, whether that's where he went or not, I couldn't say."

"All right, I'll start there. Thank you."

"Sure, good luck finding your friend."

"Thank you." I nodded as I walked out the door.

The weather outside seemed to reflect how our emotions had been. No matter which direction you looked there didn't really seem to be an end to the dark clouds, and the rain put a chill in the air. There was one benefit to it though, the wet dirt roads held footprints well. There weren't many sets but hopefully if I followed them long enough, I could separate Varen's from the other.

"Hopefully the rain kept enough people inside that Varen won't be too hard to track." I thought.

As I made my way through the mostly empty streets, I couldn't help but wonder how much Varen's power could have affected. I watched as things died and rose up in the clearing, but could his emotion and power be causing this storm? It didn't seem likely. I didn't know much about magic but even in bard's tales I had never heard of a lone wizard being able to affect things that much. And Varen himself had said before that he and Celenia were Novices at best. Even so, the kind of power he released, he could do a lot if he learned to control it, but if he didn't what would happen next time. I couldn't help but feel a twinge of fear at that thought, even though Varen was my friend, and I realized for the first time, why it was so critical for them to find someone who could teach them.

I looked up and saw the Academy ahead. I still hadn't been able to pick out Varen's footprints from any others and I had no idea where he would have gone. Earlier I had seen some children milling about the area but now the street was all but abandoned.

"It probably wouldn't help to ask anyone anyway." I muttered, "He took the cloak with him, he probably put his hood up as soon as he was out of sight of the Inn. For all I know he could have doubled back and gone to the healers cabin."

I felt a hand on my shoulder and immediately spun around, my hand automatically reaching for the hilt of the elven blade at my waist.

"Sorry," it was the man who had given us directions before, "I didn't mean to startle you, boy. You seemed lost. I wanted to make sure you're okay."

"It's all right." I relaxed, "I just was lost in thought and didn't hear you coming."

"Apologies." The man smiled, "What are you doing out in this rain? Do you need directions to the Inn again?"

"No," I shook my head, "I'm actually looking for someone. Tall young man with dark hair and glowing eyes. Have you seen him?"

The man cocked his head slightly, "You know, I may have seen someone like that." He stroked his beard in thought, "What was the name he gave? Valor? Valbrador?"

"Valbrandr?" I asked.

"That was it." He snapped his fingers, "He made his way into the Academy there. Let me show you" He began walking toward the building. I followed close behind, relieved that I had found him. He opened the door and motioned for me to go ahead. I hurried in, eager to see Varen.

The building was dark aside from a few windows letting in what little light there still was outside. I heard the old man close the door, then I heard a latch click, sending chills up my back. I turned to face him but with a speed greater than his age would let on I felt myself pinned against the nearby wall. The man's face was illuminated by the glowing orb of flame he held in his other hand. An Eerie smile was plastered across his face.

"Stupid!" I mentally berated myself. *"Have you forgotten all your training? When following a stranger never be the first one to enter the building!"* Then the man spoke.

"Nordak is getting sloppy. He'll try to make anyone one of his agents now, won't he?"

"Who?" I grunted.

"Don't play dumb. We've been keeping tabs on him for a while now, but I never thought one of his undying would be dumb enough to come looking here and use the name 'Valbrandr'."

"What are you talking about? I don't work for anyone, I'm just looking- "The fireball was brought closer to me interrupting my sentence.

"If that's true then why are you looking for Kaden?" He growled, lifting me higher and slamming me against the wall.

"Kaden? I'm looking for Varen!" I shouted.

His eyes widened in surprise "How do you know that name? Death's embrace, Nordak already knows about the kids."

"Kids? What are you talking about?"

The heat intensified. "Silence. How much does Nordak know?"

"For the last time I don't know any Nordak."

"Then who are you?" He growled, "Answer me before I lose my patience."

"Hjalmar. Hjalmar Brunsvold. I was a guard in Astor but have been travelling with Celenia and Varen. Our friend Kaja got hurt so we brought her to the healers and got a room at the inn, but Varen got upset and stormed out. I was trying to find him to talk some sense into him."

"You mean they aren't gone yet? The Reaper's Frozen Kiss!" He looked me in the eye. "Prove it."

"What?"

"If you have been traveling with them, prove it. Tell me about them."

"What? You assault me out of nowhere and then expect me to tell you about my companions? Why would I do that?"

"Fine, you won't talk; We'll change tactics. I'll get what I want." In an instant the fireball vanished. The man said something, and his hand began to glow. He brought it to my forehead and suddenly I felt a pounding headache, I cried out. I tried to twist and contort to escape his grasp, but the man had incredible strength for his apparent age. Moments later the headache subsided, and he released me and stepped back.

"What was that?" I growled, drawing my sword in case he tried to attack again.

He held up a hand. "I'm sorry. I had to know for sure."

"What did you do?"

"I read your memories. Not much, but enough to know you are who you claim to be."

"Why did you attack me?"

"You were looking for a Valbrandr." The man shrugged

"You say that like it should explain everything. Start giving me some answers or I swear on my sword-"

"What? You'll fight me?" The old man chuckled, "You may be skilled with a sword, but I've been practicing magic far longer. The fight wouldn't last long. I suppose I do owe you some explanation though, if only because my actions were rash."

He pulled a chair from nearby and sat down, motioning me to do the same. I shook my head, preferring to be at the ready despite his comment.

"How much do you know about your friends?" He asked.

"I have only known them for a couple weeks so not a lot. I know they got kicked out of their hometown, but I also know they are good people."

"You know they're mages, don't you?"

"Yes."

"Do you know what kind? What they practice?"

I hesitated, unsure whether to answer honestly, but the way this man spoke suggested he already knew; and if he truly looked at my memories, there was no question.

"Necromancy." I finally answered.

"That's right." He smiled. "Where did they learn it?"

"They said they had a teacher back in their hometown that taught them." I started, then thought back to when I met them. "They also said they descended from Necromancers."

"All correct. Do you know anything more? About their family? Where they come from?"

I thought for a minute. "No, I don't." I looked at the man. "But I get the feeling you do."

He smiled and nodded slowly. "Their parents were Kaden Valbrandr and Altea Eirasin."

"Altea Eirasin? I've heard that name. She left when was young, but she was well known in Astor. She was a healer they called Altea the Blessed. Did you know her?"

The man shook his head, "I only met Altea once. She was a very kind woman and she put you at ease just being around her; but no, I don't know her story. Kaden, however, was a very close friend of mine. We attended school here together."

"So you were their father's friend. That still doesn't explain why you attacked me or who this Nordak is."

"Well, there's quite the story to that, and it would take me some time to tell."

"We have one friend being looked after at the healer's cabin and one who could use some time to cool off. I have plenty of time."

"Very well. To begin, you need to understand us as children. There were three of us: Kaden, Nordak, and I; and we attended this very Academy. I was local to this region and had some talent with magic. Kaden came from a well-known mage family nearer the capital. Nordak was the son of a regional noble family. They sent him here because the teacher we had at the time was widely acclaimed and taught at a prestigious university in a major city before coming to help teach in our small town."

"So if Nordak was your friend, why are you so afraid of him?"

"Well the three of us started together, on similar ground as far as magical understanding. Both Kaden and Nordak were specifically studying the field of Necromancy. I dabbled in it a little extra due to their influence, but I was a general student of magic. Kaden's family had some powerful and very skilled mages of a variety of magical schools, and it proved to be a great advantage to him. While Nordak and I were learning from the classrooms and books Kaden was learning at home too as the time passed the gap widened between ourselves and Kaden. He would come up to us before class with excitement in his glowing blue eyes, eager to show us the newest spell he learned." The old man smiled at the memory, "It was fun, and he had never meant any harm from it. In fact, Kaden was nothing but supportive of our own progress as well. But Nordak grew jealous of Kaden. When I discovered this, I tried to warn Kaden to tone it down a little, but he shrugged me off telling me that Nordak was fine and that a little competition was good for them. That it would push Nordak to improve."

"And what happened?" I asked finding myself invested in the man's story.

"Well, at first Nordak seemed to distance himself. He started spending more time studying. It wasn't too surprising; we were only a couple of years from graduating the academy and then if we were skilled enough, we may be picked up by one of the larger mage schools or move on to a trade if we weren't. We thought he was just eager to impress. Kaden kept up his usual attitude and exceled at just about any necromantic spell he tried his hand at as well as many non-necromantic ones. Graduation continued to approach. We still thought of Nordak as a friend up until the duel."

"Duel?"

"It was about four months before our graduation. Kaden was doing a demonstration out in the schoolyard for a necromantic spell his father had taught him the day before. Nordak had missed the morning's classes but he suddenly showed up and called out to Kaden who turned to our friend. Nordak told him that he believed that his own power now rivaled that of Kaden's. Nordak challenged Kaden to a necromantic duel. Still believing Nordak to be our friend, Kaden welcomed the competition. He accepted; Kaden had never been one to turn down a challenge. They set the duel to be two nights from then, with a 24-hour period for preparations. Nordak wanted to keep it secret, the rest of us were unsure, but with some assurances from Kaden and thanks to his charm, we were convinced to go along with it."

"Are duels like that a regular practice among mages?"

"Fairly normal, yes. Usually for students they are overseen by an instructor, or at the very least a more skilled mage. There are usually also magical protections in place to ensure the safety of the participants. They are used for practice, or to see how a useful a spell would be in a real situation. Some, like this one, were used to determine who was a better mage."

"So why the 24-hour preparation period? Why didn't they just duel right then?"

The old man cocked an eyebrow at me, "You've never seen a necromantic duel, have you? No surprise, even then they were highly frowned upon. These days anyone caught participating would likely be arrested and executed." He sighed, "The period for preparation for a necromantic duel is to prepare corpses. Normally longer is given but they did it quickly so no one would find out about it."

"Prepare corpses? For what?"

"Necromancy is magic over death, and the peak example of this is the ability to animate a corpse. In a necromantic duel combat is done through the animated dead, not the mages themselves. Whoever can create the strongest undead wins. That night Kaden and Nordak met here in the schoolyard. Kaden managed to get his hands on three Corpses; Nordak had five. At the time we weren't sure how he managed that many but looking back he probably used previously raised undead as grave robbers. Both approached their ends of the dueling ground. Nordak smiled and shrugged off his robe, revealing strange tattoos on his arms. He clasped his hands together and began to chant. Kaden quickly followed suit. Kaden's was familiar, it wasn't the first time he had raise something, although for class purposes it was normally much smaller. Nordak's chant was strange and something about it disconcerting. The dead rose and were commanded to fight. It didn't take long to realize there was something strange about Nordak's animation spell. Kaden's risen were holding them off fairly well to be sure, but Nordak's had a sort of intelligence that should not have been present in a basic animation."

"What do you mean?"

"Well to put it simply using necromancy to animate a corpse is much like using other types of magic to animate normally inanimate objects. Simply put, Necromancy is required simply because it also acts to hold the body together, an effect that's not generally necessary when animating other objects. But because it's only magic animating the corpse, it can only follow basic commands. It has no will of its own and without command will simply stand there doing nothing.

Nordak's were different. While they were indeed under his command, they also seemed to have the capability of higher thought. As the duel continued it was clear that Kaden would be overpowered. Then one of Nordak's undead seemed to slip from his control. It turned to the crowd of onlookers. One of the students, a son of a member of the guard, stepped forward with sword and shield and held off the creature, commanding another student to run for our instructor, Egil. Kaden altered his commands and the undead under his control moved to protect the other students. Kaden shouted to Nordak, conceding the match; he wasn't willing to put his classmates in danger for pride and he believed this would be enough to satisfy our friend. He was wrong.

Seeing the opening, Nordak commanded the undead still under his control to advance. It was clear that defeating Kaden wouldn't be enough. Nordak wanted to kill him. Kaden knelt down and picked up the long bone staff he always brought with him. He held it up, planning to fend the undead off by hand if he had to. Kaden was good at combat, but these undead were something else. He fought hard and managed to hold them off suffering only a deep gash in his cheek from one that would later leave a scar. But it was clear if it lasted much longer Kaden would be overpowered, and so would the undead. Lucky for everyone involved, it was that moment that a student returned with Egil. With a blast of his own magic the corpses were reduced to ashes and Kaden and Nordak both collapsed to the ground."

"What happened to Nordak? Was he punished?"

"Both Kaden and Nordak were taken to the Inn and placed under guard. The next morning, they were taken before Egil and the town Elders. While it was clear that Nordak was to be blamed, Kaden was not guiltless. Nordak was to be ejected from the school and the town and would be escorted home under armed guard. Kaden's position was under scrutiny; His graduation would be postponed pending the full investigation of events, and it was questionable whether he would be allowed to graduate at all. The only reason he was not being escorted home like Nordak was because of his own actions to protect his classmates when they were in danger, but he was just as guilty in participating in an unsanctioned duel."

"So Nordak was escorted home? And Kaden?"

"Nordak was supposed to be escorted home, but the night before he was to leave, he managed to get past the guards and vanished into the night. No one here has heard from him since."

"What about Kaden?"

"When Nordak vanished, and it was clear that he still held a grudge against Kaden. Egil and the Elders encouraged Kaden to leave, both for his safety and for the town's. Shortly after that Egil stepped down from teaching."

"Was he under scrutiny as well?"

"No. I believe he held himself responsible though; as their teacher he felt he should have seen Nordak beginning down the darker path, and should have put a stop to it before it got as far as it did."

"I see. I suppose it makes sense, and it explains a lot about Celenia and Varen. What it doesn't explain is why you attacked me and accused me of working for Nordak."

"The less you know about that the better." The old man's face grew serious. "All you need to know right now is that we've come to discover some people who work for Nordak and we believe that you and your friends are in danger because of it. They need to get as far away as they possibly can."

"Well, Varen stormed off a little while ago very upset. I have no idea where he went."

The man sat back and stroked his chin in thought, "If he's anything like his father, you should try the graveyard." He walked over and opened the door, "Keep following this road, you'll see the large iron archway. It isn't too far."

"Thank you." I stepped outside back into the rain.

"Oh, one last thing before you go, boy. It would probably be better if your friends didn't know about all this. For their own protection."

I watched as the man stepped back into the academy building, closing the door behind him. I turned back to the muddy street and started following down in the direction he pointed.

"Keep a secret from Celenia and Varen… about their father? That doesn't seem right. We're here in the town where their father was taught necromancy for years, and they have no idea. But the old man had a point. If they knew they would want to stay, and we have Olmar on our tails already, let alone this Nordak that has some quarrel with their family."

I saw the gateway up ahead and slowed to a stop just outside.

"I guess I don't have a choice. I can't give them a reason to stay."

I stepped around the corner, into the graveyard. As I passed through the rows of headstones, I noticed that they were unlike any I had seen. Each plot had a headstone of some sort, but atop each headstone sat a shallow brass bowl. Each bowl rose upward at the center into a small pedestal with a candle atop every pedestal. None of the candles nearby were lit but looking around I spotted Varen leaned against a tree, the headstones all around him were lit. Varen's head was leaned back, looking toward the sky, but his mouth was moving.

"*Is he casting a spell?*" I thought.

"Varen!" I called out, making my way over. He looked over at me, and as I approached, I could see small blue orbs, some floated above the candles and some were scattered near Varen. "What are you doing?" I gestured to the candles.

"I just, needed some people to talk to." Varen smiled, looking around, "It's kind of a shame not everyone has easy access to people who have passed on. They are good listeners, and very good at comforting and advising."

"You're… talking to the people here in the cemetery?" I looked around, suddenly understanding what each of the orbs must be.

"Yeah, you can see them right? The orbs? If you were here when I cast the spells you could have seen their full spiritual form, but their presence is strong enough you should be able to see the wisps."

"Yeah, I see them. Listen Varen, I just came because I wanted to make sure you were okay. You were pretty upset back there."

"Yeah, I'm okay now. Well, not entirely, but as okay as I can be right now. Have we heard anything from the Healer's cabin yet?"

"I'm not sure." I shook my head. "I left not too long after you did, but it took me a little while to track you down. Celenia stayed behind though so she should know."

"I see." He sighed, "All right then, let's go back. Thank you, Hjalmar." He stood from the tree and moved over to each headstone, thanking the respective spirits as he put out the candles. Finally, he turned to me. He was much calmer, but there was a sort of melancholia to him too.

I turned and started out of the Cemetery, and Varen caught up and matched stride with me. We spent most of the way in silence, Varen held his head back, letting the rain gently pelt his face.

"So did you come here planning to talk to spirits?"

"No," he chuckled, "How could I? I don't know this town any better than you do. I just needed to get out of that room, I didn't care where I went. I just kind of happened by there by mistake; But when I realized that it was already prepared with all the materials needed to speak with them, I decided to stay and hope at least one of them would listen."

"You have me, and Celenia. Why couldn't you talk to us?"

"It's different, Hjalmar." Varen shrugged, "You guys are part of the group, and we're all stressed about her. The dead are already dead. They are good at giving objective advice and just listening. They have no ties to me or even this world. Although…" He let the sentence trail off.

"What?"

"They knew my father, Hjalmar. I think he went to school here.

What are the odds of that?"

"Are you sure? What did they tell you?"

"They said I looked just like Kaden. That was my father's name. They wouldn't tell me much aside from the fact that some of them were his schoolmates, but they knew him."

"The world's a lot smaller than it seems I guess."

We reached the inn and stepped inside, both of us dripping wet from the rain. The tavern was busy now, the dinner rush in progress. I don't even think the staff noticed us as we walked past them toward the room. I opened the door and stepped inside. The room was empty, and a small piece of parchment sat at the edge of the bed. Varen stepped past me and picked it up, as he did the paper reacted and a symbol appeared. Varen breathed a relieved sigh.

"Is that from Celenia? What does it mean?"

"It's an arcane symbol. It means life. Kaja's going to be okay."

"Well good for you." A voice growled at us from behind, "You better hope the same can be said for my sister."

Chapter 19

Parting Ways

Amara

I had spotted them as they passed by the entrance to the town and silently followed them back to their room at the inn. The rain made it easy to mask my footsteps, though I needed to stay toward the drier ground at the edge of the streets near the buildings. They stepped inside where I heard them say Kaja, the girl we had previously captured, was going to be okay.

"Well good for you." I growled, "you better hope the same can be said for my sister." I couldn't help it. After what I saw in the clearing, I didn't expect them to act like nothing was wrong. It infuriated me.

They both jumped and turned, raising their arms to protect themselves, but they were slow. In a flash I was past Hjalmar and had the Ugathri knife up to Varen before he could fully react.

"You better start explaining boy, or this knife is going to puncture your body thrice for each elf you harmed."

"What are you-" He stopped, understanding in his expression. "The clearing."

"Yes." I hissed, "The clearing. Now talk."

"It was an accident."

"An accident! Undead were guarding the clearing, what elves weren't killed and raised were collapsed unconscious on the ground looking paler than the moon, and no living plant life remains. How could that possibly be an accident?"

The boy looked at me with his glowing eyes and spoke. "Listen, I am happy to explain what happened in that clearing, but I am going to see Kaja at the healer's cabin. You can accompany us, and I will explain on the way, or you can attack me. It's your choice."

I hesitated, torn. I was furious about what happened to my sister and her rangers, but something about him made me think there had to be another explanation. Or perhaps part of me just wanted to know what happened more than anything else.

"Fine." I finally responded, pulling away from Varen, "But if you try anything you will be dead faster than you can blink. And with this knife, even necromancy won't be able to bring you back."

The boy glanced at the knife and nodded mutely. He motioned to follow out the door and I obeyed staying close behind but keeping a keen ear for his friend. They explained about magical mutations and Varen's reserve, they explained about Kaja getting hit by an arrow fired by my sister. They spared no detail in their retelling of events including how Varen's sister had to protect both of their friends to prevent the effects from reaching them too. I wanted to deny it, to think that they were making up a story just to appear innocent, but the events fit too well with what I saw. When we reached the healers cabin, they turned to me.

"Well, what are you going to do now?" Varen asked.

"I don't know. It was a rather extreme accident but clearly it was an accident. My loyalty should lie with my people, but the event occurred because my sister wouldn't heed the decision of the council. This situation is a bizarre tangled mess of events. For now, I want to see your friend for myself and ensure that she will be okay. I don't know how I will return to my people with your story though, it's farfetched and I wouldn't have believed it if I hadn't seen the effects myself. For now, I can't find good reason to try to bring you back; Besides, you're technically beyond the bounds of our laws as long as you are in human lands."

"I see, well you are welcome to come and see Kaja. I'm sure she'll want to thank you herself for helping us." Varen replied.

I nodded, and Hjalmar led us inside. A young woman sat at a desk near the entrance.

"Erinis, right?" Varen asked, "My sister left us a message saying that Kaja was okay."

She smiled and nodded gently, "Your sister is already here, and your friend is waiting for you. Follow me." Erinis led the way back down the hallway to a small room where Celenia was seated next to a bed where Kaja stood up, a bandage could be seen under her shirt around her arm and torso.

Varen smiled and put his arms around her, careful of the injured arm.

"She is okay to leave as soon as you are ready to do so, but she needs to take it easy on her arm. No heavy lifting, no fighting. As for her bruises she needs to use the same salve I gave you." She looked at Hjalmar. "Her personal items are in the basket here on the dresser, and if you have any other questions you can feel free to call for me." She retreated out the door, leaving the group alone.

"I'm okay Varen." Kaja pat him on the back. He released his grip and stood up. She turned in the bed and let her feet dangle off it. "Let me get dressed and we can get back on the road."

"No." Varen said putting his hands on her uninjured shoulder.

"What?" Kaja smiled at him, but her smile quickly disappeared when she looked at his face.

"Kaja, Hjalmar, I want to thank both of you for everything, but you can't continue on with us."

The room erupted with voices. Kaja, Hjalmar, and even Celenia protesting but he held up his hand, silencing them.

"Celenia told me when Kaja joined us that she didn't like the idea. That we were exiles and there was a good chance of her getting hurt. She was right. And it applies to you too Hjalmar."

"I'm not letting you go Varen." Kaja said sternly.

"Kaja, you have a family back in Vellara and they are probably worried to death about you. They hired Olmar to bring you home. They just want you back Kaja, and you deserve someone better than an exiled necromancer. And Hjalmar, you had a whole life back in Astor. You were city guard with a whole career ahead of you. I can't let you throw that away with us."

"What about Amara?" Kaja cried, looking at me.

"Amara's not part of the group. She came in here to see that you were okay and then is going to return home. In fact," He turned to look at me, "Amara, I know you don't owe us anything and you're home and your sister need you; I don't mean to delay your Journey, but Kaja is in no condition to fight should something happen, it would mean a lot to me if you, if both of you," he looked at Hjalmar, "Would accompany her home and make sure she is safe; or at least take her as far as you can."

I looked Varen over. His voice was firm, and he was going to stand by his position, but I could also see the pain in his eyes. He didn't want to push his friends away, but I could tell he truly believed it was better that way.

"I will help take them as far as I can, and I will stay with them as long as danger remains." I nodded.

"I will too. But Varen, are you sure about this?"

"I'm sure." He turned away and began to walk out the door, and while I wasn't sure I thought I heard him mutter, "I have to be."

Celenia looked just as shocked as the rest of us were but followed after her brother once she recovered.

Hjalmar and I looked at Kaja who stared at the floor.

"He doesn't... want me here?"

I stepped up and helped her off the bed. "Hey, come on. Let's get your things and we'll get on the road. Things will be better once you're back with your family."

She stood and put her arms around me, I felt her wince at the movement, but she refused to let go for a minute. I pat her back as her body shook.

"Can you give us a minute Hjalmar? I'll have her out and ready as soon as I can, but she needs some privacy right now."

"Right. I'll be outside the cabin. Come find get me when you're ready." He left and closed the door behind him.

A few minutes later the real crying started.

Varen

"Varen wait just a second." Celenia said as she caught up to me.

"What is it Celenia?" I asked, trying to keep my voice steady.

"What was that?" She stepped around to cut me off, "That's how you are going to end things with them? What has come over you? Before you were attached to them like they were family and now you're pushing them away?"

"What's come over is that Kaja was beaten and shot by elves, because of me!"

"That was not your fault, they were the ones that ran off and got captured."

"Yeah, and we broke them out. That's why they chased us."

"And if we didn't, they might be dead instead of injured!"

"That's beside the point! They wouldn't have gotten captured in the first place if I had listened to you from the start and we got out just the two of us. You were right Celenia, we are exiles being hunted and because of that we are a danger to anyone who we let get close."

"But- "

"It's done, Celenia. Just drop it." I pushed past and continued to the inn.

"Fine. Let's get our stuff and get out of here." She growled.

We gathered our stuff in silence. I didn't want to talk over what had happened; I was worried I might change my mind. I kept telling myself that Kaja would be better off at home, with her family. That she would be safe and find someone else. That she would marry someone who could support her and protect her. They would probably take over her parents' shop, or maybe start their own. It didn't stop the pain I felt, but I tried to convince myself that it didn't matter. She deserved happiness, I didn't. I didn't know how long my sister and I would be running; I never did. With a paladin on our tails, would it be enough just to go to another nation? How far would he chase us? As much as it hurt a life on the run is not what Kaja deserved.

"I have my things together. You ready?" Celenia asked curtly.

"Yeah. I'm ready. Let's go."

We walked out the inn into the muddy streets making our way to the south side of the town.

"How far do you think it is before we reach the port town?" Celenia asked.

"A few days at least. I doubt if there are any places to stop along the way though."

"We'll have to make do. We don't have any of our tents either. We'll have to find caves or just sleep out in the open."

"We could go without if we needed to. It might be miserable, but we could get there faster. And we wouldn't get caught off guard if Olmar catches up to us." I pointed out.

"Do you think he's already been here?"

"I doubt it. I haven't seen any posters about us around town, nor have there been any whispers among the few people we pass by. If Olmar had already been here, I think we would have been stopped by now."

"You're right. It has been quiet." Celenia agreed.

"That doesn't mean we can relax though. We have no idea where he is. He could be close behind us for all we know. Or maybe he'll find a way to catch us up ahead."

Celenia nodded in agreement and we continued in silence. I decided to break it once more.

"I want to come back here sometime. When we're not being hunted, and people forget about us."

"Here?" Celenia scoffed, "Why would you want to come back here? It doesn't seem like there's a lot to a place like this."

"No, but I spoke to some of the spirits here, and they told me something interesting."

"What could they have told you that would make you want to come back?"

"They told me that dad was taught magic at the academy here in this town. They wouldn't tell me much else, but they told me that."

"Varen stop joking around." Celenia looked at my face for a moment and realization spread across her face. "You're not joking. Don't you think that's kind of important information to tell me? We should stay."

"We can't stay Celenia."

"Why not?" she shouted.

"Two reasons: One, we're being hunted, Two: the longer we stay, the harder it is for me to walk away because the more I want to run back to them and beg them to come with us again. We can't stay."

Celenia's expression of anger softened into understanding. "Okay, we won't stay. But we will be back one day Varen. Maybe someday soon, and maybe you can get her back."

"Maybe…" I let the word trail off, unconvinced.

Amara

After I had managed to help soothe Kaja and get her dressed, the three of us went back to the inn where they were staying. Hjalmar paid to stay for the night, and we went back to the room in hopes of catching Celenia and Varen for a final goodbye. When we arrived, however, their things were gone and there was no sign of them remaining.

"They must have already left," Hjalmar sighed.

I glanced over at Kaja, concerned she might break down once again, but she seemed emotionally drained. She moved across the room and crawled onto the bed, curling up.

"I'm assuming you want to stay then, since you've paid for the room."

Hjalmar nodded, "It's too late to start moving now. We wouldn't get far before needing to stop and make camp. Besides, I thought a night's sleep in an actual bed might do her some good." He gestures to Kaja.

I looked at Kaja. "You're probably right. Best to wait until morning, but let's leave at first light and try to make the best time we can."

"Agreed." Hjalmar let out a sigh, looking out the window.

"Is something the matter?"

"Well, yeah, I guess. Something Varen said has been bothering me."

"Something he said before he left? What is it?"

"Well, he said that I was a city guard and had a whole life back in Astor before I left."

"Was he wrong about that?"

"No, not necessarily. I had a life. I was a guard which paid well and supported me well enough. But what kind of life will I be able to have going back?"

"You can't just get your old job back?" I tilted my head in confusion.

He laughed, "Amara, I was a guard, a soldier. I have been gone for more than a week now. To them I abandoned my troop. If I return there's going to be some severe punishment, and that's if I'm let back in the guard at all. I decided when I left that town. In all honesty I had lived in Astor all my life, and it's a great city, and I enjoyed being a guard. It's just..."

"What?" I coaxed.

"Those two, as well as Kaja, quickly proved themselves trustworthy to me. And, exiles or not, they were on the brink of a journey to go and see the world, and I realized that I wasn't as happy with my life as I thought I was. I wasn't appreciated in the guard; I was just another body. There was no chance for promotion, I just would've stayed a footman all my life."

"Is that a bad thing?"

"Not necessarily, but I realized didn't want to live in the same town my whole life. I wanted to accomplish something in my life, and I was never going to be able to do that in the guard. We dealt with thieves and drunks mostly. Occasionally we dealt with a bandit or two, but I've experienced more in my time with them than I would have learned in years of training with the guard. That's why I left. I wanted something more and I thought I could find it with them."

"I see," I nodded, then looked directly at him, "you still have a choice, you know."

He laughed, "Varen made it pretty clear he doesn't want us around anymore."

I shook my head, "I don't mean with them. Sure, he asked you to help get Kaja home safe, but after that if you don't want to go back to Astor you don't have to. There is a lot to see out in the world, but if you wait for someone to take you then you are probably never really going to see it. You are still fairly young for a human; you can make your life whatever you want it to be. You just have to make the decision yourself, don't wait for someone else to make it for you."

Hjalmar looked back at me, a small smile on his face. "Yeah, I guess you're right about that. Thank you, Amara."

"You're welcome." I smiled back. I spread my arms out in a stretch, "Well, I think I'm going to get some food. I haven't eaten much today. Do you want anything?"

"Sure just something simple is fine, thank you." He glanced at Kaja for a moment.

"I was already planning on getting her something too," I chuckled, "It may be cold by the time she gets it, but at least it will be food. Stay here and keep an eye on her. I'll be back."

With an arcane word I altered my appearance to look more human. I examined myself in the mirror and, satisfied with the result, walked out the door and made my way down the hall to the dining area. It didn't feel like we had been in our room long, but it was apparently long enough for the excitement of dinner to have calmed down some. I saw a few empty seats at the bar and approached. Two humans were working the bar, one male and one female.

After a few moments the woman working the bar walked up, "What can I get for you tonight?"

I pulled a few coins from my pouch, "Just three soup meals please. And I'd like those on a tray so I can take them back to my room."

"Will do. I'll get those out to you as soon as I can. Would you like something to drink while you wait? It's on the house."

"Tea, if you would please." I smiled and she turned and walked through a doorway behind the bar. I sat there for a few minutes musing on the experience of the last couple days.

Moments later, the tavern was engulfed in a deafening silence. I looked around, concerned that my magical disguise had somehow faded. No one, however, was looking at me. Their attention instead was drawn to a large, armored figure at the entrance.

As the figure approached the bar, several individuals made for the door behind him. Others attempted to push themselves into the wall in an effort to avoid drawing his attention. Every elven instinct I had screamed for me to get away from this man, but I held my ground.

"One fish meal please, with the house ale." The man took the seat next to mine and placed a few coins on the bar. The barman looked at him and nodded in acknowledgement. He gathered the coin and started to walk toward the doorway when the man stopped him.

"Hold sir. One moment please." He pulled several more coins from the bag at his waist, "I'm looking for someone. You haven't seen a tall young man accompanied by two young women, have you? They would possibly have a member of the Astorian guard with them."

The man scratched his chin." We've had a few outsiders come through recently, but I can't say I've seen an Astorian guardsman. What did the boy look like?"

"Tall, as I said. Would have likely been wearing some mage robes, and bright green eyes."

"Unnaturally green?" The barman asked.

"As if they glow."

I felt my body freeze, and my stomach knot. I only knew one individual who matched that description. *"Who is this man? And why is he looking for Varen?"* I had no answers but knew it wouldn't end well for me to ask him directly. I had to figure out how to enter the conversation without drawing suspicion.

"I know of the lad you describe. Can't say I saw him personally, but a few members of my staff haven't been able to stop yappin' about him. Seems he passed through today, but I can't say for certain when he left or even which way he went."

"I see..." The man nodded, "That's actually very helpful. Thank you."

"Anything for a paladin." The barman nodded, "I'll get your meal to you as soon as I can."

As the barman left, I sat stiffly in my chair. I didn't dare look at the paladin directly but, I tried to peek at him out of the corner of my eye. He was taller than Hjalmar, and a little broader in the shoulders. He looked haggard like he had been travelling without rest, and his gear was scuffed and dirty; except for his shield, which looked like it had been polished to a shine.

"Here's that cup of tea ma'am. We'll have your food out to you as soon as we can." The barmaid set the small cup before me. "Would you like something as well sir? A mug of Ale perhaps?"

"No, I've got an ale coming with my food, thank you. If you have some water though, that would be appreciated. I don't want to drink too much while I'm on a job."

The barmaid smiled. She turned and took a clay tankard and filled it from a pitcher nearby. She turned back and set the cup in front of him.

"Let me know if there is anything else." She gave a smile and walked across the bar to help someone else.

The paladin took a couple fingers and touched the surface of the water, speaking a single word. The water gave a small glow for a moment then faded until the light was gone. He took a sip and caught me staring.

"Just a small spell to cleanse the water." He smiled, "Most taverns do a pretty good job of making sure their water is clean, but a little extra protection never hurt."

I nodded in response. I didn't trust myself to speak.

"You don't look like you're from around here. What brings you to a small town like this?"

"Well, so much for not talking to him." I set down my cup, "Just travelling." I smiled.

"Ah, I see. Odd for one such as yourself to be travelling these lands. Do you travel alone?"

"Of what matter is that to you? You think me incapable of handling myself?"

"Oh, no. I just meant it was odd for an elf to be travelling here."

I froze again. I couldn't help it. Did he have some ability to see through my glamour? I regained my composure quickly and tried to shrug off the comment. "I may not be from around here, sir, but where you get off calling me an elf is a mystery."

The man laughed, "your illusion is good, I'll give you that; But you clearly haven't been here long enough to actually disguise yourself. Your appearance is human, but your clothing is not of human make. At least, not any that I've seen; but it's the sword at your side that gave you away. An elven longsword, if I'm not mistaken."

I grunted, "All right, fine. But how do you know so much of our people to be able to identify our weapons and clothing?"

"I've done some work for your people before. Well, probably not your people, judging by the clothing, but elves.

"I see. And tell me, which elves have you done work for?"

"Ah, let's see. I believe they called themselves Vessi."

"Well that makes more sense. The Vessi *do* tend to have more contact with outsiders than the rest of us." I replied, searching for any way to extricate myself from the conversation.

"I suspect that's true. And what of you?"

"What of me?" I asked, cocking an eyebrow.

"You're elven; yet not Vessi. So, what are you doing in a human city?"

"I still don't see how that is any of your business, friend." I gave a strained smile that I hoped looked more sincere than it felt.

"My apologies if I've overstepped." He smiled, "Perhaps instead of telling me why you are here, it may be more acceptable to ask how long you have been traveling and from where"

"Why is any of this any concern of yours?" I saw my chance to go on the attack. "You may have contact with the Vessi, but that doesn't mean that I am going to trust you off hand. No detail of my travels are your concern. Nor do I particularly feel like discussing them with outsiders."

"I see. I knew your people generally avoided outsiders, but I wasn't aware they were so defensive about it."

"Well, I wasn't aware that humans enjoyed sticking their noses in the business of others." I shot back. "Or is this your way of trying to get my attention?"

He smiled. "You're hardly my type, miss."

"Then what exactly is it you want?"

"Very well. Straight to the point then. As you may have heard me ask the barman, I'm looking for someone. A few someones, actually. Two of them are siblings; a boy and a girl, both magic users. There's a girl with them and possibly a guardsman."

"Why is someone like you looking for them? Are they in danger?" I tried to pull off the wide eyed worried look as best as I could.

"Kind of," He nodded, "That's why I need to find them as soon as possible."

The barmaid returned placing a tray of bowls and plates on the counter before me. "Here's your food miss, when you have finished just leave the tray and dishes against the wall outside your door and someone will be by to pick it up."

"Thank you." I smiled and took the tray. "*Finally, a way out.*" I thought

"My, that's a lot of food for one person." The armored man commented.

"But sir, I never said I was travelling alone." I smiled and took my leave.

I walked down the hall, careful not to move too fast. I needed to warn Kaja and Hjalmar, but I didn't want to attract this man's attention any more than I already had. I reached the door and, my hands full, I gently kicked it a few times. Hjalmar opened the door and I pushed past him into the room.

"Get up, both of you." I hissed, setting the food down on the dresser.

Kaja sat up groggily while Hjalmar closed the door behind me.

"What's going on?" He asked.

"There's a man here fully clad in armor. He's looking for Varen, and the Bartender told him that they just passed through."

"Olmar," Hjalmar whispered, looking at Kaja.

"Who's Olmar?" I asked.

"You were told all about Varen and Celenia's magic right? That they practice Necromancy?" Kaja asked.

"Yes," I nodded, "They told me when they explained what happened to my sister and her men in the clearing.

"Good," She nodded, "that makes the rest of this easier. See, they were exiled from our town because of the necromancy they practice."

"Did they do something bad with it?" I asked, remembering the clearing.

"No," She shook her head, "They were cast out because the leader of our town believed they would do something bad with it in the future.

Claiming that Necromancy would cause the destruction of the town or some such nonsense. So, they were told to leave."

"Which they did." I was following so far.

"Yes. But we found out shortly after that a paladin had been sent after them."

"A paladin?" I asked.

"I'll field that one Kaja." Hjalmar stepped in. "A paladin is usually sent to kill a person or creature too dangerous for the local guard to go after. They are powerful warriors, often wielding enchanted gear and wielding their own minor magic to help them take down their foes. It's not uncommon for one to go after a Necromancer, but they are usually hired for the job. My guess is their town leader hired him to go after them."

"If Olmar knows they have been here, then it sounds like Celenia and Varen are in serious trouble." I said.

Kaja stood off the bed and pulled her hair back. There was intense look in her eyes as she moved toward the door. She drew close to me as she passed and reached for the Ugathri blade at my belt. I only just managed to grab her by the wrist before she was able to draw it.

"What are you doing?" I hissed.

"I'm getting rid of Olmar." She growled back, "If Varen doesn't have to worry about Olmar than he doesn't have to worry about continuing to run after they get to sea. If he doesn't have to worry about that then he has no reason to leave me behind. I'm going to solve all of our problems in one strike."

"Kaja snap out of it." Hjalmar spoke sternly, stunning both of us.

"Olmar is a fully equipped, fully trained paladin. I'll be first to admit that you are leaps and bounds better than when you started but even the three of us together couldn't hope to beat him. If you go in against him with only a knife, no matter how big it is, you are only going to get yourself killed."

"So what do you suggest, Hjalmar?" Kaja snapped, "I go home to Vellara as Varen told me to and let Olmar catch up and kill both of them? That sounds like a great plan."

"I didn't say that. All I said was that we couldn't take him. Celenia and Varen's best chance is if we can get ahead of Olmar and warn them. Between their magic and our combat skills hopefully we at least have a chance. If nothing else, we have a better chance with them than we do on our own.

"I'm with Hjalmar." I turned to her, "The job I was asked was to do was to keep you safe as long as I could. That doesn't mean that given these rather extreme circumstances, we can't go and warn them of the danger."

"Okay," Kaja sighed, "you two are probably right. So, when do we leave?"

"As soon as most of the Inn is asleep, I'd say." I suggested.

"Why wait?" Kaja asked, "The more of a head start we can get the better off we'll be."

"He spoke to me, that's how I know who he is. If we go out now, he'll recognize all of us and he's bound to follow us. If that happens, we'll lead him right to them."

"I guess we don't have any choice then." Hjalmar said, "We wait."

"Then let's eat up, because we're not going to have time to eat once we hit the road. And once we do, I have something that just might help us."

Chapter 20

The Princess and the Paladin

Celenia

After travelling as far as we could before sundown, we decided to rest the night on the road and recover from all the madness of the past few days. I woke in the morning to find that Varen must have dozed off sometime during his watch that night. I wasn't too worried; The wards we had put in place would have woken us up had anyone approached, but we still felt better having someone on watch. I considered waking my brother, but I decided to let him sleep, his emotions were surely drained after everything and he needed the rest.

I started a small fire trying to pull my mind off the events of yesterday. I felt guilty for what had happened. Over time I came to see Kaja and Hjalmar as valuable allies; and Varen had been happier travelling with Kaja than I had seen him in years. I couldn't help but wonder if things would've been different if I hadn't sewn the seed of doubt by expressing my concerns to him at the beginning. Part of me knew it probably wouldn't have made a difference, but I still couldn't shake the guilt. He blamed himself for what happened in the clearing, and it wasn't just Kaja. Though we practiced necromancy we always practiced on creatures that had already been dead. The few times we attempted a human raising we received permission from the sprit whose corpse it had been. Whether they were a threat to us or not, those were people's lives, and his loss of control ended them.

Finished with the fire, I took my spell book out, hoping that studying would help take my mind off it, but my mind kept returning to recent events and our current situation. The trees nearby shook slightly, probably from the wind, but the hairs on my neck still stood up.

"I am so tense." I half sighed; half groaned to myself. "The stress is killing me. We need to hurry and get to port."

"Agreed," Varen groaned, sitting up. "Although I'm not sure if that will be enough."

"Sorry, Var. did I wake you?"

"No, I've been awake for a few minutes, just didn't want to get up yet. Sorry I fell asleep on watch." He smiled softly.

"That's why we have the wards. How are you feeling?"

"As well as I can feel after sleeping on the ground for a few hours." He shrugged. "We don't have any supplies for breakfast or anything, so should we get on the road?"

"Yeah. The sooner we get to port the better." I stood, dusting off my robes, "What did you mean that you weren't sure getting to port would be enough? We were just exiled from here. Once we're across the water we're free."

"Legally speaking, yeah." Varen nodded, "But I've been thinking about Olmar. He's a paladin and they are usually hired to do something. If he's after us, will his contract be void just because we crossed the ocean? Will the fact that we've left kingdom borders really stop him from hunting us?"

I was silent for a minute. The thought hadn't even crossed my mind. I thought crossing the sea would solve our problems but would someone like Olmar be stopped by that?

"It doesn't matter though. We've lost Olmar. As long as we can leave the kingdom before he finds us, he will lose our trail permanently." I said.

"And if we don't?"

I sighed, "Can we just focus on one problem at a time. Olmar is a problem but if he comes for us after we've left, we can deal with it then."

"Okay, you're right," Varen held up his hands in surrender, "one problem at a time."

We put out the fire and finished gathering what few possessions we still had before continuing down the path in relative silence. I still couldn't shake the feeling that something was wrong, but I shrugged it off as stress once more. Maybe if I could relieve some of my guilt, it would help.

"Varen." I started but stopped, struggling to find the words.

"What is it Cel? Is something wrong?"

"No." I replied too quickly, "Well maybe. It's just, what I told you before, back when Kaja joined us. I was wrong. Kaja and Hjalmar were great companions, and even better friends. I know I was unsure at the start, but I think you were right before, and you shouldn't have sent them off."

Varen was silent for a moment before responding with a sigh. "No, Celenia. You weren't wrong. We are sentenced to live a life of exile. There's no changing that fate; but just because we have to live it doesn't mean they do. I love Kaja and I was overjoyed to have her here with me; but I was selfish. If she came with me, we could be together, sure, but we can never go back to Vellara. She could never see her family again. I don't regret practicing necromancy Celenia, because of that I've been able to talk to mom and dad since they died; but I would have given anything to have them actually there for us. Kaja has the opportunity to still have her family there, I can't take that from her. It would be wrong. And Hjalmar should never have gotten involved in the first place. He met us on accident telling us that because of spells we cast, his town was in danger."

"We never intended that, Varen."

"No we didn't. I know that, but it doesn't change the fact that we're inexperienced. Until we can learn how to control our spells better, and I can control the reserves within me, we are a danger to anyone around us. I killed people, Celenia. I didn't mean to. I didn't want to. But I could feel the energy rising within me and I was powerless to stop it. If it wasn't for you knowing what was about to happen, I could have killed our friends too. I can't allow that to happen, and if sending them away is the only way I can make sure they're safe then so be it."

I don't think I had ever seen my brother near tears since we were children, but I could see them welling up and hear his voice quivering. I pulled his towering frame in close and wrapped my arms around him. He gently hugged back.

"I'm sorry Varen." Was all I could say.

He nodded first before he could find his voice. "It's okay. I just… don't want to talk about it anymore. It's hard enough as it is."

I nodded my head in understanding. We stood there in the middle of the path for a moment when we here a voice in the trees nearby.

"How sweet." The voice dripped with sarcasm. "He pretends to feel bad."

Korryn and several elves emerged from the trees to our left and spread out to cut off the path behind us. We turned to run down the path, but she spoke a word and in an instant tree roots broke through the ground and created a wall blocking our path to the south.

"You're not the only one who can wield powerful magic, boy. You simply caught me off guard last time."

I pulled my scepter from my robes, but a loosed arrow knocked it from my hand.

"You've come back to get revenge then?" Varen stepped forward, covering me as best he could, "I am sorry for what happened, it was an accident. But if this is the only way you'll be satisfied, take it. Simply recall that I was the only one that harmed you and your people. Your qualm isn't against my sister."

"As much as I would relish taking your life, I'm not here for you." Korryn sneered. "I've been following you since this morning in hopes you would lead me to my sister. But I've grown tired of waiting and my patience grows thin. I know she left to seek you out, so, where is she?"

"Amara? She found us yesterday, late in the evening."

"What did you do to her?" Korryn snarled.

"Nothing! We talked. She wanted to know what happened in the clearing and I told her as best as I could. She was supposed to be on her way back home."

Korryn leered at us. "What reason do I have to believe you. You invaded the sanctity of our lands and tried to circumvent our laws. What assurance do I have that you speak truth? You killed my rangers without a second thought. How do I know you didn't kill her just as easily?"

"I offered to let you have your revenge." My brother responded, "If I'm not concerned for my life, then what reason do I have to lie to you?"

Korryn looked my brother up and down, scrutinizing him. The elves Korryn had brought with her had bows at the ready. Most were aimed at my brother, but I could see a couple pointed toward me, watching my every movement. I stayed as still as I could and whispered arcane words, hoping they wouldn't hear. I didn't need my scepter to cast, that was just a focus. I could feel my palm heating up, with a word the air near it would ignite. If they decided to fight, I hoped I could at least take them by surprise. I glanced over as one of the elves took their focus off me and looked toward the woods from which they emerged.

"Korryn, something approaches from the elven pathway, it sounds like a mounted individual. They are closing in quickly."

"Who would take a mount on an elven path? They aren't designed for that." She turned as a dark horse came crashing through the trees. Kaja and Hjalmar rode atop it and Amara dropped from the trees just behind them.

"What are you doing here?!" My brother and Korryn shouted in unison, though their questions were directed at different people.

"Korryn?" Amara looked shocked, "What are you doing here? Are you okay?"

"I came looking for you." Korryn replied, "Amara, you need to come home."

"I was going to. I just had to do something first." Amara looked at her sister's face. "Is something wrong?"

"We don't have time for the reunion!" Kaja shouted, "Varen, we came to tell you that Olmar is coming."

"Kaja, we knew Olmar would still be looking for us. That's not news." I pointed out.

"No, you don't understand. He came into town last night. Amara ran into him at the tavern. He knows you were there; he could be here any time. Amara took us down the elven paths in hopes we could get ahead of him, but I'm not sure how far ahead we are."

"Not far," one of the elves interjected, "Someone is approaching down the road, and they are riding hard."

Korryn looked at Amara and sighed. "You won't leave unless we stop this man, will you?"

Amara shook her head, "What happened in the clearing was an accident, we both know that. These humans are innocent of any purposeful crime you accused them of. Knowing that, I find it likely they are innocent of whatever this man hunts them for as well. I can't leave and let innocents be killed."

Within moments the hoofbeats became audible to even myself and moments later Olmar broke through the ranks of the elven archers. He road atop a large white warhorse donned in armor. Olmar's own armor shone in the sunlight, covering him head to toe. He stopped, eyeing everyone there.

"I am Olmar Bengtsson, and I am here for the mages and the human girl. If the rest of you stand aside you will not be harmed."

Korryn sighed once more, "I will never understand what you see in these humans, sister." She turned to her elves, "Encircle my sister and the humans, and protect them at all costs. Failure is not an option." The elves moved to follow her instructions, though many tried to keep some distance from my brother and myself.

"You are making my job more difficult." Olmar growled, "But I will not be stopped in my mission. You have thus chosen your side." He drew a large sword from his side and raised his shield. Kicking his horse into a charge.

The elves launched a volley of arrows, but they bounced off Olmar's armor with a chorus of ringing. We dove out of the way, but a couple of the elves took some hits from his shield as he passed. His horse spun to face us again. The elves stepped back into his path. As Olmar began to charge I hurled the spell dancing across my hand. He raised his shield and I watched as the flame struck the shield and explode back in our direction. We scrambled as Olmar rode again into our midst swinging his blade.

Hjalmar used the chaos to get behind the paladin, and attempt to strike at his mount, but was rewarded with a kick to his chest plate, knocking him back. The elves had changed tactics, dropping their bows and now fending him off with elven longswords. Amara pulled back, away from the throng and drew her own bow. She spoke a single word as she let the arrow fly. It struck Olmar's shield with a thunk. Rather than deflect like all the others, Amara's arrow had sunk into the shield, though didn't fully pierce it.

Olmar looked at his shield in surprise, then turned his attention to Amara.

She drew another arrow in response, nocking it. Olmar's horse reared up and came down on our group who scrambled to get out of the way. We regrouped as Olmar's rode away for a moment. He sheathed his sword and rounded toward the group. He kicked his horse back into the fray as he drew a club. He swung as he approached, catching and knocking aside a few of us as he did. Kaja, who had been hurling knives with her good arm to little effect, caught a blow to the stomach and fell back gasping for air. Varen released his own spell which, reflecting off Olmar's shield, showered Ice and snow back into the group.

Korryn shoved Varen out the way of one of Olmar's swings. "Stop casting." She commanded.

"I was trying to help." Varen argued.

"Well it's not. That shield is Ugathri make and your magic is just getting reflected off of it. You may have powerful magic but leave this to the skilled combatants. Stay out of our way."

Varen nodded mutely.

The elves used their short swords to find exposed spots on Olmar's horse, effectively driving him back. Amara loosed a couple more arrows; one again embedded itself in Olmar's shield and the other ricochet off and found its home in Olmar's leg armor. Olmar let out a grunt and pulled back, pulling the arrow from his leg as he went. He began to retreat up the road. We all relaxed as we watched him ride away.

Hjalmar grabbed my arm and started to drag me toward the tree line.

"What are you doing Hjalmar?"

"We have to get back into the trees." Hjalmar yelled, "Everyone."

"What do you fear, human?" Korryn chuckled. "Our enemy flees before the might of the elves."

"He's not running. He's getting ready for a full mounted charge."

We looked up the road and saw Olmar rapidly approaching once again, a lance held steady in his hand.

"Everybody into the trees." Korryn commanded, "Stay together and watch for him."

We ran into the trees, attempting to follow Korryn's orders and stay together, but it proved difficult in the underbrush. I only hoped it would prove more difficult for Olmar on horseback. Stumbling our way through, we found a small clearing on the other side the woods sat on one side and some rocky hills on the other.

"Amara, you take any rangers who still have their bows to the top of the hill, be ready to launch a volley down on him." She turned, "The rest of you, with me. Swords ready. Do not let your guard down." Korryn looked at me, Kaja, and my brother. "As for the three of you: Stay back and try not to get yourselves killed."

Everyone scrambled to get to Korryn's ordered positions. Olmar rode into the clearing. With a whistle arrows began to rain down on him from above. Too many for how many elves were atop the hill. I looked and watched as each arrow Amara released seemed to split into several as it arced through the air. Several arrows seemed to dig into Olmar's armor, but none seemed to pierce through it.

Korryn swore. "Since when do humans have armor so resistant to our arrows?"

"It's been a while since you've fought actual human warriors, hasn't it?" I replied.

"This is hardly a time to laugh at our expense. If it doesn't look good for us it looks even worse for you." She turned back to her men and shouted as they bore down on Olmar, swords drawn.

If it wasn't so terrifying, it would have been incredible to watch as a single Paladin fended of an entire group of elves. It seemed he was supernaturally aware of where each blow would land and deflected any that would have actually been effective, while those he ignored glanced harmlessly off his full plate. If we hadn't evaded him previously, he easily would have killed us before. Even now it was as Korryn said. Our chances of success rapidly seemed to be dwindling. Olmar once again wield his sword but seemed to be using the flat of his blade to strike at the elves knocking them to the ground battered and bruised, but not dead. I was certain he would not be using the same methods when he reached us. As Korryn's men started to fall Amara began to bring her archers down the hill. They were still too far as Korryn's last man fell and Olmar raised his blade toward Korryn.

"Your highness!" one of the elves called out as they loosed a spell that caused a bright flash between Korryn and Olmar. The horse reared back, putting a few feet between them.

Olmar looked to the approaching force then back to Korryn. He sheathed his weapon and pulled back on the reigns, his horse backed toward the tree.

He made a motion and his voice echoed through the clearing. "I yield for now. I do not seek to start a war with your people by attacking a royal." He turned and looked directly at us, "But know this, I will return, and your lives will be forfeit. Evil will always be struck down, and I will see righteousness done." He took his reigns up and rode his horse back into the woods.

"Korryn! Are you okay?" Amara grabbed her sister by the shoulders.

"I'm fine." Korryn batted her hands away.

"Why did he just leave like that?" I asked, "And what did he mean about starting a war?"

"Relations have always been tense between humans and elves."

Korryn explained, "If he attacked me or my sister outright our people would not hesitate to retaliate, which could very likely lead to war between our people. And we are particularly volatile at the moment. You need to come back with me Amara."

"Why? What's going on Korryn?"

Korryn took a deep breath, as if to steel herself, "Mother's dead."

"What?!"

"It occurred during a private meeting between her and Eizel Avareen. He's the one that told me the news."

"What happened? How?"

"I'm not sure of the exact details, or what they were discussing; but it seems that during their meeting Shehazari assassins entered the chamber. They tried to fight them off, but in the end, mother was killed and, just as the legends say, the Shehazari vanished as suddenly as they arrived. You need to come home. To be present for mother's funeral," Korryn hesitated, "And for the decision of succession."

"What do you mean? Are you not the successor by default?"

"It seems there is some difference of opinion in regard to who should lead the Vene'ta'ri next. I have my supporters, but some feel my views of outsiders are too harsh. Most certainly my recent actions in defiance of council decision do not help my case. In any event we both are needed back home. Your friends are safe for now, but at this moment our people need you; need us."

Amara looked at us.

"There is no decision to be made here." Varen said, "You know that, right? If your people need you, then you have no right to abandon them. We appreciate your help, but with Olmar driven off we can handle ourselves."

"What of when he returns? He swore he would."

"We'll face that when it comes." My brother shrugged. "Maybe by then we'll have the skill to face him without help. Go be where you need to be right now Amara. And thank you for all your help."

Amara nodded and turned to her sister. "Okay, let's go."

Korryn smiled and nodded then stopped, "We need to stop by the south gate of that town along the way."

"Why do you want to stop by a human town? That's not like you."

Korryn smiled, "I didn't say in the town. I left a couple of men near the southern gate in case you came up behind us."

"And I completely passed them by taking the elven trails." Amara laughed

"You always have been unpredictable, sister." Korryn shook her head, a slight smile on her face. The two of them began to walk toward the tree line.

"Korryn." My brother called and she turned to face him. "We know that one day we are going to face Olmar again; but what about you?"

Korryn turned and scrutinized my brother for a minute. "As much as I would still like nothing more than to see you pay both for your actions in the city and the harm you cause myself and my men, I acted rashly previously. The council had decided to allow you to leave which was a decision I could not accept. Where elven law is concerned you are free, and we have more pressing matters to attend to in our kingdom. But know this." In a flash, Korryn drew and loosed an arrow from her own bow. The arrow whizzed by Varen's head missing by inches, "If you ever think to cross our people again, there is not a hole deep enough to hide in. We will find you." She turned and walked away, her sister close behind.

Kaja and Hjalmar approached my brother.

"Varen, I'm sorry." Kaja said, "I know you wanted me to go home, but I had to warn you. Although, I guess any excuse would have been enough for me to come back. You can hate me if you want, but I don't want to leave."

"I don't hate you, Kaja." Varen sighed, "I never hated you and I wasn't mad at you."

"But you sent me away."

"I sent you away because I'm too dangerous to be around. You were unconscious for what happened in the clearing when we escaped, but if it weren't for Celenia I would have killed both of you. I didn't wat to put you in that kind of danger."

"That's not just your choice, Varen. You never coerced me to come along, and I was always ready to accept the dangers that were bound to come with this kind of journey. I know you love me Varen, and I feel the same way, but you don't get to make decisions for me even if it is out of love. If it's dangerous you have to let me decide if I can handle it, or if I'm willing to face it."

"Kaja, you could die."

"Yes, I could." Kaja agreed, "But I'd rather live a short life being where I want to be than live a long one always wishing I was somewhere else. It's my choice Varen, let me choose."

Varen sighed, but nodded his head in agreement. "All right. I'm sorry Kaja." He turned to Hjalmar, "What about you? You're in a completely different situation. Will you still choose to accompany us rather than go back to your life in Astor?"

"Varen, you've been wrong on that from the beginning. As far as the guard are concerned, I abandoned them. There's no home for me back there anymore. I made my decision when I helped you out of the city. Even if I could have gone back before I'm pretty sure Olmar is going to eliminate any chance of that now. I'm stuck with you."

"Well, it sounds like you have both made your decision." He smiled, "Okay, let's get together what we need and head for the port."

"Um, Varen. You may want to reconsider that course of action." I said.

"Why?" Varen asked, his face scrunched in confusion.

I pointed to Korryn's arrow which had stuck itself in the rocky ground at the base of the hill. The shaft had already turned grey and brittle.

"What would have caused that?" Kaja asked.

"Necromancy," Varen responded, "something similar happened when I lost control in the clearing after you got shot."

"That was on a much larger scale though." Hjalmar piped in.

Varen nodded in agreement as I took a deep breath and opened my mage sight. I could see the necromantic energy as it flowed outward. It wasn't enough to really harm anything, in fact it was probably just barely enough to accomplish what had happened to Korryn's arrow, but it seemed to be emanating from a stone no larger than my palm.

"Varen, that stone there." I pointed at it. He knelt down to pick it up.

"Yeah, I can feel the magic coming off it but…"

"But what?" I looked at him, dispelling the magic keeping my magesight open.

"Celenia, it's relayed magic. It's second hand."

"It's a waystone." I concluded. My brother nodded in response.

"Secondhand magic? Is that real?" Hjalmar asked, "and what's a waystone?"
"Secondhand magic definitely real," I chuckled, "but most people don't recognize it as that."

"So what is it?" Kaja asked.

"It's determined from where the magic originated. A spell cast from a mage directly would be considered firsthand magic, because the magic came directly from the source. Secondhand magic is less direct. Take the rings Kaja and I wear, for example. If a mage had cast the spell directly on the two of us it would be a firsthand spell."

"But because it's coming from the ring it's secondhand magic." Hjalmar finished.

"Kind of. It's a secondhand spell." Varen corrected. "Which is more commonly known as an enchantment" I responded.

"There's a difference between secondhand magic and a secondhand spell?" Kaja asked.

Varen nodded, "The first is the distinction between magic and a spell. Magic is the energy that is focused and commanded to create a desired effect: the way to focus and create the effect is the spell."

"Put simply," I said, "The magic is the energy, the spell is the process."

"So the stone here is putting out just the pure necromantic energy? That's why it's having a similar effect to what happened in the clearing."

"Right," Varen nodded, "When I lost control in the clearing, I released a massive amount of necromantic energy, or necromantic magic. I didn't cast a spell."

"So is it safe to be by this stone?" Hjalmar asked, concern in his voice.

"Yeah, you're fine." I smiled, "The amount put out from the stone is very low. Enough to do what you saw to the arrow or kill some small insects if they get too close, but not enough to hurt you."

"But there's another important difference between a secondhand spell and secondhand magic." Varen said.

"What?" Kaja asked.

"A secondhand spell lasts as long as the object it's enchanted on. Secondhand magic dissolves over time. Usually a pretty short amount of time." I replied.

"So the magic coming off the stone will eventually stop?" Hjalmar asked.

"Yeah. Usually only hours after the time it absorbed the magic." Varen said, looking closely at the stone.

"So, what is a waystone and why is it important?" Hjalmar asked, slightly irritated at Varen's partial explanations.

"A waystone is a stone that has both an enchantment and uses secondhand magic, they are also only attuned to a certain type of magic."

"So what do they do?" Kaja asked, coming close to get a better look.

"First you attune several stones to the type of magic you use. Then you link them to each other, one at a time, in a certain sequence. Finally, you set them along a path. When you release a burst of the attuned magic at one stone it will be absorbed and relayed, then the next stone in the sequence will also start to radiate the magic."

"But you two haven't used necromancy around here." Hjalmar said, "Why would it be reacting?"

"It means another Necromancer used these," Varen said, "And it was recently."

"What do you want to do?" I looked at my brother.

"We need a teacher." He said, "We may as well go take a look."

Chapter 21

Egil

Hjalmar

We followed the trail. Varen released the magic at each stone as we found them and Celenia used her magesight to lead us to the next one in the series. Whoever had placed them didn't make it easy, the path took some extreme turns at times and wove its way through the woods. I could only assume they tried as hard as they could to make it so only those who already knew the path could follow it. As we followed the paths the rocky hills turned larger and the undergrowth made traveling the path even slower than it had been. In the Early evening we finally reached the end of the waystone path and found ourselves standing before a cave dug into the hills. Even I could fell the necromantic energy within, or maybe it was my own nerves.

"Are we really going in there?" I asked.

"Are you scared Hjalmar?" Kaya teased.

"Aren't you? All we know is we followed a very difficult path that whoever is here obviously didn't want found, to a cave where we believe another necromancer is. One that is skilled enough and hopefully willing to take Varen and Celenia as students."

"Okay, you two stay here while Celenia and I check it out- "

"Absolutely not, Varen." Kaja interjected. "You already tried to leave us behind once. Where you go, I go. I'm not afraid of anything we may face in there."

Varen opened his mouth to argue, but the look on Kaja's face silenced any rebuttal he may have had.

"Okay, but will the two of you at least stay behind us? There will undoubtedly be magical wards and other spells in there and Celenia and I are our best chance of getting through it unharmed."

Kaja and I nodded in agreement and Varen and Celenia led the way into the cave. We didn't get far before the cave became nearly pitch black. For a moment I could actually see the glow of Varen's eyes. They weren't as bright as they had been before, but they certainly had some of their luster back. Varen spoke an arcane word and an orb of light burst into existence floating just above his outstretched hand. He moved his arm until it was stretched in between and above us; the orb followed. He spoke another word and the orb hovered in the same spot as he dropped his arm. It followed him as we moved deeper into the cavern. Occasionally Celenia would stop the group and she and Varen would weave spells, disabling wards and defenses most likely. After what seemed like an hour, we arrived at an open chamber that split off into several paths. Torches sat at the entrance of each branch.

"What now?" Kaja asked.

"Anything Celenia?" Varen turned to his sister.

Celenia shook her head. "It's odd. This would be the perfect spot for a spell trap or any other type of defense but… I can't sense anything of the sort. The necromantic energy seems to be emanating from down that pathway." She pointed to one of the paths on the left-hand side.

She and Varen led the way once more. We passed several gaps along the corridor that looked to open into various rooms, though with only the few moments they were illuminated by the orb of light, I couldn't tell what they were being used for. Finally, Celenia held up her hand stopping the group.

"Up ahead," she whispered, "Room to the right."

Varen nodded and dispelled the orb of light. It took our eyes to adjust but once they did, we could see a faint light coming from the room Celenia had directed. We moved slowly, making as little noise as possible. Even the sound of my own breathing seemed loud in my ears and I wondered if anyone else was feeling as tense. We reached the edge of the opening and Varen leaned over Celenia, peeking around the corner. He paused for a moment then slowly passed his sister and entered the room. After a few moments we heard his voice from within.

"It seems clear. Don't drop your guard though."

We entered the room. The light we had seen before was coming from lit torches mounted in the cave walls. The room was furnished with a few stone tables. There was a smaller table off to one side with a set of drawers connected to it. Sitting on a rag atop the table were some small knives and other tools. On each of the small tables a collection of small bowls and baskets sat at one side filled with what looked to be various herbs and powders.

"What is this?" Kaja asked.

"It's a lab." Varen responded looking peeking into one of the baskets.

"For what?" I asked.

"Well, a lab used by a mage is usually to experiment with magic." Celenia rolled her eyes.

"What do you mean experiment? Isn't magic something you are taught?"

"Only in the beginning." Varen explained, "More skilled mages use labs like these to try to develop new spells or improve the ones they already know."

"Is that safe?" I asked, "I thought you said magic was Volatile."

"It is volatile; and no, magic experimentation is not completely safe. That's why it's done in a lab where you can try to make it as safe as possible. Usually a lab like this is—" Varen stopped and spun around toward his sister.

"Filled with all sorts of protective wards." She grimaced.

"A bit late for that revelation, isn't it?"

Varen

The old man entered the room. He was thin, pale, and looked like a good breeze could knock him to the ground; but the air of confidence he exuded told a different story. His eyes seemed alert and there was a frightening intelligence there. Every time he looked at me it seemed he was thinking of a million different ways to end my life.

"Who are you?" Kaja seemed unaffected by the man's aura, her daggers were drawn, and she seemed ready to strike at any given moment.

He leveled his gaze at her. "I believe that is a question for me to ask.

You are the ones trespassing, after all."

Pushing through my own fear I stepped forward. "I am Varen. This is my sister Celenia, and our friends Kaja and Hjalmar. You're a Necromancer, aren't you?"

"If you know that much then you know that I can easily kill you and use your corpses to serve my own purposes. Give me one reason I shouldn't, boy."

"We are necromancers as well" Celenia spoke, "but we were discovered and exiled from our home. We've been looking for a new teacher."

"So, you came to a cave where you felt necromantic magic and expected whoever was there to teach you?" he scoffed.

"...Will you?" Celenia asked nervously.

"You and your friends are foolish and should never have come." He turned and looked at me for a moment. "Do you have any idea who I am?"

I shook my head quickly, unable to get my voice to respond.

"I am Egil Frostad, because of me a town was nearly ravaged by undead, and you think I would be willing to teach you?"

"Wait." Hjalmar tilted his head in thought. "You said your name was Egil?"

"Do you know him Hjalmar?" Celenia asked. Everyone's gaze turned to him.

"I know of him, maybe." Hjalmar shook his head. "Varen, if he's who I think he is, this is the instructor who taught Kaden."

Celenia and I turned to look at him and he gazed back at us.

"You taught our father?!" Celenia finally broke the silence. "Then you can teach us!"

"Idiots!" He growled, "it has never been a matter of can, rather a matter of will. I don't take students anymore."

"We have nowhere else to turn. If you don't take us on, then we have to leave the Kingdom. We had never been outside our town, let alone the region. You are the only other Necromancer we've found. I don't know that we'd be able to find another."

"If you can't find another, then don't learn. You are young, find another path." He waved the air as if he was shooing off flies.

"That's not possible for my brother." Egil turned and looked at her expectantly. "He's a source Necromancer."

"A wellspring?" Egil looked at me intently and stroked his white beard. There seemed to be some sort of internal debate, but he gave little hint to his actual thoughts. Finally, he turned and placed his hand on the wall next to him and an arcane symbol glowed. He spoke a string of arcane words that I was unable to discern. An uneasy feeling gripped me. Our surroundings began to twist and distort, finally just becoming out of focus. The uneasy feeling was replaced with a momentary weightlessness and the unfocused room contorted and transformed. As everything settled and refocused, we found ourselves in a different room. It was large and open with some arcane writing in a circular method at either end of the room. Torches lined the walls to either side and two torches were mounted with even spacing at either end. Some small storage spaces seemed to be carved into the wall to the left, and unlike the rest of the cavern we had seen, this space had a door carved out of stone. Egil stood in front of the doorway, still facing us.

"Where are Kaja and Hjalmar?" Celenia gasped.

I looked around once more. In trying to understand our new surroundings I had failed to notice the absence of our friends.

"Your friends are fine. I moved them to another room where they could watch safely. You should be more concerned about your own fate." Egil said flatly.

"What does that mean?" The question came out a little more irritated than I intended it.

"You wish to be taught. Then you shall have a chance. One." He studied us out of the corner of his eye as he crossed to the other side of the room.

"You said you don't take on students." Celenia eyed him back, "What changed your mind?"

"Don't get ahead of yourself." Egil growled, "I have not changed my mind yet. I am simply giving you the opportunity to prove why I should."

"But why even give us the consideration? You were so opposed to us before."

"My reasons are my own and I will speak of them no further." He stated, "Do you wish for this opportunity or not?"

I looked at my sister who sighed and nodded. "What do we need to do to prove ourselves? Animate corpses? Speak to the dead?"

"While both are abilities of necromancy, I don't care about your abilities as Necromancers. Necromancy can be taught. I want to see your abilities as mages."

"How are we supposed to do that?" I asked, again unable to hide my irritation with this man. He knew that he had the advantage. Even if we wanted to get out, I was sure that door had some sort of wards on it, and even if it didn't, we were in a completely different section of the cave. I had no idea how to get back.

"Have you ever been in a duel?" He asked.

"We dueled a lot during town defense training back in Vellara." Celenia replied. She made the wisecrack out of nervousness, but it still managed to irritate Egil.

"A mage duel," His even tone was starting to get strained. "Tell me you at least understand how they work."

"We know the concept." I held back my own irritation in an attempt to ease the tension. "Due to the dangers of our previous situation though, we have never participated in one."

I thought I saw a hint of a smile at Egil's lips, but it was gone fast enough that I wasn't sure if I had imagined it.

"Let me explain it for your benefit, then." He approached us at the center of the room. "This room here is to be our dueling ground. Normally, another individual aside from the duelists is here to oversee and prevent serious harm. This duel, however, is to be a little different. I will stand in one of the magic circles at one side of the room, the two of you will take position in the other. The circles have duel layered spells. The first will prevent any harm from occurring to the duelists."

"So, our spells won't do anything to each other? That doesn't make for much of a duel." My sister scoffed.

"Don't be so quick to make assumptions, girl. That is where the second layer comes in. The first layer absorbs the spell that was cast, and the second layer is a necromantic spell that drains that same amount of energy from the duelist. You lose when you lose consciousness."

"How do we know you won't kill us if we lose?" Celenia eyed him suspiciously.

"You don't, nor do you know what happens to your friends. So, if you choose to duel, duel as if your lives depend on it." He grinned, then returned to his stoic expression. "This is your final opportunity to back out. If you do, you and your friends will be allowed to leave, but you are never to come back here."

I looked back at my sister who took a deep breath and nodded at me.

"We're not turning back now." I looked at Egil.

"Very well, then the two of you take your place in that circle over there, but first remove any magical items you have on you and put them on the shelves in the wall this includes your staff and scepter. They are warded so no harm will come to them."

"Why do we have to do that?" I asked.

"It is to be a duel between mages. No aides allowed." Egil responded simply. He turned and took his place across the room.

My sister and I walked over the shelves and placing our things on them.

"He really doesn't want to teach us," she muttered, "He's a master, and won't give us any advantage."

"But it's the only shot we have. We have to try. Maybe we'll get lucky."

Celenia rolled her eyes but nodded. Having placed everything on the shelves, we turned and took our place in the circle opposite Egil.

"There is only one rule, and it's for your own safety. Do not leave the circle under any circumstances. The circle is what protects you, and I cannot guarantee your safety should you leave it."

Celenia and I nodded in understanding. Egil spoke a word and I could feel the magic in the circle coming to life.

"Ready? Begin." Egil called.

Celenia began with a fire spell lobbed in his direction. Egil countered with ice and the spells fizzled out leaving some water on the floor between us. Before we had a chance to react Egil struck again as lightning arced and struck the field generated by the circle. The sensation was odd; it was as if hours had passed in moments. I quickly opened my mage sight in hopes of being able to counter the next spell before it came. I was able to recognize just as he lobbed a fireball in our direction. Quickly I cast. A wall of Ice materialized in front of our circle. Celenia let out a breath of relief but a moment later the wall collapsed, and stone struck our field. He was preparing air element spell next. Rather than counter, I sent shards of Ice from our wall soaring to his end. He threw his spell off to the side and I was certain I had him. Suddenly one of the torches nearby flared up, its heat intensifying and the ice melted, losing momentum and dropping to the floor ineffectively.

"What happened?" I asked.

"He threw his spell at the torch, using the wind to superheat it." Celenia shook her head.

"This isn't working, we need to think of something else."

"Quick casting." Celenia said.

"Let's give it a shot."

We both prepared spells. Celenia threw hers. She once again began drawing on energy. As she did so I lobbed mine. We continued that way, alternating our casting and varying our spells. Egil held them off at the beginning but they began to come to fast and a few struck his field. He lashed his hand out and a sudden light burst before our eyes, blinding us. As we lost our focus on our spells the backfired in our hands. He began to retaliate in a similar fashion. Strike after strike hit our field and I could feel the drain.

Celenia set another Ice wall. We knew it wouldn't last long. We began casting more ice spells to reinforce it as it continued to be bombarded with spells.

"We can't outlast him Varen. And it seems he can cast alone as fast as we can together."

"I know, we need something big."

"Cast with me." I said.

"What?"

"Cover me. I'm going to use it."

"Varen..." The warning in Celenia's voice was clear. I chose to ignore it.

I knelt down and began to chant. I slowly released the flow of magic from within me that I normally attempted to suppress. It wasn't as strong as usual. I hadn't had the time to build back my reserve, but it was there. I was terrified to use it, but I saw no other option.

"The wards should protect us." I reasoned, *"And we're all necromancers so even if the wards fail it shouldn't do any lasting harm."*

I began to weave my spell. There were no corpses around, so I'd have to release the energy in another form. I decided to alter a fireball spell. I could hear the battle raging as my sister attempted to hold Egil off as best as she could. I could feel the ward sap my physical strength and exhaustion started to grip me. I shook my head and kept my attention on the spell.

The preparation finished, I stood. Raising my hands in front of me I spoke the final word. The spell emerged as a huge green ball of fire began barreling toward Egil. He tried to toss his spell, but it was of little effect. The Spell struck and I watched as Egil dropped to his knees.

"Yes!" My sister shouted.

"Don't celebrate until you are certain it's over." Egil growled. "He raised his arms and our field was engulfed in flames. My own spell had already taken a lot out of me and as the field continued to drain me, I felt consciousness slip from my grasp.

Chapter 22

Return to Vellara

Varen

As I woke, I bolt upright. I analyzed my surrounding and saw I was still in the caves. Celenia lay nearby, both of us on bedrolls. Our personal items lay in a pile nearby, no attempt had been made to separate them out.

"You're awake!" I heard Kaja's voice I turned toward the room entrance as she rushed forward and pulled me in an embrace. I hugged her back.

"Well, we failed." Celenia grumbled rubbing the sleep from her eyes as she came to. "But we're not dead, so at least that's something." She got up. "Let's get our stuff together and get on the road."

"Actually Celenia, Egil wanted to talk to us. Hjalmar is already in there; I was just sent to see if you two were awake yet."

"How long were we out?" I asked.

"A few hours, I think. It's hard to tell in these caves." She stood, pushing the wrinkles out of her clothing.

"What does Egil want to talk about?" Celenia asked incredulously.

Kaja shook her head, "He wouldn't say. He said that he wanted everyone there before he said anything."

Celenia looked at me and I shrugged. I walked over and started picking my things up from the pile. Celenia joined me an a few minutes later we were ready. I felt much more comfortable with my staff in hand. My cloak and ring gave no small feeling of security either.

"Let's go." I said, "Whatever he wants, it's probably best to not keep him waiting."

Kaja led the way down the winding corridors until we reached what looked like a large conference room. A grand table was centered in the room with chairs all around. Egil sat on one side and Hjalmar sat opposite him. We took the seats nearest Hjalmar. For a few moments we sat in silence as Egil just looked at us. Finally, Celenia broke the silence.

"Look just ask us to leave already. We lost the duel, just let us get on our way."

"If you would like to leave far be from me to stop you; but I never said that I would teach you if you won. I said that the duel would be what makes my decision. I never expected you to beat me." He chuckled.

"Oh." Celenia said sheepishly, then realization his, "So you will teach us?"

"Well, that's up to you. I am willing on a condition." He looked toward me. "We need your help, Varen."

"My help? I don't understand."

"I am part of a group actively seeking a certain Necromancer. He poses a great threat, and he's been looking for you and your sister."

"Looking for us? Why? What did we do?"

"Nothing. It has to do with a grudge against your father. I can explain more on that later. The point is that there is a group of us that have been trying to figure out how to stop him. With training, I think your ability as a wellspring mage could turn the tides in our favor. You don't have to decide right this moment, but I want to show you why we are trying to stop him. Follow me." Egil stood and led us down the hallway a small distance. He turned into a room where he had a teleportation circle prepared.

"Where are we going?" I asked.

"Home. I must warn you. It will not be a happy visit. What you are about to see was the doing of the man we are trying to stop. I'm sorry to show all of you this, but I feel you deserve to know. The circle will activate again about an hour after you arrive and will remain active for another hour. Return to the circle at that time and it will bring you back here."

I nodded, feeling a knot in my stomach as I wondered what we would find. Wandering undead? The town under attack? Egil spoke the command to complete the spell and our surroundings once again blurred around us. The weightless feeling lasted a bit longer this time but within moments we arrived just outside the town. As everything shifted back into sharp clarity, none of us could move.

There were no sounds of combat or fighting, but it couldn't be denied that one had occurred here recently. The walls were charred, and some spots still smoked from embers struggling to stay alive. Kaja tuned and buried her head into my chest. I could feel her tremble, but she wouldn't cry, not yet. The shock still held us all transfixed, the tears would come after.

"Kaja, do you want to stay here while we check it out?" Hjalmar offered.

Kaja took a deep breath then stood upright, "No, I have to see this." She turned to me, "I am going to my families store. I need to know if they are okay."

"Do you want me to come with you?" I asked.

She shook her head, "If this happened the way Egil said it did, the two of you are our best chance to figure it out. Look around and see what you can find. I'll take Hjalmar with me."

The two of them took off toward the town entrance and were soon out of sight.

It took another moment for Celenia and I to get the courage to move toward the town. We did so slowly, horrified at the scene before us. As we entered, we passed the bodies of a few of the townsmen who must have been assigned guard duty when it occurred. Celenia knelt down to look at them.

"It looks like they were killed by the sword. The injuries themselves don't seem magically inflicted." Celenia said.

"Yeah, but that doesn't tell us much."

"No," she shook her head. "It doesn't. If this was done by a Necromancer, I'm going to go check the graveyard outside town."

"Okay," I stood. "Egil said they were looking for us. If that's the case I'm going to go check our old home."

Celenia nodded and I watched as she left then turned my attention down the path. Looking around I noticed that a lot of what was actually destroyed were the town walls, or fields, some carts sat abandoned in the road, destroyed. I finally made it to our home. The gate was broken and hung off a single hinge. I hopped the fence and walked up to the door. As I tried to open it, I heard something scrape behind it. I peeked behind the door and I saw our table laying on its side against the door. Before I had time to figure it out, I heard snap of a string and ducked out of the way as a crossbow bolt embedded itself in the door.

"Plenty more where that came from!" A gruff shout came from inside. I recognized the voice, but I couldn't place it.

"Who are you and what are you doing in there?" I called in.

There were a few moments of silence before the voice responded. "Varen?"

"Leif?" the recognition suddenly hit me. I shoved my way inside to find that leaf had sat himself in a chair at the far side of the room, ready to take shots with a crossbow at anything that attempted to get in.

"Varen, it is you." Leif chuckled then winced, "What are you doing here, boy? You and your sister were supposed to leave these parts."

"Yeah we did, but we heard something happened and we came back."

"Ya don't just come back from being exiled boy." He laughed, then clutched his stomach.

"You're injured."

"Am I?" He feigned surprise, "I hadn't noticed."

I ignored the sarcasm, "Let me help you. I think we have some bandages in here somewhere."

"I already raided them boy. Whatever weapons those things were using create wounds that don't heal. How's Kaja? How's my daughter?"

"What things? What happened here?"

"Varen, please. I'm not going to last the day. I'll tell you all I can but first I have to know, is Kaja okay?"

I took a deep breath to calm myself and nodded. "She's fine. She went looking for you and her mother. She went to the shop."

"Her mother's already gone." Leif sighed, "So's the rest of the town I'd wager. I'm probably the only one left."

"Leif, what happened." I asked again.

"It was last night, just after midnight, I think. Most the town had already gone to bed; I was checking stock at the shop. An order had come in wrong. The alarm bells started ringing. We thought it just another goblin raid or some bandits or the like. I took a sword from the rack and set out, determined to see that whatever it was, was finished quickly so I could finish my check and go home. No amount of training could have prepared the town for this though."

"For what? What attacked the town?"

He shook his head, "Couldn't tell at first, the first ones that came were wrapped head to toe in bandage and carried odd blades, the likes of which I had never seen before. It wasn't until the shambling skeletons joined that we realized we must have been dealing with undead. At first many in town thought it to be you two, come to take your revenge for your exile."

"What about you? Did you think it was us?" I asked sadly.

"Nah." He smiled, "Varen, I've kept an eye on you and your Sister much more than you think, that's why I gave you the book. Did you find that?"

"My father's spell book? Yeah, we found it."

"Good. I promised your father I'd look after you. It was the last thing he asked of me before he died. Sure, finding out you were necromancers came as a shock to me, but I knew your heart. The two of you wouldn't do something like this. Whoever did though was looking for you. A few living men came among the dead, and they were asking for your dad. Someone caved and told them your father had died years ago, all that was left of the family were a couple kids. Then they started asking after you. They tore the town apart trying to find you. Once they figured out you weren't here nothing stopped them from killing everyone and destroying everything they could. I came here in hopes to find a clue myself and maybe send word you were in danger. Unfortunately," He looked down at his stomach, "They caught me before I was able to. I got away and made my way here. With the strength I still had I pushed the table against the door and set myself up here."

"Was one of the men who came a mage named Nordak?"

He shrugged, "The ones I saw didn't give their names and most of them wore armor and blades. Not impossible for a mage to have been here though. With undead being involved there was certainly a mage behind it. That doesn't just happen naturally."

Leif coughed and clutched his stomach. It was clear as he spoke that he was growing weaker. He realized it too. As the coughing fit passed, he looked at me.

"Varen, will you do something for me?"

"Of course, what is it?" I knelt next to him.

"On the bed there is a letter for Kaja, I wrote it in case she ever returned to find this. I didn't suspect it would get to her so soon." He chuckled weakly, then turned serious. "Tell me something Varen. How has your relationship with my daughter grown since you have been gone? Do you care about her? Do you love her?"

"I'm not going to lie to you, Leif. I do love her. We have hit a rough patch or two along the way, but I love her and would do anything for her. I know you never approved of me,"

He cut me off, "Varen, I was concerned for your ability to provide for her, but that is not all that's important. She loves you. As her father I have known that for a long time, and now she will have no one else to turn to. In our home a sword stands displayed on the wall. If you are serious about wanting a life with her take that sword and my blessing, but only if you swear to care for her and protect her above all else."

"Leif don't act like that, we can get you a healer, there's still time to help you."

"No Varen, there's not. We both know it. You love to hold out hope and I've always admired that trait in you, but my life is about to end. Promise me."

"…. I promise, I will take care of her. I won't let you down."

Leif smiled gently and nodded, satisfied. He leaned back in his chair and I watched as he took his final breath. I rested my head in my hands. I was upset, but I knew Kaja would be devastated.

"There's no time to mourn now. I have to see if there are any other survivors. And..."

I looked at the bed and saw the letter, neatly folded. I picked it up and carefully placed it in a pocket of my robe. I looked at Leif one last time before gently closing his eyes. Looking down I caught a glimpse of a leather bracelet under his cuff. Kneeling down I saw it was well worn and leaving the house. I would have liked to give him a proper burial. Maybe once we finished, we could do that and bury him with his wife. I took the bracelet for now made my way toward the Valtr home a couple streets away from the shop. The front door was missing, torn off its hinges like our gate. I entered cautiously. The house seemed very torn apart. Furniture was overturned and objects were scattered across the room, heavily damaged. On the far side of the room I saw an overturned table and a glass box shattered on the floor.

"That must be where the sword was displayed. But where is it?" I searched and finally found it near the entrance to the next room. I picked it up. The blade was heavy, and definitely would take some practice to get used to. Checking the edge, I found it would also have to be sharpened before it could be of any use.

"That's probably why it was cast aside." I mused allowed, "Someone tried to use it not knowing it was dull. I took several minutes and searched the house, but I didn't find much. The rest of the house was the same as the front room, and I found spots of blood where injuries occurred, but it looked like whoever fought here, Kaja's mother no doubt, had gotten out. Satisfied that there was nothing more here, I left the house.

"Varen!" Celenia shouted in a panic running down the road. "Varen, we have a problem."

"What's wrong Cel?" I asked putting my hands on her shoulders and she caught her breath for a moment.

"Kaja and Hjalmar. They're unconscious at the church. Something's wrong. I think it's," She shook her head rather than finish the last sentence. "Just come see."

She grabbed my hand and took off running down the street. I almost tripped but managed to catch my footing and find pace with her. I kept trying to ask her what was going on, but she would only shake her head and keep going. Several minutes later we reached the church. Immediately I could feel the massive amount of lingering magic emanating from it.

"Death's embrace." I swore, "What happened here?"

"I'm not sure, but whatever it was, it wasn't good." She walked in, motioning me to follow.

As we entered the stench of death was strong. It looked like a good portion of the town had retreated back here in an attempt to make a stand. It made sense, the church was fairly easily defendable, and those who knew the church well enough knew a few of the hidden passages to get out. We were always told in trainings that if the battle got too rough and the enemy breached the walls to make our way to the church. A pathway to the altar was cleared through the pews and bodies and Hjalmar and Kaja lay on the floor unconscious only a few feet short. I ran up to them, kneeling. I felt for their pulse. It was there, still strong; but their skin was cool to the touch. I saw next to Hjalmar's feet and his helmet was off, laying a few feet away.

"Celenia, get Kaja. I'll grab Hjalmar. We have to get them out of here."

Celenia followed my lead, knowing better than to ask any questions at the moment. We managed to drag them out into the street.

"How long were they out?" I asked.

"I'm not sure." Celenia shook her head, "As soon as I saw them, I came and got you."

"Why didn't you get them out immediately?" I growled.

"I panicked, Varen. The only thing I could think of was telling you. By the time I realized what I should have done I already saw you down the road.... Is it what I think it is?"

"My guess is as good as yours, but with the amount of wild necromantic magic in there, it's likely. We should take them back to Egil, though. He should know for sure."

"The teleportation circle should just be activating now." Celenia said. "The sooner we get them back there the better."

"Right." I nodded, then had a thought. "Celenia, I didn't get a good look at who was in there. Did you see Kaja's mother?"

"She's not there." Celenia assured, "When I came back, I passed their store. I saw her mother's body with a smaller group that took a stand there. I'm sure Kaja already saw her body. Did you find Leif?"

"Yeah, he was alive. He passed while I was talking to him though. Had some last requests for me." I hoisted Hjalmar onto my shoulder. He was awkward and heavy, but I knew it would be faster than trying to carry him in front of me. "Let's get them back to Egil. But I need to make a stop by the store. It should only be a second."

Celenia nodded. We made our way down the streets as fast as we could. Once we made it to the shop, I saw the many bodies scattered around. Kaja's mother was easy to spot. Like Kaja she was an excellent fighter and was likely leading the stand. I searched quickly and, finding a small pendant that looked well worn, I pulled it from around her neck, snapping the chain. I looked at Celenia and nodded, signaling that I was finished, and we made our way back to the Circle. When we stepped inside our surroundings immediately faded and the stomach-turning weightlessness took effect. Moments later we stood inside the caves once more. Egil sat waiting for us off to one side.

"Egil! Kaja and Hjalmar need help!"

Egil jumped to his feet seeing them in our arms. "Follow me."

He led the way down the corridors back to his lab, where we first ran into him.

"Lay them on the tables there." He rummaged through a drawer nearby, pulling out some papers.

We did as we were told, and he stepped up between the tables looking at each person. He reached into a few of the baskets grabbing out ingredients and putting them in a mortar, then grabbed a pestle and began crushing them up.

"What happened?"

"We split up to explore the town, looking for survivors or any clues to what happened. Kaja and Hjalmar went together. Celenia and I went our own ways. After a while Celenia had tracked me down again in a panic. She took me to the church where we felt strong Necromantic energy, like a ritual spell or something. There was no one there casting, but there were a lot of townsfolk lying dead. We found Kaja and Hjalmar unconscious inside. We pulled them out as soon as we could, but I have no idea how long they were there."

"He used the agitated necromantic energy from the battle to create another one." Egil muttered to himself. "He must have used too much and did nothing to restabilize the magic. Varen, Celenia, I'm going to do what I can but, as I'm sure you already suspected, they cannot be cured."

"We were right then." Celenia said woefully.

"Yes. Your friends have contracted the Necromantic disease. What was left behind after Nordak's ritual spell was wild magic. This unstable Necromantic energy infected them. How the disease will progress depends a lot on how much of the wild magic their bodies absorbed. I can slow down the progression, but I cannot stop it."

"Is there anything that can?" I asked.

"No. No ritual or spell ever found has been able to cure the disease." He stopped for a moment in thought. "Well, stories tell of one thing that has, but it's a bard's tale."

"Please Egil. I'll do anything I have to." I begged, "What is it."

"It's a magical artifact called 'The Eye of the Guardian'. It's said to be thousands of years old, if it ever existed at all, and that is a very big 'if'." Egil sighed, "If you are really determined to try to find it, I'll do some research."

"Thank you." I smiled slightly.

Egil nodded, "But Varen, don't get your hopes too high. The chances of an item like this actually existing are incredibly slim." The herbs crushed, he set the mortar on one of the tables. "Listen, this is going to take a while. Why don't the two of you look around? You should get yourself acquainted with the caves, and then get some rest. I'll come find you when this is done. Then we will begin your training. When you are practicing, I'll direct my time toward finding out what I can about the Artifact. Also, the two of you have now seen what Nordak is capable of, and I will have much more to tell you regarding that. Prepare yourselves; There is great difficulty ahead."

Celenia and I nodded in agreement. We stood and left Egil to focus on helping our friends, and I couldn't shake the feeling that we were getting into something far over our heads.

* * *

To Be Continued in Journey of the Exiled Book 2

Epilogue

Kaja

I sat on the stone bench, drenched in sweat and draining my waterskin. I still felt sick, but from the sound of it, that wasn't going away anytime soon, and I wasn't about to let it get in my way.

"You're really improving." Hjalmar commented, sheathing his sword and taking a drink of his own skin.

Egil had created this training room for me and Hjalmar to keep our skills sharp. It took some begging to get him to do it; He was pretty adamant about us resting. But eventually he gave in.

"Thanks." I gasped after a drink. "Can't let Celenia and Varen be the only one honing their skills." I smiled.

"Speaking of whom," Hjalmar jerked his head to the door where Varen stood waiting.

"Varen! What are you doing here? Aren't you supposed to be studying?"

"I am, but I need to show you something."

"What?"
He shook his head "It's easier just to show you. Come on."

He took my hand gently and began leading me through the cave's mazelike corridors. Over the past weeks we slowly began to learn the layout of the caves, but it was still easy to get lost. Varen had to stop a few times to make sure we were still on the right path to… wherever he was leading me. But without fail he would eventually nod to himself and continue to lead the way. Personally, I suspected that the siblings used marks only they could see and understand in order to find their way around, though I could never prove it. Eventually we made our way to the entrance of a small, dimly lit room. Varen turned and motioned for me to go inside.

The room was mostly bare, lit by torchlight at either side. In the center was a cushion; Probably where Varen wanted me to sit. A few feet in front of that, to either side, were some strange looking bowls. Behind each bowl sat a piece of wood with an object atop each. I stepped up to examine each more closely. On one was a small leather bracelet, the other a small pendant necklace.

"Varen, what is this?" I turned as he entered the room.

"You'll see in a minute. Just have a seat there."

I did as I was told, taking a seat on the small cushion.

Varen placed a candle in each bowl and lit each with a word. He then stood between the two objects and began to chant. As he did so the candles began to glow brighter until the torches looked dim by comparison. Next the light rose off the candle and pulsed for a moment before disappearing. Varen ceased chanting after that and, for a moment, the room was as still as it started. I was about to ask Varen what the point of that was when to figures shimmered into existence before me.

"Mom! Dad!" I choked back tears and smiled the largest I felt I had in a long time.

Pronunciation Guide

People

Aderon: ʌˈderɒn

Aelton: ˈeɪltʌn

Altea: æltiːʌ

Amara: ʌˈmaːrʌ

Anabelle: ænʌbel

Astra: æstrʌ

Avareen: ævʌriːn

Brunsvord: ˈbruːnsvɔːrd

Celenia: Seˈleniːʌ

Daleen: Dʌliːn

Egil: eɪdʒɪl

Eileen: aɪˈliːn

Eirasin: ˈeɪrʌsɪn

Eirinis: ˈeɪrɪnɪs

Eizel: ˈaɪzʊl

Ellara: eˈlaːrʌ

Erlend: ˈeɪrlʌnd

Frostad: frɒstæd

Galan: geɪlʌn

Garron: gˈeɪrɪn

Hjalmar: Jɑːlmɑːr

Ingrid: iːŋgrɪd

Kaja: ˈKɑɪjʌ

Korryn: Kɔːˈrɪn

La'vee: lʌˈviː

Leeya: ˈliːjʌ

Leif: leɪf

Miavel: ˈmiːʌvel

i

Na'var: nʌ'vaːr

Nalia: 'naːliːʌ

Nordak: n'ɔːrdæk

Olmar: 'ɔːlmaːr

Siele: 'siːel

Talise: tʌ'liːs

Tavaran: 'tævʌræn

Tei'ara: teɪ'ɑːrʌ

Terramane: 'teərʌmeɪn

Li'nar: lɪ'naːr

Ciara: siː'aːrʌ

Tevar: te'vaːr

Thaias: t'aɪʌs

Thistelle: θɪs'tel

Ureya: uː'reɪjʌ

Valbrandr: Vælbr'ændɜː

Valtr: 'vaːltɜː

Varen: 'vɑːren

Vestil: Ve'stɪl

William: wɪliːʌm

Za'rola: zʌ'rəʊlʌ

Groups

Shakari: ʃʌˈkaːriː

Shehazari: ʃehʌˈzaːriː

Ugathri: uːˈgɒðriː

Vene'ta'ri: veneˈtaːriː

Vessi: veˈsi

Vetri: veˈtri

Place

Astor: æstɔːr

Njord's Port: nɔːrds pɔːrt

Vellara: velaːrʌ

Other

Mercharı: mərˈtʃaːriː

Mirkoya: mərˈkɔɪʌ

Made in the USA
Middletown, DE
29 May 2024

54846815R00265